D1572370

THE STRING

CONSPIRACY

—·—

RESONANCE: BOOK 1

CANDACE FREILICH

RHEA PRESS

Previously Published as "The String Conspiracy" episodes 1-46 on Kindle Vella

Copyright © 2021, 2023 by Candace Freilich

Cover Image by Tithi Luadthong

ISBN: 8-9871577-1-8

ISBN-13: 979-8-9871577-1-8

To Grandpa Bill
who filled our shelves and minds with stories

CHAPTER ONE

— · —

Jo

J o wasn't a thief. Really, she wasn't, though some of the tools in her equipment bag might have suggested otherwise. A set of lock picks. Two pairs of gloves. A small blow torch capable of cutting through metal...

She glanced at the security guards busying themselves a few meters away. Normally, you'd be hard-pressed to find one, as the university budget couldn't afford to trim bushes or fix cracks in the pavement, much less hire competent security. But today, a full six defended the physics building with a tight barrier of yellow cones and a bag check station. No doubt they were there for the same reason she was: the Resero artifacts.

Such a silly thing to call them, by the way. "Artifacts." Like Resero was some prehistoric priest on the Rudian plains and not the physicist who'd single-handedly modernized interdimensional travel. But that was the term the media had picked up, and it covered all the odd tools, designs, and prototypes his estate had donated to lucky schools.

Behind the security guards, dozens of bubble-like lab rooms floated at various heights. A crisscrossing web of glassed-in hallways and stairs linked and supported them, like the sticks on a giant molecular model. Some rooms hovered bare meters above the bushes, while others reached seven, eight, even a dozen stories high. The university's artifacts waited in one of them, Jo was sure of it. The presence of security guards only confirmed her suspicions.

She hiked the strap of her equipment bag higher on her shoulder and tried not to look conspicuous. She was here for a legitimate job, after all. A piece of lab equipment had broken down and, as usual, the university didn't have money for a certified tech. Who could blame her for wanting a peek at the artifacts while she was at it?

She took another look at the security bag check and bit her lip. Rows of hedges ran to either side, hiding pesky machinery like the massive A/C unit and the transformer that would otherwise ruin the building's aesthetic. If she backtracked and went around them, perhaps she could pass as a student using the side entrance and avoid the security checkpoint altogether. Of course, her oil-stained jumpsuit and giant leather bag weren't exactly covert amidst a crowd of book bags and lost freshmen, so she soon drew the stare of a security guard. *Don't panic. You have permission to be here.* He took a few steps closer, and she gave him a tight-lipped nod, making it clear she wasn't approaching the front.

The man was on his com now, undoubtedly describing her shifty green eyes and face full of freckles to his colleagues. Probably her grimy boots as well. And she'd so hoped to avoid any attention. She quickened her pace around the overgrown shrubs, but he quickly overtook her.

"Sorry, miss. I don't mean to alarm you, but I'm going to need to search your bag." He blocked her path with his broad shoulders and gave her an apologetic smile. He looked young, possibly around Jo's age, and fresh out of whatever two month course they gave budget security guards. "Special circumstances, you know?"

No, I don't know, Jo wanted to say, or something equal parts coy and clever. But one glance at the electric baton on his belt brought forth a nod and hesitant compliance. It took all of her focus to not look guilty.

"So, uh, what's the purpose of your visit?" the guard asked, leading her over to one of the bag check tables. He unzipped the oil-stained canvas and was immediately met with a pile of diagnostic tools and a set of hex wrenches. Hopefully he wouldn't dig much further.

"Maintenance job. Fixing the lab's amovoscope."

"Oh, Orin mentioned something about that." To her horror, he started pulling out wrenches and power testers to make it easier to search the deeper areas. He handled the dinged and dented tools with care, more than Jo usually used, but she wanted to cry out for him to stop. The next layer held the lock picks.

She needed to focus on something else to hide her anxiety, but her eyes kept drifting to the baton at his waist. "So, uh, is that com you're carrying an Argoit 3000?"

"This?" His hand went to the black device beside the baton. "I don't know, maybe?"

"Does it ever do that thing where it crackles for no reason? Like, it almost sounds like someone's rubbing sandpaper over their microphone?"

"How'd you know?"

She shrugged. "I've seen it a few times." She picked up a small multimeter to demonstrate. She hoped he didn't notice her sliding the lock picks into her sleeve at the same time. "See, there's a spring inside the top corner that can warp over time and mess with the speaker. So what you do is, you take a weaker magnet, like from your fridge, and you rub it over the call button a few times like this."

"Is that so?"

"Yep." Now that his hands had stopped moving, Jo began absentmindedly repacking her bag. "Works every time."

"Huh. Here, let me help you with that." He started repacking as well, as if this small demonstration was enough to save her the trouble. Or perhaps he'd simply forgotten he hadn't finished. "Thanks for the tip."

No, thank you, Jo thought to say, but she merely nodded. She didn't think the blow torch would have fit in her other sleeve.

Once they'd finished, the guard gave her a smile and waved her on to the entrance. Two of his colleagues flanked the wide glass doors, checking IDs and watching each visitor scan themselves in. That was something Jo couldn't do. Although she'd done a few jobs for the university, it was on a case-by-case basis and only regular contractors got access cards. Usually, she'd wait to follow a student in or hack the card reader—one simple twist on the panel corner with the broken latch, unplug all the blue wires, and put a hair pin across the empty space while jamming the alarm signal—but no. With security guards present, getting in would be infinitely more difficult. She'd actually have to talk with someone.

Someone she knew would be preferable. She kept her distance from the door and pulled out her transcom to dial the maintenance supervisor. *"Hey, Orin? I need access to the resonance lab."* She rehearsed the line in her head as the transcom rang and one of the guards slid his hand to his baton. Shit. Could the old man please answer before the guy with the weapon started asking questions? Or at least before she found herself stumbling through an excuse, littering it with technical terms and hints of her planned mischief.

"South entrance, right?" Orin's gruff voice cracked on the line, preempting her practiced response. "Security guard wants to know if you're the one with the cat t-shirt or the thief purse."

"Thief purse, obviously." Jo knew better than to trust the university to keep their instruments calibrated, so she always brought her own. It wasn't her fault the bag had room for more than she needed. Out of the corner of her eye, she spotted the cat t-shirt lady on the other side of the bag check. She appeared to be selling either drugs or exam answers. Possibly both, if she was a chemistry major.

When Orin radioed to let Jo in, the guard seemed hesitant, but did little more than glance at her bag suspiciously. She shuffled inside and met the maintenance supervisor at the bottom of a chipped, salmon-colored staircase. He didn't look much different than he had when she'd been a student here. Same dingy work gloves and apron. Same deep creases at the eyes. More hair on his face than his head, though not much on either.

Orin pocketed his com. "Sorry about the extra security. It's for the artifacts, you know? Everyone wants to take samples."

"Yeah. So unreasonable." She certainly hadn't smuggled in her own resonance meter in case she got a chance at a sample herself. Rumors suggested they held clues to a bigger prize. "You said the amovoscope's gone out again?"

She didn't wait for Orin to answer before heading up the stairs. They were long and echoed horribly, a slanted tunnel of glass and steel that ended at the first bubbled lab. The building design included safeguards to seal off individual rooms, in case of a fire or radiation leak, but judging by the cracked tile floor and flickering lights, she suspected the seals were too rusted to shut. She took a scan down the hall before the old man caught up with her. No sign of artifacts or extra security.

They continued on and her mood picked up on the third floor. She'd found the room she'd be working in, with a beat-up door and a shiny new set of locks.

"Do you think what they're saying is true?" Orin asked, using a mix of keycard and code to let her in. The old version had only used a keycard, and sometimes students would leave it propped open so they didn't lock themselves out on a bathroom break. "You think Resero was working on a new prototype when he died?"

Jo shrugged and took in the familiar smell of dust and old oil. Patchy sunlight filled the room, drifting through broken blinds and old notes that had been taped up to block the glare. Desks and chairs sat scattered about, clearly dragged around so students could monitor the machinery. It hardly looked like the place to store precious artifacts, but they had arrived on such short notice. The yellowing lower cabinets had new latches. Perhaps one of them held her goal?

Orin nudged her shoulder. "Used to be that I couldn't shut you up about Resero."

She slipped off her bag and started prepping her tools. That was back when she still thought she had a chance of following in his footsteps. Before her grad project had failed spectacularly and all the research companies turned her down. "The D.I.C. said there wasn't anything."

Of course, the D.I.C. wouldn't be the best source of information. Everyone knew Resero and the department had fallen out a few years back. Something about the department claiming broad powers under the 'Interdimensional Counter-terrorism' part of their name. They'd claimed the right to commandeer any piece of technology they saw as dangerous.

Now it was Orin's turn to shrug. "Didn't stop the big tech companies from offering a prize to anyone who finds it."

He let the words hang in the air, his implied question clear: Was Jo going after the reward money?

Did he mean would she try to make a name for herself so she'd never need to freelance again? She sure as hell wanted to, but she wasn't telling him that. "Can you give me a hand pulling this cover off?"

She handed Orin her extra screwdriver. If he was going to hang around and chat, she'd put him to work. And not just because she was ticked he wouldn't leave her alone to check for artifacts. The piece she was fixing—the amovoscope—was one of the most complex devices the school owned. Since its purpose was to test how new devices fared during interdimensional travel, the containment chamber required a shell of solid steel, and the access panel alone weighed twenty kilos. A certified repair team would have sent two technicians to repair it (and a hefty bill to match). Orin's extra pair of hands meant not throwing her back out for her own modest fee.

They leaned the cover against a counter by the door, and Jo set to work testing the various wires and switches and motors inside the device. All the while, Orin watched over her shoulder like a gossip with a juicy rumor he was dying to share. He kept trying to corner her into making eye contact. Perhaps he was keen on showing her the artifacts, granted she promised him a share of the prize money.

A buzzing rose from the depths of the machinery, and Jo yanked her arms out. She confirmed that it'd been switched off and unplugged, but something inside hummed with life.

She rounded on the old man. "Tell me you didn't try that old fix of yours. If I find you've bypassed a fuse with a wire, I swear I'll—"

"I haven't done that in years!" He sounded indignant, if not a little guilty. "Though I suppose a student might've tried something."

If one had, it was his own damn fault. He'd likely been ignoring the maintenance complaints again. Sure, he had a dozen other buildings to take care of, but how hard was it to call in a tech? It used to drive Jo crazy when she was a student. She'd had to design all her projects around whatever equipment happened to be working, and that only stopped when she started fixing the machinery herself.

Nothing to do now but try to pinpoint what was powered and where the power was coming from. She pulled her resonance scanner from the bag, ignoring Orin's *"I knew it!"* look. The palm-sized device was mostly screen, perfect for displaying the spectrometry and frequency breakdown of whatever she held under the pen-like wand, but having it with her wasn't enough to prove her intentions. Its algorithms also let it stand in for a circuit tester in a pinch. And based on the whirr of the machinery, they were about to need it.

See, in order to test how well devices functioned during interdimensional travel, they had to actually be transported. Which meant if you were touching the wrong part while it was running, you might find your hand drifting to another dimension without the rest of you.

She used the scanner wand to move aside some wires and quickly jerked it back out again. Bright blue streaks arced across the inside of the machine, racing around a spiral module near the top. An erratic energy field. They sometimes formed when anti-friction components shut down incorrectly. They also tended to expand the range of those 'touch me and I'll send half of you to Rudu Five' mechanisms. As if the powered circuitry wasn't bad enough.

"Is that what caused it to break?" A finger pointed near the edge of Jo's vision.

She batted Orin's hand away. "Not likely."

Fields like this relied on nearby capacitors to maintain themselves, and even in a big machine, one would last a few hours tops. Half that, if it kept growing at the current rate. So if this was the problem, it should have burnt itself out well before she arrived. But instead, the little streaks of lightning crept toward the opening, building up strength. If it hit one of the transportation components, both Jo and the lab would find a few of their own pieces missing.

"I need an adjustment panel. Quick."

"Uh, okay." Orin stood and looked around the room, rubbing his stubble with the back of his hand. "What's one look like?"

"What's one look like?" She didn't have time for this. She needed a trained technician, not a leveled-up janitor. "Never mind. I'll get it. Try to keep yourself and anything metal away from those sparks."

She sprinted to the cabinets and tried to picture where everything had been when she opened them last. It'd been in the center top, hadn't it? Though the new locks here suggested it could've been moved. She thought about asking Orin for the keys, but the man had a thing against organization. Kept the whole campus on one single ring. She pulled the lock picks from her bag and had it open in seconds.

A screeching alarm sounded throughout the room, echoing off the windows. The old man yelled something, but his words were lost in the droning. At least the adjustment panel was exactly where she'd expected it to be. She grabbed the trapezoidal plate and its accompanying wand.

"What'd you do that for?" Orin asked again when she rushed back. "I had the keys with me."

She stuck the wand inside the amovoscope. The erratic field had grown to half a meter in diameter, and melted plastic dripped from a nearby control circuit. If she didn't take care of this now, it could take half the room with it, not to mention the artifacts likely hidden in the cabinets. "No time."

Her hands flew over the adjustment panel, attempting to get the field stabilized so it could drain the remaining power safely. The blue streaks flicked in defiance. If only she could get a better angle on it. She didn't notice the security guards rush in until one of them knocked the amovoscope's panel cover onto the floor.

"Put your hands up and—"

"Don't move!" Jo pointed to the field, which had crept down the side of the steel and stretched out toward the cover. Just a few more adjustments.

The guards hovered at the edge of her vision, their stun weapons drawn. As if that was a threat when this field could take them out at any moment. She crouched down, trying to find a better angle to dismantle the damn thing.

That's when she spotted it, a large crackling hunk of deformed plastic and metal that might have once been a capacitor bank. It hung by a cable in the middle of the crackling field, supported by two rapidly melting brackets. She needed them to fail faster.

She rolled to the side, slamming her arm into the panel cover, and gave the side of the amovoscope the biggest kick she could muster. Pain shot through her heel, but one of the supports came free. The bubble wobbled as the capacitor bank fell, and she whipped the wand back up. A few frantic twists of the adjustment knobs and the field flickered and popped, forming a perfect sphere in the final moment before it disappeared completely.

The adjustment panel fell to her lap as she leaned back into a desk. A drop of sweat ran down from her hairline.

One of the guards approached, taking the long way around the scorched metal cover. "I'm sorry, miss, but you'll have to come with us."

"It's all a misunderstanding." Orin waved his hand at the amovo-scope's wreckage. "We didn't have time for the keys when the sparky stuff happened."

"But Talavar said—"

"Let me talk to Talavar." Orin took the guard's com, practically snatching it from his belt, and went to inspect the locks on the cabinets. Nothing was broken, of course. Years of practice ensured that.

She turned back to the guards and wiped sweat away with her sleeve. Only a pair of them had come, though there'd been at least six on duty. The artifacts weren't in this room, were they? It was just supposed to look like they were. But if they weren't here...

Orin tossed the com back to its owner and motioned for Jo to grab her bag. "The dean wants to see you."

Chapter Two

— · —

Jo

Two buildings over stood the administration office, looking like a giant marshmallow with windows. A giant toasted marshmallow, thanks to decades of buildup and the starlings who nested in the solar panels on the roof.

Jo still had the option to turn back. Technically, the dean didn't have any authority to detain her, and it was only Orin as escort. Even with the weight of her equipment bag, she could easily outpace him. And if they tried to press charges, well, she'd taken enough scans of the amovoscope to prove her innocence. But if she ran, she wouldn't get paid. Or have a shot at the artifacts.

That didn't stop her from considering it as they trudged up the wide spiral staircase at the building's center. Getting grilled with a bunch of questions wasn't how she wanted to spend her morning. The whole experience reminded her too much of college. Getting ordered into the dean's office because Professor Fennit "doesn't appreciate getting called out in class over technicalities" and "Jo must have plagiarized because her project used components we haven't covered yet." It wasn't her fault Fennit wasn't used to students reading ahead in the textbook, or actually checking out the "Additional Resources" section on his syllabus.

Administrators in floral skirts and jewel-toned suits brushed past, but Jo kept her eyes on the steps. She hated doing that tight-lipped nod thing people expected when seeing someone they barely knew. All she wanted was to tell Talavar the amovoscope wasn't her fault, confirm her payment, and go home.

She paused mid-step on the landing. Up ahead, a pair of buff women sat outside the dean's office, sporting t-shirts baggy enough to conceal all manner of security tech. The door also had a shiny new lock. Perhaps she could stay for a bit more after all.

"Jo! So good to see you." Anita Talavar burst out of her office door with a smile. She wore her usual belted dress, with a row of big red buttons running down the left side. Dean Talavar's smile was peculiar, though. Too many teeth. Especially for someone whose most expensive piece of lab equipment was now a charred husk of metal.

Orin cleared his throat. "Now as I was saying on the com, when we—"

"Yes, I'm sure Jo had nothing to do with the amovoscope failing. It's only her own inventions that melt podiums and burn faculty members." Talavar chuckled at her own quip and motioned for Jo to come in. Orin was pointedly left outside when the door closed. "But enough about the past. How's freelancing going? Any interesting projects lately?"

"It's been going well." Or at least it had been, until a poorly maintained amovoscope almost killed her and the dean thought to mention the worst day of her life. The day her thesis project spewed a fountain of acid, burning away any shot she had at joining a big tech company. Talavar's office looked the same as it had then. A curved, cushioned bench ran along one side, littered with paperwork, spare shoes, and tangled charging cords. Oval bookshelves held debate trophies and diplomas, and the collection of self-improvement books looked to be in the same order, if not a little dustier. She half-expected her parents to be sitting in front of the tangerine desk. Mom rambling on about how they'd pay whatever it takes to make it right. Her dad arguing that the school's insurance should cover everything, and wasn't it actually her adviser's fault for not checking the grad project over first?

Jo took a deep breath. In the end, they did let her graduate, even if she didn't get to shake Professor Fennit's still-bandaged hand. Big help the diploma was when she couldn't get any recommendation letters to send in with her job applications.

Talavar took her place behind the desk and mustered one of those smiles drenched in fake sympathy. "I was so sorry to hear the freelance business has been rough lately. It must be hard on you."

Rough lately? "I'm afraid I don't kn—"

"I know it's difficult for me, as someone with a long-term, stable position, to truly empathize with your plight, but I want you to know that we're here for you. That assistant maintenance position is still on the table, should you change your mind."

"I'm good, thanks." So this is what she got called in for. Talavar was always trying to save money by adding her to the staff. It was a steady job, but at half the hourly she charged freelancing. Any other day, Jo would have walked right out, but today she spotted a new Kisgy 427 security cabinet behind Talavar's desk.

The dean pursed her lips. "You know, we have a research opening, too. Same great benefits, but more flexible hours."

And possibly the same workload. "Oh? And how's Fennit's flex migration project going?" The one he'd been working on for over a decade because he never seemed to receive enough funding.

"Fine. He's just fine." Talavar pushed her chair back and rapped her hand on the cabinet. The keypad flashed at the ready. "You know, there are other benefits to working here. Quite interesting and rare ones."

The Resero artifacts. Jo tried to keep her interest from showing on her face. "Such as?"

"Oh, I'm sure you've heard about them."

"Nope. Not a clue."

"You couldn't possibly not have—"

"Nope." Jo forced herself to grab her bag and stand. She'd have to push Talavar's buttons if she wanted the dean to show her the artifacts without making any promises. "If there wasn't anything else?"

"The Resero artifacts, Jo. I'll let you work with the artifacts. All you have to do is sign a two-year contract."

She swallowed back a *yes, absolutely*. "How do I know they're legit?"

"Oh, they're fully authenticated and documented." Talavar swiped a card through the lock, then used her body to block the keypad as she typed. The door cracked open just enough to slide something small out before it shut again. "But you have to leave your equipment bag by the door."

Jo complied, more than a little annoyed that she hadn't thought to hide the resonance meter in her sleeve. They both knew the resonance was the most valuable part of the artifacts; that any trace of materials or their interdimensional imprint could hold clues to whatever Resero was working on last. What Talavar didn't know was just how much Jo could do with that information, given she could get her own prototype working back home.

Once the dean was back in her seat, she revealed a metal shaft with a blue and gray etched handle. A Venaen crystal probe. Her hand blocked the tip in case Jo had devised a way to get a sample without the scanner, but she didn't pull back when Jo leaned forward for a better look.

"And where's your proof of authenticity, then?" Jo asked. She already knew, of course. All the news articles said Resero's niece had stamped the artifacts before sending them off. But pretending to inspect the stamp gave her an excuse to touch the handle. She held it steady, playing at twisting her head so the swirl of the 'R' was right side up while her fingers crept up the other side.

Talavar pulled it out of her hands mid-twist. "I think that's enough proof, then. If you agree to my terms, you can help Fennit take samples. Maybe even work with him to make history. What do you say?"

She wanted to say was that she already had samples, and that Talavar had helped her get them. While the dean had pulled the probe away, Jo had scraped her nails to collect residue from the handle's etching. "I'll think on it."

She collected her bag and bid the dean farewell with a smug little smile and no further explanation. It wasn't easy to manage while keeping her hand half-closed to protect the dust beneath her fingernails, but it was worth it. Oh, so worth it.

Outside, the air felt cool and damp, but victory was close at hand. Sure, Talavar had kept the probe's tip covered, but residue from that wouldn't have been much help anyway. Who knew if Resero had even used that specific tool on the rumored prototype. But the handle? That almost certainly had Resero's residue on it. If there was enough of it, the prototype tracking device that had commandeered her living room could deduce where he'd been before he died, and that opened all sorts of possibilities.

Her resonance scanner beeped from her bag, letting her know it had finished processing the amovoscope data. She was tempted to take it out to check the handle residue as well, but it was better to get further from campus first. There were still security guards about.

She kept her hand cupped around her nails to protect the sample as she hastened past domed lecture halls and cylindrical dormitories to the edge of campus. One of the buff women from Talavar's office appeared to be following her, but it was too late to stop Jo now. Her escape route beckoned from across the street.

A large brick building rose before her, with wing-like additions sprouting from its sides to hold row after row of transport rooms. It had been a train depot once, but now the tracks that ran under the road were silent and no one ventured in intending to remain in this dimension. She'd heard in her grandmother's day the idea of this sort of travel was quite scandalous, but for her generation, sliding between dimensions was as safe and commonplace as flying. And the building's proximity to campus meant students didn't have to live on the same planet, much less the same city. This sliding station was one of the few things the university had going for it, really. Just that and the fact that they charged less tuition than any other accredited tech school in the quadrant.

She pushed through the door with her elbow, protecting the grit under her fingernails. Footsteps followed her to the side stairs, but they'd drop off soon enough. She was off campus now, and out of the domain of any overly zealous security guards. If the footsteps belonged to another traveler, well, most people didn't bother heading to the very top. Even during rush hour, commuters were inclined to choose the rooms closer to street level, which meant Jo could avoid impatient people huffing about how many devices she needed to lay out on the scanning bed.

The transport officers tended to be huffy about that, too, sometimes. As if she was holding up the line on purpose. But it wasn't like she could take her equipment through without getting them cleared for transport. A few stray bursts of energy could send her traveling off in the wrong direction, or get her lost in Stringspace entirely.

She reached the conveyor belt to unload, only to find the footsteps hadn't faded after all. The buff security guard had followed her in and was quickly approaching the security line. The room wasn't large, only about twelve meters square, and its lack of furnishings other than the security equipment meant Jo had no place to hide. Not that she had a reason to hide. Slipping her hand behind her back was a perfectly normal part of getting ready for the pre-transport scan. But how was she supposed to get a scan of the residue now? She couldn't chance losing it during transport with no backup scan. If she was seen, would the woman accuse her of stealing in front of the security officers? Would she try to drag Jo back to Talavar's office?

She had to think of something. The best she could do was pretend she hadn't noticed the woman and start wiggling her bronze metimur out of her bag and onto the rubbery conveyor belt. Compared to the simple scanning bed, the device was huge and heavy, and turned out to be just the thing to give her an idea. The rest of her equipment followed, carefully arranged in scanner bins to block the security guard's view of her resonance scanner. Take that, Miss Muscles. A flick of the switch and a spin of the knobs to select settings, and Jo took the readings in less time than it'd take to set the scanner to travel mode. The sample would be finished processing by the time she got home.

Talavar's guard stayed back from the security line, which was expected, but also somewhat unnerving. The woman moved like she was taking a picture and sending it to someone. Talavar? Jo repacked her bag and hurried to the transport area. She had to act innocent. She *was* innocent. There were no laws—that she knew of—that prevented her from touching the probe when it was offered. Still, her heart beat a guilty rhythm as she took her place in one of the many blue transport circles. Like the others in the surrounding tile, her circle was two meters wide and barely more than a painted line. Somewhere, hiding in the lines and cracks of the ceiling, cameras and sensors were detecting her presence and preparing to send the data through satellites and interplanetary nodes. Other nodes, the ones positioned around the yellow arrival circles, were confirming their availability for travelers sliding in and flashing through Stringspace like lights on a runway.

Once in her circle's center, Jo swiped a finger across her nav bracelet. She kept her back to the security guard to block her view of the destination dials projected by the thin bronze band. She set the first two numbers to her target dimension, a quaint little world she called home. The third and fourth numbers pinpointed the station by her apartment. Her screen blinked twice to confirm, and she started to sense the interdimensional string through her wrist and finger.

With her destination set, she reached for the familiar tingle of the trans-dimensional link. It had a greenish-yellow taste that kind of stuck to the roof of her mouth like sour honey. One of her college textbooks had tried to explain the sensation of the strings, but the technical jargon never felt quite right. No string felt the same as the others, and rarely did two people perceive them the same way. The concept of their use was the same, though. A traveler shifted their body's natural frequency to match the vibrations of their target dimension, gradually phasing until their adjustment was complete. She wrapped her mind around the sensation and *pulled*.

Conveyor belts, scanners, and circles slid past her. The ground disappeared, and she floated in a swirling opal mist, with whispers and a hint of cinnamon tugging at her senses. Her muscles held motionless, as if paralyzed. Even her heart ceased its beating, but she didn't need it mid-phase. She ignored her paralysis and focused on the string. Its pulse felt strongest in her chest, and she willed her equipment bag to match its frequency, spreading it through every atom of her tools and circuitry. The nav device amplified the signal, helping her focus.

A moment later, the swirling opal faded into a tile floor. Her lungs gasped for air, and a steady rhythm restarted in her chest. Had she lost anything? The bag felt as heavy as before, and a quick check allayed her fears. She couldn't be sure about the stuff under her fingernails, though. She'd only ever had a thin layer, so a few particles here and there wouldn't be obvious.

Other than the absence of Talavar's guard, this room wasn't much different from the one she'd just left. She started for the exit, but her scanner beeped from her bag. One little peek before heading home wouldn't hurt anything, right?

She scrolled through the amovoscope data first. Charts of spectrometry and composition data filled the screen, almost entirely readings she'd expected. Melted plastic. Fried circuits. Overheated dielectrics. But one energy pattern she didn't recognize. A deeper analysis might prove whether it had caused the amovoscope's meltdown.

As for the Resero residue, it did indeed have traces of humanoid resonance that could work in her prototype. Also lubricant, steel shavings, scorched silicate, and... No, that couldn't be right. She flipped back to the amovoscope data, tracing the peaks and troughs of the strange reading. How was it the same? How in the hell was the same energy signal from the amovoscope on Resero's tool? It's not like the tool could have caused the failure from halfway across campus. She must have contaminated it. What other explanation could there be? Anxiety demanded Jo be certain, so she spent a quarter hour looking like an idiot, standing beside the sliding circle with the scanner wand under her fingers and frowning at the screen. The tops of her nails and pads of her fingers didn't have any trace of the signal. Only the tiny line of residue she'd scratched off the tool did. That had to be a coincidence, right? Like, there was no way that Resero's old probe, located in a whole other building, could have caused the malfunction. Jo bit the inside of her lip. The only other explanation was that Resero had something in common with the failure. Or perhaps his missing prototype did.

This treasure hunt might be more interesting than she'd expected.

CHAPTER THREE

— • —

PRAVI

P ravi Resero knew better than to flinch when the D.I.C. director held up the bag of black powder. *If you're going to fall for a trick,* her uncle used to say, *at least make sure it's a clever one.*

Three weeks. That's how long since he'd passed. And during that time, the Department of Interdimensional Counterterrorism had tried dozens of tactics to make her admit the prototype existed. Interrogations disguised as friendly conversations. Slipping in little questions in the middle of unrelated discussions. Confining her to the house 'for her safety' with the promise to lift it once they found either the prototype or evidence there never was one.

Not that she had anything against the house her uncle had left her. It was a long, single story of white-washed concrete. Sleek lines. Perfectly square windows. A sturdy flat roof that cantilevered over the narrow slate porch.

And here was Regional Director Munus, holding the small plastic bag. This sort of "gotcha" was anything but clever. Knocking on her door, making a little small talk, then sliding out the bag as a "oh, and one more thing..." Pravi let her fatigue show as boredom. She had better things to do than play the D.I.C.'s little games. Like finding the prototype before they did.

"My agents found this on some tools you sent to Jiulin University." Director Munus held out the bag, keeping his free hand tucked into the pocket of his impeccably tailored track suit. His slim build and shadowed chin suggested mid-40s; quite young for someone in that position. Less of an ass than the last one she met. "Care to explain?"

"Not really." Just because he had evidence didn't mean he had proof. She'd learned that the hard way when she and her uncle tried to get the last director charged with corruption.

He kept holding the bag anyway. It was one of their tactics, dragging out moments of silence to make their target uncomfortable enough to fill it. Too bad for him, she'd committed their strategy guides to memory. She grinned, the kind of blank-eyed smile most people found unnerving. Guidebook E Chapter 37 suggested it as a counterattack to extended silence.

They'd been on the same side once, back when Uncle Xander was still a senior energy consultant. Identifying faulty products, recovering stolen goods, tracking smugglers... that sort of thing. For anything involving cutting-edge tech or weird energy signatures, Uncle Xander was their man. Pravi had helped too, but without the badge or clearance.

One minute. That's how long she and Munus had held their poses. Another and people might start wondering if they were mannequins.

Pravi would have made a good consultant herself, but unfortunately for them, the D.I.C. would never officially take on an insensate. Too much risk, they said, since she couldn't slide away if the mission went sideways. She didn't realize just how deep their prejudice went until after Xander's death. Keeping her locked in her own home. Trying to void Uncle Xander's will and confiscate the contents of his laboratory. Telling the judge that a woman who couldn't sense the strings couldn't even keep herself safe, much less the 'legacy of the most brilliant scientist of our time.' As if they hadn't tried to declare him incompetent just a few years before. What she really wanted to do was get her Z73 plasma blaster and tell Munus to get the hell off her porch. But that would cause more trouble than it was worth.

Instead, Pravi leaned against the front door's metal frame and crossed her arms over her olive green jacket. A light breeze teased at the hood, and her short black hair brushed the bottoms of her ears. "What is that, anyway? Mold or something?"

"Not mold. Fenmo powder. The kind that can be programmed to mimic other resonances under the right conditions. See, what you do is—"

"I know what Fenmo powder is." She flicked her dark brown eyes back to Munus. "What I don't see is what it has to do with me."

He smiled and tucked the bag into his pocket. "Why don't you tell me?"

Tell him what? That she'd been using the powder to smuggle out clues to her uncle's missing prototype? That she trusted complete strangers more than she trusted the department? The prototype was dangerous, that much was true, but better to risk the wrong person finding it than to help the D.I.C. Too many of the devices her uncle helped recover "disappeared" from storage and reappeared on the black market. Better to form her own team and get the job done right. "Xander's workshop was a mess when I got here. Toolboxes dumped out, lids only half screwed on, metal scraps everywhere..." All evidence that he'd recently finished a prototype, but she wasn't going to tell Munus that. "I wouldn't be surprised if a bag spilled off a shelf and he just left it."

"A substance that's worth thousands per ounce and he just ... left it?" Munus must have had a great deal of self-control to keep his face that emotionless. The tops of his eyebrows didn't even peek over his sunglasses.

Pravi held back a smile of her own. "Wouldn't surprise me in the least."

It wasn't entirely a lie. Her uncle had gotten lax in his final years. Notes scattered between rooms. Groceries left on the counter instead of put away in the pantry. An easily corruptible prototype left unsecured and stolen from an off-world locker... And the worst part was, he hadn't thought to tell her about it until he was on his deathbed. One moment she was grappling with the possibility that his heart condition would kill him, and the next, he was confessing that not only had he not retired, but he'd been conducting illegal experiments with cosmic radiation. It was the only way for her to slide, he said, to finally sense the strings. He didn't mean to lie to her, he just wanted her to be surprised.

Because only Xander would get her a birthday present that involved breaking a dozen research regulations.

"I see." Munus shifted his weight forward and then back again. "So you're saying you were not aware of this at all?"

"Should I have been?" It was an interesting staring contest. Munus acting like he didn't have a multitude of more pressing cases and Pravi pretending the doorframe wasn't digging into her shoulder.

"If there's nothing els—" Pravi's watch beeped a proximity alert. She swiped across the screen to see a woman running a long, pole-like device through the ornamental grasses in the side flower bed.

Munus cleared his throat. "I suppose there was one more thing. We're conducting a security scan of the premises. With how many people came to pick up the donations, we wanted to make sure no one left anything behind."

Wanted to test her security perimeter was more like it. And all the while, Munus had used the bag of powder to distract her. A much better ruse than she'd given him credit for.

"I see." She needed a way to spin this in her favor, or at least make it less advantageous for the department. "Correct me if I'm wrong, but I believe I have a right to be present for such scans?"

He froze for a moment. "I believe so, yes."

"Give me a minute, then." Pravi slipped into the house, careful to block the director's view of the interior as she closed the door. No sense in giving him an excuse to barge in and claim he saw some phantom threat.

Inside, the sparse entryway opened into a museum-like hallway, with lighted nooks and alcoves on either side. Xander's favorite inventions had once stood on display, at least the ones the embassy didn't deem dangerous to the local population. His first nav prototype. A broadband scanning array. An electronic secretary that would write on his whiteboard while he ate lunch. He'd spelled out where to donate each in his will. And, surprise, surprise, the D.I.C. had insisted on scanning them before they left. As if she'd try to sneak out the real prototype right under their noses. Let them chase false leads then. It meant Pravi had more time to stay ahead.

Chasing leads... Pravi checked her surveillance feed again, this time on high speed and pausing whenever the agent stopped to check the grass. Sure enough, the woman had planted at least three penny-sized devices. Probably to take out a section of her security net. If that's how they were going to play this...

She strode to the third alcove on the left and ran her finger along the side. Uncle Xander had loved the classics, so of course his mission supply closet had a secret door, opened by pushing sections of the wood trim in the correct order. Inside, cubbies, hooks, and cabinets lined the walls, leaving just enough space in the room's center for a pair of benches they'd once used for staging missions. She looked longingly at her Z73, but grabbed a metal detector-like scanner instead and stuck a handful of listening devices in her jacket sleeve. She could use this opportunity to get a leg up on the D.I.C.; to spy on their patrols as they'd tried to spy on her.

Once ready, she met Munus in the side yard next to the firepit, at the center of a checkerboard of concrete squares and grass. The patio chairs had been stacked far in the corner, replaced by folding tables and a large white canopy that served as the D.I.C.'s makeshift command center. Munus still had one hand in his pocket while the other held his transcom, and the only sign he noticed her arrival was a pause in the scrolling of his thumb across the screen. The agent with the scanner stood beside him.

"So we're ready to start, then?" Pravi asked, holding her own scanner in front of her like a cane.

The agent gave a self-satisfied grin. "I'm almost done, actually. Just this little patch of patio left."

"Oh? Sorry to trouble you, but owner's right to be present and all that."

"But it doesn't make sense to—"

Munus tucked his com in his pocket. "We're ready to proceed." He gestured toward the yard and took a step back out of the way. If he suspected Pravi knew about the penny-sized disks they'd left, he hid it well behind a look of boredom.

Pravi mimicked the sweep of his arm and smiled at the other agent. "After you."

The agent flashed her teeth back, more gritted than grinning, and started a careful scan of the nearest flower bed. Something about the way she moved made Pravi suspect she was legacy—the kind of agent who measured their career in tasks completed and cases solved. Other than passing over the planted disk a tad fast, her motions were precise and professional. Almost like the familiarity of the action had made her forget her annoyance with Pravi.

Couldn't let that last long. Pravi started up her own scanner, setting it to a special program Xander had come up with himself. It would still beep for the items and resonance patterns in its database, but would also alert if she gave the side of the handle a squeeze. She swept it twice over other flowers before hovering over the planted disk and hitting the switch. The beeping drew the agent's attention.

"Oh, what's this?" she said in faux surprise. As much as she wanted to exaggerate it, she kept her voice low and steady. Munus would probably know she'd seen it planted, but it helped to practice keeping her expressions in place. Her three-year sabbatical had come with a little rust.

The agent craned her neck to see and nearly dropped her probe into a tangle of creeping moss. She looked from Pravi to the disk and then over to Munus. They exchanged a quick flurry of eyebrow movements while Pravi took the resonance data from the disk and added it to her list of scanning targets.

"It's a good thing you thought of scanning, Mr. Munus," she said, intentionally dropping his title. "Might want to have your agent expand her search parameters, though."

Munus nodded, and the agent gritted her teeth, pretending to flip through the scanner screens. Unfortunately for her, Pravi had no intention of leaving it at that.

They spent the next two hours passing scanner probes over the flowers and grass, with the agent trying and failing thrice more to keep

Pravi from finding the planted disks. When she finally gave up, Pravi let one of her own devices slide from her sleeve into her palm and pretended she'd just picked it up.

"Ooo, new version this time."

This drew Munus' attention, and he responded with a stern look at his agent. Her russet cheeks took on a pinkish hue.

Good. Now that Pravi had thrown them off guard, she could focus on expanding her own surveillance. She worked her way through the D.I.C.'s usual rotations, pretending to check the foliage for devices while secretly planting some of her own. The disks' dark brown exterior blended cleanly with the surrounding soil and mulch. She made sure to keep her back to Munus and the agent each time, but it didn't really matter. The agent had returned to scanning with a renewed vigor—much too focused to pay attention to Pravi—and Munus was likewise distracted with supervising. Pravi would have smiled if it wouldn't give herself away.

Work done, she made another few passes of her scanner before brushing off her hands. Hopefully, her new surveillance net would be enough to let her move from defensive to offense when it came to the D.I.C.'s tricks. The prototype was legally hers, both by her uncle's intent and a broad clause in his will for 'the remaining estate.' Any supposed 'authority' that tried to claim otherwise, or that treated her like a second-class citizen, wasn't worth her respect.

Munus caught up with her before Pravi reached the porch. "Excuse me, Ms. Resero."

"Yes?"

"You dropped these." He pulled another evidence bag from his pocket and let it unroll with a flick of his wrist. Four metal lumps sat nestled in a scattering of mulch and dead grass. The surveillance bugs. Four of the six she'd planted, anyway.

Munus presented a tougher adversary than she thought. "I guess that's what happens when you find more than you can hold. Just toss them in the bin with the others."

"Are you sure?"

"What else would I do with them? I don't want whoever planted them to be spying on me."

To this, the director could only open his mouth to respond, then close it again. He hadn't expected her to keep up the act. It felt like a small victory, catching him off guard enough to make him drop his emotionless facade. Not to mention the two surveillance bugs he hadn't found.

She hung her scanner back on its hook. As for the Fenmo powder, well, the D.I.C. couldn't have intercepted all of it. Somewhere out there, an enterprising young scientist could be analyzing her message. Assuming Pravi hadn't messed up the frequency or programming, they'd soon find out what her uncle had been working on. As a sliding device, it was relatively harmless. But the battery... In the wrong hands, it could become a weapon.

CHAPTER FOUR

— • —

Jo

Jo pinched a stubby bolt and grounding wire in place inside a bear-sized carcass of metal, while her other hand searched the tile around her knees. She'd spent the last three days in this position—back arched, head ducked inside the half-meter-wide frame while her arms scraped against rough-cut panels. It'd taken much too long to realize she needed a pad to kneel on, when the purple on her knees turned out to be bruising and not oil stains.

The scraping from the Resero artifact waited on her workbench. There'd been something weird about the ratio of materials, but she had successfully isolated the physicist's resonance. All she needed now was for this junk heap of a prototype to actually function, so she could use it to trace his last movements.

Her teeth gripped a thin flashlight while she worked. If she turned even slightly, she might lose sight of the grounding bracket amidst the tangle of wiring and components. Her searching fingers found cool metal. Rounded head, eight millimeter profile. She pulled the wrench inside the opening, careful not to let her spotlight budge even when her sleeve snagged against the edge of the opening. One new fabric run among many. The shirt's gray canvas almost looked like it was meant to have that texture, though the splotches of lubricant and oil stains were anything but intentional.

Her prototype, dubbed 'the cryptoscope,' was a gangly thing. Lanky arms sprouted from the sides like the jagged limbs of a patchwork octopus. She'd harvested most of the components from scrap shops, and spare cuts from old jobs served as the plating. Even if she could afford it, she couldn't have made it much prettier. But maybe if she'd spent more, the blasted parts would actually fit on the first try. Two more screws. She just needed to install two more screws, and then she could do a test run with the Resero sample.

Her bracelet buzzed as she finished tightening the bolt. Either her mom was texting about family dinner night or someone had posted a news article about the missing Resero device.

"I wouldn't get that if I were you," Nik said from the kitchen. She'd almost forgotten her friend was there, though he came by most days between classes—always with a big stack of papers to grade.

"And why's that?" Without turning around, Jo swiped on the tiny screen to see 'Viral Inventor Claims He Cracked Resero Case.'

Nik shrugged. "Just trust me on this. It's just another braggart making vague statements for attention." He sat with his back toward her. Curly brown hair piled atop his head, while the cuffed sleeves of his button-up rested on the kitchen island—it was barely a kitchen, really. Simple white cabinets and a fridge cowered in the far corner, with a two-stool island used more for Nik's papers and laying out components than eating. His arm moved as if marking someone's homework, but he didn't turn the page or add it to the stack.

Jo became keenly aware of the room outside her prototype. The workbench along the wall of windows opposite the kitchen. Cluttered shelves of spare parts and tools to either side, with wires running up to the ceiling. And Nik's trancom, no longer visible on the counter. "So, which braggart was it this time?"

"No one you'd care to hear from."

Jo's hand paused halfway to grabbing the next screw. There'd been many claims lately; some from less popular universities, some from tech bloggers, and many from small-time inventors looking for attention. *'Oh, it's in this octave of worlds.' 'Oh, it's by this sort of city or land formation.'* Always too vague to be helpful. But Nik had never held her back from looking before.

"Now I've done it." Nik turned around, his red pen capped and held tightly in his fist. "I was too insistent, wasn't I?"

"Yeah." Jo fiddled with the screwdriver for a moment before setting it down. She couldn't risk messing up the install if her focus wasn't there.

"You can use my com, if you want."

That would make it easier to walk away and disengage if she needed to. "You know me too well."

"Fifteen years will do that to you."

Fifteen years. Over half their lives since twelve-year-old Jo moved into the apartment next to his. That might have been when Nik's counter habit started, coming by when his mom left for work and staying until his dad came back home. Doing homework while Jo fiddled with whatever broken device her mom had brought home last. It was more than enough time to know how Jo would react when she looked over his shoulder. She should have trusted him when he said she wouldn't want to know.

Kniel Jacron grinned at the top of the article, his trademark computer chip logo in the bottom left corner. 'Jacron says followers in for a "wild ride"', read the caption. 'Vlogger's new video series will follow epic journey to retrieve missing Resero prototype.' It was all too easy to read the quotes in Jacron's voice. One of his old videos ran on repeat in her mind any time she fumbled with the cryptoscope. One of those reaction videos, the kind where the vlogger records themselves over a clip sent in by followers, laughing and gasping at how someone's invention failed spectacularly. Jo usually laughed and gasped along. Except that last time, the invention had been hers.

Another student had recorded from the back row during the thesis presentations, far enough away that Jo hadn't noticed the familiar auditorium with Jacron chattering in the foreground. She hadn't even recognized herself until the camera zoomed in on the messy-haired and sleep-deprived figure on stage. From there, it felt like the video slowed to half speed. There was her thesis project, shiny and pristine, being loaded with a sample for chemical analysis. Then it was shaking, whirling the way it had in the tests, but a little faster, a little hotter. A wisp of smoke, a hiss of venting. Her face sinking from anxious energy into petrified dismay.

'Well, that wasn't supposed to happen,' Jacron had said with a laugh. *'Poor girl. Sounds like she might have the wrong size motor. Just a bit too big and it can start to— Sweet mother of destruction, what the hell is that?'*

Molten yellow melted a hole through the shell, quickly pooling on the podium and spilling onto the professors' tablets as they frantically tried to shake it off.

What was it Jacron had said? *'This chick should not be allowed around a soldering iron. What did she do, weld a detonation device to it?'* Though not nearly as dramatic, the truth was just as amateur. She'd missed a decimal when she'd calculated the pressure for the emergency release valve.

Jo pulled herself away from the transcom. She couldn't take the same risks with the cryptoscope. "Time to put the suit on." She pulled a hazmat suit and goggles from a cabinet of dusty baking dishes and tossed them to Nik.

He sighed and lifted a yellow sleeve. "What if I just hide behind the counter?"

"And what if one of the limbs flies off and sprays hydraulic fluid?" She picked up the last two screws and knelt back at the base. "Just do it for me? Please?"

There was a rustle from the kitchen, and by the time she'd finished putting in the last component and had double-checked the wiring, Nik was mostly in the suit. He'd only pulled his zipper to mid-chest and the hood hung down his back, but at least the goggles sat tight on his face. She checked the fit of her own safety glasses and flipped the power on at the control station. Images of spilled acid and molten metal threatened to steal her attention, but she pushed them aside to focus on the cryptoscope.

The initial hum sounded promising, and after a few moments, she let her hand drift away from the emergency shut-off and inserted the Resero sample into the analysis tray. Another small whirr, but no grinding yet. The limbs lifted, and she kicked a few stray tools out of their way. The base protested a bit, but that was expected. Soon, if the arms didn't pop or explode first, they'd start phasing in and out as they rotated around the base. She'd gotten the idea from the amovoscope. Send the sensors just barely into Stringspace, clear of the signal distortion from the surrounding world, and add that extra dimension of triangulation to the scan. The algorithms alone had taken three years to write. This was her first chance to test it all together.

Her hand hovered over the emergency switch. At first, the joints jerked and clicked in a stuttered attempt at life, but soon the movements grew smooth, gliding upward and down as they danced around the base. Some sped and some slowed, phasing in and out to avoid collisions. It was working. The confounded thing was really working. Sensors blinking, looking for traces of Resero across the known worlds. Lines of code filled the screen, mapping out a path between them. What would she find by following that path? The limbs spun and lifted in an intricate dance, tracing delicate lines with their blinking sensors. *Who was the one who should avoid soldering irons now, Jacron?*

A large popping sound echoed from the base, and whatever had failed sent smoke pouring out through the gaps in the plating. *No. Please, not an actuator.* Jo slammed down the emergency shutoff switch, but it was too late. The limbs unphased and crashed into each other at odd angles. Glass sensors shattered. Joints bent. Pieces of plating grated and rolled, sprinkling metal shavings across the tile.

As if that wasn't bad enough, the fire alarm beeped as the smoke reached the ceiling. Jo had under a minute before her makeshift override let the signal pass and the sprinklers poured gallons of water over the prototype's fragile circuitry. Extending the override could save the electronics. Or, if the smoke's source was a true fire and not the dying breath of a component, it could doom the frame and joints as well.

Disappointment rang in her ears, sounding an awful lot like Jacron's voice. Maybe she should just let the water take it and find something else to do with her life. The scent of melted rubber oozed across the floor. It had a chemical edge to it, like the puffs released by dying transistors, and not at all like overheated grease. So much would need to be rebuilt, anyway. Maybe stalling the sprinklers would be worth the risk? She hit the override extender and slid open a window.

There was too much to take in. The jagged joints. The shards of glass and dull metal shavings. It'd take days to fix everything, or weeks, if the interior damage had hit the harder-to-source components.

"At least none of the limbs flew off." Nik came up beside her, goggles on his forehead and arms crossed. "So what are we thinking about for your new career? Hippotherapist or Vitruvian goat farm tour guide?"

Jo snorted in spite of herself. "Goat farm tour guide?"

"Ah, yeah, I forgot. Tour guides have to talk to people." Nik smiled, the mischievous one he always did when he was trying to cheer her up. "Guess you have to stick to engineering."

"Guess so."

No sense in delaying the inevitable. She grabbed her diagnostic pad from the desk and plugged it into an undamaged port on the back side. Orange light flickered on the plating, and she jumped back. It wasn't flames, was it? It took her a few frantic seconds to realize it hovered around the holoprojectors.

A map. The blasted thing had the nerve to spit out a map.

Several hundred orbs wavered into focus above the broken device, bathed in a spectrum of red, violet, and blue. In a way, they were all the same planet, occupying the same relative position in the universe, just in parallel dimensions. Minor differences between them had compounded in the millions of years since their creation, resulting in varying landmass sizes and geography.

Jo zoomed into the octave containing Resero's homeworld. A bulging cloud of gold shimmered around it, with a faint strand of green twisting inside. Weird. She'd only been expecting the green. She must not have isolated the resonance from the tools as much as she'd thought.

"Is there a problem?" Nik craned his neck over her shoulder. He smiled when he spotted the map. "Or is this the opposite of a problem?"

"A bit of both, I think?" She prodded the floating ribbon of green. "This streak traces out Resero's movements. You can see how it hops between Terran and these other worlds, but it's too faded to tell which he visited and which he merely passed by. Plus, there's this."

Jo gestured to the sweeping gold puff. "It's tangled up with Resero's movements and screwing with my readings."

"Can you filter it out?"

"I'm trying."

"Could it be a broadcasting channel?"

"The dispersion doesn't match any registered bands." Jo lowered the diagnostic pad and bit her lip. "It must have been present in the Resero sample or the scope wouldn't track it."

Nik raised an eyebrow. "The missing prototype?"

"Only if it's still running. The gold is so bright while the green is so—" Oh. Oh no. There were her hopes, getting themselves up again. What was she thinking, considering following the path? Why would she think this was anything but the dying outputs of her own failed invention? This wasn't anywhere near where Jacron said he'd be heading.

"I'm coming with."

"What?"

"To investigate." Nik took the pad from her hand and started running an algorithm of his own on the data. "Look at the dispersion patterns. The eddies. Project or not, you found something."

Jo didn't need special effects overlapping Nik's face with numbers and equations to know what was going on behind those eyes. Modeling natural processes and patterns was his thing, just as much as machinery was hers. She wouldn't have been able to crack the cryptoscope's algorithm without his help.

"I appreciate the offer, but where would we start? Even if we assume I didn't mess up the cryptoscope, we have this huge mass of gold to wade through." Better to rebuild and try again later. It'd take a while, of course. She'd have to order new sensors, fabricate new limbs, identity which parts failed inside the main body and test for cascading failures. Not to mention figuring out how to pay for it all.

"This one." Nik handed her back the diagnostic pad.

The screen had amplified a section of the model, zooming in on a cluster of planets near Resero's home planet. In the center lay a shimmering blue orb with a cracked land mass on one side and ocean on the other. Bright white letters labeled it "Yerin," and four threads of green stretched from the golden haze to its surface.

Nik slid his hands into his pockets. "It has only a handful of sliding stations, so it shouldn't be too hard to search."

"Unless he went to a private one."

"Private sliding equipment is prohibited. The main industry is tourism to some sort of nature preserve."

Jo caught herself searching for another excuse, but the truth was she was scared of being wrong. Of wasting their time. Of that bit of hope welling up in her chest. She glanced up at Nik, but his attention zeroed in on his transcom. His fingers flipped between time zone maps and weather charts, then hopped over to tourist blogs and travel tips. He wasn't giving her the option of saying no.

And that bit of hope thanked him for it.

CHAPTER FIVE

— · —

ZAHIRA

A flurry of sand swept through Tilman Yar, battering at Zahira's window. No storm coming, at least not yet. The sky didn't have that dusty orange tint, and hovercraft still flew through the gaps between yellow-brick buildings. When the winds hit Yerin's capital, they'd block out her view completely, and even the tightly packed apartments and HighTrak tubes would disappear in the dusty fog. Two days. She needed the weather to hold for two more days while she completed her errands and staged her and Grandmother's escape.

Though her face stayed turned toward the sky, her attention darted to the street below. No people or vehicles she didn't recognize. The window sheers fell back into place. Their thin gauze was the opposite of a shield, putting up little resistance to glaring light and prying eyes. The room had a set of heavier curtains, but she used them as rarely as possible. She needed everyone to think she had nothing to hide. It was a lie her life depended on.

She took two deep breaths, forcing herself to remain calm. How devastating would it be to give herself away now, when she was this close to leaving this prison of a planet?

Though the street seemed clear of police patrols, Zahira angled her body to block the view of her dresser as she opened a secret panel in its top. Inside sat a pile of cash and a tattered diary, its pages carefully abused, bent, and coffee-stained to look as though the scores of entries spanned decades rather than days. If someone found the compartment, they wouldn't think to dig further. She pushed it all aside to reveal a second latch hidden in a knot of wood. The ceramic box inside held the true secret. Its golden finish was old and faded, and when combined with the diary, one might expect it to contain sentimental treasures from a long-lost love. What it really held was the truth of who she was. What she was.

Grandmother sighed from the bed. "I can't imagine how you filled the old ones so fast. Have you been doing the breathing exercises like I taught you?"

Zahira nodded, but couldn't help her anxiety. After living in fear for twenty-three years—for her whole life—they finally had a chance to leave Yerin behind. Grandmother was getting too old for life in hiding. Even the foam mattress, once considered a luxury after years spent in desert camps, had grown too hard on her joints. And Zahira, well... Never having to run anymore might be too much to hope for, but those hunting her would find their task exponentially more difficult once she made it off-world.

She sat cross-legged on the bed and set the box beside her. A dozen metallic coils rattled inside, each one small enough to wrap her pinkie. When her grandmother had first brought them home, she'd thought of them as tiny shields. As if hiding who she was could keep her safe. She later learned safety was an illusion she couldn't afford to buy into.

She unwrapped her hair, letting her springy black curls free from her silk scarf. Most of it poofed upward, while a row of pinned twists around her crown hid a second set of coils. They buzzed at her scalp. She'd tried placing them elsewhere, but with how klutzy Zahira had been as a girl, everywhere else had proven too prone to breakage.

Grandmother sighed again and started untwisting Zahira's hair and removing the coils. "This time you may have collected enough nguvu to power the apartment."

It wasn't a criticism, but it felt like one. Zahira couldn't prevent her body from harvesting the stray radiation, but she could control how fast it happened. If she had remained calm, she would have filled the coils more gradually. No matter how stressful the morning had been, she should have kept her emotions in check. Zahira didn't realize her shoulders were drooping until Grandmother gave a light tug to make her sit up straight.

"There was a field fluctuation on Jedvi Avenue," Zahira admitted. "Something massive inside the tech café." The whole street had been blocked off when she went out for supplies. Security officers held back the crowd as vested men filed out with singed monitors and fried server racks. "Do you think it could have been...?"

"A hatari?" Grandmother finished the question for her.

The possibility of meeting someone like her tickled at Zahira's mind like the remnants of stored energy against her skin. The last coil caught and she flinched.

"Best not to look, my noya. You're as likely to find Boliska as someone who shares your markings."

Zahira let her gaze fall to her hands. The gold charms on her wrists used holograms to make her skin a smooth ebony, but she knew where the amber lines twisted across her palms and fingers. Centuries ago, babies born with the markings were abandoned in forests or sacrificed to deities. Now, instead of superstition, the biggest threat to hatari was government labs. Boliska labs.

Comb teeth pressed into Zahira's scalp, separating the hair for a new twist. Grandmother's agile hands worked swiftly, smoothing the ends of each strand with a mix of argilla and piptree oil before inserting a new coil. The earthy scent rekindled Zahira's hopes. "If we found someone else like me, and if we all got off Yerin, and we went to the Senate to testify—"

"That's a lot of ifs for what was more likely a collapsed friction field," Grandmother spoke with all the authority of the engineer she'd been decades ago. Before Zahira was born with the markings. Before both their lives had changed.

Grandmother started reworking the twists around Zahira's crown, pausing after each sentence to insert a pin. "Let's say it was another hatari. What would you have done if Boliska had been on site looking for them? If the agents had their scanners running as you passed by?"

"I guess I..."

Grandmother stopped her with a click of her tongue. "It doesn't matter. Not what you could have done to escape or what you could do if you met someone else like you. Neither of those things happened and, strings willing, they won't have time to happen. We have to stay focused on the present and gather the last of the supply caches." Another pin slid against Zahira's scalp, but quickly slid out again as Grandmother pulled back on the twist. Hard.

"Ow. I get it, focus on the present."

Grandmother continued to pull backward for a few more seconds, tight enough to loosen two more pins before the twist slipped through her fingers. Her weight shifted heavily on the bed and something thumped against the headboard.

Zahira spun around to find Grandmother lying rigid, the left side of her face slouched and drooped. How...? She'd been fine mere moments before. No sign of tranquilizer darts or sniper wounds. Zahira hadn't heard anything either, and a quick check showed the window and apartment door still closed.

She raced over to check Grandmother's pulse. It was slow and her breathing ragged. Her wrinkles appeared deeper, even on the side that slouched. The woman was nearing eighty. Only Zahira's paranoia would assume it was a Boliska raid and not her age. Grandmother had spent so much of her life keeping Zahira safe. She couldn't lose her like this, not when they were so close to leaving. Panic rose in her chest, and her mind went to the emergency bag tucked under the side of the bed. She could call an ambulance and get herself safely away before it arrived.

"Nah noya," Grandmother murmured, movement returning to her face.

"Shh. I'll get help."

"No. Nguvu. They'll know," Grandmother warned. She'd have the traces on her fingers.

"But you'd be safe." Grandmother wasn't hatari, and though the Boliska would try to question her, she'd be no use to their experiments and Zahira would be long gone. She brushed her fingers against the weathered face. "If you don't see a doctor, I'll lose you."

Zahira reached under the bed skirts for her bag, the canvas sack packed with everything she'd need to disappear. New name, passports, stacks of cash... By the time the ambulance arrived, she'd be a ghost.

Even Grandmother wouldn't know where she'd gone. Trembling hands checked that nothing was missing. Her foot snagged on another strap. Grandmother's bag. How many times had they escaped discovery together? For the first time, she'd be starting a new life alone.

Her heart raced, and the amber lines prickled across her skin, raising tiny hairs across her arms and back. She had to leave the only family she'd ever known. Zahira forced the panic down, and the nguvu with it. At least Grandmother could finally rest. Only the spare coils left to pack.

Grandmother stopped her hand. "The numbness is fading. No need to be drastic."

"You need a doctor."

"What I need is to get off Yerin. What good does a doctor do me if I spend the rest of my life worried whether you're safe?"

Zahira slid the pack over her shoulder anyway.

"And what about the devices?" Grandmother continued, her voice gradually losing its slur. "The signal disruptor? The resonance echo? Years of work confiscated in minutes." She gestured at the closet. All the caches Zahira had collected so far sat behind the row of coats. They'd been stored separately for a reason, so that a single random inspection couldn't wipe out all their preparations. If the hospital found the traces of nguvu, it'd only be a matter of time before they checked the apartment and confiscated everything.

"Careful. You only have half the coils in." Grandmother took her arm weakly and stroked the side of her face. "At least let me finish. No need to run off looking like a hare fleeing a sandstorm." She was putting it nicely. In her panic, Zahira had been ready to leave in a way that would surely draw attention. Even if her scarf could conceal the mess of her hair, the heightened emotion and missing coils were a catastrophe waiting to happen. Any stray nguvu could make nearby electrical systems flicker, alerting the Boliska to her presence.

Grandmother combed slowly, putting less tension into the twists. "It'll be alright, I promise. I'll make an appointment as soon as we get off-world. We're too close to give up now."

"Are you sure?" Zahira wanted to insist she see a doctor now. Although the numbness had come on fast, it hadn't looked like something she could get over as easily. She wouldn't put it past Grandmother to lie.

"I'm sure. If we miss our window to leave, we'll have to wait a whole year to try again." The eggs wouldn't wait for them, she meant. Tourism was Yerin's biggest industry, fueled by the giant lizards living on the second continent. All the other worlds had lost theirs millennia before, but somehow the comet that hit Yerin killed only half of the prehistoric creatures. And Grandmother's plan hinged on leaving while planet security focused on hatching season.

"What if something happens before then? What if you have another episode?"

Grandmother worked a pin into the latest coil. "We'll worry about that if it comes. If the Boliska find me, it won't just delay our plans. It would make them impossible." She meant the Boliska would know everything she did.

"But would they really administer the truth serum?" Zahira asked. Would they risk losing their only lead if her aging body couldn't handle it?

"Yes." Grandmother's answer was a whisper. "And they'd watch the sliding station even more closely, especially at hatching time."

As if security wasn't already the size of a small army. Their plan had been to wait for the hatching crowds to peak, but what if Grandmother's health couldn't last that long? Could they risk leaving early? She glanced toward the dresser. "Is the powder ready?"

"Almost." Grandmother twisted the last coil tight against her scalp. It'd taken half their savings, but they'd procured a dusting of fenmo powder, a substance that mimicked other resonance patterns when exposed to the right programming pulse. "It still needs a few hours to set."

And once it set, the security scan would believe it was an egg shard. As the security officers converged on the faux contraband, Grandmother and Zahira could use the resonance echo and signal disruptors to slip past the scanners to the sliding circles.

"We leave tomorrow then. Or tonight." Zahira snatched her scarf off the bed and quickly re-wrapped her hair. "If I grab the cache of power packs now, we can leave as soon as we're ready."

"Waiting two days is less risky. The sliding station will be packed and—"

"Packed isn't that much better than crowded."

"Breathe, Zahira."

"Moving will help burn off the anxiety." She grabbed her bag and checked that it held her transcom. "Promise me you'll be ready." She wasn't leaving Grandmother much choice. Even if the old woman wanted to argue, she'd always cave if it meant calming Zahira down.

"Alright."

"I'll be back in an hour." *Please hold on for an hour.*

Zahira closed the apartment door behind her and turned left, following a trail of rusty sand to the stairwell. It gritted under her sandals with every step. She wanted to hurry, but that might attract attention or make the nguvu build faster.

Outside, the wind whipped sand into drifts along the buildings, mere puddles compared to the sandstorms that flooded the streets every winter. She scurried west, following the clear tube of the HighTrak as it wrapped its way to Mugambe station. Mumea ferns shaded most of the sidewalk with wide, yellow leaves as their thick red trunks stretched as high as the surrounding apartments.

The buildings grew taller as she approached the HighTrak station, standing four or five times the height of the trees. She wouldn't need to pass the security scans, thankfully. Her target was in a locker on the first floor. She walked in and out as fast as she dared, alert to any sign of police or Boliska.

Once she turned the first corner toward home, throngs of tourists blocked her view, pouring from a sliding station a few blocks away. They were easy to spot, standing a full head or two taller than the native Yerins and sporting tank tops and shorts. Their bare arms prickled against the chill. It was amazing how many foreigners thought a desert biome implied heat, even this far from the equator.

The voice of one of them rose behind her, "Holy crap, Nik. They have dinosaurs."

And the woman was only learning this now? Zahira's brow furrowed. What else would tourists come to see? The grand fields of solar panels?

The woman started reading from a tourism pamphlet, stumbling over the price of the Grand Reptile Tour. "Ten thousand monettes a person? That's over half what I made last year."

Her companion shrugged. "We could come back when you win the prize money."

"If we win the prize money," the woman corrected.

Perhaps that was their reason for visiting, some sort of Stringspace scavenger hunt. She'd heard of broadcasting channels paying people to travel between worlds, completing various tasks while filming. While she waited for the light to change, Zahira put a few people between her and the foreigners to avoid any cameras.

Only four more blocks to home. Hovercraft hummed along in rush hour traffic, and perfume and body odor blended with the grimy scent of the street. The woman fumbled with a zipper behind her. Maybe she'd forgotten to turn on her camera. Something mechanical whirred and started beeping.

"Wow, I've got something already." Knobs clicked and the beeping grew louder, and Zahira's stomach tightened. "This can't be right. It says the signal's right here."

Please not a resonance scanner. Zahira risked a glance behind, revealing her worst fear. The waveform on the small, square screen was unmistakable.

Distance. She had to add distance. The light changed and the crowd pushed forward, allowing her to whisk away down a side street.

The beeping continued. She took a turn to the right, looping back toward the station to get out of the scanner's way and keep them from following her home. But still the pair turned when she did. The woman's scanner must have been tracking her. *How the hell was it tracking her?*

"Hey! Wait!" the woman called.

But Zahira couldn't wait. She ran.

CHAPTER SIX

— · —

Jo

J o's workmen's boots slapped and gritted against the sandy pavement as Nik and the Yerin woman got further and further ahead. She would have worn better shoes if she'd known chasing down leads would mean literal chases. Office buildings and quaint shops passed by in her periphery, their occupants drawn to the noise. She'd been worried her sneakers would let sand seep into her socks, but that would have been better than drawing this much attention.

The sidewalks weren't packed, but people kept turning to see what the clomping was, and she could have sworn some of the native Yerins intentionally blocked her. They were easy to spot as they were a full head shorter than the off-worlders and most wore scarves to keep their hair clear of sand. Her transcom translated snippets of sentences. *'Cloud heads.' '... thinking they own the place ...' '... got more height than brains.'* Her cheeks flushed from more than exertion.

She caught up with Nik two corners down, but the Yerin woman was nowhere in sight. Her friend braced one hand against the nearest building and shook his head as he struggled to catch his breath. The woman was fast. Too fast. And she knew the area.

Jo pulled out her scanner, fumbling to untangle the wand's cord from the zipper. Only a faint signal in any direction. Yerins and off-worlders strolled and hustled through the intersection, muddying the resonance trail.

Once he was breathing easier, Nik straightened his clothes and dug his hands into his pockets. A scanner of his own bulged against the fabric. "She took us this way before, you know. Over there's the place we first saw her."

He nodded to the right, and Jo followed his gaze. Sure enough, there stood the glass building that looked like a giant hex wrench, its bottom floors arching over the street. The nearby stone and brick buildings felt familiar as well. By her estimate, they'd taken at least two trips through this intersection, enough for the scanner to pick up traces along every street. The woman would be a kilometer away by the time they checked them all.

As disappointed as Jo felt losing their lead, a little burst of excitement pulsed in her chest. She'd been right. Or more accurately, *the cryptoscope* had been right. As quick as she'd been to dismiss the map as the machine's dying sputters, she couldn't deny the scanner readings. Somehow, Resero was connected to Yerin.

Nik pulled her into the throng of pedestrians heading for the intersection. "So which way do we try?" Nik pulled her from the throng of pedestrians heading for the intersection.

"Left?" The light had only just turned green going straight, and she'd read somewhere that all things being equal, most people would choose right over left. The Yerin woman seemed like someone who'd know that.

"Seems as good as any."

The next time the light changed, Nik stayed close to Jo as she shuffled across, both of them prodded along by elbows and shoulders. She clutched her scanner to her chest. She wasn't a screw-up after all. Even if they never found another trace of Resero or the woman, Jo at least had proof of that.

The scanner flickered, picking up faint traces across the street. The source wove back and forth, as if dodging through the ghost of the previous crowd. Here, the sidewalk was wider and roomier, and a row of brightly colored trees shaded the half nearest the street. The orange and magenta leaves hung low, forcing Jo to duck when she followed the trail away from the sunny areas. She didn't mind, though. Every scrap of the resonance trail suggested her years of work were worth it.

"You okay?" Nik asked as she ducked under the twenty-somethingth branch. His scanner still rested in his pocket, taking background measurements for his own theory about the golden cloud. "It's not like the woman's the only trace, you know. The trail touched other worlds."

"I know."

"And we can check out that science museum the booklet mentioned, if you want to. So the trip's not entirely wasted."

"Maybe later." The chances of finding the woman again were slim, but she wanted to keep trying for now. Every flicker of the scanner readings gave her a little burst of joy.

"I could automate that for you." Nik nodded to the screen. "Wouldn't take long. Maybe a dozen lines of code."

Jo bit her lip. It could save her neck pain to have a program direct them down the path with higher levels, but then she wouldn't see the readings herself. "I'm good."

Nik sighed and fell back a pace, hands still in his pockets. His steps were surprisingly agile when he walked like that, bending and twisting his way through the crowd without showing more than his wrist. He continued glancing over at her face when he thought she wasn't looking. "You sure you're okay?"

Was her smile so maniacal that it looked like a grimace? "She ran, Nik. You know what that means?"

"She has overdue parking tickets?"

"People are looking for her, and she knows it." Jo spun her finger in the wand's cord. The woman had to have something to do with the missing prototype. She just knew it. "Maybe she spent time with Resero before his death?"

"Or she's a pickpocket and he was one of her victims."

Jo rolled her eyes. "Then whatever she pocketed is still on her, and it has something to do with the prototype. Either way, we're on the right trail."

A brief flicker on the scanner meant they were about to start on the wrong trail, but Jo retraced their steps back to an alley. Nothing here looked or smelled familiar. A scattering of stalls lined the walls to either side, selling colorful fruits and glossy-looking rolls. A sweet aroma drifted between them, carrying hints of nutmeg and melted butter. According to the scanner, it carried traces of the woman's resonance as well. She'd guessed correctly. The woman had indeed turned left back at the intersection.

"So, what's the plan if we find her?" Nik whispered. "Do you go in with the old one-two while I come around with a burlap sack?"

Jo bit back a smile, and it made him grin.

"I assume I'll be doing the talking?"

"I was thinking neither of us will." She tapped her transcom. "Seeing as our target's so keen on avoiding us, we'd probably get more out of a picture." She explained that if they could get a clear shot of their target's face, a reverse image search could pull up who she was, where she worked, and how she got in contact with Resero. All infinitely more helpful than the sound of the woman racing away.

"Gotcha. I should have counted on you to come up with a plan that didn't involve talking to people." He opened his mouth to tease her more, but as they stepped out of the alleyway, Jo held up a hand to stop him. Was she seeing this correctly? There, just one shop down, a patch of yellow and mauve stood out from a group of off-world businessmen. The woman's headscarf? The group waited to cross the intersection, and the scanner pointed right toward them.

She looked up at Nik, who nodded that he saw it, too. They both set their transcoms to record. If the woman turned to check over her shoulder, they might be able to get a shot of her face.

But before they could get closer, a group of tourists approached from the other direction. A family, from the looks of it. The dad had a sunburnt nose and a sweaty visor and was practically dragging a reluctant toddler. A pouting girl clung to his other arm, followed closely by a preteen typing grumpily on his transcom. The only one with even a hint of a smile was the curly-haired woman lagging behind. She smugly flipped through her own transcom, pausing briefly to retrieve bagged snacks from the man's knapsack and toss them at the kids. Other wrappers fell out as she rummaged, but she ignored them.

No wonder the Yerins hated tourists. Jo considered stopping to pick up the trash, but Nik was already on it, scooping up the wrappers while the woman stared at him like he was stealing. He walked a few steps over and deposited them in a bin.

The light changed, and Jo and Nik hastened to keep up with the businessmen. Unfortunately, the couple and their children got there first, and the Yerin woman was almost entirely out of reach, with only the top of her scarf visible between the bronzeray and navy suits. Jo tried walking on her toes to get a better angle.

"Harold." The curly-haired woman shoved her partner's shoulder. "Harold, I think that woman's recording us."

The man rolled his eyes and picked up the whining kid around his waist.

"Do something, Harold."

Harold picked up the other child and started walking faster, cutting around the side of the businessmen. Thank the strings. Jo almost had a shot of the Yerin woman. If only the curly-haired lady would move a little to the left.

But the tourist was too busy hassling her husband and tripped instead. For a brief, glorious moment, Jo's transcom had the perfect view of the Yerin woman's face as she turned to witness the commotion. Then the businessmen started falling like toy blocks. They knocked into each other as they fell, floundering in a tangle of knees and briefcases. A jolt of horror swept across the Yerin woman's face, and the side of her head slammed into a light pole as she lost her footing.

Shit. Jo stuffed her transcom down her shirt and went to see if the Yerin woman was okay. Before she could reach her, a flash of amber crackled up the lamp pole and sent a stutter into Jo's steps. What in the name of...

Before she could finish the thought, the Yerin woman was on her feet, scurrying away as a loud cracking noise from the light pole sent glass raining down on the crowd.

Jo ducked and popped her collar to protect her neck. By the time she lifted her head, the Yerin woman had disappeared again and traffic stood at a standstill. The lights had also gone out at the surrounding intersections, though only the nearest one had a base littered with glass shards.

The businessmen dusted glass off their sleeves, and while Harold's two younger children sniffled, it didn't look like anyone was injured. No signs of blood, anyway. Nik made it to Jo's side, standing as though his hands hadn't left his pockets.

He raised an eyebrow and tilted his head toward the pole.

'*No idea,*' she mouthed. Light poles weren't supposed to do that, at least not for anything short of a lightning strike or insane power surge. Bursting the glass should have required a high temperature inside the bulb, not a relatively light impact to the pole. She crept forward to inspect it, grateful she had her workman's boots. They might be junk for running, but there was zero chance of any glass getting through.

The first thing she noticed about the pole was the smell. It burned sharp and metallic-y, like galvanized wire. She could almost taste the remnants of an energy discharge. And energy discharge it must have been, for the arc had left scorch marks where the woman's head had hit the base. *How the hell did she walk away from that uninjured?*

Jo slipped out her scanner, waving the wand to either side of the marks. There was something oddly familiar about the readings. No. It couldn't be, could it? She flipped back through to her readings from the university lab, comparing the graph from the amovoscope's damage to that of the pole. A near match. She almost dropped the scanner in surprise. That couldn't be right. She tried scanning further up the pole, but the readings were the same. The light pole had suffered a field fluctuation like the amovoscope, though much smaller in scope and very short-lived.

She crouched to swipe the wand nearer the base and a glint of metal caught her eye. A small, broken coil of wire sat among the shards. Coincidence? She ran the scanner wand over it to be sure it was safe to pick up, but it hummed with residual energy. It had the same reading as the Yerin woman.

"Hey, Jo?" Nik nudged her arm and motioned for her to back up. An emergency HoverMed was coming in for a landing.

She turned back to the pole, but the coil piece was gone, blown away by the air currents from the hovercraft's quad fans. Glass shards and street debris were already spinning circles around her feet, and she wouldn't want to be there when the currents reached full force. She shoved the scanner into her backpack.

"About time," someone said with a harrumph. Jo didn't need to turn to know it was the curly-haired woman. "It's bad enough to have faulty equipment like this on a street corner, but they should at least have the decency to keep the ambulance times short. Isn't that right, Harold?"

Harold barely had the energy for a dismissive shrug. "I think it's a sign to head back to the hotel pool."

"Not until my babies get checked over by a doctor." She stood firm, even as the wind from the fans battered at her tunic and forced her to raise her voice. "Those shards of glass flew everywhere. They could be stuck in their hair or between their fingers."

"I see." Harold turned back to the kids, looking them in the eye one by one. "Any of you have a lawsuit-worthy injury?"

They shook their heads.

"Pool it is, then."

"Harold. Don't you dare, Harold." The curly-haired woman moved to stop him, but spun around as the fans died down and the hovercraft latch clicked open. She was probably hoping to snag an EMT to check her children before they got any further away. Instead, the door lifted to reveal a green-vested team of police responders with weapons in hand. They were the energy discharge kind, meant to stun rather than injure, but the woman's face went pale.

Jo didn't feel so great either. Who sent a police force to deal with a broken light pole? Behind the handful of armed responders came another half-dozen with scanners, the expensive models with twice the sensitivity level and wireless wands. They surrounded the light pole and started right to work. Only then did a pair of EMTs disembark to check on the witnesses.

"I think we should go," Jo whispered to Nik. "Give our testimony if we need to and hightail it back to the sliding station."

"Or to the museum?"

"I don't want to remain on this planet any more than I have to." Even as she said it, it sounded irrational. But where was the logic here? A young woman had hit her head, and instead of the typical ice pack and aspirin, they got a minor explosion and a detective squad.

Nik looked at her questioningly, but all she could do was shake her head. It had to have something to do with the readings. The woman. The amovoscope. The golden clouds on the cryptoscope's map. How were they connected? And Resero. How could she forget him.

Her transcom buzzed, creating a sudden symphony with the transcoms of the surrounding crowd. A security alert for her current location. All persons at transport hubs would be subject to an additional search.

Jo and Nik exchanged glances and started back to the sliding station, their pace just quick enough to blend into the crowd. A glance behind showed a handful of emergency responders setting up some kind of perimeter. Short, green barrier blocks now lined the broken pole, with "Boliska" in big, bold letters on one half and "Do Not Cross" on the other.

Nik bent down to pick up a wrapper and empty cup someone dumped right next to a trash can and then stayed there. "Um, Jo..."

"Yeah?"

"Look at this."

Inside the bin was a yellow and mauve scarf.

And just when Jo thought it couldn't get any weirder, all the transcoms buzzed again. This time a picture of the Yerin woman popped up, her face mostly turned away but her scarf wholly recognizable. It looked to have come from a traffic camera.

"Arsonist suspect in the area," the caption read. "Believed to be unstable. If spotted, call the authorities and do not approach."

CHAPTER SEVEN

— · —

PRAVI

P ravi stabbed her shovel into the ground, making a show of weeding her garden bed while waiting to hear from her contact. It helped to picture the spiky, smelly vines as D.I.C. agents. The shovel blade tore through the thinner roots and pried the giant tangle from her yard. If she had a bigger shovel and plausible deniability, she could do more than imagine their removal. But that was just frustration talking.

What she needed was to get out from under the D.I.C.'s thumb. The second her wrist buzzed, she opened her transcom, expecting it to be her ride out of there. But no, her algorithm had flagged another field fluctuation. Yet another possible link to the missing prototype. The trail of events had taunted her for weeks, dangling dozens of leads she had no way of following. Where was it this time?

Yerin. Pravi would have dropped her transcom if it wasn't connected to her wrist.

Yerin. The world where her uncle had stored the prototype before it was stolen. Of all the places to tempt her away from her current plan...

Her wrist buzzed again, this time with a text from her contact. The black market weaver was on her way. Pravi had hired the woman to guide her through the strings—to take her far from the reaches of the D.I.C. She could worry about the new lead after they reached the first waypoint.

She pulled up a heat map of the D.I.C. agents. All remained at their post except one of the pair manning the stakeout car across the street. A quick scan of the surrounding area found him strolling back from the strip mall a few blocks down. Agent Beni, Munus had called him. A bag of something warm swung from one of his hands. Presumably he and his partner's lunch.

Pravi texted the weaver to wait an extra minute for the agents to get into position. Other than setting off her schedule, Agent Beni was a pleasant fellow. Always very polite and quick to offer assistance. Not too good at noticing when the lady bringing him a plate of thank you cookies also slipped a surveillance bug between the seats.

She heard his knock on the car window through her earpiece.

"Did I miss anything?" Agent Beni's pants squeaked against the leather. *"The sandwich place was closed, so I grabbed us some burgers."*

"Burgers?" His partner's voice dripped with disdain. Agent Clive, if she remembered correctly. He'd picked out all the dried krellaberries from the cookies.

"Cheese and meat patties on a bun."

Wrappers crinkled in Pravi's ear. The agents appeared adequately distracted. Just in time, too, as her contact had turned onto her street.

"What kind of meat?"

"Bovine, I think." Beni licked a finger. *"It's not so bad. Kind of like grilled lurefe."*

Any second now. Pravi checked her scanner for signs of the weaver's transport van. Just as it glided onto her screen, Clive let out a surprised yelp that suggested his burger tasted nothing like lurefe.

"What the— What in Yemia's name is this?"

"That's a pickle."

"A what?"

"A delicious gourd soaked in vinegar brine. I ordered mine with extra."

This was why Pravi had picked the front for her exit point. Just last week, they'd been too busy discussing game miniatures and the finer points of deck building to notice a reporter setting up cameras in the tree above their car.

The weaver's van filled most of her screen now, and Pravi checked inside the gardening tote to confirm her go bag held everything she needed. Weapons. Snacks. Various bandages and detoxifiers in case she ran into bounty hunters hoping for information on the prototype. Also, miscellaneous doodads and gadgets her uncle had made for her over the years. The resonance echo and blocker set was her favorite, and she pulled it from the tote. The echo she planted behind the tree with her shovel and the blocker she tucked down her shirt.

"You've got to be kidding me." Clive's voice. He must have spotted the weaver's van pulling up. *"That's it, I'm calling headquarters."*

His partner unwrapped another hamburger. *"Go ahead. Munus could use a good laugh."*

"This is serious."

"'Target keeps shopping online. Delivery trucks block view. Please advise.'"

"It's been twelve this week!"

Pravi grinned and switched to the security cameras. Her contact exited the faux delivery van and started up the front walk. So far, so good. The weaver was a uniformed woman of about Pravi's height and laden with packages. Packing peanuts, mostly, plus a dictionary or two to make the balance believable.

So close to freedom. After a D.I.C. agent scanned the delivery driver, she readied for part two of her plan: tempt him and his colleagues away from her front walk. The day before, she'd let it slip to Munus that proximity sensors lined the yard, programmed to give an auditory alarm if someone approached from the outside. Pravi pulled up the security app on her transcom and triggered two of the fence posts to beep for ten seconds. As soon as the faux delivery woman started back down the front walk, the agents' heat signatures headed for the perimeter.

Once the delivery woman got halfway back to the van, Pravi stripped off her baggy sundress and ditched it in the gardening bag. From behind, she now looked just like another delivery woman, uniform and all. She popped open a collapsed cardboard box to hold the go bag in front of her and hurried down the stairs to join the weaver.

"Oh, come on." Clive's voice whined into her earpiece. As she'd hoped, he and his partner were staying in the car. *"You saw the*

donation pickup van. She had piles of extra stuff. What more could she need?"

"I don't know, groceries?"

"Nah, that's the green truck on Saturdays."

"Probably shoes then." Two thumps echoed from Agent Beni's side as his feet went up on the dash. *"You can never have too many shoes."*

The man had no clue Pravi was about to slip past his guard, but he also wasn't wrong. Though their thick soles hid knives, a multi-tool, and a compass, Pravi's black boots moved silently across the sidewalk. The spare pair she carried held expanding pouches that doubled as a parachute and flotation device. Regretfully, she'd had to leave the rest of her collection back in the house.

The weaver's passenger door waited for her, and she slipped in before the other agents returned to their posts. She sat low in the seat, out of the view of anyone outside. Hopefully, it'd be a while before they noticed her missing. For the next thirty minutes, any D.I.C. scans would show her still digging in the garden bed.

Pravi now had a better view of the weaver. Short red hair framing a stoic face. A forest green beret tilted to the right. The woman came highly recommended from one of the few contacts Pravi could still trust after her uncle's death. Supposedly, the woman had ferried thousands of insensates between the strings.

She didn't speak until they'd put a few kilometers between them and Pravi's house. "That was a bit of a ride, wasn't it? I've never pulled one over on the D.I.C. before."

"Eh. You get used to it." Pravi took her pack from the box and climbed up into the seat. She'd pulled a sucker out of her pack when the door closed and now popped it in her mouth. It tasted bland and kind of bitter, but it'd keep her conscious if any potential kidnappers brought knockout gas.

The woman laughed. "Easy for you to say. Some of us haven't conned worse than a border control agent. Speaking of which, where to?"

"The sliding station in the market district." A fifteen minute drive if they didn't hit traffic and the rear-view mirror stayed clear of tailing cars. She wiggled a sucker at the weaver. "Want one?"

"I'm good, thanks. I mean, like, where are we going after?"

"You'll see when we get there." Hadn't they been over this already? Pravi wouldn't disclose the destination until they were actually inside the sliding circle. She couldn't have the weaver making some side cash by leaking her plan.

The woman looked Pravi up and down. "Hopefully no place cold, unless you have a jacket and some pants in that backpack of yours. Essaun, maybe? Or Nerrut?"

Or maybe it was none of the woman's business. If she'd been this pushy in her emails, Pravi wouldn't have hired her.

Pravi gave her backpack a little hug and slipped her hand into the side pocket. "Wasn't that the turn for the market?"

The weaver nodded. "Before I picked you up, I got a traffic alert about a three car pileup. This way should take us around it."

No, turning a street earlier would have taken them around it. If there even was an accident to begin with. It appeared Pravi would be reviewing her technique for jumping out of a moving vehicle.

"So, where are you from?" she asked, surveying the sidewalk. There would be a stoplight coming up in the next five hundred meters or so with a nice patch of grass. "Khilsh, was it?"

"Khlarn, actually. You ever been to our salt fields?"

"Nope."

"I highly recommend it."

The lady was good. She'd obviously studied Pravi's real contact well. Preferred hair and outfit. Place of residence. Possibly all the main tourist stops and a few quieter ones. Definitely a professional.

But Pravi was professional too, and the woman had missed the fact the real weaver spoke one of Khlarn's southeastern dialects and not a Pirrlish one from the north. The two sounded similar, but Pravi's translator easily told them apart. Not a typical setting for translators, as most just converted your language to hexbit and then translated other hexbit signals back to your language. But being typical wasn't what kept Pravi alive on her missions.

"Closest I've ever been is Khilsh." Pravi swiped a knob on her watch, then reached her left hand up to twist the stem of her lollipop. The movement brought the watch camera to the right height to scan the woman's profile and check it against the public database. Her other hand went back to her knife. "Xander and I went for a run there once and got to see the short-tailed mockingbirds and blue speckled thrashers. Quite pretty against a sunset background."

Her transcom confirmed it heard the voice commands (Run, mockingbird, background) by blinking red twice. No match in the database.

She let her watch hand drift back around her backpack. "We were at one of those nature preserve places, you know? The kind where you ride around in open vehicles and count how many animals you see."

Open. Vehicle. Count. Another voice command, this time to listen to the number of people breathing. The light blinked three times. She and the woman weren't alone.

The woman and her colleagues must've installed resonance and heat blockers in the back of the truck. Quite costly for a vehicle they'd have to ditch as soon as the D.I.C. realized what had happened. Which meant an organization with resources. Strange that the fake weaver's profile hadn't popped up on her database.

Pravi's eyes went back to possible escape routes. They approached the stoplight where she'd planned to bail, but a dark brown van had parked suspiciously close. If her guess was correct, it held the rest of the fake weaver's team. She'd need to get out before then.

She sensed movement behind her chair and pulled her knife from her pack as a thick wire swooped over her head toward her neck. It caught on her blade.

The wire tightened. "Agree to cooperate and we won't hurt you too much."

A man's voice. Pain dug into the side of her neck, but Pravi pushed back with her blade. A couple more centimeters and she'd be able to duck her head back out.

THE STRING CONSPIRACY   57

Before she could manage more than a wiggle of room, a light fog rose from her feet and around her chair. Knockout gas, by the smell of it. A quick glance showed the driver had slipped on a mask. Of course, neither of her kidnappers would know her lollipop meant Pravi didn't need one.

She struggled more with the knife, pretending to hold her breath against the gas. What were the rules for this one? Coughing fit? No, that was the one with a hint of fruitiness. This had more of a woody scent...

Hiccups. Hiccups for thirty seconds and then out.

Pravi obliged them with a show, letting the knife push harder with each hiccup. Her free hand slipped into another backpack pocket. A multi-tool this time. With ten seconds left in her performance, she flipped it open to wire cutters. The lollipop stem fell from her mouth and she rolled her head to one side, leaving room for the cutters to swing up and snip.

The head roll turned into a body roll, with Pravi swinging open the van door and doing a tuck and tumble out onto the street. Her shoulder slammed into concrete and the curb dug into her back. She should have worn a bullet-proof vest that offered more padding, no matter how obvious it would have been under her shirt.

Van tires squealed as she stumbled to her feet. Goals: Gain distance and call Director Munus for backup, ignoring his "I told you so" about needing them for protection.

Pravi swung her pack over her shoulder and started off at a run. The shops to her left were all boarded up, leaving no hope of using them for cover. The street to her right moved too fast to risk darting through. Straight down the sidewalk remained her best bet.

As expected, her transcom was jammed. The joke was on the fake weaver, though. Unless it got a kill code, her resonance echo would turn off as soon as it lost signal from her app, and any second now, it'd broadcast her last known position to the nearby agents.

She pressed on. A jolt hit her back, but her backpack took most of the blow. Three more in rapid succession caused her to stagger. Screw this. Pravi reached into her pack, pulling out a blaster of her own—set to stun, for legal reasons, though she wouldn't be opposed to increasing the damage if she needed to. Two blind shots over her shoulder sent a stutter through the pursuing footsteps, but the closest set didn't falter.

They'd need her alive if they wanted clues to the prototype, but that didn't mean Pravi had to make it easy. The footsteps were dead on her heels now, so she did the only thing she could do. She stopped.

The redheaded woman stumbled past as Pravi spun out of the way and fired. The beret fell to the ground, but the woman rolled to the side into a defensive stance. They had protective vests, too. Yay.

Pravi threw her knife at the woman and shot an oncoming man in the face. She counted at least three more attackers, two men and one stocky woman, before the larger man came at her with a stun rod. She ducked twice and kicked just above his groin. The point where the edge of a protecting piece would be. He doubled enough for Pravi to slip between him and the rod, slam his forearm, and throw her elbow into his neck.

Her heart beat frantically, threatening to throw her out of her rhythm. How much time did she need to buy before the D.I.C. arrived? The redhead was back on her feet, wielding what looked like a small energy cannon. Pravi chose to take on the other two and make herself harder to target. Her body moved on instinct. Block, punch, block, block, kick. Some of their hits landed, only somewhat muffled by her vest. Duck, block, kick, punch. A misread left hook became a shooting pain across her jaw. But she couldn't stop. Dozens of scars across her back, chest, and legs knew exactly what would happen if they ferried her off the planet. They only needed her alive. And there was no Uncle Xander to save her this time.

Her next move snagged the non-redheaded woman's arm and a quick twist snapped it at the wrist. The sound always made her flinch. The man took advantage with a swipe to her feet and her hip slammed into the concrete. She rolled away before he could pounce and gave one of her backpack straps a quick yank. The side pocket unzipped with a whoosh of air and the squeal of plastic. The man staggered back.

A three meter round inflatable popped up between him and Pravi, buying her time to cut the cord and get back to her feet.

It wasn't enough. A thick arm caught her over her shoulder and across her neck.

"Who else knows?" The red-haired woman twisted Pravi's arm behind her back, keeping her grip just loose enough for Pravi to breathe. "Who knows what the prototype is?"

"It's... it's..." Panic threatened to take over, but Pravi forced herself to bring one foot up instead. She stopped prying at the woman's arm just long enough to get a knife from her shoe. The blade sliced at her attacker with an upward stroke. Blood splattered down her chest while the woman screamed and Pravi gasped for air. A boot slammed into her back.

The woman repeated herself through clenched teeth, her hand canon once again aimed at Pravi. "Who. Else. Knows."

Heat whizzed past her cheek, leaving a scorched hole in the cement as big as Pravi's head. A warning shot. Adrenaline pumped through her system, and she turned slowly with her hands raised. She scolded her racing heartbeat. They needed her alive. How else could she tell them what the prototype really was? Except that wasn't what they were asking.

"You start naming names, or I'll start blowing pieces off one by one. Feet first. The ankles, shins..."

Pravi struggled to both talk and breathe. Did they already know what the prototype was? Did they know who had it? "I'm sure... we can reach an agreement."

"The only agreement is you complying. Three. Two—"

Pravi ducked to the side, and dual blasts went off, one burning past her side, while the second—a stun shot from Director Munus's pistol—sizzled against the woman's jugular. He holstered his weapon as his agents rushed in to arrest her attackers. "And here I thought with Xander gone, there'd be fewer messes to clean up."

Pravi pushed herself to her feet. The traffic was garbled, with cars that had tried to turn around blocked by others whose occupants eagerly filmed the scene.

"A territorial fight between rival gangs, perhaps?" There were few cases the D.I.C. couldn't clean up with a good cover story. She brushed herself off and took an icepack from one of the agents. Her teeth ached as she pressed it to her chin. "Or would you prefer indie film fight scene gone bad, like that time on Serei?"

"Serei had extenuating circumstances." Munus crossed his arms and surveyed the bloody sidewalk. "Though claiming there was a shipment of tainted mushrooms might work." His face was too stoic for Pravi to tell if he was kidding. "So, what was the real reason? I assume they were bounty hunters?"

Pravi nodded. He didn't need to know the truth. Not yet, at least. If the people with the prototype had sent her attackers, that meant they had a plan—a plan they didn't want anyone to know about. Most people wouldn't kill just to get their names on a patent.

"Is it worth it?" The suddenness of Munus' question pulled her from her thoughts. "Is it really that important to keep mum about the prototype?"

Her gut said of course it was, but new factors had entered the equation now. Would it be worse for the D.I.C. to have it than whoever had it now? A little voice in the back of her mind questioned her motives. But if she had the prototype in her possession, none of this would have happened. She wouldn't have needed a weaver—wouldn't have been trapped on Terra waiting for someone, anyone, to respond to the message she'd planted on her uncle's old tools.

She didn't answer Munus, even as he ushered her into a D.I.C. van and personally chauffered her home. Swatches of ideas of swirled inside her brain. Not until she was safely back inside her security system did the next step became clear: If none of the people who had access to the tools had thought of contacting her, maybe they needed a shove.

CHAPTER EIGHT

— • —

JO

J o blinked, unsure if glare from Yerin's sun had distorted the words on her transcom. She ducked into the shade of the nearest tree to read them again.

"Resero's niece says vlogger Kniel Jacron is full of 'rodent excrement'," the news article said, its words unchanged. *"Anyone who provides proof he's wrong will receive lab space on Rygal."*

Someone shook her arm. This was it. Soon, she would wake up on the floor of her apartment and discover she'd used the ultrasonic heater on the coptonium solder again. Hallucinogenic vapors were the only explanation for the absurdity of the day. A woman becoming a fugitive because she tripped. Her fall taking out a four-block radius of traffic lights. Resero's reclusive niece wanting so fervently to take Jacron down a peg that she broke the media silence she'd held for a decade.

Nik nudged her arm again. "Jo?" His voice sounded normal and not at all like when the last coptonium-induced stupor had made her miss three days of classes. "We just passed the turn for the sliding station."

Jo looked up from the article. Orange and magenta branches arched over the sidewalk while drifts of rust-colored sand gathered along the street. She was still on Yerin. And the article about Pravi Resero's offer was there, too. She passed it to Nik. "This has to be fake, right?"

The Rygal Lab had over four dozen offices, all rented out to major patent holders and prize-winning researchers. And, according to the article, the prize wasn't just getting a lab there. No. The person with proof would also get a research stipend worth fifty thousand monettes a year.

Nik scrolled his finger down the page, too fast to be doing more than skimming. "Has Jacron responded yet? You'd think he'd want to clear his name as soon as possible."

Before Jo could say 'Good point', Nik pulled up the news on his own transcom and started comparing notes between various articles while Jo watched over his shoulder. Every site confirmed it as more than a rumor. Although Resero's niece had refused interview requests, she'd responded to every inquiry with the same official statement. Yes, it was from her. Yes, she was serious about giving up the space at Rygal Lab. And yes, she intended to press fraud charges if Jacron continued using his search for the prototype to get views.

"So, should we go home and see if we have enough proof yet?" Nik tapped the pocket with his scanner. "Or did you want to wander around a bit more?"

"Home, I think." If they stayed, all they'd do was wander. Jo's scanner had a limited range, and it'd been a miracle they'd run into the Yerin woman in the first place, especially with all the background interference. Still, that slim chance of finding her again nagged Jo as they approached the sliding station stairs.

The tiered station rose imposing before them—built to mimic the ruins of a stepped temple, complete with a two-story slog to the top. Jo didn't know much about architecture, but she didn't need to. Every bit of it screamed 'this was made for tourists'. The faux-sandstone panels poorly mimicked the defects of age, and the raised frieze along the top repeated patterns from five different worlds instead of telling a story. She also doubted ancient builders would have left space for recessed screens advertising 'authentic' eateries and other tourist traps.

Scores of people shuttled in and out through the entrance, as they did at every major sliding station. *Was it just her, or were more security guards mingled in than there'd been before?* The station stairs stood broad and crowded, enough that she could have missed them when she'd slid into Yerin. She sighed and resisted the urge to turn around. Yerin hadn't been the only world touched by the green thread on the cryptoscope's map. There were other places to hunt for clues and proof that Jacron was wrong. Places that didn't try to arrest people for accidents, and that weren't swamped with guards in green and yellow vests.

Yes. There were definitely more security now than when she and Nik arrived. As Jo dragged herself upward, guards pulled a reluctant tourist aside for extra screening. She was an off-world investor, the woman asserted as the guards tried to guide her away, and wouldn't the tourism board like to hear about this harassment?

Jo watched agape as guards converged on her from other areas of the stairs, and the flicker of metal caught her eye. A small coil shone in the gloved hand of the man searching the tote—a coil not unlike the one at the base of the light pole. She hurried up the stairs and turned to Nik. "She's here," she whispered hurriedly. "The Yerin woman has to be here."

She couldn't be sure, but it was too much of a coincidence, wasn't it? What better way for the Yerin woman to slip by than to distract the guards with the signal from the coil? Jo checked the stairs from the upper landing, but found few signs of native Yerins in the swirling mass of off-worlders. Hovercraft zipped by on the street, stirring up eddies of sand. The grains glinted in the sunlight before falling and mingling with the others, disappearing as easily as the woman had. Maybe she was already inside?

Jo had no better luck past the large glass doors. Only tourists waited under the massive stone ceilings, toting children and wheeled luggage. Above them, suspended monitors warned travelers to prepare for extra screening. Maybe she was wrong. Maybe the woman had planted the coil to disguise another destination. And if the authorities couldn't find her, what were the chances Jo could?

She checked the crowd again as she stepped into line. Other than a pause to put her scanner in travel mode, her eyes didn't stop searching for the Yerin woman. Not much blocked her view. The bag conveyors here were sleek and smooth, almost sculptural, and balanced on thick, single-legged supports. The security checks were stream-lined as well, looking more like carved arches than doorways, though still labeled with "Schlau Industries" like the ones she was used to.

Just past the scanners, a frosted glass pyramid rose from the tiled floor. Its walls stretched as long as a lüftball field and soared through the lofty ceiling, enclosing most of the station's interior. Scores of people used the sliding circles inside, clearly visible through openings on the south and east sides. A man's voice came over the intercom system, saying something about an arm swab and a separate line for allergies. Though the security lines backed up almost to the door, it didn't seem to add much time, and Jo soon reached the front of the line where a sign told her to roll up her sleeves.

"This may cause a tingling sensation," the security officer said, taking Jo's wrist. "Do you have any sensitivities or contact allergies? Malo oil? Tibo? Lycrial astringents?"

She shook her head. "Only lavandula and nuciferas."

"Should be fine then." The officer wiped a cool cloth across her skin, and her forearm prickled. Warm violet light flashed from a bracelet emitter. After inspecting her skin, the woman released her wrist and ushered her forward.

Such an odd test. It couldn't be aimed at the Yerin woman, could it? Her picture occasionally flashed across the announcement monitors. Jo grabbed her scanner bag from the security belt and hurried to where Nik waited inside the pyramid.

"It might be a while," he said, nodding at the floor. Few of the circles glowed blue, and lines formed outside them while tourist after tourist stepped out of yellow arrival circles. He and Jo picked one further along the wall, shimmying between other travelers while shadows danced across the waiting faces. Above, the top of the pyramid served as a skylight, and robotic cleaning beetles scurried across its surface. A flock of pigeons perched on the nearby ridges, leaving feathers and streaks for them to sweep up.

Something wavered at the edge of Jo's vision. She turned back to the glass walls and searched for its source. The pristine panels stared back, casting long reflections of Jo and the other travelers. Except one panel lacked any reflection at all. Jo stepped closer and her eyebrows furrowed at the small flecks dotting its frame. Field emitters? An emergency exit, perhaps? A closer inspection confirmed her guess —an energized panel made to look like glass. She'd fixed some of those before, but nothing this sleek and well-hidden. It flickered again, this time accompanied by a low hum. Jo tensed, but no one else seemed to notice. She motioned Nik backwards. Possibly unnecessarily, but she'd learned to never underestimate energy fields.

They took slow steps back while the humming rose, increasing in pitch until it reached a full-blown moan. Jo covered her ears, as did those around her, but it buzzed in her teeth and went chattering down her spine. Never a good sign. Several children started wailing and those inside sliding circles hurriedly stepped out in case the transport system itself was the cause.

Over the course of minutes, the sound built into a screech, echoing up the walls until the light fixtures exploded in a shower of sparks. The emergency lights kicked on, followed by silence. Or a near silence. Her ears still rung from its echo.

Startled yelps echoed through the space, and the security officers seemed equally spooked. Jo stepped closer to Nik as tourists pushed past them, heading for the exits. Frenzied questions drowned out urges to remain calm, and the skylight cast streaks of sunlight over frightened faces.

"Power outage?" Nik suggested.

"More like a power surge." Jo nodded to the flickering gap in the pyramid wall. A separate train of thought compared the broken glass to the shattered traffic light. "The transport systems should have been protected, but it might take a while for the other systems to reset."

As they watched, several tourists tried to cut through the emergency exit panels, but officers with field modulators swept in to seal the breaches and direct traffic through the scanners. She considered them for a moment and turned back to Nik. "Hey, do you think...?"

But he had already strolled away. She spotted his teal shirt weaving through the crowd and scurried to catch up. His scanner was out of his pocket, and his fingers tapped wildly across the screen.

"What's going on?" she asked as she came up alongside him.

"I think I found her." He nodded to a sliding circle a few meters away. A Yerin woman stood in its center with long streaks of black hair frizzing out in all directions. Her chest rose in hurried breaths. Long, thin fingers danced awkwardly across a navigation device.

"Are you sure it's her?" Jo wanted to believe it was. Though everything else about her outfit was different, her top and shoes looked the same.

Nik tapped the scanner screen. "Readouts are the same."

Jo thought of calling out, but the woman slid away before they could reach her. Still, they couldn't give up their chance at the lab that easily. "Give me the scanner."

Nik passed it over, and her fingers cycled through the settings until she found the one she needed and directed it at the circle. *Please be enough to find a destination.*

The screen spewed out numbers.

"Ready?"

Nik nodded, grabbing her wrist so they could slide together. As she translated the data into destination coordinates, a group of security officers jogged toward them. They hadn't given the all clear yet, but the woman was so close. She couldn't risk losing the trail again. The second her scanner decoded the data, Jo set her nav device, found the string, and yanked.

The scent of pale pink and rosemary whirled around them and the string carried their feet to packed earth. Jo wavered, nausea rising in her throat. It'd been a while since she'd felt the effects of sliding this strongly, but she forced herself to look around. Shoulder-high shrubs grew to either side, and their thick roots crowded the arrival circle. The air smelled sweet and earthy. Above them, steel frames held a wired navigation system and a grubby, glass-paneled roof. Patches of sunlight filtered through decaying leaves.

She found the Yerin woman two rows over, spewing heavy splatters into the bushes while her frazzled hair caught on the branches. The scent billowed out before Jo could plug her nose and she had to take a moment to push down her own nausea.

"Are you alright?" she asked, tapping the woman's shoulder.

She jerked away. Another heave and the puddle grew, spilling across the ground toward their shoes.

Jo inched back and started digging through her scanner bag. "I have some Slydwell, if you need it?" The small pink pills were meant for sliding-induced nausea, and she popped one herself.

The woman's black hair bounced in a nod, and Nik held his hand out for one, too. Their navigators said they'd traveled twenty quizzets, which explained the side effects. It was a good distance for a single slide, but shouldn't have been enough for the woman to get this sick. Unless she wasn't used to sliding?

"Maybe we should find her a bench or something?" Nik tried to hold the branches back so the woman's hair wouldn't get caught as much. "Or maybe a trash can?"

Jo nodded and started searching the room for something suitable. The scant furnishings looked more like those of a greenhouse than a sliding station. No concession stands or visitor desks. Only a rack of tools and baskets sat by the front door. Grooves from carts and wheelbarrows ran into and out of the circles, suggesting the station saw more harvest shipments than travelers. Bushes of red berries took up most of the space, well out-numbering the sliding circles and leaving stains across their faded outlines.

A blur of green solidified two rows over, and Jo blinked in surprise. It looked like security guards from Yerin, but they couldn't possibly have jurisdiction. And even if they did, she and Nik hadn't broken any major rules. Sliding that soon after a crisis was a misdemeanor at best.

Leaves crunched behind her. "That'll be fifteen monettes." The speaker's voice was hoarse and bored.

Jo turned to find an older woman, her skin more tawny than Jo's olive tones and hair even darker. Loose, embroidered fabric wrapped her narrow frame. Jo blinked. "Excuse me?"

"It's four monettes each slide fee. Cash only." The woman gestured to the pile of vomit. "Another three for the mess."

"But we have autopay..."

"No autopay. Cash."

"Who the hell carries cash?" Jo complained as Nik pulled a stack of coins from his wallet.

The stationmaster tucked them in her pocket. "Exit code is 234. Pleasure doing business." She turned and strolled back down the aisle, her sandaled feet padding softly on the dust.

The Yerin woman fumbled for her backpack. "I can pay you back."

"Don't worry about it. How are you feeling?"

"Fine. I'll be fine in a minute." She pulled herself up by the branches. Her legs wavered beneath her, and her stomach heaved.

Nik wrapped his arm under the woman's. "Take it easy. No need to rush."

"I... I have to go." She pulled her navigation dials up and stumbled toward the nearest exit circle.

"You really should wait. It takes a while for the medication to kick in."

The woman tried to respond, but gagged instead. Why wouldn't she listen? If Jo was reading the dials right, she planned to go another ten quizzets, or over eight dozen frequencies.

Voices rose on the other side of the bushes, and Jo stood on her toes to peek over. The guards didn't appear to have any cash.

"Payment or no exit code," the stationmaster repeated.

One of the guards whipped something out from his side. It looked like a blaster, but transport officers weren't supposed to have anything more than a taser? And they had no reason to draw on someone just doing their job.

Jo jerked her head back to the Yerin woman. Unless they weren't transport officers? The woman did have traces of the Resero project. She elbowed Nik. "We have to go."

He lifted an eyebrow, but her fingers were already dialing the coordinates for the next world over. "We can't leave her like this, Jo."

"We aren't." The woman shouldn't be sliding that soon, but she was in no condition to face whoever was chasing her. Bounty hunters, perhaps? An uneasy feeling in Jo's stomach told her to run without the Yerin woman, but she didn't feel any better about the idea than Nik did. And not just because the woman might hold a piece of the Resero puzzle.

A blast rang out before she could think of an alternative, and the station manager crumbled to the ground.

"Jo—"

"Trust me." She grabbed Nik, the Yerin woman, and the string. As soon as she had a hold on all three, she pulled.

CHAPTER NINE

— · —

ZAHIRA

Zahira got only a hurried yell as warning before a new frequency forced itself into her body. She'd recognized the voices too late. Damn sliding sickness. She'd thought the pair were fellow travelers until they grabbed her and forced her to slide. The couple who'd tracked her that morning now held her hostage, dragging her back to Yerin. To the Boliska.

No. She couldn't let them take her.

Her fingers tore at the bushes while her mind struggled to hold on to the string she'd escaped to, to keep her body vibrating firmly in its frequency. This wasn't how it was supposed to go. She'd only headed for the station to give Grandmother a chance to leave town. She'd thought if she left via the strings, they wouldn't set up blockades on the main roads or increase security at the other stations. But if they captured Zahira and gave her the truth serum...

She shouldn't have let Grandmother convince her to continue with the plan. Should have said to hell with the Boliska threat and found a way for them to leave together. Every cell, every molecule of her body threatened to betray her, screaming to return to the frequency they'd called home. Maybe if she'd had more time to adjust, if she'd found equilibrium with the new string, she would have had a chance. The branches disappeared from her fingers and the slide held her captive.

She grasped for a new string, any string, but the signal from the couple washed over her with too much force. Hope faded as the ground grew solid beneath her. Her feet and stomach went different directions. Knees hit cold stone, jolting nausea into her throat. She scrambled to run, but her arms collapsed beneath her, shaking as the muscles tried to adjust to the new world.

"It's okay," said the woman's voice. Joan or something, wasn't it? The one with the scanner. "I think we lost them."

"Lost them?" The man's voice. He seemed as confused about the phrase as Zahira was. She hadn't seen anyone following her, not even the couple that now held her captive.

She struggled to rise, but the best she could do was push up to her hands and knees. Why did her body have to betray her like this? Her head felt like it was swimming in circles.

"Are you all right?" Pale gray eyes peered into Zahira's half-open ones, inducing another wave of dizziness as she tried to focus. "She's all green, Jo. We should get her to that bench."

No. Zahira wasn't going anywhere until she figured out what the hell was going on. She tried to push herself up again, but all she managed to do was roll onto her back.

"It's okay. I've got you." The man slid one hand under her shoulders and the other behind her knees.

Too dizzy to fight, Zahira called for the nguvu. It responded with a whisper. Not even enough left for a small shock. She must've spent it all overloading the sliding station scanners. Her nausea rolled with his steps. Ten paces later, he set her down again, and cool metal pressed against her back. A jolt of surprise ran down her spine. Yerin's station didn't have benches.

The man started fanning her face as he turned back to his partner. "What the hell were you thinking?"

"She—" Jo's coveralls swished at the edge of her vision. "I mean, they... Godsdammit. Didn't you hear the blaster shot as we left?"

"Blaster shot? You mean the thump of a tool falling?" Nik bent to dig through Jo's scanner bag. "You're lucky we didn't lose her mid-slide."

"I saw it, Nik. One of the bounty hunters shot the stationmaster."

"Shot the— What bounty hunters?" Nik's words echoed Zahira's thoughts, and she pinched the skin between her thumb and forefinger to force the fog from her mind. Though the room was still blurry, she saw neither glass nor sandstone. Instead, stripes of grey and blue wrapped the rounded walls. *Where was she?*

"They followed us from Yerin." Jo snapped back. "I thought they were security officers at first because of their green vests."

Green vests? Zahira's heart raced as Nik pressed a pink pill and a wet wipe into her hand. "So you helped a fugitive escape?"

"Station officers don't carry blasters, Nik. They shot the stationmaster back on Rudu."

The sliding sickness medicine nearly dropped to the floor as she pretended to take it. The Boliska were supposed to be powerless outside Yerin, no more than contracted peace officers, and certainly too prudent to risk an interplanetary dispute. She slipped a SlydWell of her own out of her pocket. One that she could be sure was real. The pill's sugary, plastic taste dissolved quickly, but did little to ease her pounding head.

She turned to face her... captors? She hesitated to think rescuers, but neither looked even slightly Yerin and her wrists were free of restraints. Their height alone suggested off-worlders, plus their noses weren't nearly arched enough for a northern lineage, nor rounded enough for coastal ancestry. And that Jo woman had so many freckles that they'd escaped her face and traveled down both arms. What reason did either of them have for tracking a hatari?

She snuck a look at her nav device. There were on a world called Trivate. Station 6. The name sounded familiar, but she couldn't remember how far it was from Yerin. At least they hadn't dragged her home. "What do you want from me?"

Nik shrugged and turned to Jo. "Might as well tell her. Since apparently we already have bounty hunters who know we're on the trail."

Jo flushed. "What was I supposed to do? Let them take her?" She took her satchel back from the bench and angrily forced it over her head and shoulder. "And who's to say they saw our faces? I didn't see any looking back at the bushes."

Whatever they wanted, these strangers clearly didn't know who the Boliska were or what they were capable of, and Zahira wasn't about to correct them. It did feed the worry growing at the back of her throat, though. Why had the woman assumed they were bounty hunters? Who else would be after hatari? She used her natural confusion to feign innocence. "What would they want with me?"

"The project." Nik leaned forward and lowered his voice to a whisper. "You know, the one Resero was working on before he died."

This time, Zahira didn't have to feign ignorance. "I have no idea what you're talking about."

"Xander Resero, the astrophysicist? We understand if you don't want to tell us about it. I mean, you've probably been bothered by dozens of—"

"You have the wrong person." She sat up to leave, but the world wobbled. She'd have to take it slow to get to a sliding circle without fainting.

"I set my scanner to pick up his traces, and it pointed straight at you." Jo offered a hand to help, but Zahira ignored it. "I get that you can't talk about it, especially with everybody wanting it. I mean, for all you know, we could be bounty hunters, too."

"Are you?"

A smile cracked at the edges of Nik's face, and his eyes twinkled at Jo.

She didn't appear to notice. "Of course not. I mean, I guess we thought the reward would be nice, but it was really more scientific..."

Zahira's hand paused over the nav dials. "How high of a reward?"

"Senxi and Neskin are offering 200,000 monettes a piece. Word is that black market prices are even higher."

She choked. Whoever was after the project wanted a hatari pretty bad. She'd have to warn Grandmother. "Where's my backpack?"

Nik handed it over, and she dug through for the transcom. Jo watched with interest, but tried to pretend she wasn't. Did she think Zahira had the project in there? She sent a quick coded text, "Golden Spears", so Grandmother would know she'd made it safely away and to proceed with caution. "So what kind of project are we talking about?"

Jo shrugged. "No one knows, except maybe his niece."

"Then how could you—"

"Know what resonance to track? I found a sample in one of his old tools."

Zahira was going to say 'How do you know it wasn't something lame, like a nose hair trimmer?' But she didn't mind the unsolicited information. It told her Nik and Jo were far from professionals. It shouldn't be too hard to get away from them now that her stomach was settled. The nearest circle waited less than a meter away, and they didn't seem like they intended to stop her. It did make her curious, though. What did the physicist's project have to do with hatari? Could he have been hatari himself? "Can I see his picture? This Resero guy."

Nik pulled up an image on his transcom. An older gentleman, late seventies, with more laugh lines than wrinkles. No signs of nguvu lines and definitely not Yerin. He did look familiar, though.

Jo watched her eagerly. "Have you seen him before?"

"No, I don't think so," she lied.

"Are you sure?" Nik pulled up another one, but this time the smiling blue eyes twinkled above a chest-length nest of a beard. Now she was even more sure she knew him. It'd been years ago, but Zahira had watched from the apartment while he spoke with Grandmother at the park across the street. She'd brought the box of spare coils.

Zahira's chest tightened. "Sorry, I can't help you."

"But you have to have met him." Jo went to pull up another picture on her own transcom, but Nik stopped her hand.

"She said she's sure," he said. "Maybe the scanner malfunctioned?"

"Triple checked before we left." Jo tucked the transcom back into her pocket. "And I recalibrated after the arrival scan."

Nik stuffed his hands in his pockets and shrugged. "Midley's Theorem?"

Zahira could only shrug. She hadn't even talked with the man, much less had contact that could leave his traces for years. As for Midley's Theorem, Grandmother had mentioned it before. Although resonance patterns were even more unique than fingerprints, Midley argued that between hundreds of worlds, there was a minuscule chance of two matching. A one in ten trillion chance, she'd said. And yet neither Jo nor Nik accused Zahira of the obvious. That she was lying.

Jo twisted her scanner strap. "No, it couldn't be Midley's. There's a trail between Terra and Yerin, remember? It could have something to do with the background interference, but we —"

"Wait." What was it Jo just said? A trail between Terra and Yerin? "You can track resonance patterns between worlds?"

Jo's face froze. Zahira assumed she hadn't wanted to let that slip. All the reason to press further.

"If you show me how, I'll tell you everything I know." It wasn't much of a promise—Zahira fully intended to make up a story on the fly—but Jo seemed eager to believe her. And Grandmother would want her to investigate. If the Boliska had something similar to track her, she needed to know its weaknesses.

Chapter Ten

—·—

Jo

Three Slydwells later, Jo took the Yerin woman to see the cryptoscope. She'd given her name as Noya, but her translator was registered to a Dede Lesedi, and Jo had no idea which was the pseudonym, or if they were both fakes. She also couldn't guess what the woman had against hovercraft travel. Noya/Dede had insisted on walking the entire way from the sliding station to Jo's apartment, as if she hadn't already spent the afternoon leading Jo and Nik on a wild chase through Yerin's capital. The trek had given Jo entirely too much time to second guess herself. This wasn't just any strange woman she'd invited into her home. She was a Yerin fugitive, wanted at a high enough priority to justify text alerts and additional travel screens. Sure, she seemed connected to the much-desired Resero project, but might the bounty hunters have other reasons to hunt her?

On the other hand, what danger did she pose? Jo had no doubt the woman could overcome her in a physical match, but what would be the point? She had nothing the woman would be even remotely interested in, other than the cryptoscope, and that lay broken and mangled from its first and only scan. She'd only done a brief assessment to order new parts before she and Nik headed off to Yerin.

"You tracked me with this thing?" The woman squatted next to one of the cryptoscope's deformed limbs and reached into the projection—the only part of the device that still worked—and ribbons of green wrapped across her palm. An apple-sized sphere floated just past her fingertips, its emerald land masses swirling into cobalt seas.

"Not exactly. The precision faded once the trail hit the surface." Jo leaned against the storage racks and watched the clouds of gold curl between the worlds and the woman's fingers. In the light, it looked like strings of gold also wove over the woman's hands and face. "Tilman Yar has only the one station, so we figured we'd start there."

"You were planning to search a whole city with a hand scanner?"

Jo's cheeks went warm. "It was a test run, you know? To see if I've got the kinks worked out." She waved her hand at the golden clouds. "And to figure out what this mess is."

"This bit of green is the frequency you used to track me?"

Jo nodded.

"But I've never been to any of these places."

"I know." That was the most frustrating part. Unless it was a true case of Midley's Theorem, that green should have been Resero's trail only. And it should have led them to a place he'd visited, not this strange person who claimed to have never met him.

Unless the dean had lied about the probe being one of the Resero artifacts? Jo scrambled for a scrap of paper and sketched out the rough shape of the tool.

"Have you ever owned one of these before? Or just touched one?"

The woman frowned at the sketch, turning both it and her head at angles as if to jog her memory. "Not that I recall. What is it?"

"Just the tool I got the sample from. Maybe if I scanned you, that might help narrow—"

"No." The word came out with all the force of a bullet train. "No scans."

"It's completely noninvasive, honest."

The woman stepped backward and her cheeks flushed. "I'm not your lab rat."

"I wasn't suggesting you were, but it'd help to—"

"I'm not doing it." Her voice cracked at the end, and the air buzzed around her. Bright lines of amber flashed across her walnut skin. They wove in circles on her face and spun across her knuckles like fire.

Holy shit. "Okay, okay. No scans."

"Good. Back to the crypto-seeker."

The woman gestured to the clouds and asked another question, but Jo couldn't stop staring at her hands. Was that normal for a Yerin?

The hand moved to wave in front of her face. "Jo?"

"Yes?"

"Could you zoom in on Yerin, please? I'd like to—" The woman jerked her hands behind her back. She must have noticed Jo staring.

"I have an epinephrine shot, if it's an allergic reaction to something? Or there's a clinic down the block." Jo hadn't served her anything, but a lot of the lubricants she used for the cryptoscope were plant-based.

"No. It's, umm... It's fine." The woman tugged her sleeves down past her wrist and took a backward step toward the door. Her eyes darted between Jo and Nik.

Could it be something contagious? Was that Resero's project? Some kind of virus? It could explain why the resonances would match. "We can get you antibiotics, if you need them. The clinic isn't that far."

"No, no. I'm fine." The shakiness in the woman's voice said she wasn't as she took another step toward the exit. "It's a genetic mutation, that's all."

"Are you sure? If Resero infected you with something-"

"Jo." Nik's voice came low and uneasy from the counter.

"What?"

"Take a look at this." He held out his transcom, eyes never leaving the woman's face as he angled it so she could see it too. The screen held a picture of a scaled creature. Labeled "Hatari," it was dark, menacing, and barely humanoid. The caption read 'Ancient Yerins believed creatures like this roamed the deserts at night, feasting on nguvu, sheep, and runaway children.'

"Seriously, Nik? This is hardly the time for random factoids..." Then she saw it. All across the creature's skin crawled thin red lines, weaving and swirling like the woman's amber ones. "You can't be serious."

He nodded at the woman. The lines on her face had brightened at the sight of the picture, flashing fire across her skin.

The woman lifted her hands like some fantasy wizard, ready to cast a spell as she backed uneasily toward the door. "Like the myths say, these lines contain nguvu, and I'm not afraid to use it."

"Well, shit." Nguvu radiation. Why hadn't Jo thought of that? That it wasn't the woman the frequency was leading her to, but something smaller. "This explains everything." The amovoscope back at the university. Stray radiation could have caused the energy field to destabilize, leaving traces that overlapped with the readings from the Resero sample. And because nguvu was a radiation rather than a stable substance, of course it'd read as clouds instead of a single path. And that'd mean... "The Resero project. It has to contain nguvu."

Nik glanced over his shoulder. She'd barely noticed him stepping between her and the woman. "Given the situation, I don't think now is the time to—"

But Jo's mind was already racing. "It has to be slightly off, mutated somehow, otherwise the program would have been able to identify it..." She dashed to the terminal to confirm. The resonance patterns didn't quite match, but they were close.

The woman's lines flashed out of the corner of her eye.

"Do you know what causes it?" Jo asked. "Your lines I mean. Is it some kind of biological reaction?"

The woman shook her head slightly, eyes wide. She'd frozen halfway to the door.

"If it is a chemical reaction, then that explains why the pattern deviates. Resero probably used something else, maybe some kind of crystal or metal alloy, to harness the flow." It all made sense now. That's why he hid it from his colleagues. Everyone knew nguvu studies were forbidden.

The woman cursed. She reached under her headscarf and pulled out something small and metallic. "This. Is this what you were tracking?" She tossed the coin-sized coil to Jo. A coil like the one from the light pole.

The metal wasn't as light as Jo'd expected, and its wire wrapped as thick as a ring band into double spirals. She gave it a pass with her scanner. While its surface shone silver, almost platinum in color, it showed no signs of vibrations as it buzzed against her skin. "Perfect match."

"Of course it is." The woman crept back to the cryptoscope, sporting the same look Jo imagined herself having whenever an extremely frustrating problem turned out to have an insanely simple solution. "Does anyone else have one of these seekers of the hidden things?"

"The cryptoscope? No. That's my research project." She looked closer at the coil's composition. Silver, copper, palladium, and... silicon?

A soft buzzing sent chills up Jo's spine. She turned to see the woman staring at the device, head tilted to one side. Her brown eyes seemed at once focused and contemplative. Jo's chest tightened. The woman's fingers pinched together and amber spirals traced her thumb and forefinger. Before Jo could move, the woman dropped her hand and threw her backpack back over her shoulder. "I have to go."

Air rushed out of Jo's lungs. "Were you...? Were you going to zap the cryptoscope?"

Noya, or whatever her real name was, scrambled for the door. "Thanks for the Slydwell," she called over her shoulder.

Jo cursed and rushed to her project. No signs of surface scorch marks. She grabbed the scanner, but no traces of nguvu either. Had she imagined things? But then why had the hatari rushed off?

Nik looked over her shoulder. "How bad is it?"

"I don't know. It doesn't look like she touched it." Jo swiped back to the readings from the coil. "And I think we have bigger things to worry about."

"You mean with her coils causing all those clouds on the projection?"

"No, these tiny things couldn't leave a trail like that." Jo tightened her fingers around the coil. "But Resero's project could be like them, but bigger."

Nik brushed aside the implications. "Are you sure all the clouds are from something man-made? Yerin isn't the only part of Stringspace with background levels of nguvu, and it's not too much of a stretch to assume most of it is natural."

"Pretty sure. Check this out." Jo pulled up three fuzzy graphs side by side on the screen. She gestured to the first. "So this is nguvu's typical resonance, and this is the sample pattern from the tools. Note how these sections are similar, but with a phase shift."

"That could be due to the different geological origins."

"Yes, but..." She enlarged the third graph and re-initialized the scanner, keeping the scanner wand hovering two feet above the coil. "If I take the background resonance readings, the pattern is similar to nguvu. But look what happens when it gets closer." The graph morphed, shifting phase to be a closer match to the sample. "The coil physically changes the nguvu's resonance as it's stored. So that cloud must be nguvu that's been altered."

"Then an asteroid or dwarf planet, something with the right composition? I find it hard to believe Resero would risk dealing with stored nguvu of this magnitude."

"He might not have intended to. Check this out." Jo tapped the number showing the coil's signal strength. It wavered upward by a fraction of a decimal point. "The reaction inside isn't stable, Nik. It's risen 0.0023 telsas since the woman left."

"What?"

"I don't know how, but the coil's attracting more nguvu to it." Her eyes drifted back to the cryptoscope's projection. The golden clouds were thickest at their centers. "Maybe it's like Xisi's theory of gravity, or like how water condenses into bigger droplets. The concentration itself draws more nguvu into it. So, over time, something like a planet or asteroid would have gathered enough to knock out all the surrounding systems."

"But why would Resero want to collect nguvu?"

"Maybe he didn't mean to?" Gods, she hoped he didn't mean to. "It could have been like a nguvu net? You know, something to keep radiation away from sensitive equipment?"

"It'd still be breaking the Code of Ethics."

"Yeah. And that would explain why he kept it secret."

"So you're suggesting that, instead of using a controlled environment, Resero traipsed through all those worlds with a prototype nguvu net?" Nik gestured to the projection. The clouds covered at least a dozen worlds, including Domun.

"It does sound a little crazy when you put it like that."

"A natural source makes more sense." He jammed his hands back in his pockets as if to emphasize his point. "Maybe a new asteroid, recently pulled in by a gas giant. A discovery like that isn't something to sneer at, you know."

She'd never suggested it was. But her gut said an asteroid couldn't explain the distribution of the clouds. And with the risk it would pose to nearby worlds, why would Resero keep it a secret? Unless he hadn't...

Jo flipped back through her scanner data to the sample from the artifact. There, hidden deep within the resonance data, she found the altered nguvu pattern from the coils. No wonder she hadn't been able to separate the gold clouds from the green strand. It appeared to be embedded in the mesh of frequencies. Could it be fenmo powder? She rushed over to the workbench for some mixing plates and the bits of dust she'd scraped from the artifact. "I need the frectyl wine vinegar and a pinch of potassium bicarbonate."

"Pantry or supply shelves?"

"Pantry for the bicarbonate. I think the vinegar is in the fridge."

Nik rushed into motion while she grabbed a dropper and an acid test. She really didn't deserve him. Anyone else would have demanded an explanation first. "No vinegar here. But there is a model hovercar."

"Chilling it helps the adhesives set faster," she explained. Though to be fair, a week would have been plenty, even in warmer temperatures. She really should let her nephew know she'd gotten the axle fixed. "Maybe try the top left cabinet?"

She set out the items she'd collected on the counter, careful not to spill the sample. There wasn't much, just the bit she'd scraped from her fingernails, but even a few flecks of fenmo powder would cause a reaction. And if they found fenmo powder, that meant someone had planted the frequency on the artifact. Someone connected to Resero. She scraped a few bits of dust into the mixing tray and gradually stirred in the potassium bicarbonate until it looked like white powder flecked with ground pepper. A few drops of the vinegar and it started bubbling.

Pale lavender at first, but then it shifted to green. A dark, rich green that confirmed her suspicions.

"Is that proof enough for you?" Jo tossed the dropper in the sink and popped the lids back on the bottle and canister. "Someone planted the sample. Someone wanted us to find out what Resero was working on, to find whatever these golden clouds are. If it was an asteroid, why wouldn't they just tell someone? Why would they keep it all covert like this, with frequencies hidden in fenmo powder?" She didn't look to see if Nik was still in denial before scrolling back through the scanner. Surely whoever had planted the frequency had left some sort of clue of what to do with the information.

Lubricant. Steel shavings. Bits of iron and aluminum. All things one would expect from a workshop. But something about the distribution of elements felt off.

"Look at the graph of the sample's composition," Nik said, popping his head over her shoulder. "Eight percent. Five percent. Two percent. Why not eight point two or five point three? It's too perfect."

It *was* too perfect. The compositions of the elements were all whole numbers. 8 5 2 7 1 3 2 4 5 9 7 8 6 9 5 7 8 4. Eighteen digits. Like what you'd need for a transcom number.

Chapter Eleven

— • —

Pravi

To no one's surprise, Pravi's house gained more D.I.C. agents after her failed escape and the attack on her life. But at least one good thing came of it. No one protested when she started carrying a Z73 plasma rifle on her security rounds.

Their mistake.

See, there were a lot of non-lethal options when it came to plasma rifles—slamming the butt into a pressure point being the most obvious one, though that usually came across as intentional. Another was stabbing the charged plasma barrel into someone's gut or back. It caused a decent amount of pain and stun damage, but again, it would be hard to pass that off as accidental. And there were laws about "incapacitating officers" and "interfering with ongoing investigations."

Incapacitating and interfering was not her intent. By all means, Pravi wanted the D.I.C. to continue searching for whoever hired her would-be kidnappers. The department had more resources and crime scene data to analyze than she did. Allowing their investigation to continue outsourced the work, and it was time for her to collect the results.

She eyed the command center on her side patio. It had grown busier over the two days since the attempted abduction. According to the conversations she'd overheard from Beni and Clive, the D.I.C. director now used the side patio as his main office. A new white tent had replaced the previous canopy, which seemed to support the theory. And if that wasn't enough, they'd oriented the entrance to block the view from her security cameras.

Pravi now stood a few meters away from said tent, pretending to watch the neighbors' yards with suspicion. She was really waiting for movement from Munus. He'd been leaving at around this time most days, presumably to meet with other teams he supervised or to grab a few hours of sleep. Pravi didn't care why he left, just so long as he did. The point was getting rid of the person most likely to foil her plan.

She held the plasma rifle in front of her, one hand resting inches from the trigger and the barrel angled toward the sky. Her other hand supported the shaft a good distance from the charged rings at the end. No point in stunning herself before her plan even started. The screen on her wrist showed Munus's shadow enter the area where they'd set up a transport circle. A few seconds later, it disappeared.

At that moment, Pravi froze, creating as much visible tension in her body as she could. It'd be ideal if it looked like the blood had drained from her face, but she'd have to settle for a look of intense concern. After holding the pose for half a minute, she slowly crouched down as if trying to make herself less of a target, as if she'd spotted a distant enemy. Through it all, she made sure not to make a sound. Munus' agents would be wary of her now, so any ploy for attention would raise a flag. She needed them to think she didn't care whether they noticed her or not. That her focus was on something more important.

Movement at the corner of her eye said her plan was working. Yurik, the agent who usually hung around the south-east corner of her house, approached with caution.

Pravi continued her charade, lifting her rifle closer to the ready position, but not quite high enough for the sight to reach her eye. In her mind, the character she was playing was hesitant, not sure whether she was seeing a true threat. In reality, she didn't want to block her view of Yurik. He came closer now, half crouched against whatever adversary Pravi had seen and trying to line up his view with hers. In half a second, he'd be a barrel-length behind her, his shoulder nearly down to her level.

She turned as if startled, swinging the rifle around so that the charged rings bumped into Yurik's left arm. A minor injury, though intensely painful. "Sorry, I'm so sorry." She dropped the rifle so the tip hit Yurik's thigh on the way down.

His already contorted face filled with deeper crease lines. To his credit, he only let out a muffled yelp.

Pravi cursed. "I am so sorry. It was an accident. I thought I saw... and then you..." She moved her hands as if she wanted to do assist, but had no idea how to. "We need to get you some help."

She reached for his comm, but he batted her hand away to press the button himself. "Green Tree down," he said through gritted teeth. "Condition minor. Need eyes on Eagle and transport to First Aid."

"Minor? Your bicep's as tense as a brick! Why'd you have to sneak up on me?" She pinched his arm above a nerve cluster and pulled a numbing patch out of her vest. She always carried them around whenever she had the plasma rifle. Keeping it charged carried the risk of accidents, and as far as anyone else would know, this had been an accident.

She tore the patch in half, slapping one on his arm and one on his thigh. It'd be better with exposed skin, but the point wasn't to actually help, just to make it look like she'd tried.

"Why didn't you say anything?" she asked, helping him to his feet. As she'd hoped, one of the agents from the command center was rushing to his aid. The woman took Yurik's other arm. "Plasma rifle sting. Left arm and thigh. I didn't see him, honest."

The woman merely nodded and did her own check for injury while Yurik recounted the "accident." He blamed himself, but Pravi continued to express remorse, saying as the one holding the weapon, she should have been more aware of those around her. She tried to help, even as the woman subtly brushed her off and headed for the command center.

At that point, Pravi stopped paying attention to her words and let herself ramble. Trails of apologies poured forth, giving the impression she cared as much about the possible repercussions as she did Yurik's injuries. Another agent waited at the entrance to the command center, intending to block Pravi from entering, but Pravi took him for just another person to babble to. He didn't stand to listen for long, though.

With Yurik's leg paralyzed, they needed both agents to guide him through the flap.

Pravi followed closely, wringing her hands and craning her neck to see the extent of the injuries while Yurik's fellow agents provided him aid. She set the cameras on her wrists, jacket collar, and earrings to record. Although she had seen it on her security cameras, this was her first time being inside the command center. Fourteen monitors hung along the far wall, with four desks and chairs set up with keyboards. They carried Yuirk to a conference-type table in the center of the space, and Pravi kept her eyes focused on that to hide her true purpose. "Is he alright? No nerve damage?"

"No nerve damage." The female agent pursed her lips at the medical scanner and then at Pravi. "But you need to leave."

Pravi nodded and started for the exit. Every few steps she turned back, as if hesitant to leave without being sure of Yurik's recovery. In reality, she'd given the cameras more angles to record from. As she exited through the flap, she found herself facing Director Munus.

"Good evening, Ms. Resero." He didn't look surprised to see her, though there might have been a hint of disappointment in his voice.

"Munus." She nodded her head in greeting. He moved to the side of the doorway as she shuffled past.

"They're off-tilt bifocal, you know."

Pravi forced herself to not stutter at the revelation. "What are?"

"The monitors. Every square millimeter is positioned at a slightly different angle so that if you aren't using two cameras, positioned directly in the center at eye level, you'll only end up with patchy blurs. And of course, we have a back-end program that randomizes angles to make each monitor unique, so you can't use an algorithm to fill in the blanks."

Pravi's recordings would be useless. "Why are you telling me this?"

"Because rather than ask me for updates on your case, you decided to stun gun my detective."

"It was a—"

"Accident. Yeah, yeah. Plausible deniability and all that."

Pravi was going to say 'plasma rifle', but okay.

"Point is, you don't trust me. And I get it. After what Agents Foxley and Brekhart did when you were a kid, I wouldn't trust me either."

Oh, that ploy. D.I.C. Guidebook C, Chapter 32. "Congrats on being able to read a file."

"They leaked your location to bait your uncle's enemies. You were only fifteen, and they didn't have the brains to protect you." He dropped his usual stiffness for a posture that mimicked empathy. "The idiots took three days to track you down and ended up with a mere slap on the wrist. Foxley got offered early retirement and Brekhart moved to a desk job."

"Not quite the right story, but okay."

"Then what's the right story?" The question started out sarcastic, but it faltered at the end. Everyone knew Foxley didn't get early retirement over one messed up case. Munus dropped his icy facade and motioned for her to go on. If he was being genuine, she might as well give him something back. It could buy her some sympathy points for later, and anyway, it's not like the truth would get him any closer to her uncle's prototype.

"No one took the bait at first." Pravi sighed and crossed her arms against the memories. The window breaking while she was doing math homework. The calloused hand over her mouth. The cold, dank feel of the concrete bunker. "After two days of no bites, they spread the rumor that I knew Uncle Xander's algorithm. The one he was using to track their smuggling operation."

If Munus' face paled at the revelation, she didn't notice. She was too busy shivering at the ghost of drafty air and a dull scalpel.

"Foxley and Brekhart never saved me. They didn't even tell Xander until I'd been gone for half a day." She shot Munus a look that held a touch too much hatred. "They said they didn't want to interrupt him in the middle of the algorithm."

Xander had been the one who found her. The one who broke into the bunker and pulled her out. "Ms. Pravi, I'm so sorry. On behalf of the entire D.I.C., I'd like to—"

"I was in the hospital for two weeks. Even with the stitches, some of the cuts never healed right, and half my back twitches when it gets cold."

Munus sighed and put his hands on hips. "It isn't BlackTek, Rangle, or Lienets." It took Pravi a second to realize he was talking about the investigation into the ambush. "Rangle and Lienets always use their own crew, and though your red-headed attacker had done work for TekMech, they had a falling out last year over a late payment."

"Well, that narrows down the options." And not in a good way. Munus had named all the usual suspects. Pravi bit the inside of her lip. Unknown players were the most dangerous.

Munus waited expectantly with his hands on his hips. What, did he think this little heart-to-heart meant she'd tell him about the prototype?

"I appreciate the update," she said, picking up the rifle and starting back to her front door.

"Listen, if you could just give me one hint about the danger it might pose..."

"I know as much about that as you know about my attackers." Pravi felt so tired, so worn from holding old memories at bay, that the lie sounded true even to her.

Her transcom and Munus' watch chose that moment to vibrate, diffusing the tension. Another hit off the field fluctuation algorithm. One had hit an amusement park ride, injuring the operator and trapping at least a dozen people inside. She glanced up at Munus. She could tell from his face that he'd gotten a message about the same event. In that moment, when his gray eyes met hers, she knew she'd given herself away. Munus now knew, or at least suspected, that the prototype and energy events were connected.

He swiped away the alert. "I'd ask, but I'm guessing you'd just lie again."

Pravi's mind went through every curse word she knew, but Munus didn't wait for an answer. She was still cursing herself when she got inside, too upset to check whether her hidden cameras had picked up anything useful. She'd lost her edge the second her transcom went off.

Her spare transcom sat silent at the side of her desk. The one she'd tied to the planted fenmo powder. Even after offering the fellowship, she'd received no messages. Pravi had blown the whole thing. Gaining allies. Hiding the info from Munus. Getting off this rock. The spare transcom blinked low battery as if to mock her, and she buried her face in her hands.

As she leaned forward, a soft purr vibrated through the desk. The spare transcom showed one... two... three new alerts and kept buzzing.

"Hi," the first read. "We found your message." The sender had attached several images. A graph of the elements where Pravi had hidden the transcom number. A readout of the fenmo powder resonance. A side-by-side comparison of the hidden resonance pattern and the pattern for nguvu radiation. Pravi frantically scrolled through everything, but if all they did was repeat back the information she'd given them, they might as well have sent nothing at all.

But wait... Pravi did a double take of the last image. It took her nearly a minute to decipher what she was looking at. Big clouds of gold, floating around a map of Stringspace. No. That couldn't be right. The legend said all the gold was concentrations of nguvu. First off, how could they have taken those readings? The only thing Pravi could think of was jumping between worlds with their scanners running and then extrapolating the points, which would obviously be prone to excessive error.

And secondly, even if they'd used some more accurate method, there was no way that much nguvu could build up between planets. All of her uncle's notes said gathering nguvu had been painfully slow. Each battery needed to charge in a high-nguvu area for a month in order to power a single slide. This much radiation should have taken centuries—hell, millennia—to reach these levels.

Either this contact was an idiot or they were pranking her. But that didn't mean they couldn't be of some use.

CHAPTER TWELVE

— • —

Jo

J o wiped sweat from her forehead with the back of her wrist. Oil or lubricant streaked every other part of her body. She'd worked on replacing the cryptoscope's mangled arms for at least a day and a half, measured by the three small meals she'd rushed through and the quick nap and shower Nik insisted on. Might have been even longer, if Nik's disapproving look and recently-placed carryout order were anything to go by. Which they usually were.

She tore open the last actuator box, once again fuming over the response they'd gotten from their mysterious contact: "These results aren't possible. Run it again." That was all it said. No "Wow, congrats on solving my puzzle!" or "Can I see the full data set for these coordinates?" Not even a "Who is this?" Usually, Jo dreaded small talk more than she dreaded conversations in general, but it seemed warranted here. The contact hadn't even introduced themselves and they'd started giving orders.

As you wish, your majesty. Jo wrangled the actuator into place on the newly welded limb and attached it with a handful of salvaged bolts. The wiring and sensors stretched across the tile under it like veins, laid out for easy installation. Luckily, very few of them had needed to be replaced. As it stood, she'd be paying off the new parts for at least a year.

Nik collected the discarded packaging. "Did you ever respond to the message?" he asked.

"And say what? 'Well, actually, we followed the trail and found a nguvu-wielding superhuman, so it can't be that far off'?" She tossed her wrench to the side in favor of a smaller one and picked up the first of the sensors. "If they want me to run it again, then I'll run it again. It's not like you liked the results the first time, either."

"I displayed a healthy dose of skepticism. A perfectly valid reaction to being told a giant cloud of nguvu is building up around dozens of worlds."

"Yeah, well, hopefully your skepticism is well-founded." Jo finished securing the sensor and grabbed a zip tie to anchor the wiring away from the moving parts. "Because otherwise, that cloud could be growing unconstrained while I drain my bank account trying to prove it even exists."

Nik tucked the actuator box into the recycling bin and grabbed his transcom. "Rather than rehash this argument, I'm going to pick up our sandwiches. Is there anything you need while I'm out? More wiring? Gyroscopic sensors?"

"A winning lottery ticket?" Maybe a robot who could finish the rest of the work for her?

"I don't know that the parts store will have any of those, but I can check." He opened the door, then turned back. "Don't die of existential dread while I'm gone, okay?"

"Can't make any promises." Jo moved onto the next sensor as Nik closed the door behind him. She bit the inside of her lip as she worked. Nik didn't deserve her frustration. When they received the contact's message, there hadn't been even a hint of "I told you so" from him. She needed a better way to vent it. One that didn't involve ranting at Nik or giving the cryptoscope a good kick.

And maybe she'd been wrong about the nguvu cloud. Though Nik had rechecked the algorithm and said it was fine, there was always the chance that one of the broken wires had mutated a signal somewhere and shifted a decimal point or two. The sensor data taken while sliding in and out of Yerin suggested otherwise, but there was always the hope.

Two hours and a near collision of the arms later, the clouds hadn't faded at all. They were bigger. The latest projection floated in the air beside Nik, taunting Jo for doubting its validity. The planets had shifted clockwise since the first run, but the golden shimmer still loomed over its territory. The edges had bubbled out in new directions, and at the center, the densest areas swirled like snowdrifts in a storm. She'd never felt so awful about being right. There was no way the contact would accept the new data.

She wandered over to the brightest eddy and poked at it as if that might make it disperse. "You see this swirl? This beautiful, glittery wisp? It could take out a whole data center and make the light pole back on Yerin look like child's play."

Nik shrugged and put his hands in his pockets.

"We're lucky it's not touching anything." She frowned at the mass of gold. "As far as I know, nguvu can't do anything in the middle of space. Except maybe zap an asteroid or something."

"What about these?" Nik gestured at eddies further into the projection. "They look like they're close enough to graze a planet."

She bent closer to inspect the swirls, taking note of their locations. "You don't suppose they already hit? They look less dense at the center."

"I would expect an epidemic of power outages to be headline news."

"Good call." Jo pulled up the news on her transcom, searching for field fluctuations on the planets closest to the eddies. The first one looked promising. *'Power Surge Derails Downtown Entertainment.'* "Two dozen people were trapped on a roller coaster after the anti-friction field collapsed on Denali. Happened around two this morning, which makes sense with the dispersion pattern."

"Coincidence?"

"Not if it happened twice." She scrolled further down. "The planet to the right had a hit on a distribution center."

Would that be enough proof for their contact? Or would they claim Jo and Nik had reverse-engineered the data to fit the events? "Do you think there's any chance of predicting the strikes?"

"Location wise? Yes." Nik stared thoughtfully at the swirling clouds. "When, however, is a trickier question to ask because we don't know what the threshold is for the eddies. Or if there even is one. We could end up waiting days for a strike to come."

"Nik?"

"Yes?"

She gave him the biggest smile she could muster. "Got any plans for your weekend?"

He sighed. "I guess I do now."

Chapter Thirteen

— • —

Nik

Early the next morning, Nik slid shivering into Domun station. He'd spent three hours exposed to the winds of northern Fressia, and the blast of warm air came as a welcome shock. He pushed back the hood of his parka and searched for Jo.

Her cobalt snow boots appeared a few circles closer to the entrance. Drops of melting snow flakes speckled the surrounding floor, and mittened hands pulled her woolly coat closer. Snow covered every inch of her. Or at least, every inch that didn't have an oil stain to repel it.

Her scarf muffled a string of curses. "Why'd I think waiting in a blizzard was a good idea?"

Because she couldn't resist a puzzle any more than Nik could? He brushed a chunk of snow off her shoulder, and it fell to the tile in a moist clump. "At least we got the data."

"Of somebody's snowmobile failing! It's hardly newsworthy. So again, it looks like we're making this up." Jo's teeth chattered as she spoke, and she stomped more snow from her boots. He tried not to cringe thinking about the puddle it would melt into.

Her transcom buzzed from somewhere inside layers of insulation.

"I'm surprised that's not too frozen to work."

"I wish it was." She pulled it from her sleeve and turned the screen toward him. "I told my brother about the snowstorm, and look what he sent me—a picture of him and the kids. On the beach."

Typical Naom. When they were younger, he'd derived great joy in leaving crumbs and wrappers out for Nik to find. In a way, it was still better than the empty and pristine house he went home to.

Jo crossed her arms back over her coat. "Honestly, I don't know how Piowins do it, living in the cold like that."

"It's the yeeti." He walked over to a trash can to shake the snow from his coat and hat.

"The what?"

"Artificial whale blubber." He'd learned about it from one of those natural documentaries when he was ten. His oceanographer parents were on back-to-back submarine expeditions at the time, and he'd thought if he studied enough, he wouldn't be left behind for the next one.

Jo turned toward the coffee shop instead of the exit, and Nik followed without question. Scents of cinnamon and roasted nutmeg drifted toward them, emanating from row after row of knotted buns and baked puddings.

She shuffled into line. "I'd rather have a heatwave than another blizzard."

"I didn't think it was that bad. We did experience the majestic glory of the Fressian moose."

Her sideways glance asked if he was kidding. "Oh yes, because a scenic vacation is never complete without a seven-foot beast defecating two yards away from you. One small hot chocolate, please."

The cashier turned to Nik.

"I'm good, thanks." He shrugged off his sweater and tucked it under his arm with his coat. In all honesty, he was also a bit bummed it was a small strike. The output energy data of a larger one would have been fascinating to see.

Jo wrapped her fingers around the disposable mug and took a deep breath of steam. Small drops condensed on her cheeks and nose. "What are you grinning at?"

"It's really quite balmy in here."

"So?"

"I would have thought you'd be warmed up by now."

"And I would have thought we'd have more to show for our time." She peeled off her mittens. "At least the last one didn't make us wait as long."

"Ulg." He cringed, remembering the way his shirt and shorts had stuck to his skin as they'd waited outside the nature preserve. "Too damp."

"It was a rainforest, Nik. It's supposed to be damp." She smiled, her cheeks pink from the cold. "I can't believe you thought you'd grade papers."

"I brought an umbrella."

"Should have worn a wetsuit." She took another sip and unfastened her coat. "I guess it's settled, then. If the next biome is anything less than comfortable, we let someone else handle it."

"Good plan." Nik held open the door for her, wishing it could be that simple. But from the way she obsessively checked the cryptoscope's scans, he knew that wouldn't be enough to sway her.

Sure enough, Nik awoke the next morning to rattling—his transcom buzzing against his nightstand. He couldn't drag his eyes open, the lids were too heavy, so his head fell back to the pillow. Undeterred, the caller tried again, sending vibrations echoing through the bedside.

He fumbled for the device. "Hello?"

"Hey! Can you meet me at the station in an hour?" Jo's voice sounded like she'd been up for a while—or like she'd never gone to sleep.

"Good morning to you, too." He checked the time on the transcom. 6:27. He'd have to call the physics professors to say he'd be missing their VR session.

"I got another hit from the algorithm."

"Would you call for any other reason?"

"I've got a good feeling about it. No rain, no snow... no precipitation whatsoever."

Nik yawned. "It's not a desert, is it?"

"Nope." Excitement spilled from her voice. "Can you make it?"

So much for sleeping in on his day off. He stretched, letting his toes point out from the covers. "Yeah, I can be there."

"Awesome. Oh, and you'll need to wear something nice."

Nice? "My family nice or yours?"

"Mine."

Dress shirt and slacks. Got it. "Anything else?"

"Don't bring papers to grade."

"Already finished them." He'd stayed up until two in case this happened.

The call ended, and Nik let the transcom fall to the mattress so he could wipe the sleep from his eyes. Maybe he should've said no. The pillows looked so tempting. But in spite of his complaints, this whole nguvu cloud situation wasn't all that bad. Sure, it was a deviation from his plan (publish two data analysis papers a year until he could buy Jo a lab, then fund an official partnership with research grants). But if they succeeded, it could cut years off his timeline, and he wouldn't have to follow Dr. Inio to Kerr to study the sleeping patterns of cave mice.

He forced himself to shave and shower, waking up in the warm steam. Dress nice, she'd said. Hopefully that didn't mean a tie. He tucked a folded one in his pocket just in case.

Jo was waiting for him at the station. He'd expected her to wear one of her nicer jumpsuits, the kind made of silky fabric instead of canvas, but instead she sported a shirt and trousers. Her pants were black and cropped, tapered to just above the ankle, and her striped shirt had a shallow neckline that followed her shoulders. Something about the creases on the front made Nik suspect they'd been a birthday gift. One that hadn't been taken out of the bag until that morning.

"So where are we off to?"

"It's a surprise." She bent over her nav device, covering the coordinates. A tight bun held her hair off her neck. Surprisingly, she wasn't wearing the scanner bag. Instead, her shoulder supported a bright red, leathery tote, its smooth shape interrupted by the bulge of the device. She never carried a purse. He hadn't realized she even owned one.

"Ready?" She offered her hand with a grin and his fingers clasped around hers. "You're going to love this." Jo led the slide, passing the frequency through her palm as the station blurred into the color of paprika. The string itself felt like a mountain of feathers, but something twisted in the pit of his stomach. His mouth tasted like cotton.

Moments later, the world came into focus with a whirl of commotion. Shades of red, orange, and blue danced against white-washed walls as large chandeliers hung from the ceiling. The station's visitors wove between circles with lively gossip and even livelier clothing. More voices joined them from a second-floor balcony with intricate, wrought-iron railings. Nik pinched the bridge of his nose. His insides felt too shaky. "How big was that jump?"

"Only ten quizzets." Jo fumbled through her bag and passed him some Slydwell. "But the frequency is a near ratio of our homeworld."

"You could have warned me." Forcing one's body to vibrate at a multiple of its natural frequency did weird things to your insides.

She took a dose of her own. "I didn't think it'd be an issue. I've never traveled this close to an octave pair before." Her head turned to the nearest blue circle, but her feet still pointed at the door. "I guess if it's that bad, we could go back."

"Nah. I'll be fine." At the very least, this data meant he could publish three papers this year instead of two. And he'd take the whole pack of Slydwell if it meant getting away from Inio's rodent obsession. "Which way are we headed?"

"The target is out the doors and to the right a few blocks." Jo's hopeful smile crept back to her cheeks. "It's near the original downtown area, so lots of things the nguvu could hit."

Outside, the cool breeze helped clear Nik's foggy head. Wispy clouds painted the sky, and the sun hovered low over the buildings. More likely sunset than sunrise—something he and Jo rarely saw, tied as they were to their projects and research. Wouldn't it be nice if they didn't have to grind? If Jo got the Rygal fellowship, could they have more evenings like this?

Rows of shops ran to either side, connected by strings of flickering lights. Balconies wrapped the upper floors, and a grid of windows punctuated their facades. The buildings stood shoulder to shoulder, distinguishable only by a change of color. Coral and cantaloupe and lime green. He could hear the buzz of traffic behind them, but bicycles were the only vehicle in sight. The air was tangy and sharp, suggesting the start of supper time. A normal, casual supper oblivious to the threat of nguvu. Restaurants had their doors propped open, and clusters of outdoor tables were set with napkins and candles. Couples strolled the street in pairs, chatting and drifting closer to each other. The men wore well-cut suits and the women's attire balanced striking jewel tones with sleek, black shoes.

Outdoor tables crowded the sidewalk, keeping Jo close by Nik's side. It'd be easy to reach out and brush her fingers, but he shoved his hands deeper into his pockets. Laughter and music seeped from the doors and windows, and street performers warmed up along the avenue. The smooth croon of jazz floated through the air, punctuated by the tapping of a drum brush. He closed his eyes, and his steps slowed. His translator tried to make sense of the vocals. Perhaps he should disable it. The words sounded so heartfelt in their native tongue.

Jo's voice pulled Nik from his trance. "Come on, we don't want to be late."

He opened his eyes and found her striped shirt several meters in front of him. Her strides bordered on prancing. She must have been very confident in the incoming strike. "How long until the eddy brushes the planet?"

She checked her bracelet. "About forty-five minutes."

"Then why are we running?"

"The reservations are in five."

Reservations? He turned the corner, and the path morphed into a plaza. Strings of lights swooped from the surrounding buildings, spinning a web around a tall, black pole at their center. Hovercraft flew along the street at the far side, but music piped in through speakers muffled their sounds. Nik followed Jo to one of the outdoor patios. Flower boxes hung from ironwork railings, and the restaurant leaked rich, savory smells. She gave her name, and the server led them to their seats. The tables were bistro-style, woven and metal, and set with a dainty vase of flowers.

Jo pulled out her own chair before he could reach it. "We'd like two coffee noisettes, please, and a retior pastry to share."

"I'll have them right away." The server tapped in the order. "Anything else I can get for you?"

"That's it, thanks." Jo pulled out her scanner to recalibrate and turned back to Nik. "Have you figured it out yet?"

"Figured out what?" His chest tightened. She was staring at him like he'd forgotten her birthday.

"Cafe Rosita? The theory of Stringspace relativity?"

"Wait." Coffee noisettes and a pastry... Something tickled Nik's memory. "You mean Otmoniset? Otmoniset's Theory of Relativity?"

She beamed. "I ordered us his usual. This very table is the one where he noticed the ripples in his coffee, leading him to posit the movement of the worlds relative to their frequency." Her eyes lingered on the scanner knobs. "I know it's not much, but you've been such a sport with hunting the strikes..."

Her voice drifted off as the server arrived with their order. Two coffees swirled with cream plus a powdered, flaky heap as large as a dinner plate. It smelled like heaven.

Nik tore a corner off the pastry. The flaky texture was a pleasant mix of lightness and crunch, and worth all the prior worlds Jo had dragged him to. Too bad shattered glass echoed across the plaza before he could take another bite.

CHAPTER FOURTEEN

— • —

ZAHIRA

G randmother always said if you wanted to hide, head for the crowds—the more boisterous, the better. Zahira couldn't think of a refuge more boisterous than the Ballisium, with voices unrestrained and drinks sloshing as fans cheered in delight or protested a referee's call. A sports complex wrapped around a sliding station, hundreds of screens lined its main transport area, allowing guests to purchase concessions without missing plays. Cheers and commentary reverberated from the dozens of adjoining fields while drone-mounted cameras soared high overhead. Though its circles could handle hundreds of transports per minute, the Ballisium served more as a destination than a travel node, which made it perfect for Zahira. Sure, the major transfer stations held more people and thus safer crowds, but they also had a high turnover rate. Most people were either coming or going, leaving anyone waiting exposed. But not here. At the Ballisium, everyone was waiting. Mostly in line for greasy carbs, but others hovered in front of the plethora of screens, their steaming nachos and foamy beverage in hand. The next timeout or commercial break would see them scurrying back to stadium seats.

Zahira waited behind a half-melted drink at one of the busier bars. Her cold metal stool sat within view of the sliding circles, but also offered an intense game to use as cover. The screen before her showed women in green and orange jerseys dodging around a circle field, turf flying at their feet. An orange player dunked a yellow ball into a raised basket, and, having purchased a tee with the green team's logo as part of her disguise, Zahira groaned in response.

She risked a glance to the circles. Grandmother should have arrived by now. She'd left Yerin two days ago, and the dinosaur egg tourism should have kicked into high gear. With Zahira gone, the station security should have been lighter, leaving an opening to escape. Yet the sliding circles showed no signs of Yerins at all, much less the gray-haired one who'd raised her.

"Mind if I sit here?" The voice belonged to a man around Zahira's age. He had spiked blond hair and deep amber eyes, and he'd been glancing at her while he waited for his order.

Zahira scooted her stool to the side. Less to give him space and more to make sure she still had an open path to the exits.

The man cleared his throat. "Nice tattoos, by the way."

She looked down at her arms, almost forgetting she'd added on to the nguvu markings with an ink pen. Trying to hide them with a long shirt or gloves would have drawn too much attention, but she still fought the urge to tug down her sleeves. "Thanks."

He gave her a nervous smile. "I've gotten a few myself, but none of the bioluminescent kind. You get them on Jalur?"

"Maybe?" She should have thought about that detail. Grandmother would have. "I was a bit drunk when I got them."

"Gnarly. My name's Silas, by the way."

"Dede." She gave his outstretched hand a curt nod. At least she'd remembered the name on her translator this time. She'd given Jo and her friend the nickname Grandmother had always used.

He returned the hand to his pocket and bowed back. "Pleasure to meet you, Dede. I, uh, I'm sorry if I'm bothering you..."

"No worries. Just trying to watch the game, you know?" And the sliding circles. Which he'd continue blocking if he didn't sit down.

"Oh. Sorry." He rocked on his feet for a moment and stared at his drink. To her surprise, he left the neighboring stool empty and instead headed back to the other side of the bar.

Had he... had he been trying to flirt with her? Zahira exhaled into her drink. She was so used to judging people by whether or not they were a threat that the thought hadn't even crossed her mind. He had been attractive, though. That much she'd noticed. Maybe now that she was free of Yerin, it wouldn't be as risky to try a relationship. She turned back to the screen and sighed. The green team was now down 2-7. She probably wouldn't be picking them if she ever had the leisure to follow a sports team.

At the next score, a new, shorter figure slid into focus back at the transport circles. Zahira noted hair the right shade of gray and a red hat like they'd agreed to. She reached into her pocket to pay her tab, but stopped. The figure was walking weird, kind of bent over like she was trying to hide her face. Either something was wrong with grandmother, or something was really wrong with grandmother. Wrong in that she'd been apprehended and the Boliska had sent a decoy.

She pushed down her concern and called to the bartender for another round. Because everyone knew fugitives hid. They didn't do anything that drew extra attention to themselves. A fugitive from Yerin certainly wouldn't be baring her arms, wearing bright green, and calling out in her native tongue.

The old lady walked on to check a quieter table.

Grandmother would have known better. She would have at least known Zahira's voice even if she wasn't the one who'd come up with their strategy. Zahira tightened her fist. She shouldn't have listened when Grandmother said to leave Yerin without her. Shouldn't have abandoned her to cling to the chance of a normal life. There was only one way to remedy her mistake, but she'd have to get herself to safety first.

She took a swig of the fresh drink, using the reflections in the glass to check for more signs of Boliska. Two men were skirting the sliding circles, hovering within view of the decoy. They weren't the right height for Yerins, but they weren't interested in any of the screens, either. One kept looking at his watch, then looking up. She guessed it linked to a scanner in his pocket.

Zahira paid her tab and headed for the other side of the bar. She didn't like the idea of using bystanders, but she told herself that anyone in her vicinity was already in danger. And anyway, she'd used up her sympathy guilt when she chose not to fry Jo's crypto-thingy. "Hey."

The man with amber eyes looked up as Zahira set her drink at the seat next to his. She leaned against the counter.

"Sorry I was abrupt earlier. A bad game can really get to you, you know?"

His look of surprise morphed into a coy smile. "Yeah, no, it's fine. I, uh, should have checked the score before coming over." Yep. That goofy grin was definitely attractive. Didn't change her plan for using him, though.

She tucked a stray strand of hair behind her ear and took out a piece of paper and pen. "I think their odds are better for their next match. If you'd want to meet up or something?"

He stuttered his interest as she made like she was writing down her transcom number. Instead, she wrote, *'My ex just showed up. Would you mind walking me to the sliding circles?'* She folded it and slid the paper his way. "Sorry, I don't usually do things like this."

He smiled, but as he read the paper, his face turned to one of concern. "Oh, uh, yeah. Of course." He dropped a tip by his drink and got up to walk with her.

When he whispered to ask where, she pointed out the man with the scanner watch. "But don't let him see you look. I don't think he's noticed me yet."

"Oh, okay." He then immediately looked over his shoulder to find the man. Cute, but definitely not clever enough to be a hatari's boyfriend. They hastened to the sliding circles, with Zahira pulling up coordinates for a jump. Only a few more steps to those blue lines. She started to thank the amber-eyed man when an arm grabbed for her wrist. It seemed the Boliska with the watch had another friend.

Zahira yanked her arm down toward her assailant's thumb and twisted out of his grasp. She followed it up with a quick elbow to his gut. He groaned, but his leg swiped at Zahira's feet. She managed to dodge it enough to stumble instead of trip.

"Hey now." The amber-eyed man cut in to block her assailant as she stepped into the circle. "Do I need to call for security?"

The Boliska shoved him aside. Zahira reached for the string, only to find she hadn't hit 'Confirm' on her nav device. Shit. She ducked the man's swing for her face and got a good kick in at his leg.

"Help! Help!" she called, scurrying to another circle. That was one good thing about being off Yerin. If a uniformed Boliska had come after her back home, the crowd would have helped him take her down.

Instead, a man with nachos helped the amber-eyed man to his feet, and two more bystanders dragged their eyes from the screens to hurry over. Her assailant was hesitant now, with so many eyes on him. The crowd could clearly see who was chasing who.

Within moments, Zahira had a protective ring around her chosen sliding circle. She whispered a quick thank you and grabbed the string. Her transcom buzzed with a set of coordinates as soon as the slide ended. *'Turn yourself in if you want her to live.'*

Zahira didn't bother looking up the location. The Boliska wouldn't be keeping Grandmother there, not when they had the upper hand. But she couldn't just slide back to Yerin and start zapping things, either. She needed to figure out where they were actually detaining Grandmother before she did anything else. Thank the strings she hadn't fried her chance at that.

Zahira set her nav for Jo's homeworld, hoping the inventor was already fixing her device. She'd rather not have to use force, or a hostage Nik, as incentive.

Chapter Fifteen

— · —

Jo

The air crackled with electricity. Jo had been wrong about the strike's target. Though the music and dancing had stopped, the strings of lights remained intact, glittering over frightened faces.

She grabbed the scanner and raced to where the plaza met the street, hoping the crash hadn't been as bad as it looked. A quadcopter lay on the ground like a cracked egg, with all four rims of its fan blades bent and fragmented. One still spun from the impact. Traffic angled to avoid it, but also slowed to watch.

Halfway to the curb, bits of glass and carbon fiber crunched under Jo's feet, growing larger the closer she got to the crash site. A quick scan confirmed it—a nguvu strike. White sparks darted across the quadcopter's panels, revealing cracks across its windows and a blood-splattered airbag inside. The cabin shook as if someone was trying to get out, but the live currents prevented rescue. She had to do something. All she had was her scanner—useless for anything other than taking readings—but there had to be a way to redirect the sparks.

"Don't touch it." The stranger's voice was sharp, though Jo had kept a safe distance from the wreck. A towering, dark-haired man brushed past her and knelt to inspect the damage. The center of his dress shirt was wet with sweat as he angled his head to check for leaking fluids. Sweat lined the edges of his beard and hair. "Looks like one of the engine fields failed, or maybe the gyroscope."

A blond-bearded man came up beside him, panting. He was also dressed too formal to be an emergency tech, though his shirt had some sort of paisley pattern instead of solid blue. He hastily set a black duffel on the ground and unzipped it. "Any fire risk?" he asked.

"No, thankfully." The dark-haired man rose to his feet and took to rolling up his sleeves. "Now wipe that self-satisfied smirk off your face and toss me the field sensor." His voice was so sharp that Jo reached for her nonexistent tool bag to get him one. Who were they to carry such a thing to a place like this? Off-duty mechanics, perhaps? Some kind of high-end handymen?

The blond man pulled out a small ball of gears as sirens echoed from the right. There must have been an emergency response station nearby. Jo shoved her scanner in her pocket but kept it running, the wand tucked neatly in her sleeve. A bright-yellow ambulance sped over the trapped cars, flanked by two pairs of hover bikes with "Police" emblazoned on their sides.

The dark-haired man ignored them. He unwound the field sensor from its chain and waved it toward the sparks. All three of its lights blinked green. High energy discharge. The man's lips twisted into a scowl and he flicked his wrist to reel in the sensor. Two lights would have meant it was safe enough for basic protection gear, but they'd need a large adjustment panel to fix this one. Jo nearly gasped when the blond man pulled one out of the duffel bag. Who the hell were they? Field sensors and adjustment panels weren't things you just toted around in case you needed them, high-tech mechanic or not. Had they expected the energy distortion? Did they know about the nguvu? Her curiosity grew as the dark-haired man started directing the responders with a quick flash of his ID.

She shifted to her toes for a better look, but an officer stepped in front of her, unwinding a roll of caution tape. It formed a chest-high line in front of the growing crowd.

"I hope no one's injured," someone said.

Another voice agreed, while others whispered in speculation about what caused the crash. Transcom lights lit the edges of Jo's vision.

The nearest responder moved and she once again spotted the dark-haired man. He turned the knobs with practiced ease, quieting the energy field's erratic bursts. She tucked away her scanner wand

and angled her transcom. With any luck, she'd match his picture to a database.

The sparks faded from the windshield as more responders reached the scene, and the dark-haired man gave the all-clear. Carefully, a pair of firefighters pried open the cockpit, untangling the passengers from the mangled craft. Jo and the crowd watched with bated breath. Blood gushed from the first passenger's leg, and she tumbled into the waiting arms of a paramedic. The other held an injured arm, red staining the gaps between her fingers. Paramedics quickly ushered them onto stretchers, and once the ambulance doors shut and its lights sped away, Jo and the transcom-wielding crowd turned their attention back to the clean-up crew. Yellow- and blue-vested officers sifted through the wreckage, photographing the debris and taking smaller samples for further analysis. What Jo wouldn't give for those readings.

The dark-haired man stood at the edge of the scene, appearing to coordinate the clean-up. A neon blue vest now covered his shirt, but Jo couldn't make out the markings. He waved to someone in the crowd. The blond man stepped forward, ducking under the caution tape to take the adjustment panel and duffel. Now that she was paying more attention, something felt familiar about his face. She lifted her transcom to snap another picture.

Nik snuck up behind her. "Whatcha doing?"

"I'll explain in a minute." She passed him the scanner and ran both images through a reverse image search. The results pulled up faster than expected.

"Did you get what you wanted?"

"Maybe more." She showed him the screen. "You were right. We're not the only ones looking into the distortions."

The dark-haired man was Zave Danu, a consultant for the D.I.C. His company dealt with unusual energy readings and field fluctuations, and the blue-vested responders had its logo printed on their backs. His friend in paisley was Dr. Peikarean Froum, two-time winner of the McKeni prize for physics. Jo had used his equations for modeling Stringspace energy transfers in one of her college courses.

"See. I told you the experts are on it." Nik handed her the purse with the scanner tucked back inside. "We had nothing to worry about."

The second search result suggested otherwise. *'Award-winning Physicist Loses Grant Over Crackpot Theories.'* Jo felt her face pale. "One of his 'crackpot' theories is that hatari are real, and the Yerin government is locking them up for experiments."

Nik jammed his hands in his pockets. "So he might need more proof, too. What do you want to do?"

"I don't know." Her Resero contact was waiting on her data, but what help had the contact been, anyway? Other than making snappy demands. There was also the Yerin woman to consider. "What do you think?"

He shrugged. "D.I.C. connections sound promising, given that we can convince them."

Jo nodded and bit her lip. With how the contact had reacted, she suspected that would be difficult. But what other choice did she have? She held the scanner out to Nik. "Here, you talk to them."

He shook his head and kept his hands in his pockets. "You're the one who's convinced the world is ending."

"And you're the bright, caring friend who knows I hate talking to strangers." She gave him a big grin.

"How else can you fix it but with practice?" He nudged the scanner away with his elbow. "Just tell them about the scans and see if you can get a business card or something."

"Nik..."

"Here they come. Pretend they're the Star Ranger figurines you used to practice presentations with."

"That was one time," Jo started to say, but the men's presence stopped the words in her mouth.

"Rude of you to kick me from the scene," the blond man, Dr. Froum, was saying. "I wasn't the one putting innocent lives at risk."

"I could hardly ask the precinct to cordon off the area over a hunch." Mr. Danu shifted the duffel to his other hand and ran his fingers through his hair. "We still don't know what we're dealing with."

"Does it matter? As long as we can predict the strikes, we can prevent—"

"Prevent what? You think precincts are going to close whole business districts over one little accident? Do you have any idea what kind of manpower that takes?"

Dr. Froum huffed, and Jo found herself following a distance behind. Even without knowing about the nguvu, they'd known the strike was coming. What data did they have that she didn't? Was there some pattern she wasn't seeing?

"We've picked up a tag-a-long." Dr. Froum gave her a sideways glance and stepped aside to let her through.

She took a few steps past, embarrassment gathering in the pit of her stomach. Why couldn't she just text them the data and be done with it? Or plant a bug in their pocket so she could hear their conversation from a safe distance away? She turned on her toes and shoved her scanner at the physicist. It's not like she could feel much worse.

He flinched away like it was poisoned. "Can we help you with something?"

"I, umm..." She cleared her throat. "I heard you say you predicted the energy strike."

Mr. Danu shot him a look. "I think you misunderstood. What my colleague meant was..."

"We knew it was coming, too."

"You what?"

She glanced at Nik and took a deep breath. "We've been tracking an anomaly through Stringspace that appears to be a large nguvu concentration. I think when the pockets accumulate enough charge, they cause field fluctuations. Like this one. Or the circuit surge on Ninel, or..."

Dr. Froum's face regained its color. He snatched up the scanner and started scrolling through the data. "Hold on... Does this mean you can prove it isn't an ion storm?"

An ion storm? Jo nearly stumbled in disbelief. Matching incidents scattered across a dozen worlds, and he thinks it's some random energy flares from Stringspace? "Well, yeah."

Froum grinned at his friend. "Told ya."

Mr. Danu rolled his eyes. "The nguvu concentrations are in **String-space**. Therefore, it was a previously unexplained Stringspace phenomenon."

"Yes, but—"

"And nguvu is a naturally occurring energy form, yes? So you can't keep blaming these incidents on lightning people—"

"Hatari."

"—and felons who somehow override their neural block. There's no conspiracy here."

"That's not true," Jo protested. She felt as steamrolled as Dr. Froum looked. "These concentrations aren't natural."

"Don't encourage him."

"I don't know anything about paroled felons, but I do think I know what's creating the nguvu clusters."

"Is it an evil corporation with ties to the government?"

Uh, what? Jo backed up uneasily. "Not that I know of..."

"I rest my case." Mr. Danu hefted the duffel bag and turned back toward the sliding station.

"I think it's the Resero project." The words slid out unbidden. She'd meant to keep that part quiet, or at least wait until they heard the more reasonable sounding parts of her spiel.

Mr. Danu's head swung back so fast she could have sworn she heard his neck crack.

Dr. Froum grinned and rolled his hand. "Please continue."

Jo swallowed. Both men stared at her intently, clearly intrigued by her theory. She tried not to let her voice shake too much as she explained about the sample and the cryptoscope. "I think Resero found a way to store and convert nguvu. I don't think he intended to keep it running, but the clusters are building up all over Stringspace."

Mr. Danu glanced at the physicist. "But you don't think it's a secret government-funded project?"

"No."

"Don't let him convince you otherwise." Mr. Danu sighed and put his hand in his pocket. A few seconds later, he handed her a business card. It was gray and square and had the same symbol as the back of the responders' vests. "Send me what you've got on the clusters, and if you can predict any more strikes, send me that, too."

Jo nodded.

"And don't let Pekke here corrupt you with all his talk of lightning people and shadow governments."

Dr. Froum gave a sly grin. "I'm sure these brilliant young people are more than capable of seeing the truth for themselves."

"I do hope so." Mr. Danu and Dr. Froum held out their hands as if to shake them, but instead turned their palms to the outside to brush knuckles. "Call me if there's another hit on the algorithm."

"I will," the physicist replied.

The men bowed to each other, and Mr. Danu hefted the duffel, heading back toward the station.

"Now then," Dr. Froum said, turning back to Jo. "Would you care to explain exactly how you managed to break the Stringspace barrier with your tracking device?" His gaze was sharp and unnerving, like a teacher accusing her of cheating.

She smiled anxiously. "Perhaps it'd be better if you saw it yourself."

The cryptoscope's arms whirled and spun, updating the nguvu map while Dr. Froum stood transfixed. Jo fidgeted on her stool at the counter. If only she could feel as calm as Nik looked. She should have tidied up before she left. Bits of wire and packaging still littered the floor from her repair work, and she hadn't dusted the shelves in ages. She imagined the physicist's lab would be much more organized, with spare parts in bins and drawers instead of re-purposed boxes held together with duct tape.

His gaze lifted from the glowing orbs. "How'd you account for the phase variance?"

"Integrated resonance filters." A requirement for moving any sort of heavy equipment through Stringspace. "The algorithm uses Thwin's phase-shifting equations to extrapolate the coordinates."

"From his Theory of Chaotic Variables?"

She nodded. The idea sounded simple in theory. Have the limbs take turns sliding partway into stringspace, far enough away from all the planetside interference, and then use a series of equations to extrapolate the data. Of course, coming up with the equations took over a year of modeling and a great deal of help from Nik.

"Hmm. Wouldn't have thought of that." He stroked the sparse hairs on his chin and squatted for a clearer view of the base. Each section bent and spun in an intricate pattern, their joints narrowly avoiding collisions. His eyes widened. He must've seen a joint pass through the glass. "Okay, that is legitimately cool."

Really? The brightness of his smile suggested he wasn't exaggerating.

"How long does it take to run?" he asked.

"A full, detailed scan could take a couple days, but since we've narrowed it down to a ten quizzet range... Twenty-five, maybe thirty minutes?"

"Thirty minutes? Even to get it down to a half block radius?"

"Not exactly. The strike was a special case." The buzzing faded and the arms started to slow. "Here, I'll show you on the new projection." She let the arms click back into their slots and stepped over to the console. With a few keystrokes, she pulled up the nguvu cloud and zoomed in on one of the eddies. "We looked at where the clusters are densest, then predicted when and where they'd collide with a world." She stepped up to the model and pointed to the cluster that had taken out the quadcopter. It looked a bit like a leaking egg yolk. "But I'm not sure what other conditions you need. The area over here has passed a couple worlds without striking, but this other one struck at half its density. That's why I wanted to scan the strikes, to see what environmental factors could affect it."

"It seems a lot more straightforward than my method. I was analyzing the amount of interference on radio signals and cross-referencing them with geographical energy sinks." He waved at the projection. "Would you mind zooming out again?"

Jo obliged.

"I think I have most of these, minus Trekio and Roufty." Dr. Froum slipped his datapad from his pocket and started comparing something in his notes to the locations of the collapsed eddies. "Are you sure there's nothing outside this quadrant?"

"I'm not positive, but it seems limited to this range."

"Strange. They matched the profile..." He tapped the datapad against his chin, eyes lingering on the center worlds. He gestured at a dense patch near Domun. "Did you happen to scan this one as well?"

"I... I didn't notice that one was about to collapse." It couldn't have done more than graze the planet, which was exactly what they'd been looking for.

"An anti-friction field failed on the subway. It happened a day or two ago."

Jo blinked at him. "How'd we miss that, Nik?"

Nik lifted his head from the counter. "Sleep. Sleep is good."

Dr. Froum continued poking around the model, assessing the affected worlds. "This is pretty impressive. You got all this from one of Resero's old tools?"

"Yeah, sort of." Jo bit her lower lip. How to explain without mentioning the hatari or their contact? "We also took some, um, samples on Yerin, and the readings matched. Once I'd confirmed its source, the pieces kinda came together."

The man's head perked up at the mention of Yerin. "What kind of samples?"

"I, umm..." She swallowed. She couldn't lie and say a strike because the light pole didn't match any of the clusters. Thankfully, a knock on the door bought her some time. "Sorry, let me get that." She'd never been so happy to have an unexpected visitor. Usually, she'd go completely silent and wait for them to disappear. Or she'd check the security feed to see if it was a package she'd forgotten about ordering.

As soon as she opened the door, she wished she'd done either. There stood the hatari, bright lines glowing.

CHAPTER SIXTEEN

— · —

PRAVI

"*Hey. Hey, Clive. The mail's early today.*"

"*Hmm?*"

"*Packages.*" Agent Beni took a long slurp of something icy that crackled through the surveillance speaker. "*The truck just pulled up. Ten monettes says there's at least six.*"

Clive yawned and creaked the leather seat with what sounded like a big stretch. "*Sure. I'll take a bet of five or under. It's been pretty slow lately.*"

Pravi tapped her fingers on the desk as she glanced at the shipping tracker. She'd placed the order only an hour ago, right after the strike her contact predicted made the news. If the data was right about the nguvu clouds, they'd need to move fast to counter them. While the D.I.C. team had been busy "ensuring her safety," she'd been compiling a personnel file. Jocelyn "Jo" Incerti, Masters in Trans-world Engineering and Janston Merit Finalist. Size medium for blaster-proof vests. The resume lacked field experience, which meant Pravi would have to do some training. Or possibly find more allies.

Beni slurped again, this time louder and more crackly. He must have turned toward the driver-side window to watch the postman. "*Did you hear about the distribution center on Euri?*"

"*Let me guess. Another field disruption?*"

"*Yep, and what a mess. The main priority warehouse backed up before they caught it. Package delays over forty-five minutes.*"

Pravi's source said an hour or more, with some packages arriving days late or not at all. She'd put it at the top of her list of suspicious events, and even more so now. Euri was on the edge of Jo's nguvu cloud.

"Four. I win." Clive's voice was smug and she pictured him nestling back into his seat. *"Senator Trenton says it's terrorists."*

"I doubt it. My buddy says it's all failing sensors and relays." Beni drummed his hands on the steering wheel. *"We could see a massive recall in the next few weeks."*

Well, didn't that sum up the recent response to the strikes. Half of the pundits declared they were malicious attacks, while the others blamed it on manufacturing issues. Pravi got up to get her mail, keeping the agents' conversation streaming through her earpiece. On the surface, she was on the side led by Senator Trenton. There had to be some sort of mastermind behind the nguvu cloud and the prototype's theft. But on the other hand, Trenton had a habit of seeing terrorist threats everywhere, thanks in large part to his colleague Edmond Schlau. Senator Schlau had founded of one of the first—and most profitable—trans-world security companies.

"Munus certainly has his hands full between Trenton's grandstanding, the strikes, and the Penderfyn case." The finger drumming stopped. *"Ope, hold on. He's going back for another load."*

"What?!"

"Seven total. Pay up."

Pravi grinned as she took the second set of packages straight from the postman's hands. In her ear, Clive insisted that the constant ordering was suspicious and that they needed to examine the contents. Beni responded by hitting the lock button every time his partner tried to exit. How nice it would be to have a partner of her own again, even if they turned out to be as picky and obsessive as Clive.

She scanned the packages for tracking bugs before depositing them in the office. Body armor. Military boots. One of those low-powered blasters that wouldn't put Pravi at too much risk of friendly fire. Worst-case scenario stuff, really. Everything had been sized for Jo's height and build, including a fake ID and matching nav device. What was taking the inventor so long, anyway? Pravi had expected her to send the data by now.

For curiosity's sake, she pulled up all the videos recorded at the event. It had been a minor one, compared to the Euri distribution center. Only a small gyroscope was affected, rather than the main drive for a web of conveyor belts. Still, the distribution center's single leaked security tape proved no match for the plethora of images and social media clips. Not only were there shots from the plaza, but also security footage from nearby restaurants and videos taken from passing craft. Even a live stream from a food blogger suddenly turned news reporter. Broken glass and flashing lights filled Pravi's screen.

She spotted Jo's clear green eyes and freckles at the edge of one of the debris shots. From there, it didn't take long to triangulate her position relative to the crash site and find more images of the inventor. At least two showed what appeared to be a scanner tucked into her sleeve. Good. Jo had at least collected the data, even if she hadn't sent it. Pravi scrolled further, checking out more clips that pointed in Jo's direction and might hold clues to why the woman was taking so long. All seemed fine at first. Jo had been close enough to the field, practically stepping on the debris, and had a clear shot while the rescuers worked. She even made eye contact with the rescuers once or twice... oh. Oh, no. She'd spoken to one of the rescuers. One video showed an influencer going off about how traumatized they'd been, and there, in the background, was Jo and the lead responder.

Pravi's anxious tapping became a tight grip on the gear that she'd ordered too early. Worse than talking to him, Jo had followed his colleague back to the sliding station. Pravi knew those responder vests and had even met the lead responder, Zave Danu, a few times. If Danu's company had responded to the field disruption, they were no doubt reporting to the D.I.C. The blond man she didn't know personally, but his connection to Danu's company was clear. Which meant Pravi's one and only contact was cooperating with the D.I.C.

She shoved back from the keyboard. There had to be a way to get ahead of this. Discredit Jo? No. Her data would be too complete by now to poke holes in, and it's not like the inventor should have known better. Not to mention any antagonism from Pravi would be suspicious.

Could she stage an event that didn't fit the data? No. There were already a few of those, and Munus could spot her tracks.

Pravi bit the inside of her lip. A dull ache in her gut said this wasn't wholly a bad thing. If Jo was right, if that nguvu cloud proved to be even half as big as she thought, Pravi couldn't fix it on her own. Even if she could slide herself between worlds to chase the thief. When it came down to it, did she really care if the D.I.C. knew about the nguvu cloud? She wanted the prototype. To be able to live like a normal person, without worrying about escape routes and whether transport aids would turn out to be human traffickers. The nguvu cloud and field disruptions just added complications.

There was one way she could spin this to her advantage. She could go to Munus right now, make a show of swallowing her pride, and tell him what she knew. Or at least, tell him a little more than what Jo knew, so it gave the impression she had taken the initiative to cooperate rather than getting exposed by a contact.

She forced herself up out of the chair. That was the best tactic. Sure, she'd be giving up whatever advantage she had in getting to the prototype first, but they'd be getting that from Jo soon anyway. This way, she at least had a chance. Maybe she could worm her way onto the team and make a plan to get the device back from them later. Let the D.I.C. clear away the obstacles first.

Her body moved while her mind was still convincing itself of the plan. Down the hall, out the door, and around toward Munus' staging area. He wasn't such a bad guy when you got down to it. She'd heard Beni and Clive say he used to work in internal affairs clearing out corruption. And even if she couldn't entirely trust him with the information, he'd have it soon enough, with or without her. She barely registered that the staging area had been reordered.

"I'd like to speak to Munus," she told the woman on duty. Agent Jandra, if Pravi's memory served her. The one who'd tried to plant surveillance devices in her yard. She had her dark brown hair twisted up tight and a crisp white blouse under her track suit.

"Is it something I can help you with?" Jandra put one hand on her hip and leaned her other arm on the door frame to block the opening.

"Munus is currently working on other cases, leaving me as the new lead here."

Something about her condescending smile said she was enjoying it immensely.

"When will he be back?"

"Perhaps I should have been more clear. The personnel change is permanent. But I'd be happy to—"

"So he's like gone gone?" Pravi's mind went through a half-dozen curses. Of course he'd move on. Why wouldn't he shift his focus to other more pressing cases? To more cooperative leads? What had she expected him to do, keep vigil in her yard like some abject suitor? Her uncle would have chided her for missing the clues. Beni and Clive's gossip. The D.I.C. showing up right away to fix the field fluctuation crash. The way the field office was sitting a half meter further back from the street.

Always be aware of your surroundings. Uncle Xander had drilled the idea into her since she was small, and after surviving the abduction, she'd made it her creed. But oh, how she'd wavered. She hadn't noticed that the stack of patio chairs now sat on the opposite side of the entrance flaps. Scuff marks on the stones suggested the change in command had required some change in furnishings or equipment, the most likely cause for the shift in the tent's location. The only thing that hadn't shifted were the damn D.I.C. security cameras, which had caused a half-meter wide gap in the surveillance net. A small mistake, but one Munus would never have made. Because minor or not, it put Pravi's life at risk.

"If it's about the case, I'd be more than happy to assist in any way I can." Jandra's lips curled into a smile that suggested she was both eager to have Pravi at her mercy and totally oblivious to her own ineptitude. How she'd managed to make team lead was anyone's guess. She either had a few lucky breaks or connections.

"No."

"No?"

"No, it's not something you can help me with." Pravi sighed. Jandra would never qualify for the strike team. Even if she lowered herself into the agent's favor, it'd never provide an opening to retrieve the prototype. She flipped out her transcom and dialed the number Munus had given her. She could take a few jabs at her pride if it meant speaking to someone competent. Someone who'd be conscious of the inherent dangers of the project.

Jandra's pocket vibrated. "Hello?" The agent stared cheerfully into Pravi's eyes as her voice echoed in the earpiece. "As I said before, all leadership and authority for this case has been transferred to me."

Pravi ended the call, but the agent continued.

"Honestly, I don't see what the difference is. Either you want to co-operate with us, or you don't. It's not like Munus won't pass everything back to me."

No, but Munus would at least have some tact in how and when he passed on the information, rather than using it as an overconfident power play. "I'll tell Munus or no one. Take your pick."

"Hmm, how about tell me or get held in contempt? A week or two in a holding cell might change your tune."

A puff of air forced its way through Pravi's nose. Her uncle's lawyer had decades of experience dealing with D.I.C. obstruction charges. A few days was the most it would be. But she didn't have a few days, and arguing with Jandra would get her nowhere. She had two options. Give up her slim chance of retrieving the prototype or make a power move herself.

Jandra moved first. "Yurik, Euros," she snapped to the two nearest agents. The first went rigid at his post at the perimeter and the other peeked out of the field tent. "Please transport Ms. Resero to a holding cell at Command."

They looked at each other, then over to Pravi. The urge to question the command was written clearly on their faces, but with an outsider present, that could mean two months' probation.

"Yes, m'am," they murmured. Yurik started towards Pravi first, his face all apologies.

She backed away from him, heading straight for the new gap in the surveillance net. They didn't seem to notice. Three meters. Two meters. The agents closed the distance as she edged a knife out of a strap by her ankle. Once they were fully clear of the cameras, Pravi sliced the back of her hand.

Jandra froze, her self-satisfied grin morphing into a mix of horror and confusion.

Pravi held the blade against the arm of her jacket, ready to slice through her forearm. "Wouldn't high command just love to hear how your team forced me into a discreet corner? How they threatened me at knifepoint?" She lifted a finger to point to the gap in the cameras. There'd be no way for Jandra to prove her innocence. The gap was damning all on its own.

"I want to see Munus. Now."

CHAPTER SEVENTEEN

— • —

JO

A mber swirled across the hatari's skin, glowing with all the intensity of an electrical fire. Of all the things Jo had hoped the knock would be, a walking EMP wasn't one of them. A door-to-door salesperson, sure. Or the superintendent complaining about her excessive use of electricity. But certainly not the nguvu-wielding fugitive she'd planned to hide from Dr. Froum.

Unfortunately, the woman pushed past before Jo could warn her about the physicist. So much for using the interruption to avoid his pointed questions. Like how exactly she'd discovered the connection between nguvu and the prototype's resonance pattern. Or what she'd found on Yerin. Or who she'd planned to send the crash site data to...

"I need to use your seeker of the hidden things," the hatari announced. She pulled a data storage stick from her pocket. "You can search from a digital pattern, right? Please tell me you don't need a physical sample."

Jo hastily closed the door to follow her. "You don't, but—"

"Good evening." Dr. Froum gave the hatari a nod. At some point, his paisley dress shirt had come untucked, and his sleeves were now rolled to his elbows, revealing arms even paler than his face. His grin faltered when his eyes fell on the hatari's skin.

"Phosphorescent tattoos," the woman lied. Her pace barely staggered as she hurried past him to the cryptoscope's control tower. "Pretty cool, aren't they? Is it this slot or..."

"The one below it." Jo rushed over to help program the cryptoscope, giving herself an excuse to act as a buffer between the woman and the device. Hopefully the hatari's request to use the cryptoscope meant she hadn't second-guessed her decision to leave it in one piece. Still, Jo didn't want to take any chances. Not with how much the woman's nguvu lines were flickering.

"Phosphorescence indeed." Dr. Froum winked at Jo like it was a joke they were both in on.

She scowled back. No, they could not be in on the joke. There was no joke, not with a crackling lightning rod standing within a meter of her recently repaired prototype. Even without the warning glow of the hatari's nguvu lines, it was obvious the woman was distraught. The data stick shook as she pocketed it, and she didn't seem to know what to do with her hands. They jumped between fiddling in the front, hiding in the back, and readjusting her backpack straps. Eventually she settled on leaning against Jo's workbench, her hands gripping the edge to either side.

"I think maybe we should pick this up again some other day." Jo set the program to run and turned back to Dr. Froum. He watched the hatari with such interest that she feared he would make the situation worse. "As much as I enjoyed our conversation, I have something personal to attend to."

"Something personal?" He glanced between Jo and the hatari, then back over his shoulder at the spinning cryptoscope. "Oh. I see." His shoulders slouched a bit, but he hesitated to move toward the door. "Perhaps it's something I could help with?"

"I'm afraid not. It's... um... a private matter." Yes, that phrase should work. Jo's mother used to say it like a warding spell whenever her older sisters were crying or especially snappy with her. They'd been much older than her, and once she became a teenager herself, she learned the phrase held some sort of dismissing power. One that guaranteed people would stop asking questions like *'Are you sure you're okay?'* and *'Would you like to go to the party at the quad this weekend?'*

It appeared to be working on the physicist. He took a deep breath to say something, but the words froze in his mouth. One nod of agreement from the hatari, and he'd be right out the door.

The woman shook her head instead. "Please don't leave on my account. I'm only here until the scan's done."

Jo could have screamed. Did the woman not understand what she'd been trying to do? Dr. Froum was both a potential witness and a potential victim. If she did her zappity zap thing with him present, he'd not only recognize it, but know who to call to have her arrested.

"Don't you think it'd be better if—"

"It's fine, really." The hatari reclined back, letting her legs slide forward to block the path between Dr. Froum and the door. "Just go back to whatever you were discussing when I got here. I'll be out of your hair shortly."

Jo couldn't help but feel trapped. Even if she managed to avoid the hatari's feet, her glowing arms rested within easy reach of Jo's diagnostic tools. One accidental zap and a thousand monettes' worth of equipment would turn into charred paperweights. She looked to Nik for help, but he was still snoozing on the counter.

"What we were discussing before, eh?" Dr. Froum turned halfway to Jo. "I had been planning to ask Miss Incerti about her attempts to sidestep my questions, but it seems that's answered now. Perhaps I should give a few answers of my own." He emptied his pockets onto one of the equipment shelves. "I know regular ID cards are easy to fake, so here's my access card to the Redikin University library and my parking pass for Abrani Research Center. My membership cards to The Black Dragon comic book store, Saves-a-Lot, and Desden holographic theater. Also, a punch card for a coffee place I visit daily. And if that's not enough to prove that I am who I say I am, I can update my blog with a post of your choice."

Jo stared at the colorful key ring tags and the pile of plastic cards, unable to comprehend what they were supposed to mean. "Why are you showing us this?"

"Because I want in." He stuffed his hands back into his pockets. "I know I don't look it, but I'm actually well prepared for subterfuge and espionage. I have not one, but three safe houses. Also four sets of personalized fake IDs, a custom-fit set of body armor, and a guy who does unregistered nav devices for cheap. I can put it all in resume form if you'd like."

"I... I'm so confused. What exactly do you want in on?"

"Playing hard to get, eh? You want me to prove my deduction skills?" He put one hand on his hip and flipped out his transcom. "Okay, then. Jones Slai." He flashed her a picture of a man with short, black hair and a scruffy chin. His arched nose and thick eyebrows looked like a bit like the hatari's. "He disappeared last year after an electrical fire killed his wife." Dr. Froum swiped to another photo, one of a preteen girl with bright green eyes. "Noru Yezza, taken after her brother visited the hospital with minor burns. Jess Ritru, Kiele Manne, Zadio Panwel..." More faces sped across the screen. "Every hatari lead ends in a missing person case, yet here you have one, alive and well, and not on Yerin. And not just any hatari, no, but Zahira Nacitè, the one whose face has been plastered across all the conspiracy forums for the last three days."

Jo glanced over to the workbench. The woman—Zahira—had stiff-ened, and her nguvu lines now flickered like a strobe light. No wonder she'd run the second she'd heard Jo's scanner.

Dr. Froum seemed not to notice as he continued. "So somehow you've been able to do something none of us have ever managed. You swept in and shuttled a hatari to safety before the Boliska could get her. I'd love to be there for the next attempt."

"The next attempt?" Jo asked at the same time Zahira gave a dismis-sive snort.

"Shuttled me to safety? I would have gotten off without all the fanfare if it weren't for her." The hatari crossed her arms, and though the lines flashed as hot as fire, she didn't look injured in the slightest. "You're crazy if you think the getaway was anything but botched."

"It was an accident," Jo mumbled. "We didn't know who she was until we brought her back here."

Dr. Froum gave Jo a sympathetic look. "Was it really botched, though? Zahira's off Yerin, isn't she?"

"I wasn't the only one who needed to escape." Zahira's voice shook as she spoke, and Jo's thoughts immediately went to the cryptoscope.

"That's what you needed the scan for. To find the person you left behind."

"I wouldn't have left her behind if it weren't for you. Your interference means my seventy-year-old grandmother is at the mercy of the Boliska." The men in the green vests. That had to be who she was talking about. The ones who had followed her off Yerin and shot the stationmaster.

Jo bit the inside of her lip. "What do we need to do to get her back?"

The stool creaked from the counter as Nik wiped the grogginess from his eyes. "What are we doing now?" He tensed when he spotted the hatari.

He wasn't going to be happy with her plan. "I'm going to help Zahira get her grandmother off Yerin." Somehow the words came out more confident that she felt. Her mess up had caused the problem in the first place, and there was no guarantee she wouldn't make things worse. Especially since the plan would undoubtedly involve sneaking past armed guards and fighting their way back out again.

"I'm helping as well." Dr. Froum's shoulders slouched as he turned to Zahira. "That is, if she'll have me."

He and everyone else looked to the hatari for the final word.

Zahira looked a bit like a mountain cat cornered mid-hunt, her face a heavy mix of apprehension and surprise. She pulled her feet in to more of a defensive stance. "What would you do if I said no?"

"Well, I suppose I'd give you my contact info in case you changed your mind." Dr. Froum's eyes twinkled, then dropped to the floor to search for the second half of his answer. "In all seriousness, yes, I'd be disappointed. But I understand the need for caution."

Zahira's face softened, most likely due less to Dr. Froum's heartfelt response than having few other options. Like Jo being her only help. "I'll allow it, then." The hatari tightened her grip on the workbench and raised her eyes slowly. "But only if you send me everything you know about hatari."

"I'd be glad to," Dr. Froum said, then quickly added, "even if the answer was no."

A thick and awkward silence followed, broken only by the creaks of feet shifting weight and the soft hum of Zahira's coils. All they had left to do was wait for the cryptoscope to tell them where they were going.

Jo twisted the cuff of her sleeve as she watched the arms start to spin down. She'd done it again. While there was no cascade of acid this time, one of her inventions had gone and hurt people against her intent. Yes, getting Zahira's grandmother captured had been an accident, but what if she'd proved her design and put it up for sale? What if the Boliska had gotten hold of a copy? Jo wouldn't blame Zahira if she zapped the thing when they had finished.

The scan ended with a soft groan, and the projector spawned clusters of glowing orbs. It felt weird seeing the planets like that, with swirling oceans and jagged landforms clearly visible. She'd gotten so used to the bulging gold of the clouds that she'd nearly forgotten what a scan was supposed to look like: a clear, green trail weaving between worlds with only wisps of gold marking resonances that nearly matched. Wisps that presumably signaled degraded sections of the trail.

Zahira stiffened, and Jo looked closer to find the cause. After a few moments of tracing the green line as it wrapped around and between planets, a cold realization settled in her stomach. That itself was the problem. The trail led away from Yerin.

CHAPTER EIGHTEEN

— • —

ZAHIRA

Z ahira glanced from Jo to Dr. Froum. Could this be some kind of trick? Her grandmother hadn't left the planet in at least two decades, yet the cryptoscope's projection showed an emerald ribbon sweeping up and away from Yerin.

The physicist's eyes traced it meticulously, like he was searching for more than just her grandmother's location. His deep, pensive stare sent a ripple of energy across her skin. Though he didn't look like he'd messed with the sample, she suspected his offer of support came with ulterior motives.

Jo, on the other hand, looked pale and a bit shaky. Like a tourist's kid feeding a dinosaur for the first time. Her sincerity was endearing, but chances were, she'd rescind her offer as soon as it became clear what they'd be facing. Taking on the Boliska was too much risk to expect from anyone, much less complete strangers. Better to accept assistance with the planning and be prepared for when they ultimately backed out.

"Are you sure you ran my sample and not a different one?" Zahira stepped closer to the projection. Grandmother's green line barely grazed any of the planets and instead picked a tiny moon as its endpoint. A moon the Boliska couldn't possibly have jurisdiction over. *If Grandmother had gotten free, she would have sent a message, wouldn't she?*

Jo typed something into the console, causing the map to zoom in and label the moon as belonging to the Trilo string. "There was nothing to confuse it with. The only other sample I have is the Resero one, and that's all golden clouds."

Zahira nodded. Even if they wanted to, Jo and Nik wouldn't have had time to swap in a sample this accurate. The green line swirling around her home city of Tilman Yar was a given, but it also wandered out into the desert and back, matching the times she and Grandmother had emptied the coils in secret. A loop even marked a southbound trip to purchase contraband tech. If the trail was a forgery, it was a convincing one.

If the trail was real... No. That would be too much to hope for. On Yerin, the Boliska held the upper hand, with enough control and surveillance to catch her before she'd even left the sliding station. Why would they take a hostage out of their sphere of influence? What was so special about this moon? Zahira gave her backpack straps a light tug and pulled out her transcom. The only way to know for sure was checking it out herself.

"Hold on," Dr. Froum said, joining her at the edge of the projection. Had he already spotted a reason to back out? "Is this end point in the moon's southern hemisphere?"

Jo nodded.

"Interesting." He stroked his stubbled chin, his eyes seeming to stare straight through the moon. "I'd always suspected the Boliska were into something shady."

"Shady?" Zahira scoffed. "Kidnapping hatari isn't shady enough for you?"

"It's more than that. They've been working as defense contractors for what, half a century?" His words came slowly, like he was only saying scraps of the ideas swirling through his head. "They're in charge of energy disruptions, radiation leaks, not to mention protecting those giant lizards you guys have. All big, important jobs. How is it they've gone this long with no oversight or competition? Blackmail? Bribery? I can't imagine they're turning a profit on the hatari."

A shiver swirled down Zahira's back. How many nightmares had she had of exactly that? Of a Boliska surgeon standing over her with a scalpel, ready to harvest whatever organs would fetch the best price.

Dr. Froum brushed past her to tap on the moon. "There's a base here. It's billed as a research lab, but no one with adequate funding would go anywhere near it. The 'labs' are little more than warehouses with thick shielding. A place for experiments that are too risky—or too illegal—to do planetside."

Zahira nodded. Hardly the place for government contractors to take their prisoners, especially as a quick search showed no connection between Yerin and the owners. Too exposed. Too vulnerable. But whatever the catch, it had to be better than facing the Boliska on their home turf. She glanced at Jo to find the inventor's face pale beneath all her freckles.

"If they brought your grandmother here, well..." Dr. Froum went back to rubbing his chin. "Makes you wonder how much the government knows about what they're doing."

How much oversight the Boliska had wasn't any of Zahira's concern. She needed to get Grandmother out before they dosed her with the truth serum. Before they weakened her already fragile health. "How easy is it to get in?"

Dr. Froum shrugged. "Possibly too easy. When you pay to rent a warehouse, they give you an access code. I understand not needing referrals or interviews like the big labs, but the lack of oversight is asking for trouble."

"An interesting sentiment coming from a guy with multiple safe houses and fake IDs." Zahira crossed her arms. He had a point, though. The lack of oversight could help the Boliska just as much as it helped her. "How's security?"

"It's been a while, but from what I remember, the entrance check is pretty lax. Just don't bring anything that can get past the exterior shielding."

"You've been there before?"

He nodded, and a mix of emotions rippled across his face. Anger? Sadness? Regret? "A friend of mine used to run experiments there."

Nik cleared his throat from the kitchen island. "No weapons. No controlled substances without a research permit. Explosives must be insulated and secured during transport through common areas." He tilted his transcom in their direction. Zahira hadn't even noticed him pick it up, which worried her. She'd let herself get distracted long enough for him to contact someone. "They also have a reservation page on their website and a vague sort of floor plan."

"Oh, good. We should probably print that out." Dr. Froum started scrolling on his transcom, but a whirr from under a pile of blueprints said Nik had already handled it.

Jo rescued the fresh pages before the weight of the blueprints could mangle them. "Looks like at least half of the warehouses are empty, so that should make things easier." She passed Zahira a copy. Half of the oblong spaces were indeed marked "available," forming scattered blocks of blue in the sixteen by sixteen grid. Most of those marked "occupied" clustered around restrooms or emergency shelters.

"Only two exits?" Had Zahira read that right?

Dr. Froum peered over her shoulder. "Technically, only the left one is active unless the base is in emergency mode. The idea is that a single exit makes it harder for thieves, since the rest of the base is shielded to prevent free sliding."

No free sliding? Zahira had no desire to travel the strings without a nav device, but it would have been a better option than getting captured. "Is there anything weapon-like that's allowed? In case I have to fight my way out."

"I have heavy wrenches," Jo said, straightening. "And screwdrivers."

"Screwdrivers?" Dr. Froum clicked his tongue. "Sounds like someone's watched too many action movies. Do you have any energy probes?"

Jo gestured behind her. "They're buried here somewhere, but the shock output is low."

"I have something else I can grab, then." The physicist tapped his chin and started rifling through the shelves. It appeared he hadn't been scared off yet. "You don't happen to have any insulator cuffs, do you? Or a grounding bracelet?" He listed off a few more devices that Zahira didn't recognize. What an odd way to do things, gathering random tools before they had any plan of attack. Perhaps he and Jo gave themselves courage by surrounding themselves with gadgets? At least this meant she would have more time to deal with the floor plan. It wouldn't be easy. The base had over a hundred occupied warehouses, each forty meters square and spread out in a way that could take hours to traverse. A quick calculation on her transcom said a zigzag through the campus totaled nearly eleven kilometers. She didn't want to think about what the Boliska might do to Grandmother in that amount of time, but she also couldn't count on a resonance meter picking up faint traces in the midst of all that shielding.

She selected a pencil from a row on the counter. The writing utensils had been ordered by size, forming a sort of stair-step pattern with their tips. Given how messy the shelves and workbench were, she doubted they belonged to Jo. She glanced over to Nik who busily took notes from his transcom. Although he and the others would back out any time now, at least she had help with the prep work.

Zahira took a deep breath and started tracing potential search patterns, marking off which warehouses they'd pass. The base had hallways intersecting every four warehouses, so she could potentially cut the total distance traveled in half. It'd be even faster if she had Jo and Dr. Froum's extra sets of hands.

She gripped the pencil, trying not to imagine how things would be if she and Grandmother were planning it together. If the target was some piece of tech they needed to retrieve. Sitting on the bed, they'd have the blinds closed and the blueprints taped to the back of a game board for easy concealment. Blue and green chess pieces would mark obstacles and targets, shuffled around with whispered concerns and gestures. Instead of the clinks of equipment coming from Jo's shelves, the air would be filled with the sweet scent of gia fruit tea. She could almost hear the whistle of the electric kettle.

Nik sat an empty mug gently in front of her, pulling her out of her reverie. "I've found tea helps with focus, if you'd like some? Jo has a few different kinds."

"Just water for me, thanks." She tried not to eye the boxes sitting next to the kettle. If gia fruit turned out to be an option...

Nik filled her mug as more clanging echoed from the shelves. "Is that really necessary?"

Zahira turned to find Jo pulling a metal case from between two heavy boxes. It unfolded to the size of a workout mat, barely avoiding the cryptoscope's arms.

The inventor pressed some switches, and motors purred from the inside, lifting it up off the floor. "You never know. There might be something to carry."

Or someone. The device ran the length of a stretcher.

"Wouldn't carrying that much stuff be counterproductive?" Nik started steeping his own tea. "I assume the situation calls for a quick exit."

Jo and Dr. Froum exchanged glances, and the former flushed. "We figured a quick exit might be impossible without it."

They let the sentence hang in the air, neither of them making eye contact with Zahira. Her chest tightened.

"You think Grandmother might be unconscious." She didn't mean for it to sound like an accusation, but all the force of the realization came out with her words. What if she was too late and the Boliska had already administered the truth serum? Or what if Zahira got injured during the escape? She might be able to drag Grandmother out, but the reverse would be impossible.

"Yes, I mean, no..." Jo's face was a tangle of sympathy and guilt. "I'm sure she's fine. The lift would merely be a precaution."

"Accidents do happen," Dr. Froum added. "My friend said her first day there, a prototype pillow-stuffing machine exploded next door. The whole hallway buried in goose feathers. She pulled them out of her equipment for weeks after."

"Grandmother's not going to be injured by a mountain of goose feathers." She wouldn't be injured by anything, not if Zahira could help it. Still, images of the last day they'd spent together floated back into her mind. Grandmother, face slouched and drooped, unable to move. "I'll take the lift, but only as a precaution."

"As a precaution," Dr. Froum agreed. The empathic look on his face said he didn't believe it any more than she did. "I reserved a lab effective immediately, so we can leave as soon as you're ready."

Zahira nodded, then realized he'd said 'we can leave' instead of 'you can leave.' "So you are coming with?"

Dr. Froum seemed surprised at the question. "Of course, why wouldn't I?"

"Because I'm headed into a poorly secured moon base under false pretenses. If everything goes to plan, I'll be stealing a captive from under the nose of an elite security team and making a break to the one and only exit. And there won't be any free-sliding out if it all goes to shit."

Zahira noticed Jo stiffen at the words. At least she had the sense to have a normal, logical reaction when faced with this sort of situation. It was all well and good to pretend to be a hero, to imagine oneself fighting oppressors and rescuing the weak, but when it came down to it, rational people would give in to self-preservation.

Dr. Froum crossed his arms. "You weren't planning to do it all on your own, were you?"

"Of course I was. She's my grandmother." And when Zahira had been born with the nguvu lines, her grandmother hadn't hesitated to drop her life, savings, and career. The woman had smuggled her across the desert in a baby carrier, for string's sake. And afterward, once the dangers of the desert proved too much, she'd dealt with all manner of crooks and hustlers to set up new identities in a strange city. She'd never once complained when young Zahira had let secrets or nguvu slip, even when faced with repeating the whole process over again.

"You shouldn't have to save her alone," Jo said weakly. Her hands tightened into fists and she took a step forward to stand next to Dr. Froum. "You'd have a better chance if you weren't so outnumbered."

"Outnumbered? You think a few wrenches and technological do-dads will make us a match for a trained police force?" Was Zahira hearing this correctly? This timid, scrawny inventor had decided to waltz into a sand lion den for a woman she'd only met twice. A woman who'd considered frying her most precious invention.

"Zahira's right." Nik mirrored Dr. Froum's pose but on the other side of the cryptoscope. "We have no idea what we'd be getting into, and everything we do know is more than we're equipped to handle.

There's too much at risk to make a foolhardy attempt." Finally, a voice of reason. As much as Zahira would appreciate their help, she didn't want to lead anyone to jail or the emergency room. Or worse.

Dr. Froum and Jo didn't budge. "I've made my stance clear," the physicist said.

The inventor nodded in agreement, but her fists weren't clenched as tight as they had been before. She seemed to avoid meeting Nik's eyes.

He sighed. "Before you decide to go gallivanting off, can I at least have a word with you in private?"

Jo glanced to Dr. Froum and Zahira as if to ask for permission, and they both shrugged to show they didn't mind. She followed Nik to what looked like a bedroom and closed the door behind them. Zahira hoped he could talk some sense into her, maybe even talk some sense into Dr. Froum. This sort of insanity could be contagious. They planned to break into a Boliska base with only a few hours of prep work, and she had started to believe they actually had a chance.

CHAPTER NINETEEN

— • —

NIK

"Are you insane?" The words forced themselves out before Nik finished closing the door behind him. He'd simply taken a nap—for twenty, maybe thirty minutes tops—yet somehow his best friend's life goal had changed from recluse inventor to amateur vigilante.

He found small comfort that Jo's bedroom hadn't gotten the memo. Her worn headboard and hand-me-down dresser hadn't sprouted secret compartments or budged from their posts flanking the door. The cryptoscope's blueprints still littered the walls, surrounded by random sticky notes and hand-sketched diagrams. In the far corner, splotchy overalls and long-sleeve tees spilled over the side of her hamper, with no sign of masks or capes anywhere.

Jo started to put her hands on her hips, but ended up sliding them to cross in front instead. "I have to do this, Nik."

"Have to, like someone's threatening your family? Or have to, like Tayna Ernst daring you to fix the spectrograph second year?"

She shot him a sharp look. "This isn't some stupid matter of proving myself. The Boliska took Zahira's grandmother, and she's pretty convinced that something bad will happen if we don't get her out."

"And I feel for her, truly I do." He couldn't imagine losing his family, much less the one person who was always there for him. His hands tightened in his pockets. "But we're not cut out for heroics, Jo. Our lab safety classes didn't cover breaking and entering or daring standoffs with defense contractors."

"They also didn't cover exposing mystical nguvu people to the bad guys hunting them, yet I managed that just fine." Her voice shook like she was on the edge of tears.

Oh, was that what this was? He studied the way she bit her lip and checked to see if her arms were shaking in spite of being crossed. Yes, this must be just like her grad project. And when she knocked over his mother's prized moon lilies. And the time her hover taxi ran over her roommate's transcom. Crippling guilt over an accident.

And he'd been worried she'd undergone some massive change while he slept. Time for some strong condolences. "You couldn't have known, Jo. No one could have known."

"We should have. *I* should have." She took a heavy breath and exhaled through her nose. "How could I have been so stupid? I got so caught up in the excitement of being able to track missing people, I didn't even think of those who wouldn't want to be found."

"We thought it was Resero's trail, remember? What harm is there in trailing a dead guy?" The next step was supposed to be buying tubs of frozen Rydelian custard and watching a martial arts movie with horrible physics, but that might be difficult with the guests. Especially since Jo would insist on leaving when they did.

"Helping search the lab is the least I can do." Her statement seemed more directed at herself than at him, and her shoulders slumped against the wall. "And how risky is it, really? To walk around with a resonance scanner?"

Her laugh came out pained and abrupt, and his fists tightened until his nails dug into his palms. He wouldn't be able to convince her when she was like this. Maybe a distraction would help. "I sent our contact the data. Of the hovercraft crash, I mean." He watched her posture for a shift in tension, but she merely nodded. "You and Dr. Froum looked pretty engrossed in the cryptoscope."

"At least that bit of today went the way it was supposed to. Any response yet?"

Nik shook his head. "It took a while to upload, so they might not have gotten it yet."

Jo nodded again and bit her lip. "You don't suppose they're connected? The nguvu cloud and the Boliska? If they're collecting hatari..."

Shit. He'd made things worse, hadn't he? Her arms had stopped shaking, but only because she gripped her biceps tight enough to wrinkle her sleeves. Rather than take her mind off going to the lab, he'd given her another reason to do it. "A few scans would be enough to confirm that, wouldn't it? We could ask Dr. Froum—"

"I'm going, Nik." She had an edge to her voice that said that was the end of the argument. If he pushed any further, she might ask him to leave, and then he'd be stuck in a state of worry, wondering when he would get a call from the hospital or jail. Or worse, if he might never get a call at all. The most he could do now was mitigate the danger. "That's all you would do then, right? Run a couple scans, then hightail it out before the fighting starts?" Again, he watched her body language for signs of agreement. He needed her to promise him.

She shrugged. "Once we find the right door, I can open it if they need me to." Which could put her in the line of fire. Her weight shifted from foot to foot with a restlessness that said she'd do worse if it came to it. Someone had to be there to stop her.

"Count me in, then." He bumped her shoulder with his. "We get Zahira to her grandmother, and then we slide right back. Deal?"

She nodded, not meeting his eyes. Not the strong agreement he'd hoped for, but the best he was going to get.

They shuffled back out to the living room and found Dr. Froum and Zahira kneeling next to the equipment pile. Or more, equipment *piles*, as there were now three of them. One appeared to be the discards, shoved off to the side and haphazardly stacked in an old, dented toolbox. A smaller collection sat in front of the hatari, holding two resonance meters, the lift, and a set of lockpicks. As for the physicist, his hoard held almost as much as the other two combined, and he slowly nudged it closer and closer to Zahira.

He looked up when he heard them enter and raised his eyebrow at Jo. She shrugged and went to her workbench to grab her equipment bag.

"I think you'll find we have enough hands after all." The physicist slid his mound of devices forward like they were chips on a gambling table. He took a sideways glance at Nik. "Might even get that search pattern under twenty minutes."

Zahira's eyes jerked to Nik, then over to where Jo had pulled out an old messenger bag from behind a tub of oil rags. Her face brightened. For a moment, Nik imagined Zahira in a crisis, her arms pinned by Boliska agents and her eyes shooting that hopeful look at Jo. Would he be able to tear his friend away? Could he fight against both of their consciences long enough to reach the exit?

A flutter of activity swept aside his concerns. Dr. Froum and Zahira went to work, taking turns filling Jo in on their plan for the search as they passed around equipment, bags, and floor plans. Once Jo joined, it became a wild dance. People scurrying between shelves, counter, bags, and workbench. It reminded Nik of how Jo's family packed for vacation, where they had seven people trying to cram their clothes into three suitcases. Next thing he knew, he'd been loaded up with a bulging messenger bag and shoved in the back of a hover taxi.

"The nearest sliding station, if you please," Dr. Froum said, squeezing in beside him.

The narrow passenger bench ended before Nik's knees, sparing exactly the amount of floor space necessary for his heels to press against its base while his toes brushed the wall dividing them from the driver. With the addition of crammed backpacks and the lift, the physicist had to turn sideways to get the door to close. Nik ended up with Dr. Froum's back plastered against his right shoulder and a wrench stabbing into his left hip. He could barely breathe, much less protest.

The Domun sliding station wasn't much better. Rush hour crowds, zero privacy, and Dr. Froum and Zahira arguing over a cache of supplies he wanted to pick up on the way. All the while, Jo gripped the strap of her equipment bag like it was the bar of a roller coaster on its way to the summit. Her knuckles turned white by the time they reached the final station.

"We get there, we scan, we go home," Nik whispered, letting Dr. Froum get a few steps ahead. The physicist led them away from the main sliding circles and down an arched hallway with burnt orange walls and red brick tile. A dozen tunnels branched off to either side, leading to dedicated security checkpoints for remote research stations and moon bases. "Any signs of trouble and we head for the exit."

"Mm-hmm." Jo eyed the tunnel Dr. Froum had just disappeared into. They weren't the only group wanting to pass through the check. At the end of the hall, three agents wanded a device under a massive scanner frame, watched by a short woman with glasses. Behind her stood two more women, a teenage boy, and a pair of men with a crate.

Jo and Nik went to join the line, but Zahira stopped halfway down the hall, covering her sudden halt with a quick pocket pat like she'd forgotten her ID. She kept her back to the security line. Nik noticed her pull a small mirror out of her pocket, and he took another look at those who had gathered. The pair of men were on the shorter side, maybe half again as tall as their meter-high crate. One had a nose similar to Zahira, and they both sported some sort of green safety vest. Why did that look familiar?

Boliska. Like the men who had followed them off of Yerin.

He cursed under his breath and tried to send a covert signal to Jo. The plan would fly out the window if they noticed Zahira. They needed to abort. Regroup. He leaned one elbow on the wall to hide the hatari behind him and kicked at Jo's foot with his own.

"Ouch," she said, turning to give him a glare.

He pointed to the men. '*Green vests*,' he mouthed.

Based on how she tensed, she had to know what that meant. Had to know they needed to leave. He waited for her to tell Dr. Froum, but she pulled her resonance meter out of her equipment bag and walked right past him.

No. What did she think she was doing? He wanted to dash up and drag her away, but she'd already reached the men, resonance meter tucked up her sleeve. She leaned to one side and appeared to clear her throat. Nik's translator couldn't catch the exchange from that distance, but the Boliska had moved to stand side by side between her and the crate. One reached behind his back for something tucked in his waistband.

Jo motioned toward the security officers and swept her hand to gesture at the device they were scanning. The men shrugged and gave her a hesitant reply. She gave them a small bow and strode back to where Nik and Zahira waited.

"Great luck," she said, pulling out the resonance meter and opening the most recent scan. A wavy graph danced across the screen. "This ought to narrow down our search pattern."

"Can you put that away before they see you?" Nik hissed. He could see her logic, that they could more easily follow the Boliska's trail than whatever traces were left of Zahira's grandmother. But she could have suggested it to Dr. Froum and let him take the risk.

Jo's fingers continued to dance across the screen. "It's not like they can see it from here. And anyway, they'll be moving through the line soon. The Boliska said this was the last piece of equipment for the team ahead of them, and they expected security to wave it through momentarily."

A glance back at the security agents confirmed the story. It should have been a relief. They'd done what they had come to do. Jo had narrowed down the search for Zahira. It should simply be a matter of the hatari and Dr. Froum following the Boliska's trail to whatever lab they used as a base. The danger had been minimal and Nik and Jo should be free to go home.

Jo copied the signal to Zahira's scanner and sent another to Dr. Froum. That should have been the end of it. But instead of putting her scanner away, Jo switched to another screen. Nik's chest tightened as the Boliska's signal became her target scan as well.

Chapter Twenty

— · —

Pravi

Pravi stretched against her metal fence. Waiting on Munus was like waiting on an informant. Stiff legs, sore back, and a growing desire for greasy takeout. She tried uncrossing her legs, but the rubber mulch at the patio's edge dug into her like the lumpy cushion of an old hovercar. All she needed now was her uncle's usual lecture on signs of betrayal and how to blast your way out of an ambush.

She glanced at the imaginary driver's seat where Xander would keep lookout. His timer would be going by now, counting down to the moment he'd call the meeting a bust. It'd been nearly half an hour since Agent Jandra disappeared into the command tent. More than enough time to get some sort of message to Munus and for Pravi to hear back. The woman had to be planning a counter-move.

Pravi twirled her finger in a blade of grass that had wormed its way under the fence and eyed the tent's closed flaps. Circumstances had changed since she'd charged outside, demanding to speak to Munus. She had more data. Jo's data. And the inventor's nguvu cloud didn't look nearly as crazy as it had before. If the prototype's thief had found a way to ramp up the radiation collection...

She needed a consult. Someone to confirm that her apprehension hadn't clouded her judgment, and that this was indeed worst-case scenario. The nguvu cloud pointed to an entity with enough capacity to decimate any security system. Or to take down a warehouse-sized server bank. A well-armed adversary with unknown goals and motivation. With her uncle gone, Munus was her best option. He'd see the need for discretion, would understand that spooking the enemy could lead to more casualties than whatever they currently had planned. She had to get him the information before Jandra's hubris caused a massive delay.

Ideally, she should head back to her office. Someone needed to model the nguvu cloud's growth, and there was also the matter of potential targets. But Agent Yurik stood between her and the path to the front door. This left her with two choices: Continue waiting for Munus in the security gap, or risk a dash past Yurik.

She glanced over to where the agent waited. Bright green ferns and spiny trees ran to either side of him, far enough apart for Pravi to dodge through, but close enough for cover and making the agent second guess following her. If she was lucky, he wouldn't risk the paperwork he'd get for the arrest. If she wasn't lucky, or if Yurik still held a vendetta for the time Pravi had paralyzed two of his limbs, she'd waste precious hours in a holding cell. As fast as her lawyer would be, she'd be losing time instead of getting a head start on the data.

Jandra poked her head out of the command tent, sporting a self-satisfied smirk. A body camera hung from her neck. "I trust you're doing well, Miss Resero?" The agent said it like a question, but her eyes claimed it as a challenge. Pravi would have to choose her words carefully.

"Is Director Munus on his way?"

"I relayed your message to his assistant." Jandra tossed a body cam to Agent Yurik. "I deeply apologize for the injury you sustained under our watch, Miss Resero. We're taking steps to avoid a repeat of the incident."

"I see." Given that Jandra's camera recorded audio, it would be safe to assume the woman hadn't lied about telling Munus' assistant. But that didn't mean Munus had received the message.

Pravi plucked two blades of grass and rolled them together. On the surface, the body cams benefited her, not Jandra. The agents could no longer threaten her with false charges or try some of the other frowned upon manipulation techniques. She could even head inside to model the nguvu if she wanted to. But that's what made it worrying. Jandra didn't strategize the same way as Munus. She seemed to value status and results over procedural integrity. The cameras had to be for creating a false sense of security or some sort of plausible deniability.

Pravi didn't budge from the security gap. If Jandra wanted to try something there, she'd have to explain to her superiors why she had only the body cam footage as evidence. The woman's grin widened. Had she expected Pravi to make that choice?

"I want to make sure you feel safe in our hands." She signaled to an agent still inside the command tent. He walked out with two long scanner rods, both flaring out into wide fans at the ends. "So I think it's time we did another perimeter sweep. As I'm sure you're aware, you have the option to be present while we scan, or you can waive that right if you're more comfortable staying where you are."

A tough choice indeed. Either allow Jandra to assess the full extent of Pravi's defenses, and possibly find an excuse to raid the house, or leave herself vulnerable to whatever else Jandra had planned. From the way Jandra brandished her scanner, the agent preferred option two.

Pravi swiped a finger across her watch. "Or I could do both. I believe virtual supervision is allowed under D.I.C. code 2.4.7 subsection 35b?"

The agent's face fell slightly as she switched on her scanner. "I suppose that's acceptable. So long as it doesn't interfere with the integrity of the scan." She turned quickly on her heels, giving the other agent very little time to follow. The flare of her pole swept and beeped over the ground before Pravi could pull up the first security feed.

The game was on. Jandra started for the back of the house, where only a sleek wall of frosted glass stood between her and objects she could 'mistake' as conspicuous. Pravi swiped across her watch to shut the scanner-blocking shades that rested between the panes of glass. Jandra whipped around the far corner, getting two passes at the bathroom windows before those, too, were blocked. Hopefully she wouldn't try to claim that the blinking light of Pravi's toothbrush signaled some sort of bomb or that her robe had been worn by an intruder.

With the shades drawn, Jandra's next move was prowling through the shoulder-high reed grasses that lined the slatted fence, testing the perimeter for gaps. A checkerboard of concrete slabs and yellow-green turf made up most of the yard, but the agent's boots stayed on the meter-wide border of mulch and domed shrubs and succulents. It soon became clear it she wasn't testing the D.I.C.'s perimeter. She was testing Pravi's.

Scanner in hand, she got right up against the slats where she could trigger proximity alert after proximity alert. As soon as Pravi could reset one alarm, Jandra was already probing for the next. She barely gave Pravi a moment to breathe, much less shift power between relay points to keep their exact locations concealed. Not that the D.I.C. should have cared about how to dismantle her security net.

Needle-like leaves and feathered stems joined the scattered trail of mulch left in the agent's wake. The scanning process shouldn't have mattered to Jandra—it wasn't a crime to have gaps in your personal security system—so her purpose had to be more than finding an excuse to have Pravi arrested. Perhaps she hoped the destruction would draw Pravi out? Or perhaps it was a personal vendetta. Pravi's wrist buzzed nonstop as Jandra crept alongside the house, setting off one proximity alarm after another. The woman seemed to be enjoying herself, even going so far as tiptoeing inch by inch, leaving Pravi braced against the incoming vibrations. Silencing them was an option, but then Jandra might claim that someone had already disabled them.

She technically had Yurik's com for communicating with Jandra. But the sole time she attempted to call directions from her seat in the security gap, the agent pretended she heard 'push the gate hard' instead of 'don't push the gate too hard' and decapitated a patch of flowers. Pravi had no choice but to dedicate some of her focus to deepening her breaths and releasing the growing tension in her back and shoulders. If she had to reset the front porch alarm one more time, there might soon be flecks of red intermingling with the green and yellow wreckage of her landscaping. She clenched her fist and swiped away an alert at the office window as black dress boots crossed into the edge of her vision.

Her attempt to hold back her hopes failed, and her eyes followed a navy track suit up to dark hair and even darker glasses. Munus. He gave her only a cursory glance before strolling into a ready position in front of Yurik.

"Boss," Yurik whispered into his com. "The department head is here."

In the security camera, Jandra responded by stomping off the bits of mulch and leaves that had clung to her boots, leaving behind a patch of debris on the nearest concrete slab. She'd indeed been well aware of her destruction. Pravi tried to catch Munus' eye as he waited for his agent to return to the patio, but he stood as still as the fallen leaves.

"My secretary said you needed me," Munus said as Agent Jandra turned the corner. She must have passed off the scanner as her hands were now crossed calmly under her body cam.

"Yes, there was an incident." Jandra shot Pravi's injured hand a condescending look. "It appears my charge isn't satisfied with the change in command."

The top of an eyebrow rose above Munus' glasses. "I thought Miss Resero had memorized D.I.C. protocols? When investigations stall, it's standard procedure to move on to higher priority cases."

"I had a pressing matter I wanted to discuss with you." Pravi tried to remember the phrases she'd prepared prior to Jandra's power play. If she gave any hint that it had to do with her uncle's prototype, Munus would have no choice but to redirect her to the new project lead. "It's related to one of our prior discussions."

Jandra took a step forward. "I tried to tell her I'd be happy to handle whatever concerns she has, and that you shouldn't be bothered by petty affairs. But she refused to move until she saw you. Given how close she is to the perimeter and her current risk level..."

Munus nodded. "You made the right call. Your charge, however..." He gave a short sigh muted by pursed lips. "I suppose it's not too surprising to find Miss Resero commandeering the department's time and resources yet again. I trust my short visit is enough to end her misguided protest."

Whatever Pravi had been planning to say froze in her throat. She hadn't expected such a swift change in his attitude toward her. Had her previous maneuvers burned away all his good will?

"Please." Pravi inched closer, staying just at the edge of the security gap. "I promise it won't be a waste of your time."

The slow turn of Munus' head carried a hint of surprise and for a moment, Pravi worried she'd let desperation worm its way into her voice. His gaze drifted down to where her feet perched firmly in the mulch, then followed the edge of the tent back up to where the camera angles left her small corner of the patio free from surveillance. Jandra opened her smug mouth to speak, but stopped as his eyes swung back to her and the body cameras dangling from both her and Yurik's necks.

"I see. I suppose I have a few minutes to spare."

"Director Munus, with all due respect, I think I can handle this." Jandra gestured back toward the tent.

Munus didn't budge. "Consider this a temporary reprieve so you can work on the Senfield and Secha write-up." He nodded toward the command center, and when she continued to hesitate, he shot her a look that said she should expect an official rebuke over her security mismanagement. He waited a moment for her and Yurik to clear out of the way, then approached Pravi. "I apologize for my colleague's lapse in judgment. Our team leads are expected to display a higher level of prudence and discretion."

Rather than push Pravi into conversation, he left a moment of silence open for her to fill. She panicked for a moment about where they should chat. Should she risk inviting him in? The alternative carried a chance of the others overhearing. Before she could answer her thoughts, Munus gestured for her to sit back in the mulch and he joined her in the security gap. He leaned back against the fence and rested his wrists on his bent knees, an unexpectedly casual move on his part. Either he was trying to make her feel more comfortable or he'd grown weary of their usual exchange of posturing. "I trust you won't go back on your promise."

Pravi shook her head and took a deep breath. Telling Munus ran counter to everything she'd done to keep the prototype's secret from the D.I.C., but her gut said to trust him. Too many people could be at risk if they allowed the radiation clouds to grow. "It's a storage device. A nguvu storage device."

He stiffened at the words.

"I know it sounds crazy. My uncle, working on something so against the laws of the research commission." Xander might have pushed and twisted the rules a bit, but he'd never outright broken any before. Pravi tapped out a nervous rhythm on her knees. How much should she hold back? How much could Munus keep confidential? "Evidently, nguvu is the key to helping insensates sense the strings."

She imagined understanding blooming on his face, but from the corner of her eye, it didn't seem like he'd moved at all. "Can you tell me where it is now?"

"It was stolen from a storage locker on Yerin approximately two weeks before his death. Since then, I haven't been able to pinpoint its location or identify the thieves. There have been traces of it, though. The Euri distribution center, for one, and more recently the crash on Xanthan. The data I've collected suggests the thief has increased the storage capacity by several orders of magnitude."

Munus' transcom buzzed, and after checking it, he sighed and peeled himself back up off the fence. "Sorry, urgent business." He stood, his face only partially toward her. Had he not believed her? Did he think this was another ploy to send him off the trail? A few strides brought him up to the tent flaps. "Change of plans, Jandra."

"Did she agree to cooperate?" Jandra poked her head out hopefully. Her lips twitched upward when her eyes landed on Pravi's forlorn face.

"It's classified. From now on, Miss Resero will be working for me on an ongoing case. You are to provide her with a private work station and continued security. Any sort of questions or interrogations regarding her uncle's prototype must be scheduled and approved by me. Interfering with her work in any way, shape, or form is prohibited. Do I make myself clear?"

"Yes... sir?" Jandra's shoulders drooped down at the words like a slow-motion avalanche, but he'd already brushed past her.

"I trust you can have everything set up within the hour. I'll be in touch, Miss Resero."

CHAPTER TWENTY-ONE

— • —

Jo

With how jittery Jo was feeling, electrified ants might as well have been crawling through her veins. The sliding station's burnt orange walls and red brick tile faded out at the edge of her vision. She'd gone and talked to strangers. On purpose. Somehow all the calculating and analyzing of the mission prep had made her forget she was dealing with people and not just another device needing fixing.

As soon as she saw the bewildered look on Nik's face, the reality of what she'd done hit her like a thousand volts to the chest. Who did she think she was, Xander Resero? A D.I.C. agent? To act like tracking down kidnappers was her day job, and that it wasn't a big deal to stroll over to trained government agents with only a scanner in her sleeve. Her hands shook as she set her and Zahira's scanners to the Boliska's frequencies. She hadn't handled this much adrenaline in years. Not since the first time she'd stayed at the lab past curfew and had to hot-wire the dorm's keypad to get to her room.

Dr. Froum—or Pekke, as the physicist had asked them to call him—finished copying the signal into his scanner and tucked it in his back pocket. Jo was amazed the man could reach any of his pockets, much less a back one, with how tangled he was in equipment straps. Not only did he have two of Jo's infrared scanners, but also three shoulder bags and a black, hard-shelled case he'd pulled from a locker at the last station. The case alone was larger than Jo's equipment bag, and warnings about electric shocks and radiation leaks plastered its sides. She gave it a wide berth. But Pekke... Pekke handled it like it was no more than a milk jug and he was trying to bring in all the groceries in one trip.

"I trust you haven't done the thing yet?" The physicist's voice was just over a whisper as he moved between Zahira and the security line.

The hatari shook her head and slipped a spare coil from her pocket. Typically, security scans didn't search for nguvu, but she hadn't wanted to risk it. Her plan was to drain everything into a spare coil and toss it in the nearest waste bin. "Just let me know when we're clear."

Pekke squinted at his transcom, appearing like he was reading something while the camera function peered over his shoulder. The screen showed two green-vested men heading through security. "You have about thirty seconds."

Thirty seconds until the Boliska transported themselves to the moon lab. Mere minutes until Jo followed and attempted to get a nguvu reading on their base. She readjusted her equipment bag and found Nik staring at her with one of those scowls he usually reserved for uncooperative bits of code. Was it because of how close she was standing to Zahira? The hatari hadn't even started the transferral yet. And anyway, it wasn't any more dangerous than what they planned to do next.

"And they're off." Pekke switched off his transcom and stuck it in the side pocket of one of his bags. "Is everyone ready? Transcom location settings disabled? IDs ready? Bathroom breaks taken?"

Nik gave Pekke the side eye and Jo patted her pockets for at least the dozenth time. Her transcom and nav device hadn't moved, nor had the scanner or tool pouch she'd taken in place of her usual equipment bag. The lockpick case was still in the outer pocket, sandwiched between a set of mini screwdrivers and a bag of tweezers for camouflage.

Her gaze drifted to the faint amber lines swirling across Zahira's skin. The coil didn't seem to change or glow, but her lines grew fainter, dimming with each breath. Nguvu was supposed to be dangerous. Erratic. Yet the hatari handled it nimbly, without any semblance of concern. What could she have done with it if she hadn't spent her whole life running?

"Next," a voice called from the far end of the room. The coil flashed a vivid orange as the noise broke Zahira's concentration. It bounced once on the brick tile, leaving a charred circle and the faint scent of hot metal.

One of the security guards tapped the scanner bed. "Either get in line or leave. This area is private property."

"Sorry," Jo mumbled, scrambling to move forward in line.

"Just a last check that's everything's in order." Pekke's voice held all the certainty that Jo's lacked, and he only followed after he made certain Zahira hadn't been injured in the transfer.

Nik stood between them in line, his face still twisted like he was pretending the taste in his mouth wasn't sour. She'd have to treat him to dinner again when all this was over, given they didn't end up in jail. On the off chance they did, maybe she could bribe the warden for a box of dried persimmons or something.

The unsettled feeling in Jo's chest intensified as she passed through the scanner. Reaching the other side did nothing to stop it, though her pack of tools went through without setting off any lights or alarms. Nik's did as well. Even Pekke got his black case through with the presentation of a few permit papers. They took turns showing their IDs to the guard before continuing on to a giant sliding circle at the far end of the room.

Zahira went last, her arms stiff and fists tight. One determined stride took her to the scanner's threshold and underneath its massive, sensor-pocked beam. It loomed over her like a robotic arm, ready to swoop down and pluck her away. Their hopes settled on the agent watching the monitor.

Jo gripped her shoulder bag until the strap pressed deep into her palm, braced against a flash of red or a warning beep. None came until Zahira reached the end to scan her ID.

"Could you try it again?" The security guard held up a hand to keep her from continuing on. "It doesn't look like it got a good read."

Zahira obeyed, but the machine still blinked red. Jo glanced at the guard manning the scanner, but he appeared unperturbed. A woman who channels nguvu walks through their security checkpoint, and they get hung up on her ID. Of all the things that could get in their way. What could possibly be so interesting about—

Oh. It was fake, wasn't it? No fugitive would risk using their real ID. Zahira still held her calm, confident pose, but her lines flashed a touch brighter and her feet had shifted to point away from the guards and toward the door.

"Yazip, I think the scanner's acting up." The first guard waved his partner over and gave Zahira an apologetic frown. "I'm sorry, miss. There seems to be a problem either with our scanner or the card. This might take a few moments."

A perturbed Yazip plucked the ID from the card reader and turned it this way and that in the light. He whispered to his partner, pointing out various aspects of the printing, then handed it back to be run again. Whatever flaw the forgery had, it didn't seem to be visible.

The first guard swiped it through his console and got a low beep in return. Still denied.

Possible repercussions ran through Jo's mind. They wouldn't take Zahira to the station's main security, would they? The guards didn't seem to suspect the ID, but there was no way they'd let Zahira onto the base with her identity in question. Would her grandmother come with them if she wasn't there? Would Jo and the others even be able to recognize her? How much of their plans would be derailed by a too-clever card reader? What brand was the darn thing, anyway? Schlister and Dranici? Jo had worked with that kind before. Their top-of-the-line fraud detection was something to envy, unless you were on the wrong side of it. Like Zahira.

Both guards continued fussing with the reader to no avail, doing the uncertain dance of low-level employees who'd rather avoid escalating the issue to management. Jo reached into the outer pocket of her shoulder bag, careful not to draw attention to herself. Her fingers hit a clasp, hopefully belonging to the lockpick case and not the screwdrivers.

"I need you to wait in the sliding circle," Yazip said, turning toward her.

Jo's hand brushed against cold metal. This was either the row of crystal probes she sought, or the row of square tip screwdrivers. "It's alright. She's a friend of mine. What seems to be the problem?"

"Please return to the circle, miss. We cannot let your friend through until we get the clearance from main."

Jo slid the nearest shaft into her sleeve and pulled her hand from her pocket. "There has to be some kind of mistake. Are you sure the issue is her ID and not the scanner?"

The guard shrugged. "The scanner worked fine for the others. I'm afraid it's company policy. Our hands are tied."

A flutter of light danced on Zahira's arm. Was she going to zap the ID reader? The scanner? The guard? She'd just drained her coils completely. How could she possibly expect to nguvu her way out of this?

"What if you ran mine again?" Jo pulling it out of her pocket, angled to hide the tip of the crystal probe. "If it doesn't work now, it has to be the scanner, right?"

The guard hesitated, but turned to offer the card slot. Nik was going to be so mad she had taken this risk. Her pinky flicked and hit the probe's switch as the ID slid in. The crystal tip burned against her fingers, and "Read Error" flashed across the card reader's screen.

Zahira tapped her ID against her palm. "Since there's a problem with the reader, could we try running it through a database instead?"

"Or we still have the old model in the drawer," the first security guard offered.

Yazip opted for the older model. Although it lacked the latest advances in catching forgeries, it'd be less of a problem with their employer than public databases. Zahira's ID passed without issue.

The hatari gave the guards a sarcastic smile before picking up her backpack from the scanner bed.

"We should go home." Nik's voice was harsh in her ear when Jo got back to the sliding circle. "The situation already escalated more than we'd planned."

She slipped the crystal probe back in its case. "I promised Zahira."

"And you said you were a mere humble inventor." Pekke interrupted their hurried whispers with a wink. "Don't worry, I won't tell anyone about your secret."

Nik smiled and nodded before pulling Jo aside again. "One Class B felony is enough for one day, don't you think?"

"Maybe, but it'd be a shame to let it go to waste." The words shocked Jo as much as Nik, but they had indeed come from her mouth. Every cubic inch of her body felt like it'd had twice the legal dose of caffeine. She should have gone home right then. She should have wanted to go home. Yet her feet found no resistance as they carried her back to link arms with Pekke for the slide. And in spite of Nik's protests, he followed.

The slide to the moon base went smoothly with Pekke in the lead. They arrived in a room that could best be described as a storage container turned on its side. Corrugated metal panels covered the walls, running upward at least a dozen meters, while the dark concrete floor measured nine square meters at best. Plexiglass doors slid open behind them, and their scanners immediately started beeping. Wherever the Boliska were, they were close.

Jo hurried to silence her scanner, expecting to find green-vested men waiting in ambush behind them. Instead, she found a hallway lined with mounds of devices on both sides. Most were no bigger than her satchel, but some of the dented and stripped machines were as massive as the amovoscope. Bare wires curled here and there, looped around missing knobs and empty slots for computer chips. Nik lifted a finger to her chin to help close her mouth.

"Where'd all this come from?" she asked, only then realizing that Pekke and Zahira had already started down the hallway. The latter walked half-crouched, as if expecting someone to jump out from the piles.

"Hmm?" Pekke stopped at a gap in the mess, one that turned off into a small alcove. "They're from the same place they always come from. A metaphorical egg laid by a busy scientist. A broken spectroscope, maybe a busted frintacy meter." He motioned them into the alcove and signaled for everyone to unload their equipment. As he untangled himself from his satchel straps, he continued, "Of course, the scientist fully intends to take it to a recycler when he gets the chance. Maybe after he gets this glitch figured out. Or after his new grant is approved—Here, take this voltmeter in case you need it for the door—Eventually, his colleague or lab neighbor adds a rusty compressor to the stack, saying whoever gets the chance first could save the other some time."

Pekke passed one pair of the UV goggles to Jo. At this point, he'd pulled on a bulletproof vest and a weird holster-looking thing from the back panel of the black case. Zahira and Nik worked on recalibrating the scanners to make sure the slide hadn't messed with their settings.

"Anyway, another egg spawns down the hall. Then another. And another. Eventually, the brood multiples until it's more useful for everything to remain. A spare motor from an exhaust fan is the perfect replacement for the busted one in the coolant chamber. Re-purposing a few knobs would save a trip to the hardware store. Certainly, the most expensive pieces are gone by this point, but what opportunist is going to waste time pulling out a few capacitors or resistors? The engine in that conveyor belt would fetch you ten, maybe fifteen monettes at a used parts store.

"Of course, smaller pieces do find a way to turn into cash when someone's desperate. You know, when a grant is canceled or some big rotor fails out of the blue. But you pay it back when you can. I've fed the collection at my lab three different models of oscilloscopes and a sub-zero freezer."

Zahira threw her backpack over her shoulders and pulled the straps tight. Jo's biggest wrench hung from her belt loop. "Everyone ready?"

"Not quite." Pekke nodded to the wrench. "I said we could do better than that, didn't I?"

The black case clicked open at his feet, and Jo leaned closer. Its interior held sixteen padded compartments, and long tubes glowed in four of them. In the rest, half-moons shone in the hallway's sterile light, with narrow slots running almost to their centers. "Are those micro-energy bands?" She pointed to the tubes, careful not to touch them. The bands were a fluke of science, created in an attempt to model the strings in three dimensions. Extremely volatile, the largest ones were rumored to release concussive force when they collapsed.

Pekke grinned. "They're smaller than the originals, but these babies still pack a punch." He pulled out a stack of the gears and pushed his thumb into their center, causing the metal to unfold into a sphere-like skeleton. His face looked almost giddy in the reflected light. He retrieved an energy band and wove it around the metal teeth. "I call this invention a 'Collapsing Energy Sphere,' or a CES. Boring, I know. Naming things isn't my strong point." He finished wrapping the loop and held it up. The jumble sizzled and glowed. "If you throw it at something, the metal structure will collapse the band, releasing a shock wave."

"Like a pulse grenade?" Zahira's eyes teamed with the possibilities.

Pekke carefully unwound the loop. "Not really. More like a taser. It won't kill you, but any muscle it hits will be paralyzed for a few minutes."

"Oh." She patted her wrench, no longer as interested. And why would she be? Her nguvu could do more than that. Of course, her nguvu had also been drained before they entered the base.

Pekke's face turned serious. "Our goal is retrieving your grandmother, not killing her captors."

"Yes, but..."

"The larger bands can cause permanent nerve damage. We're risking enough as it is, without worrying that friendly fire will leave us disfigured." Pekke carefully returned the band to its tube and handed the frame to Jo. He passed out more spheres, demonstrating how to click the pieces into place.

After a moment, Nik handed his back and looked to Jo to see if she'd do the same. "The plan is for the two of us to be away before these would be necessary."

"Eh, plans change." Pekke's eyes drifted over Jo. "Unexpected things happen. One of these could buy you time to get away should things go sideways sooner than expected. Or you could always change your mind and go a bit further."

Nik nudged the metal gear away again. "Finding the location is all that we're in for."

Jo nodded in agreement, but she slid a few frames and a loop case in her side pocket when Nik wasn't looking. Something in her gut said she might need them.

"Oh, and one more thing." Pekke pulled four small badges from a side pocket. "Clip these to your shirt, right above your heart. They should prevent permanent damage, but I wouldn't count on them for full protection."

"Awesome." Zahira plucked one from the pile and slid the clasp onto her backpack strap so it lay over her heart. "Signal's pointing that way." She started down the hall without waiting for anyone else to catch up. Her scanner was up and running, and her other hand held one of Pekke's spheres at the ready.

Jo straightened her strap and switched on the UV goggles, not bothering to see if Nik would make one last pleading motion toward the exit. She would at least finish what they'd come for. Heat signatures lit up behind the surrounding walls, with red- and purple-toned pipes leading the way forward. After the first row of lab suites, the trail branched from the main hallway, leaving the brighter lights and mounds of equipment behind. Jo felt a little guilty having the goggles on. Most of the lab suites were empty, but here and there a lone scientist hunched over a project or draped back over a chair in sleep.

After a few minutes, Zahira motioned for the group to stop. "This one. The trail leads to this door."

"I see six figures." Pekke squinted and adjusted his pair of goggles. "At least three are humanoid. The others look either too dim or too large."

Jo nodded in agreement. The two orange splotches at the far end of the room looked like a horizontal boiler tank and a piece of top-heavy machinery. The boiler tank's legs glowed nearly as bright as the body, which seemed odd, and a frill came out of one side, like some sort of cooling fin was needed to maintain the right temperature. The other machine was more foreign to her. The main body of it slanted at an angle, and a bulbous thing balanced at the top in a shape reminiscent of an animal skull. The final non-human concentration of heat appeared to hover above the ground. Possibly set atop a table or desk. It looked the right size for a person, but the temperature read at least ten degrees cooler than the others. Which left what? The two Boliska and Zahira's grandmother? Jo pulled out her scanner to confirm. Traces of her resonance did indeed float around the door frame.

"Can you get this open?" Zahira motioned toward the keypad. It was fairly basic for a secure facility. More complex than an apartment or dormitory, but nothing special as far as Jo could see.

She pulled out her lockpick set and got to work. The lock was the kind with a bio-sensor unit, so the pad would send out a small charge to read the user's resonance pattern. It didn't need it to open, just to save for future records in case someone tried to break in. Jo fed it the Boliska's resonance as her other hand used the crystal probes on the internal circuitry.

"Would have been nice if the keypad was on the side closer to the exit," Nik whispered for only Jo to hear.

A few more nudges from the crystals and the latch clicked open. Nik held her back while Zahira and Pekke rushed inside. Something similar to the smell of a zoo rushed out.

Jo glimpsed storage bins around the perimeter and a tall, barred structure in the back. The two Boliska stood surprised in the center of the room, turning to form a blockade around the third person. Jo guessed the grandmother at first, but though the woman recognized Zahira, she didn't seem to be a captive. And she shouted something at the men that sounded like orders.

Nik latched onto Jo's arm and tugged her toward the exit.

She fumbled for her scanner instead. "Readings first, remember?" A clattering came from the lab as she got it running. The two Boliska were down, one keeled over and clutching his hip and the other flopping on the floor like his right leg and arm were only half-responsive.

Zahira lifted another of Pekke's spheres to take the woman out.

"Come on, Jo. Let's go," Nik whispered urgently in her ear.

But her feet couldn't move. If the grandmother wasn't the blond woman the Boliska had surrounded, then where could she be? They hadn't moved her already, had they? All the adrenaline that had been flooding Jo's veins froze in an instant. Her gaze turned to the table where the sixth figure had laid. Bright gold, burgundy, and blue fabric draped over the side. A dark ebony arm hung limp on top of it.

Zahira rushed to her grandmother's side as a tug from Nik restarted Jo's nervous system. Her lungs pulled in shallow breaths and a weight in her chest threatened to drag her to her knees.

They'd come too late. The way Zahira shook the motionless body confirmed what Jo knew the second she'd realized the final heat signature was a person.

Pekke still hadn't noticed. He was too busy tying up the guards with all the uncanny speed and knowledge of someone who'd had practice. The one who'd clenched his hip already had his feet bound, and the physicist was working on the second Boliska's hands. The woman...

Jo looked to where the blond woman had fallen, but she was nowhere in sight. A moment later, she spotted her creeping up behind Zahira with a piece of equipment hose.

Nik tugged on her sleeve, but Jo shoved Nik off her and clicked one of Pekke's sphere's into place. She pulled a loop from its case and aimed.

CHAPTER TWENTY-TWO

— • —

ZAHIRA

Z ahira tightened her fists in Grandmother's satin skirt. Everything about the scene told her it was too late. The pallor in the woman's skin. The coolness of her arm. The way she felt more like a wax model than a person, painted with purple and gray undertones instead of rich brown and pink. Grandmother had warned her this would happen. That a lonely death in an interrogation room was the most likely end to a lifetime of running.

She clenched her fists tighter and resisted the urge to topple the nearest stack of crates. This was why they'd hatched their plan to escape. Why they'd spent years tracking down equipment and fake IDs and building up off-planet bank accounts. But now Grandmother laid cold on an icy steel table. Purple blotched her arms and cheeks, and her tight black ringlets lay askew.

A towering creature hissed from an enclosure behind Zahira, taunting her as she checked again for a pulse. Pekke had been right about the Boliska. They trafficked in more than hatari, and their merchandise watched from mere meters away. The hisser was a bird-like reptile, covered in red and orange poofs of feathers that hid dark green scales. An adjacent pen held a second beast, broader and four-legged beast with a bony frill. Their stench was overpowering, but she ignored it to hold her transcom to Grandmother's nose. No wisps of breath on the screen. No heartbeat nor rise to her diaphragm.

A bubbled drop of liquid lay just beside Grandmother's arm, with a matching needle mark on the inside of her elbow. If the truth serum had been painful, Grandmother's face showed no signs of it. The wrinkles had softened around her eyes, and her jaw held none of the tension, none of the worry, she'd had in life. Or at least in the life she'd had with Zahira.

A hand clasped her shoulder. "It was a pulmonary embolism." The stranger's voice was both soft and hollow. "A clot in her lungs. We'd have taken precautions if we'd known, but her files didn't list a clotting disorder." And of course they wouldn't have. She and Grandmother had avoided hospitals and their databases at all costs.

Zahira shoved the woman's hand off her shoulder, only to find a blade pressed to her neck.

"Such a waste, really. She could have had another five, maybe ten years with the right treatment." The blade dug a hair deeper, but didn't break the skin. "Instead, she had you."

Zahira searched the room for a way to break free, some strategy to channel her hate. But useless cargo filled half the space, metal crates that glowed like incubators and wooden boxes that appeared packed with straw. All belonging to the Boliska. Smugglers and murderers.

"Let her go." Pekke's voice rang from somewhere on Zahira's right, near a wall of data screens.

"Do you know what she is? What she's capable of?" The woman's blade urged Zahira backward, but she held tight to the steel table that held Grandmother's quiet form. She wouldn't abandon her again. The woman settled for angling the knife so she could face Pekke. "One brief lapse of control and you'll be a sizzling husk, feeling fire in every nerve in your body until your heart and lungs finally gave way."

The woman described an alternate scenario in gruesome detail, but Zahira couldn't waste time listening. She had to get Grandmother out of there. Her attacker still had one hand on Zahira's left shoulder, which meant the blade was coming over the right. She moved as Grandmother had taught her. Her hands snapped up to restrain the Boliska's wrist, yanking down and left while her right shoulder shoved the woman's elbow high and to the right. High enough for Zahira to squeeze out backward. The woman still held the knife, but Zahira's hands controlled her wrist. She stabbed at the woman's side. Once.

Twice. The knife clattered to the floor before she could strike a third time.

As it fell, Zahira willed every wisp of nguvu into the Boliska's still-captive wrist, but nothing happened. The woman's skin didn't even go warm beneath her palm.

Fingers dug into her scalp and wrenched upward with a fist full of hair. "You see what I mean?" The woman's voice sounded harsh and labored. "My arm would be charred flesh, if I hadn't come prepared."

Pain drowned out the question of how someone could block nguvu, and Zahira fought to keep Grandmother in sight through watering eyes. She scratched at the woman's wrist and arm until she bought herself a bit of relief.

The woman spun so her other arm could wrap around Zahira's neck from behind. "I told my colleagues your file was incomplete. That with how much power you unleashed into that console, you had to have some secret list of casualties. Maybe even more so than average." To Pekke, she sneered, "Since you care so much, I'll make you an offer. Let my colleagues go or I'll snap her neck."

Zahira struggled to find the woman's pinky, to pry off her fingers and break them, but they were twisted too deep in her hair. She kicked backward in search of a leg or shin, but her feet found only air. Her pleas for more nguvu came up empty.

Instead, the arm pressed deeper against her throat, blocking her next inhale. "We prefer to keep the hatari alive, but we make exceptions when we have to."

"Easy now." Pekke shuffled backward with his hands up and a sphere frame held tight against his palm. "I think we can talk this through."

The woman's grip loosened enough for air to flood into Zahira's lungs. "Release. My. Colleagues."

"No!" Zahira called before the arm at her throat cut her off again. The Boliska needed to pay. All of them needed to pay.

But Pekke bent toward the captive furthest from the door, the one he'd taken out and tied up first.

The woman rotated Zahira to match his movements like some sort of human shield. "Believe me when I say I won't hesitate. If I so much as suspect you're trying to pull something, if you even start to—" The arm holding Zahira's neck went slack and something metal clattered to the floor.

One of Pekke's spheres? Zahira took the opening to twist herself out of the woman's chokehold, forcing her to release her grip or face a broken wrist. As soon as the pressure on her scalp eased, she spun away, pulling Jo's wrench from her belt loop. But before she could strike, another of Pekke's spheres had the woman on the ground.

"You okay?" The physicist pulled a length of rope from one of his shoulder bags. He wrapped it around the woman's hands and feet in one swift movement—not as tight as Zahira would have liked, but enough for her pale wrists to grow paler—and plucked up the scorched spheres. A patch of red spread across the woman's white lab coat, confirming that at least one of Zahira's stabs had landed before the Boliska had turned the tide.

Zahira rolled the wrench in her palm. Part of her wished she had the strength to finish the woman off, but part of her wanted to lie down and sob. "Could be better. How'd you prep the sphere without her seeing?"

"I didn't." He nodded back toward the door. "Jo did." The inventor gave an apologetic smile.

Jo held another half-assembled sphere in both hands and Nik stood a few steps behind her. "I would have thrown it sooner, but I was worried it'd hit you."

Maybe it wouldn't have been so bad if it had. Perhaps it would be better to feel numb. Zahira mumbled her thanks and slipped the strap for the mechanical lift off her back. Her hands fumbled to start the motors. "Could you..." Her voice squeaked and she swallowed. "I can't seem to get it open."

Jo nodded and silently took over operating the lift. Grandmother had always said to go in with a plan, but was this worth all the time she'd spent preparing? If she'd rushed instead, could she have arrived before they administered the serum?

She and Pekke lifted Grandmother from the table to their re-purposed stretcher.

"I can stay here and wait for the authorities," he offered. "I'll make sure they pay for what they've done. If not directly, then indirectly." He eyed the crates that lined the walls. The nearest one laid open, revealing a pair of pale blue eggs the size of his head.

"A smuggling charge?" She snorted and placed one of Grandmother's arms gingerly across her chest to keep it from dangling off the edge. The Boliska had stolen away her only family, but in the eyes of the law, the illegal reptiles would weigh heavier.

"Smuggling?" Jo echoed.

Pekke stuck his hands in his pockets in a way that mirrored Nik. "The Boliska's stated purpose isn't actually hunting down hatari. It's stopping poachers from stealing Yerin's most valuable asset."

Zahira gripped the end of the lift with both hands and motioned toward the enclosures at the back of the room. The feathered lizard eyed them with interest, while its four-legged and featherless neighbor munched on a pile of dry grass. "The quorra wyn. Or dinosaurs, as you called them the first time we met." She briefly glanced at Jo and Nik. The continent they inhabited, Jura, had higher than normal levels of nguvu, which left traces on trespassers and poachers.

"And it turns out they were trespassing and poaching themselves." Pekke rocked back on his feet and sighed. "I'll make sure they face justice for Grandmother, too. Maybe even find where they're keeping the other hatari."

Zahari looked back at the woman who'd attacked her. She couldn't believe there'd be much justice in a quiet arrest, in the drawn-out appeals and those in charge shifting blame between departments and agencies. They certainly wouldn't bring Grandmother back. She wanted it all to burn. For them to feel what it was to lose everything they cared about, everything they'd worked so hard for.

The door creaked and her eyes snapped to the doorway to find two Boliska, one holding a beverage tray and the other a takeout bag. The first dropped his parcels to pull a bludgeon from the nearest crate.

"Chevier," the blond woman yelled. "Help Yob."

In the next flurry of moments, Zahira realized Yob was one of Pekke's no-longer-paralyzed captives, and he'd secretly crept toward the discarded knife. Chevier, the one with the bludgeon, went in swinging to buy him time to cut through the restraints. He hit away Jo and Pekke's first round of spheres while his partner charged.

Zahari batted the partner away with her wrench, hitting him hard enough that he stumbled to the floor. She tossed her remaining sphere at Chevier, but it wouldn't be enough. She searched the room for ideas. Only one way might clear the path for the lift. That could give her a chance to break for the exit. And even if she didn't make it out in one piece, neither would the Boliska's precious cargo.

She sprinted to release the quorra wyn. The frilled one didn't move, but the feathered one sniffed the air. It was an omnivore, if she remembered correctly, and didn't so much hunt as steal the prey from exhausted hunters. She backed away from the door as it crept out slowly, its long, fluffy tail suddenly smooth and alert. It seemed to smell the blood on the blond woman.

Once Zahira was sure its attention had shifted from her to the Boliska, she raced back to the lift and signaled for the others to follow. The woman's shrill voice shouted for someone to cut her free of her restraints.

Pekke threw a few spheres to cover their exit, with only one hitting a Boliska while the other two ricocheted off the table and the herbivore's enclosure. A low, panicked squeal rumbled from the pen, followed by the slam of bony frill on metal.

Zahira dodged toward the nearest wall, fighting to keep Grandmother's body on the lift. She was barely clear before the herbivore came barreling and kicking from its enclosure, slamming into the steel table. An angry roar and it slammed again, knocking the steel legs loose from their bolts as stacks of cargo toppled from the walls.

A yelp of alarm came from behind her, and Zahira turned to find Jo's leg trapped under an overturned crate. The herbivore charged for the exit as Nik tried in vain to lift it off her.

Zahira looked back at the door. The herbivore had shoved the Boliska aside, clearing the path to the hall. If she ran now, she could get Grandmother to the exit with little trouble. She took a few steps forward.

Jo yelped again, and Nik strained against the weight of the box. Grandmother always said to get yourself to safety first. That you could always come back for a rescue mission. But look how well that had turned out.

Zahira turned the lift around and raced back to the crate. It moved easier with her and Nik together, and Pekke offered his own quick shove in between sphere throws.

Jo wiggled free, and Nik threw her arm around his shoulder. "Is anything broken?"

She shook her head. "Just sprained, I think."

"Good." Pekke threw a final sphere and took Jo's other arm. "We need to move."

They hobbled toward the door, picking up speed once they had enough room to walk three abreast. Zahira couldn't go much faster without the lift starting to waver and shift.

Pekke helped steady it. "Remember the exit protocol." He'd given them each three sets of coordinates. Three jumps they could take to shake the Boliska from their trail. The plan was to leave together if they could, but plan on rescuing the others if they couldn't.

The nearest pair of Boliska brutes lunged forward, and Chevier grabbed for Zahira's feet. She stumbled, knocking the lift off-balance and shoving it toward the wall.

Nik caught the edge before it shot too far. Using the grip as a support, Zahira kicked backward, hitting what she hoped was her attacker's face. His hand released her ankle, and she sprinted down the hall. The lift dipped and twisted, but Grandmother's body stayed on.

Metal crunched and banged ahead of them. Hopefully just the herbivore clearing their path of the piles of junk to either side. Zahira dodged a smashed computer as the Boliska's footsteps sounded closer and closer behind. The giant lizard squealed and her heart skipped a beat. The exit was a few dozen meters ahead now, but the frilled creature was nowhere in sight. She couldn't be sure with the echoes, but it sounded like it had turned down one of the side hallways and looped back toward their rear. Its footsteps pounded closer, echoing her racing heart. The Boliska were even closer.

Pekke darted forward to grab the door, but the first Boliska was already on them. Muscled arms reached for the lift.

Zahira dodged out of his way as his fingers brushed the side. "A little help here?"

"I'm trying." Jo fumbled with an energy sphere, trying to wrap the glowing band without tripping. She was hobbling on her own now, but not fast enough to make it.

The Boliska grabbed the dolly on his next lunge, wrapping his fingers around the edge. The force jerked her to a stop. Zahira cursed, shoving the dolly back into the man's chest. He doubled over, but his grip held.

Jo hooked the last loop and sent the sphere flying. The man tried to swat it away, but it struck his upper arm, numbing it instantly, and his grip faltered.

Nik helped Zahira maneuver the lift through the door, and Pekke pulled Jo in and latched it shut behind them before the Boliska could follow. Theoretically, it would hold until it sensed them slide away. But exit doors weren't designed to keep out quorra wyn. They needed to slide away before the herbivore burst through.

Pekke grabbed Nik's elbow. "Link up. Coordinates set."

"Uh, we have a stowaway." Jo took Zahira's arm and nodded to a boy crouched in the corner—the teenager they'd seen in the security line, most likely hiding from the chaos.

"Set your nav device and get out of here," Pekke ordered. "I'm sure your teacher will understand about whatever project you have due. We're sliding in three... two..."

Nik grabbed Jo's hand as the herbivore thundered down the hall outside. A buzz rose in the chain of arms and Zahira willed her body to match, passing the frequency to the lift and wrapping it around Grandmother. The exit door shook.

Glass shattered as the room shifted to gray. Someone's hand latched onto her arm.

CHAPTER TWENTY-THREE

—·—

NIK

N ik gasped for breath as the world slid into focus. He half-expected to be sitting up in bed, startled awake from a nightmare. Instead, he and Pekke stood in the center of a warehouse-sized station, encompassed by corrugated walls and a gray trestle ceiling. Though they'd escaped from the lab, his heart still raced, drowning out the station babble. He'd told Jo they'd gotten in over their heads. He'd said the rescue attempt was something best left for professionals. But evidently she'd rather tussle with mercenaries and attempt to outrun a dinosaur than take his advice. At least they'd gotten away safe and—

He stared at his empty hand.

No, he couldn't have lost her. Nik dropped his hold on Pekke and spun around, searching the ocean of travelers for Jo's coveralls and messy bun. Faded blues, oranges, and rusty pinks rippled around the sliding room, carrying worn and weary faces. The faces of strangers.

Pekke's head lifted from his navigation dials. "Did they follow us? Or is our deceased member attracting attention?" He turned and his eyes fell on the half-empty sliding circle. "Please tell me Jo and Zahira are just looking for a tarp or blanket to cover the lift."

"I don't think they made it through." But how? Nik distinctly remembered passing the frequency to Jo and feeling her phase with him as the door crashed open. Could her concentration have wavered when the glass went flying? "We have to go back for them."

"The D.I.C. will get to them first, if they're even still at the lab." Pekke considered for a moment, then scrolled his nav device to a different destination. "I sent a message to my friend Zave as soon as I had the first two tied up. The best plan is to head to the rendezvous point and use the cryptoscope if we need to."

"But Jo—"

"Jo's an engineer. And a good one. My money is on her free-sliding rather than getting stampeded by a ceratopsid. She might even beat us home."

"Or end up at the bottom of a lake." Even if Jo had managed to grab another string before she fully phased back to the lab, traveling without a nav signal would be dangerous. They might phase-in in the middle of an ocean, or a beezlefriz cave, or a blizzard...

Pekke cursed and shoved Nik into the nearest blue circle. "Boliska. By the construction equipment."

Nik glanced over his shoulder. Yellow construction cranes arched over the crowd a dozen meters away, stark against the gray metal of the walls. Orange-vested supervisors clustered at their base, wielding tablets and ID scanners while migrant workers lined up before them. Most of the room's traffic moved in that direction, but a green-clad pair of brutes waded counter to the flow. One of them swept his hand back and forth as if using a scanner. Did that mean they didn't have Jo and Zahira?

Nik craned his neck in the other direction. There had to be some-place less crowded. Like a bathroom hallway or something. "We should try luring them away. Maybe hit them with one of your sphere things, and see if they know where our friends are."

"The spheres are a no-go." Pekke tapped his palm on the black case and got a hollow sound in response. "Even if we had some left, I don't like our chances in a head-on confrontation."

"We could find a good place for an ambush. Use the case as a weapon if we need to."

"A plucky mathematician and a physicist against two mercenaries?" Pekke hooked Nik's shoulder and yanked him back into the sliding circle. "Perhaps I didn't make myself clear. If we don't keep moving, we're going to be the ones needing rescue." He shoved a frequency through Nik's shoulders with so much force Nik had whip-lash mem-ories of being toted back and forth to grandma's house for the holidays.

Several moments of fuzzy maroon faded to a sandy tan, and Nik found himself stumbling forward. A pale wood floor rose to meet him, but Pekke held his arm tight.

"Easy now. Might want to take a SlydWell before the next jump." The professor slipped a pill from his pocket. His voice was hushed, matching the quieter station they'd slid into. Some sort of outpost for wilderness tours, by the looks of it. Long, lodge-style walls held racks and racks of hiking and camping equipment. A nearby mug read *'I Was Nearly Eaten By A Cave Bear and All I Got Was This Stupid Cup.'*

Pekke flipped through a rack of t-shirts and eyed the other arrival circles. "Funny how you were so opposed to fighting head-on when Jo was the one doing it."

Nik gritted the pink pill between his teeth. "There's a difference between getting into trouble and getting out of it."

"Is there? As far as I'm concerned, Jo got herself in trouble as soon as she designed a working interdimensional tracking device."

"What's that supposed to mean?"

Pekke smirked and held up a navy blue shirt to Nik's chest. "Let's put aside for a moment the fact that her test run searched for the Resero Project, of all things. What did you think would happen when she announced her success? Maybe a few offers from police departments and private investigators? Try an all-out bidding war between every corporate security firm and bounty hunter conglomerate. None of which would take losing lightly."

"She could sell the patent to the D.I.C. Let them decide who gets it and who doesn't."

"And then spend the rest of her life dodging a bombardment of demands and kidnapping attempts? What crook would steal from the D.I.C. when they could go right to the designer?" Pekke clapped two t-shirt hangers together and pulled a hiking backpack from a nearby display. "And even if she invested in good security, every week there'd be a new sob story. Someone's priceless heirloom or a long-lost brother. And Jo would look into every single one just in case they weren't lying for sympathy."

Nik trudged behind him to a self-checkout kiosk. "And you've figured all that out from knowing her for less than half a day?"

"You've known her for years. Would you disagree?" A blue line glowed from the base of the kiosk up to waist-height, registering Pekke's purchases. The physicist tapped his nav device on the side to pay. "I was like you once. Thinking all my best friend wanted was a cozy lab and a bunch of science awards sitting on the mantel. But sometimes... Sometimes the quietest people are a mere opportunity away from becoming vigilantes."

The physicist cursed, and Nik's gaze snapped to a sliding circle at the far end of the room. Their green-vested friends had arrived facing the other direction.

"I hope the Slydwell had enough time to kick in." Pekke toted both Nik and his purchases to the nearest blue circle. "Right then. Off we go." He linked arms with Nik and they slid again, this time along a jittery string that smelled like tobacco smoke. Once it ended, Nik coughed air back into his lungs.

The station they'd arrived in looked pretty basic. Spacious floor carpeted in black and gray, punctuated regularly with short columns and recessed box lights. Touristy off-worlders wandered from the arrival circles or peered through the large bank of windows. A mostly clear view of the sky suggested they were a few dozen stories up, and the tips of rollercoasters and pendulum swings shown at the bottom of the glass.

Nik steadied himself on the nearest column and scoured the room for signs they were followed. He didn't think his body could handle another slide. Even with the SlydWell, it felt like he'd eaten thirteen slices of Tasmisian pie. A sickly sweet taste hovered in the back of his throat, and his gut questioned his life decisions. "Couldn't we tell a security guard or something?"

"You really think those brutes couldn't take down a security guard?" Pekke tapped his shoulder with one of the t-shirt hangers. "Here, put this on. It'll help us blend in." The physicist already sported a matching tee over his dress shirt. It was one of those specialty pun tees, where the hexbit was programmed so the words would work in most languages. For Nik, it read 'The Best Camping Trips Are In-Tents.'

"You're kidding, right?" Nik couldn't imagine the shirt doing anything other than attracting eye rolls.

Pekke shrugged and got to work stuffing his shoulder bags into the hiking sack. "When in Atrylia, do as the Atrylians do. Let me see your hands quick."

Nik complied, and Pekke ran the scanner over them before packing it, too, in the hiking sack. "Nguvu traces. That must be how they're tracking us."

Nguvu traces? "But I didn't touch Zahira."

"And neither did I." Pekke threw the sack over his shoulders and adjusted the straps. "Not sure if you know, but nguvu doesn't leave traces from proximity. You have to have direct contact. And you know what we both had contact with?"

"I don't know, a million things between all the stations we've jumped through."

"That crate. The one that fell on Jo."

No wonder the man had a reputation for being a conspiracy theorist. Nik slid the t-shirt over his head. "Or we could have brushed Zahira without noticing."

"Both of us? I'd think the chances of that are pretty slim."

Nik honestly didn't care where the traces had come from. What he needed was to get home and use the cryptoscope to find Jo. He hiked up his own bag and started for the exit. The surrounding circles were all yellow, which meant the departure circles were in a different room, or possibly on a different floor.

Pekke's long strides caught up with him quickly. "I know you think this is my fault. That I somehow talked Jo into risking her life on some fool's errand. But this is so much bigger than any of us. If the nguvu disruptions spread to the sliding system—"

"So what happened to your friend? The one who became a vigilante."

Pekke's lips drew into a straight line.

"That bad, huh? And you're pushing Jo to head down the same path."

"We should stop at the restrooms ahead, see if we can get some of these traces off our hands." Pekke adjusted his already straight backpack straps and pulled them a millimeter tighter. His face had lost all trace of his mischievous grin, replaced by touches of anger and something else. Something that pulled him inside himself.

He didn't speak again until they reached the sinks. When he did, his words came out like the hush of the water. "Truth is, I have no idea where she is. I haven't seen her since I told her to ignore her gut and let someone else handle it." He cupped the stream from the faucet, letting the water run between his fingers before scrubbing them with more soap. "She ended up framed for the plot she was trying to uncover. Last I heard, she'd set up a safehouse somewhere in the outer octaves." He shook off his hands and reached for a paper towel. "Tell you what. If I'm wrong about Jo, if she really does want to stay behind the scenes, you can tell her I'm willing to take the cryptoscope off her hands for a fair price. I'll be listed as the designer and patent holder, and Jo can have a private lab and an annual research stipend. How's that sound?"

Nik didn't have to think before saying "Deal." He'd still have to find Jo and let her and Pekke flesh out the details, but it was one less thing to feel stressed about. And he should have felt at least a little relieved. Between the change of clothes and confirming the traces were gone, he should have been able to breathe a bit easier. So why did his chest feel like it had gained a few kilos?

Three steps outside the restroom, Nik nearly stopped in his tracks. There were the two Boliska, scanning the doors he and Pekke had come through. They made their way over with determined strides.

"Act natural." Pekke nodded to a hallway to their right. "This way to the stairs."

It took everything in Nik to not bolt, especially when their paths came close enough that only a few meters separated them from their pursuers. They went down three full sets of stairs before Pekke signaled that they weren't being followed.

"Another SlydWell for the road?" the physicist offered.

Nik nodded, though he wasn't sure it'd do much to combat the queasy feeling in his chest. Getting chased from station to station.

Having to plan routes to pick up disguises and ditch their pursuit. This shouldn't be something Jo wanted. He could barely convince her to leave her apartment most days. And crowded stations were always a nonstarter. Yet his mind kept running through arguments, like it might take more than that to persuade her.

CHAPTER TWENTY-FOUR

—·—

ZAHIRA

C olors and scents swirled around Zahira, and a rush of adrenaline screamed that she was falling backward and inward. She scrambled to focus on her target string—willing her body to match its frequency—but the signal fizzled weakly in her grasp. Had she lost Jo? No, the inventor's resonance still buzzed against her arm and elbow, even as the vibrations in their bodies cascaded back to the last point of equilibrium. Back to the lab.

They must have lost their connection to Pekke, and the reason dragged from Zahira's other arm. She'd barely begun to slide when the unknown hand had latched on, and between the shock of the fractured doorway and the sudden draw of an extra person, her focus wavered. Rather than leave her behind, Jo had propelled them both forward, forcing a phase shift toward the target frequency. Through their connection, Zahira could feel the inventor amplifying its remnants, but it wouldn't be enough. Couldn't be enough. They'd never reach the station without the signal beacon from Pekke's nav device. The hot pulse of the target string was already fading, its warm copper color dissolving back into blue. In moments, they'd be back at the lab. Back to Grandmother's killers.

Zahira flailed out, her string sense grasping for every frequency within reach. The links to other worlds purred against her touch. Some held, and she imagined fingers digging in like nails against the draw of the lab. Each limb of her body shifted to match a different string, tugging and pulling against the others until her chest rebelled against the strain.

A buzz came from Jo again, a signal magnified and forced through the space where their arms met. Zahira pulled back, but it tickled her wrist and teased at her grip on the other strings. The pulse grew, not like the one they'd lost, but a new frequency, loud and rhythmic, like the whirr of an engine.

A new destination.

Warily, Zahira relaxed her hold. A few strings slipped through her fingers, and she let the new pulse creep up her arm. The hum was warm and murky, nothing like the sterile feel of the lab. She released the other strings and held tight as Jo led her in a free slide. Unassisted travel was risky, but Jo moved with intention. Like she'd done it before. The inventor pulled with a steady rhythm, shifting her own frequency in spurts and giving Zahira time to adjust. Perhaps her family treated free sliding as a rite of passage? She'd heard of that, like learning to drive a hovercraft or a Tresslian's first hunt. Or making basbaa kalloonka with Grandmother...

Zahira's grip wavered for a moment. They'd never cook together again. Was this the multiverse's idea of atonement? Trudging through Stringspace with a casket? She shifted with Jo for what felt like hours, dutifully adjusting her frequency and passing the signal through to the lift. It weighed heavier with every phase shift. Yes, Grandmother had told her to run, but she didn't have to listen. She could've met her at the rendezvous point. Or picked her up at the apartment. Or...

Jo passed her the frequency with more force, pulling Zahira back to the present. The colors had morphed from grays to greens, suggesting they were getting close. Jo held their position, hovering just inside Stringspace. The greens rippled, nature scents wafted, and they... bounced?

Jo slid sideways, leading them into another smooth membrane. Their Stringspace selves ricocheted off like a ball and went floating sideways again. Jo tried another direction, and another, but the jello-like surfaces appeared to be everywhere. Zahira tried to finish the slide alone, but Jo held her back. Thank the deities the Slydwell hadn't worn off. A noodle-like strand passed through Zahira's arm, and she shuddered.

Jo moved methodically, like she was searching for something. Everything was shades of green, but the variances didn't line up with the surfaces. Tall, thick columns lined the edges. Trees perhaps? If the noodle-y bits were branches? The ground rose and sank between them. Maybe hills? A clearing? Jo seemed to think so. She slowed their movements, positioning them in the center of the grove of trees. Their feet hovered just above the ground. Zahira braced for a short drop.

The world shifted into focus, moist and vibrant, and dark blurs morphed into tree clusters. Dull light streamed through their branches. The air buzzed with life, and Zahira gasped for some to fill her lungs. It was damp, pungent... And she was falling.

Her feet broke through the surface, plunging into wetness. She thrust her head upward as swamp water threatened to envelop her. Damp crept into her clothes, and she lost hold of both Jo and the hitchhiker. Her boots sunk into spongy mud, finding enough purchase to keep her mouth above water. Jo thrashed beside her, muttering all sorts of expletives. No sign of Pekke or Nik, though something soppy dangled from the woman's arm.

"Get it off of me!" Jo shouted.

Zahira rushed to help. She shoved at the thing, realizing too late it was human. The head disappeared below water.

"Help!" came a gurgle. Long, gangly arms flailed at Jo for support.

The inventor gasped and lunged forward. Zahira joined the rescue, dragging a moppy brown head to the surface. The boy from the lab coughed and sputtered up a stream of swamp water. Mud dripped from his nose.

Zahira clapped him on the back, thanking the strings she hadn't ended the slide with a burst of nguvu for her tagalong. "Sorry, I thought you were Boliska."

He shook off her arm and reached down into the water. A backpack came up with a *plop*. "Is that what the massive thing was that smashed the door? A boliska?"

"I... No." Any more of an explanation died with one look at the lift. It hovered beside her, miraculously still holding its passenger, with only a single corner of silk stained by swamp water.

"This is the southeast tip of Norri's Lamba Province, I think." Jo moved to bite her muddy lip, but spat it out quickly. "I was hoping for someplace more familiar, but at least they shouldn't be able to track us here, not after we swapped strings."

'*Keep moving,*' the memory of Grandmother's voice whispered in Zahira's ear. '*The Boliska aren't the only things to fear.*' She wanted to argue that nothing could be worse than what they'd already been through, but there was no one to listen. She swatted at a cloud of gnats instead. "Which way to dry land?"

Jo pointed to a mossy mound bulging up a few dozen meters away. "If we can get a transcom signal, we might be able to call the coast guard or something."

Or something. Zahira guided the lift toward the mound, mud sucking at her every step. What was she supposed to do now? Let the authorities take Grandmother's body in for evidence? Find a cemetery near her latest safehouse? With all steel and concrete, it was hardly an adequate resting place.

"At least the water's warm," Jo offered.

"Yeah, could be worse." Zahira steered the lift around a floating log. "I could be dragging Grandmother through a cold swamp."

"Zahira, I..."

"You know what? It's fine." She swatted a cloud of bugs from her face and shoved the lift forward, sending ripples across the water. "We just need to get her out of this muck, okay?"

"Okay."

Zahira quickened her pace, and Jo lowered her head to follow. Hopefully the inventor wouldn't blame her for snapping, for feeling like the world had shattered around her. The mud thickened as they approached the mound. Water now lapped at Zahira's waist instead of her chest, but the silt below tugged at her shoes with every step, threatening to pull them off completely. Up ahead, the boy reached the mound and hauled his feet from the sludge, ripping them free with a moist *plomp* as the ground squished like a sponge beneath him. He kicked at the air, flinging chunks of mud from his shoes. Some splashed between Jo and Zahira.

"Almost there," Jo called, as if Zahira hadn't noticed. "Gods, I hope they don't have snakes."

Snakes? Zahira shivered and tried to wade faster, but her foot wedged under a branch and the lift careened forward without her.

Jo raced to catch it. "You okay?"

"Yeah." Zahira tried to tug herself free, but her ankle seemed to only sink lower. She bit back the urge to snap or cry. "I think I'm caught on something."

"Oh." The inventor's eyes darted between the island and Zahira. "Maybe I could get the lift to shore so you have your hands free?"

"Sure, why not?" Just leave her here with the bugs and snakes.

Jo sloshed her way to the shore, completely missing the sarcasm. "I'll see if I can find you a stick or something."

Zahira sighed and reached for her ankle, probing the mud while water lapped down her shirt. Something had hooked her heel. A root maybe? She pried off the rough loop and tugged again. This time, the mud loosened enough for movement, and her foot slid upward. She stumbled sideways with a splash. "Got it!"

But Jo didn't seem to hear. She was halfway up a tree, yanking on the thinnest branch she could find. The bark scraped and slid through her muddy palms, while the branch itself warped and flexed instead of snapping. She braced her foot against the tree and started sawing with one of the energy sphere frames.

"I said I'm free." Zahira swatted at a gnat, smearing mud across her arm. More tickled her ears and neck. "You can come down now."

"Almost... got it." The branch broke free and Jo turned in victory as her face grew pale. "Get out of there."

"What?" Zahira snuck a glance over her shoulder. A slimy, brown blob bubbled up from the water, only a few meters away. *What in the seven hells?* She stumbled back toward the mound, but the mud sucked at her feet, forcing her to fight for every step. Something gurgled from behind.

"Almost there." Jo crouched at the edge of the island, offering the branch. "I'll pull you up."

Zahira stretched forward, but a slimy limb wrapped around her leg and dragged her back. She kicked against its grip. Her other shoe dug in, and she reached for the branch. A little... further. Her fingers brushed across the tip.

The creature yanked—hard—and water rushed across her face and shoulders as she tumbled forward. It dragged her back, twisting her until she couldn't tell which way was up. A flailing arm found the surface, but the creature's grip held her tight. Nguvu pulsed with her panic. She let it flow, rushing wildly from her shin until the water boiled. Heat blazed around her calf, and the oozy grip retreated. Mud and filth slapped against the burn as her face found air.

Another arm shot forward. It wrapped her waist and rib cage, giving her bare moments to gasp for breath before the force sucked her down again. She tore at the tentacle's grip, her fingers slipping off the oozy scales. She'd have to use nguvu again. Small, concentrated bursts sparked from her fingertips, loosening the creature's grip and broiling her skin. She kicked back to the surface.

A branch smacked her nose. "Grab this!" called Jo's voice. She stood halfway down the mound, batting away tentacles as they reached for her legs.

Zahira caught the branch and wrenched it from Jo's hands. "The spheres! Get the energy spheres!" She turned to face the creature, searching for the bulk she'd first spotted. Something bubbled below the surface.

A tentacle snatched her leg as she stabbed at it, and her blow ricocheted off the water. She dug her back foot into the mud and tried again. This time, the branch made contact. A scraping, glancing blow. Still, the tentacle held tight, and another shot forward. Zahira knocked it away with a loud "smack." It whipped back, wrapping around the stick and yanking it from her hands. Bark grated against her palms. She lost her balance in the struggle and tumbled forward.

Murky water covered her face, but the tentacle released her foot. She kicked back to the surface. Something buzzed through the air, landing just past her shoulder. The energy sphere. The shock jolted through her shoulder blades and down her spine, sparks dancing around both her and the creature. The water crackled around them, and the tentacles went limp. Her muscles went numb as well, losing their ability to hold her upright.

Something surged toward her through the muck. Jo's arms slipped under her shoulders, heaving the slimy strands from her chest. Her face found air, but her lungs were too weak to gasp it. The edges of the world crept toward her, dragged her toward sleep.

Jo stumbled, and her face dipped again. Water cascaded over her mouth and nose, and the world faded into a blur of brown. Moments later, her head bobbed upward and slammed into shore.

Her thigh twitched back into feeling. Rolling to her stomach, she heaved out a stream of coughs and water. Silt lined her throat and her lungs burned. "What... the hell... was that?"

"A globson." The boy from the lab stood over them, eyes wide with interest. "I mean, technically it's a swamp globson, but same difference. You okay?"

"How in the world do you know that?" Jo handed Zahira clean leaves to wipe her face with. Her eyes were rimmed with concern.

"I saw it in Legends of Ulgor, Issue 186. Or was it 168?" He shrugged. "I forget."

"I guess I can take that off my bucket list." Zahira's muddy fingers fumbled to get her eyes free of silt. *"'Get attacked by a comic book monster.'* Check."

"And you defeated it!" The boy mimed Zahira swinging the stick. "You were like 'Pow!' then you were like 'Whack!' And then your friend threw the ball, and the globson was like 'Mzzzzzzzzzz.'" He shook himself and squirmed into a dramatic death on the moss.

"Yep, that's exactly what happened..."

He hopped back to his feet. "It was awesome! It took Yari and Ulgor practically forever to defeat theirs, and you had it in a matter of minutes. They tried fire, ice, swords... like a dozen different attacks before they figured out shock rays, but you guys knew it right away."

"So glad you found my near-death entertaining." Zahira draped her backpack over a limb and shuffled to the lift.

Grandmother's face was so pale. Splashes of swamp covered her once beautiful silks, and gnats swarmed her body and clothes. Her soul needed to be freed. She'd waited too long already. Ghaoist beliefs required a quick funeral, as close to death as possible. If that failed...

Zahira spun back to the boy. "That comic... It, umm, didn't say anything about globsons being eryti, did it?" Even as she said it, she cursed herself for the thought.

He shook his head. "What's eryti?"

"Demons. Soul snatchers."

He flinched back in horror. "You think that thing was a demon?"

"No. No, it was... It's only a superstition." Grandmother would have chided her for even suggesting it.

Jo looked up from her nav device. "What's superstition?"

"Spirits that eat the soul of the deceased. Ancient Yerins thought they'd come if you didn't perform the Death Rites fast enough. If you held too tight to your loss."

"You think the blob was coming for her soul?"

"No. Of course not." That'd be ridiculous. It was just that, well, most people thought hatari were a myth, and Zahira knew the truth of that. She spied a pair of trees at the edge of the mound and guided the lift toward it. It seemed as good a place as any.

Jo set down her stick and pulled her knees to her chest. "Do you, um... Would you like some help?"

She shook her head. The ritual had three parts, but it only required one person. Traditionally the person was a priestess, but Grandmother wasn't a Purist. Zahira maneuvered the lift around the trees and carefully lowered it to the ground, letting the branches fall back for a small curtain of privacy. She owed Grandmother so much more than this. The old woman could have had a life of ease, collecting patents and research grants while playing with the siblings and cousins Zahira had never met. A rich life. A full life. One that didn't involve digging out of tents buried by sandstorms, or drinking water cleaned only by sand and campfire kettles. Or bargaining with thugs for city-safe IDs.

Or dying alone on a cold steel table.

Breathing deep, she reached for the strings. Beckoning, pulsing. The first step of the Untying. She took hold of the stiffest one and imagined it wrapping Grandmother's body like a shield. Solid, to represent the strength of faith. The soft and fuzzy strings she draped over the body, representing the comfort of family. A lump of guilt caught in her chest as she took the third string. Erratic and wild, symbolizing the turmoil of life.

Despite all their planning, she hadn't been able to ferry Grandmother away. Hadn't used their nest egg for even a foam mattress pad to ease the woman's aching joints. It was too late now for any of their plans. For the two-bed studio on Vayin or the sight-seeing tour on Khlish. She chose a bubbly one next, for the joy Grandmother had brought to others. For the shadow puppets against cave rocks. For the hearty stews made with bargain meats. For the nights spent dreaming of a better life.

Nguvu hummed through Zahira's skin as she reached for the last string. Sharp and hot, it sliced through the others like a knife, cutting Grandmother's ties to the physical world. Her eyes cracked open. Grandmother's corpse remained, but somehow paler and more empty. There were few traces of the woman she'd once been. "Oh, Great Spirits," she mumbled. "Accept your daughter Evike into your arms, so that she might become one with the Ghao. Bless her eyes with enlightenment. May she..." Zahira choked on the words. Tears gathered in her eyes and caught in her throat. "May she live on within us—within me—and may she never be forgotten."

It all felt so final. Sadness thrust itself from her chest and down her cheeks. The last step was the return. To the earth, to sand, or to sea, depending on where the person had called home. Grandmother's body had already sunk halfway into the mud, the swamp staking its claim. Zahira wanted to pull her out, to hold her for just a little longer. She brushed a chunk of mud from Grandmother's cheek, then slowly mounded more on top of her as if tucking her in. *Your body is of earth, and to earth it shall belong.* Something soft touched her shoulder, warm and faint, like the ghost of a hug. She imagined Grandmother there, smiling, and her sobs softened.

"Zahira?" Jo whispered. "Are you okay?"

The sensation of being held spread down her arm and across her back, and her chest felt calmer as she wiped her nose. "It's done."

"So that's not part of the ritual?"

"Hmmm?" Zahira lifted her head and startled a soft something from her shoulder. A gray piece of fluff fluttered into the air, no longer than her pinkie. A pair of antennae trembled with agitation. "Oh."

A few beats of its wings and the moth-like creature settled back on her arm. More of them covered her sleeves. Dozens of tiny wings quivering against her skin, following the lines of nguvu.

Jo raised an eyebrow. "I take it that's not normal?"

"No. It's not." But their purrs were soft and warm, and Zahira felt no urge to shake them.

"They seem to be attracted to the nguvu. Are they feeding off it?"

"I don't know." She almost didn't care. This was the best she'd felt since the Boliska had taken Grandmother. "How's the kid?"

Before Jo could answer, the boy cut in. "The 'kid' is thirteen. I'm not some toddler that needs checked on." He sat criss-cross on the ground, assembling parts from his backpack. Three black pipes stuck out of the moss next to him, forming three corners of a two-meter square. Smaller pieces covered his lap and a gray box flashed red by his leg.

Zahira came out from the trees as Jo crouched down beside him. "What are you making?" the inventor asked. "It looks pretty cool."

"Nothin'."

"Doesn't look like nothing. I see a couple of directional sensors, signal lights, a power supply, and a, ummm..."

"Broad band transceiver array." The boy's eyes flashed, and a smile crept across his lips. "Gotta have that for trans-dimensional travel."

Zahira felt like that should mean something, but a fog had crept into her brain. It seemed Jo understood, as she jerked forward, checking the pieces in the boy's lap. "No way! Is this the Z3X model?"

He nodded. "Mom got it for my birthday."

"You hear that, Zahira? This kid got a sliding portal for his birthday!"

"That's nice." She watched Jo dive right into the assembly, but Zahira couldn't bring herself to care. Her head was too warm and fuzzy. She wandered to the other side of the moss, letting the excited technobabble fade behind her. Her head ached, as if stuffed with linen. A gray wing fluttered across her cheek, and she brushed it away. Startled, more lifted from her arms in unison. Her mind cleared with them. "Hey, Jo..."

"Yeah?" The inventor didn't look up from the sliding portal. The tubes and rods were assembled, with lights tracing a yellow circle on the ground.

The moths fluttered back down, but Zahira shook them off again. "Could I get a little help here?"

"In a minute." Jo's fingers danced across the keypad. "We're almost done calibrating the triangulation system."

"I don't think I can wait for the coast guard. These moths are messing with my head."

"Like freaking you out with their cuteness, or..."

"Like making it hard to think straight." She picked up her backpack and swung it at the now swarming insects. "It's like they're trying to drug me or something."

"Drug you?" Jo finally turned, watching Zahira struggle with the moths. She swatted at them with her equipment bag. "Shoo! Go away."

Zahira shook one off her elbow as another landed on her chest. "Do you think they'd follow us through a free slide?"

"Probably not, but do you really want to risk it?" She called over her shoulder. "Hey, kid! Mind if we borrow your portal?"

"Not right now," the boy said, pointing to the blinking transceiver. "Mom's already picked up the signal."

Mom? Picked up the signal? Shit. The circle was yellow, not blue. She and Jo exchanged glances, and Jo dove to reclaim her lift, but it was too late. The black rods dinged, sending half the moths scurrying about. They settled back almost immediately.

A lone figure slid into focus, a stout blond woman with a blaster in hand. "Move and I shoot."

Jo froze mid-reach for the lift, and Zahira slowly raised her hands. Her eyes searched the swamp for a way out or a distraction, but the moths refused to let her focus.

"It's okay, Mom. They're good guys." The boy started gathering all his wrenches and spare pieces into his backpack. "They helped get me out of the lab."

"The lab? I told you it wasn't safe to... You know what? Grounded. For two months. No console or comics."

"But mom..."

"No buts. You're lucky these two didn't traffic you to Frezin or sell you to Udolmian slavers."

The boy's backpack slid down as his shoulders slouched. "They're cool, Mom. Honest. They were there with Dr. Froum."

That seemed to have an opposite effect to the one the boy intended, as the blaster shot up to aim at their faces instead of their knees. "Is he safe? If you did anything to Pekke, I swear I'll—"

"Mom! He's fine!" The boy motioned for his mom to lower her weapon. "These guys can't be all bad. They saved me from a dinosaur."

"They what?"

The boy nodded, distracting her from Jo and Zahira's looks of surprise. He gave a brief explanation of their flight from the lab, with the boy serving a more active role, and making it seem like Zahira had pulled him out of the ceratopsid's path. "And oh, Mom, you should have seen the globson! It was huge, and slimy, and it wrapped one of its sticky tentacles around my waist." He raised his shoulders and sucked in like something tight was around his torso. It seemed so earnest that Zahira almost believed it had been the boy instead of her. "The short one, she took a tree branch and whack! Thwack! She started beating it up. And the other one, she pulled out a pulse grenade, and it was like ullllggggzzzzzzzz." He flopped onto the ground, shaking and reenacting the dramatic death.

"A globson, eh?" The boy's mother raised an eyebrow, checking Zahira and Jo over. "And a pulse grenade?"

"And weire moths, too," the boy added. "The short one's covered with them."

Zahira thought of shaking the things off, but the mother's finger was awfully close to the trigger. "Weire moths?"

"Yep. The insects feed off emotional energy. Mostly harmless, if you don't let them hang around too long. Least that's what it said in Issue 188." The boy picked his backpack up and threw it over his shoulder. "Anyway, I think that's enough to buy them a ride home. Don't you think, Mom? Since we have the portal right here?"

"Maybe." His mom looked to be doing some sort of math in her head, weighing her options. Hopefully she'd find that sending Zahira and Jo through first would make sense, since the sliding portal would get left behind anyway. She didn't want to think about what the woman might otherwise do to prevent them from following.

After several long minutes, the boy's mom finally nodded. She motioned him to the side, keeping herself and the blaster between them as she waved Jo and Zahira through.

Jo mumbled a thank you and finished folding up her lift. Even with the woman's permission, they cautiously approached the portal. The blaster barrel followed them the whole way.

"Tell Dr. Froum that Rafe and his mom say hi!" the boy called as Jo fumbled to set her nav device to the rendezvous point. "And make sure you don't take any of the moths with you!"

Zahira nodded, twitching away the insects as the inventor passed her the new frequency. She couldn't afford to let them cloud her thinking now, not when there was no Grandmother to guide her. Not when she had new plans to make.

CHAPTER TWENTY-FIVE

— · —

PRAVI

Within minutes of Munus' departure, the D.I.C. agents slapped together a work space for Pravi. Although the scraping noises coming from the tent had sounded promising, their efforts produced little more than a small folding table and a monitor shoved into a corner so Jandra's desk had a clear view to Pravi's screen. A trip-hazard tangle of wires trailed to the shared computer bank, and uneven pavers meant the setup tipped a finger's width to either side. The login credentials worked on the first try, though, which was more than enough for Pravi to consider it a win. She almost didn't mind dragging a spare desk chair from the house, or that it took nearly a quarter hour to wrangle the wires out of the wheels' path. She popped open a large umbrella for privacy and slid a book titled "How to Deal with Idiots" under the wobbly table leg.

Jandra humphed from her desk, but Pravi ignored her. Munus' secretary had sent over a collection of files relating to the nguvu events—files the field agent had no claim to. The umbrella was staying. She wedged its handle under the bottom of the monitor and got to work. Most of the location data matched her personal notes, but now she had access to surveillance videos and scanner reports. Numbers and graphs filled her screen. The first task involved separating the random events from those within Jo's golden nguvu cloud.

She was halfway through when someone tapped on her umbrella. A snarky reply rose to mind, but she swallowed it when she spotted the sleek black shoes standing beside her.

"Miss Resero?" came Munus' voice. "Do you have any plans for this afternoon? A beach picnic, perhaps?"

Pravi lifted the edge of the umbrella, feeling a bit embarrassed at her setup, although it had been a perfectly reasonable solution. "Just looking through the data you sent over. Why?"

She could have been imagining things, but the corners of his lips seemed to curl into the faintest of grins. "There's been another event. It's quite unique."

"Unique how?"

He shrugged via a subtle lift of his eyebrows. "Perhaps you'd like to check it out?"

"Now?"

"Are you taking my charge?" Jandra rose from her desk as if considering whether to attempt to block him.

Munus slid his hands into his pockets. "No, I'm taking my consultant. That is, if she's interested."

Something in Pravi's gut told her this might be a test, that Munus had ulterior motives for inviting her along. But she never ran from a challenge, and other than her failed escape attempt, she hadn't had a change of scenery in weeks. She signed out of her workstation and folded up the umbrella.

When she finished, she found Jandra glaring at the back of Munus' head. If Pravi hadn't known better, she might have thought he'd winked at the agent as he turned to leave. She hastened to follow. Whether or not he had winked, Munus was halfway to the rear tent flap. She caught up with him right as he reached it, and he held it open for her as if she'd been right behind him all along.

"Has the data sparked any revelations?" he asked.

"Not yet. I'm still comparing it to my notes." Pravi paused mid-step. The area behind the flap was barely a meter and a half square, with wires and conduit running up the walls and across the ceiling. Under her feet, she noticed a faintly circular chalk outline. This was why she hadn't seen anyone coming or going lately. They'd moved the circle inside.

Munus squeezed past her, letting the flap close behind them. A single bare bulb clipped to one of the support poles became the only source of light. "Preliminary reports suggest this is either the breakthrough we need or yet another confounding variable. Your goal will be figuring out which."

As he spun the dials of his nav, the room seemed to shrink. For a moment, she flashed back in time to missions with her uncle, standing in the secret sliding closet in the ready room while Xander locked in the coordinates for a reconnaissance mission. He would be rattling on about the suspected gizmo while she braced herself for the oppressing silence of the oncoming slide. The air smelled of old paper and the oil stains on Xander's coat.

Munus offered Pravi a bottle lid, pulling her from her reverie. The white plastic held two pink pills. "It'll be three jumps when you're ready."

Pravi nodded. On the surface, working with Munus didn't seem much different from what she'd had before. Combing through mounds of data with the occasional field visit. A partner who liked to use missions as some kind of test, whether on observation or strategy. The D.I.C. director appeared to be offering her the chance to have that life back. But would it last once they found the prototype?

She tossed back the pills, focusing on the sweet, citrus-y taste as they traveled down her throat. She barely noticed Munus take her hand until the sensation swiftly disappeared. Total blackness could hardly explain what surrounded Pravi next. What surrounded her every time she slid. The world had nothing but her thoughts. No lights. No sounds. No scents. Not even the sound of her lungs or heartbeat, nor the feeling of her tongue on the roof of her mouth. She struggled to rein in the stampede of panicked thoughts, noticing every lost sensation. No pressure on her skin from her clothes. No sweet taste from the SlydWell. No reassuring knife bulge at her ankle.

Focus! she screamed as nerves reported loss after loss. She was dead, they assured her. Somehow conscious, but definitely dead. They panicked again moments later when all the sensations came rushing back and Pravi fell to her knees. They'd arrived in a room much like the one they'd just left, but with solid walls instead of canvas. Part of the D.I.C.'s internal network.

Munus held her hand tight. "Bumpy ride?" he asked. His voice had a hint of teasing, but his eyes held concern.

"No more than usual." She shook out her shoulders and rose to her feet. Her uncle would have chided her for losing her composure like that. "Ready when you are."

She closed her eyes and started counting before the next slide started, letting the numbers consume her thoughts. It'd been years since she'd let her focus slip. Her longest count had been 1,267, taken when her uncle had tried a particularly tricky free slide. She was just shy of five hundred when she and Munus reached their final destination.

When her senses returned, she found herself in a tall entry area with corrugated walls. Computer chip parts and metal fragments littered the concrete floor around her, absent only in the neatly swept circle around her feet. Larger pieces trailed further down the hall, joined by D.I.C. agents snapping pictures and filling evidence bags. Munus gestured for her to lead the way.

"I take it the nguvu surge let something big out?" Pravi started toward the area with the most debris, tiptoeing through the occasional clear spot. Long dents streaked the walls to either side. "Either it took a few laps, or there was more than one." From the smooshed bits here and there, she guessed it was heavy and running on four feet.

"Organic or inorganic?" A question Munus already knew the answer to.

Pravi squatted by the wreckage, eager to redeem herself after her weakness in the slide. "The smashed pieces aren't quite flat, suggesting padded feet. Erratic steps on the turn... My guess would be organic, with a hide thick enough to not bleed all over the jagged metal."

A flash of something caught her eye. A plate of copper, half bright and the other half a dusty green sheen. A quick search found a handful of grounding wires with similar contrasting lines. "You guys got a tech leak, Munus?" Pravi asked, holding up the copper plate. "Theba flash lines. Someone came through to remove the resonance traces."

The Theba Project had been one of the last her uncle helped the D.I.C. track down. The device gave a quick flash of radiation that cleared exposed surfaces. Its effect on copper was the easiest trace to spot, but you needed clean copper to compare it to, usually found in the shadows of the flash. Rather than look at her copper plate, Munus bent down to inspect a patch of debris Pravi hadn't touched yet. It didn't take long for him to find a few copper pieces of his own.

"I'll have Holdings look into it." He glanced at his agents as he inspected a small copper heat sink, a thoughtful look that told Pravi no one else had noticed the flash's shadows. "The creature was a juvenile ghabarosaurus, a type of ceratopsid from Yerin. It injured two of our people before they got it subdued."

A giant lizard from Yerin. No wonder Munus had brought her in. "And the nguvu traces?"

"Only faint ones. One of our contractors tipped us off."

And that's why Munus had said it was either a lucky break or a wild tangent. Pravi turned her attention back to the pattern of debris. The creature had been panicked, that much was sure, though here and there equipment piles had been merely toppled rather than crushed. Past a junction with another hallway, the amount of trampled debris increased, as did the number of footprints. She followed a streak of dented wall, nodding to the D.I.C. agents as she passed.

A dozen meters on, the dents turned off the main strip, leaving the agents and the tattered equipment shells behind. "Best we can tell, the thing circled a few times before stopping to play with a water fountain. Its cage is in the room up ahead." Munus gestured to an open room at the end of the hallway. It was small for a lab, no bigger than Pravi's kitchen, and half of it was cordoned off with a row of iron bars.

"Any clue what set it into a panic?" Just getting free couldn't have been enough, as none of the dented walls led away from that room. A closer look at the room didn't help, either. It held only a water dispenser and a large pile of artificial bedding.

"Working theory is one of the debris piles toppled and set it off, but that doesn't explain the Theba marks."

Or why an informant thought a rogue dinosaur might be related to the case. Pravi went back to tracing the panicked trail. It could be that the dinosaur had stumbled into something, some other experiment going on in the lab. But the fact it originated from Yerin seemed too much of a coincidence. Other than that, the case appeared simple. A smuggled dinosaur had gotten loose, and the smugglers cut their losses and covered their tracks, leaving their pet to trample old lab equipment and scatter the pieces all over the hall. But her gut said there had to be more to it.

She froze mid-step and backtracked to the dinosaur's room. The cage door hung open, leading to the hay-filled bedding area. A *neat* hay-filled bedding area. Not a single piece had crossed the threshold separating the cage from the rest of the room.

"It wasn't kept here," she said, more to herself than to Munus. It would explain the door's lack of dents or signs of impact. A thorough search found a dented door frame a few dozen meters away. "This one. I think it came from this one."

Munus called over one of his agents to enter the master keycode. Theba radiation and enough foresight to set up a fake lab for cover up. This had to be the breakthrough she needed.

Anticipation scurried through Pravi's veins as the agent dealt with the lock. As long as the ceratopsid had indeed come from this lab, Munus would have to see that she was worth bringing to field visits. That she had earned the right to be there when they found her uncle's prototype.

A tiny beep joined the click of the door lock, and Pravi's body moved solely from instinct, shoving Munus and the agent out of the way as the floor shook and flames rolled through the doorway. A planted explosive. Pravi spun round and caught sight of spilled cargo bins and hissing fire sprinklers as a blast door slid over the opening, locking all the evidence in with the flames.

Alarms echoed down the hall, and agents sprinted through the billowing gray clouds, many of them with blasters drawn. The smell of smoke and melted plastic filled her lungs. The first wave took defensive positions while a pair broke off to check on their fallen comrades.

Pravi suspected they'd find no one to fight or arrest. The lab's owners must have rigged the door before they fled, in case the D.I.C. had seen through the decoy dinosaur cage.

"Bring in a hazard crew," Munus ordered, brushing ash off his pants. The only signs of disappointment were the stiffness in his hands and the sharpness of his voice. "I want as much of the evidence preserved as possible." He set to work arranging teams. The longer it took to clear, the more time the suspects had to erase the rest of their trail.

Pravi cursed herself for being overconfident. Of course the Theba flashes and decoy room would be only part of their precautions. She forced herself to focus. What all had she seen in that moment before the door shut? A tipped over crate and something oval. An egg perhaps? There'd been a sheen of something metal in the packing material beside it.

"Miss Resero?" Munus called, dismissing the latest round of agents. "Are you thinking what I'm thinking?"

"Exotic animal smuggling ring. This could be one of their holding cells while they wait for payment from a buyer."

He nodded. "They must have insider help to get the lizards off Yerin. I've heard the creatures can't reproduce anywhere else."

Pravi's mind went to the sheen of metal in the crate. "Are we sure about that? The missing piece has always been the nguvu pools where they lay their eggs."

A brief glance at her eyes told her Munus understood everything that implied. If the smugglers had her uncle's prototype, they wouldn't need the natural pools. It might also explain the discrepancy between the events and Jo's golden nguvu clouds. Some could be part of the collection process, while the others were incidents during delivery.

He gestured in the direction of the exit circles. "I think it's time to get you back to your workstation to have another look at that data."

CHAPTER TWENTY-SIX

—·—

Jo

J o needed a shower. Badly. Dry mud encrusted every inch of her skin, and as she turned to search for signs of Nik and Pekke, it cracked and pulled. Zahira had it just as bad, with clumps of swamp stuck at intervals from her neck to her pant legs. Hopefully their friends would show up soon. Their corner of the sliding station had already begun to smell like dried-out slugs.

To make it worse, Pekke's choice of rendezvous point had turned out to be some sort of spa resort. Other than the flurries of mud flakes that had gathered around them, the lobby was a pristine oasis. Textured mosaics flowed across the floor into artificial salt pools on either side of the sliding circles, shining bright around the swamp-encrusted lift at her feet. Soft ocean sounds hushed through hidden speakers, punctuated by occasional spritzes of briny perfume.

How long had it been now? Her watch said twenty minutes, but it felt like ages since the sour-faced attendant had sold them warm towels. Tides of customers had come and gone, usually with a curious glance at the two of them huddled in the corner. The towels on their torsos and hair were barely enough camouflage to prevent questions.

"I think we must have missed them," Jo whispered, not for the first time. By her estimate, their free slide from the lab had taken half an hour. Add in the time spent fighting the globson and being held at blaster point by the boy's mom, it seemed likely Nik and Pekke had given up waiting and moved to Plan B. She hoped that once her transcom dried out, it would buzz with dozens of missed texts. She didn't want to think of the alternative—that Nik and Pekke weren't coming because they couldn't.

Zahira gave a nod and a shiver. She hadn't said much since the swamp, and Jo couldn't be sure whether she was watching the circles for Pekke or if her mind was somewhere else. Tears had carved tiny streams in the mud on the hatari's cheeks, running dry before Jo had worked up the courage to offer her work rag as a handkerchief.

She rolled the hem of her towel between her fingers. "I think we should try heading to my place, maybe clean up and regroup." Use the cryptoscope if they needed to. "My shower's not very big, but the drain has dealt with worse than mud."

Another silent nod from her companion.

Jo's eyes fell to the floor. Stars, why did she have to be so awkward, so utterly incapable of knowing the right thing to say? "You're welcome to stay the night, too, you know. Or however long you need."

A rumbling wave rose from the speakers, crashing into rocks on a distant shore. Zahira's arms loosened from where they hugged her shoulders. "A shower does sound nice."

Lines of nguvu flickered weakly on her skin, barely noticeable under the layer of dried swamp. It reminded Jo of the dying embers of a fire. She picked up the empty lift and pulled up her nav dials before her companion could change her mind and fall back into her thoughts.

"We weren't always hated, you know," Zahira said as she joined Jo in the sliding circle, her voice barely over a whisper. "There's some artwork in a temple in Dunbi that implies some priestesses were hatari."

Jo's hand paused over the dials. How should she respond to that? The statement held too much weight. All she could think of was to ask Zahira, "Ready?"

The hatari answered by taking her hand and giving it a tight squeeze. Her palm felt cold and dry against Jo's. Even as the soft buzz of the string enveloped them, she wished her mind could think of something comforting, something that put into words everything she wished to say. But her mind came up as empty as the station where they landed.

It was evening in her part of Domun. Late enough that late-night partiers had already left for the entertainment districts on distant worlds. Jo and Zahira slid into a barren station, their disheveled appearance attracting the attention of a lone security guard and no one else.

Jo led her companion across the worn gray tile toward the front door. "Hasn't anyone tried to get hatari recognized? Officially, I mean." The Interworld Council was supposed to prevent abuses like this. When governments tried to treat people as, well, less than people.

"Someone tried once, I think. It doesn't take much to get a preliminary hearing." Zahira's voice seemed stronger now, whether from the distraction or privacy, Jo didn't know. She let go of Jo's hand and grabbed her backpack straps. "No hatari showed, of course. That would have required getting off the planet first."

Jo caught herself before the words 'You could do it now' left her mouth. That would be asking too much. Zahira didn't like getting scanned, much less whatever the council would require for proof.

Zahira reached to open the door, but then stopped. "Do you think they took them off the planet?"

"Who?"

"The other hatari. The ones the Boliska kidnapped."

Jo's mind went back to the pictures on Pekke's transcom. The girl with the bright green eyes. The man with the arched nose and scruffy chin. The blond woman had said they prefer to keep them alive. "I mean, it's possible. There's a way to check, but it could take a while."

"How?"

Jo swallowed. It was only a theory, really. "I don't want to get your hopes up, but I've been thinking about your coils and, you know, the way they change the pattern of the nguvu as they store it. What if hatari do the same thing? What if your body also shifts the pattern of nguvu, just in a different way?"

Zahira turned with a thoughtful look and opened the door by leaning her back against it. The air outside hummed with the familiar buzz of hovercraft blades. They exited to a polyglass walkway, twenty-odd stories up depending on which building you were headed to. Twen-

ty-six for Jo's apartment building a few blocks east. A handful of three-
and four-fanned hovercars zoomed high above them and in layers of
traffic below. To either side, skyscrapers rose like sharpened spears,
using the fading sunlight to slash at them with shadows. "So if we can
figure out how the nguvu shifts, we can track the others with your
crypto-thingy?"

"That's the idea, yes." It might take a decent amount of work on Jo's
part, as she'd be trying to guess what the shift was by trial and error.
But maybe it'd be worth it in the end. Maybe a few dozen dots on the
cryptoscope could help Zahira not feel so alone.

The hatari's arm shot out, blocking her path. "Let's do it, then."

"What?"

"Scan me. Let's see if I'm altering the pattern."

"I... Are you sure?" Her companion had been strongly against getting
scanned before, and even now, the nguvu swirled wildly across her
face and hands. "We could try figuring it out without one first. It might
take a while, but there are other options."

Zahira took a deep breath, her other hand gripped tight around her
backpack strap. "I'm sure." She closed her eyes tight as if braced against
a shot or a blood draw.

Jo reached for her scanner, but stopped. Burning curiosity aside, she
didn't want to take advantage of her companion's emotional state. "It'll
have to wait until we get back to my place. I want to make sure the
scanner's all dried out first." The lie felt awkward on her tongue, but
Zahira didn't seem to notice. It made sense that the transcoms being
waterlogged meant the scanner would be, too. The truth was, Jo had
spent a lot more on her scanner, and a few prior incidents had made
waterproofing mandatory.

Zahira lowered her arm and started back in the direction of Jo's
apartment. "As soon as it's dry, then."

"And maybe after we run a scan for Nik and Pekke," Jo added, to buy
Zahira more time to change her mind. "Once we're sure that they're
safe."

"Yes, of course. After we find Nik and Pekke."

They passed the next few blocks in silence, surrounded by the shadows of twilight and the soft hum of nearby hovercraft. It wasn't the same as the silence back at the rendezvous point, though. Not as... heavy? Zahira didn't seem to fold in on herself, like the gravity of her loss wasn't dragging her inward with every step.

Jo could only imagine what it had been like for her on Yerin. Never being able to relax, never being able to leave home without worrying about her nguvu and the Boliska. Had she been able to go to school? Go to birthday parties? The library? As much as Jo hated talking to strangers, she'd never had to worry they'd cart her off for experiments.

The walkway branched, and they took the turn leading to her stone-colored apartment building and its broad skirt of artificial turf. Decades of rain and sun had left the plastic grass yellowed and brittle. As for the facade, the building's anti-graffiti field was failing, and faint scribbles hovered against the gray. Not much of a home, but she'd never had to worry about it getting besieged by green-vested brutes.

She darted forward to hold open the sun-bleached door. Inside, a pair of dusty fake ferns flanked the entrance, failing to pull the staleness from the air. The atrium's carpet looked faded under the tarnished chandelier, and a series of snags pointed the way down the hall. This level had once been a fashionable strip mall, but plasterboard had long replaced the windowed store fronts. To either side ran an uneven line of gray bricks, marking out the original sills.

"Jo!" Nik shouted from the end of the hall. Beside him, Pekke scrambled to hide some metal rods in his sleeve. It wasn't hard to guess what they'd been doing with how quick he'd gone from kneeling by the keypad to standing, and how fast his frantic look had turned to a relieved smile.

Nik ran up to meet them halfway, his face falling as soon as he noticed the mud.

"No injuries for me," Jo said before he could ask. "Zahira might need some burn balm, though."

Her companion dropped the edge of her towel to hide the red welt on her thigh from the fight with the globson. "It's nothing major. Just need to get it cleaned and bandaged."

Nik frowned and turned back to Jo, his face looking like he couldn't decide whether to hug her or lecture her.

"We assumed the worst when you didn't answer your coms," Pekke interrupted. He pocketed the lockpicks he'd dropped in his attempt to hide them. "Glad to see you guys aren't fish food, but perhaps we should continue the conversation inside?"

"Inside and cleaned off," Jo agreed. She bumped Nik's arm with an unsoiled corner of her towel. "Sorry to have worried you."

He nodded and swallowed back whatever he'd been planning to say. "I'll grab some rice for the transcoms."

As soon as she got the door open, they split off in slow motion—Nik to dry out Jo and Zahira's transcoms and make tea, Pekke to return the equipment he borrowed, and Jo to get Zahira clean clothes and washcloths for the shower. The two men occasionally eyed the empty lift, but neither dared ask about it.

Zahira broke the silence instead. "We could use one of the other scanners, can't we?" she whispered. "Since the ones Nik and Pekke had didn't get wet?"

"What for—Oh." Jo had nearly forgotten about the scan in her relief at seeing Nik. "Are you sure you want to do this now?"

"Yes." Her head bobbed when she said it, as if to ward off the hint of uncertainty in her voice. "I'm sure."

"Sure about what?" Pekke dropped his hand from where he'd been about to stuff Jo's set of energy probes between a metimur and a stack of motors. "Is something wrong?"

Jo shook her head and snatched up one of the smaller scanners. "Just checking something for Zahira."

"She thinks we can find other hatari. Other people like me."

The sound of the teakettle falling into the sink shouted *Are you out of your mind?* louder than Nik ever could, but Jo scrolled through the settings anyway. "Are you ready?"

"Ready."

Curves and numbers filled Jo's screen, tracing out various parts of her resonance signature. It didn't take long to narrow down the band that resembled nguvu. "I'll have to run this through the cryptoscope to be sure, but it looks promising."

"Maybe we should talk about this first?" Nik cut in. "I mean, we only just got back from nearly getting ourselves killed."

He looked to Pekke for support, but the physicist just shrugged and looked to Jo.

"It's just a scan, Nik. It's not going to hurt anyone." Couldn't he see how much it meant to Zahira? How determined she was to see if the Boliska had left any other survivors? Jo strode across the room and entered the data into the cryptoscope. "It's not like we're going to go tracking them down. We already know how disastrous that could be, for both them and us."

Nik started to protest, but Jo's transcom started buzzing frantically from the bowl of rice. She set the cryptoscope to scan and hustled over. It buzzed three more times before she could reach it. The caller ID read: 'Pravi Resero.'

CHAPTER TWENTY-SEVEN

— • —

ZAHIRA

Grandmother always said to have a plan, but as the cryptoscope revved up, Zahira knew she'd broken that rule in the worst way. Following an emotional whim. Jumping into motion without weighing her options. She could hear Grandmother chastising her for not considering the potential consequences or how to deal with them.

Nik and Pekke were right. She was rushing out of the desert and into the swamp. What did she expect from the scan? A map to the Boliska's hideout? A suicide mission? Proof that other hatari had escaped? Zahira decided to dodge her better judgment with a trip to the shower, only to find Jo frozen in front of the counter, her transcom still buzzing in her hand.

"Something wrong?" she asked as Nik peered over the inventor's shoulder. It was just a transcom call, but Jo's face looked pale even under the layer of dried swamp.

Nik took the transcom carefully from her hands, hit the answer button and put it on speaker. Jo managed a weak "Hello?"

"Hi, this is going to sound kind of crazy, so let's just dive into it, shall we?" The woman's voice had a sort of rushed politeness to it, like she didn't want to scare Jo off, but wasn't used to being anything but brisk. *"I'm Pravi Resero, and I'm the one you've been messaging about my uncle's prototype."*

The inventor's whole body sank half an inch toward the floor, like she wanted to faint, but invisible straps held her up. If Jo had been holding the phone, she would have dropped it. Zahira scrambled through her memories for why the name Resero sounded familiar.

That man, the one whose picture Jo had showed her when they first met. The whole reason she'd been on Zahira's trail in the first place.

"I know this comes as a surprise, but I hope you understand my need for secrecy. With your revelations about the nguvu cloud, it's apparent the situation is even worse than I imagined." Something about the Resero woman's words carried a hint of insincerity, though that could have been the way they were translated. *"So first, I wanted to thank you for all your help. The data you sent me has been instrumental to my progress."*

Zahira's chest tightened. The data she'd sent? How much had Jo told her? Did she know about the incident on Yerin? About Zahira? Her mind went instantly to the scanner. Would Jo give her the hatari frequency?

"I... I'm glad it's been useful." Jo gave Nik a panicked look, like an actor who'd misplaced their script. "As soon as we saw the accumulation, we knew it had to be stopped."

And what was Jo willing to do to stop it? Give the Resero woman more data? Zahira's data? She casually edged over to the cryptoscope's control tower where Jo had left the scanner, trying to make like she was trying to distract herself from eavesdropping.

"And you made the right call. I can't imagine the devastation the cloud could cause if it's allowed to grow." A quiet thumping came through the transcom, as the Resero woman drummed her fingers on something wooden. *"I was wondering... Do you have any more data from the strikes? Any other leads we should follow?"*

Zahira cleared the last half-meter to the scanner.

Jo swallowed and glanced over to where Zahira was standing. "Umm, not at the moment. But I can let you know if that changes."

It'd be so easy to blast away the evidence right then and there. To take away the risk before Jo could be tricked or tempted into betraying her. But as her eyes found the scanner screen and started tracing the waves of frequencies and highlighted segments, Zahira knew she couldn't give it up. Couldn't fully erase her desire for connection.

"Well, that's disappointing." The air of politeness started fading from the call. *"I had hoped you took some scans on Trilo's moon lab."*

The air in Jo's apartment thickened, and they all exchanged glances. *"The fellowship is still yours, even without more data. I assume you've heard of it?"*

"I... uh... fellowship?" *How does she know about the moon base?* Jo mouthed to Pekke.

Zahira used their moment of distraction to send herself the scanner data and wipe any trace of her frequency. The Resero woman knew too much already.

"The announcement must have gotten buried in other tech news. Long story short, some cocky vlogger was using the prototype's theft for views, so I offered an award for anyone who proved he was full of gaur manure."

Jo swallowed. "You mean the Rygal fellowship?"

Zahira had no idea what they were talking about, but from the look on the inventor's face, it clearly was big and important and amounted to either a bribe or a guilt trip.

"That's the one. I think the nguvu cloud makes it strikingly clear that this is more than a leisurely scavenger hunt. It could hit a hoverbus of children. A hospital. A power plant."

Guilt trip it was then. Zahira willed the cryptoscope to finish its scan so she could safeguard that data as well.

"Point is, I'm aiming to stop it, and any scans you have would help."

Jo shot a worried glance in Zahira's direction. "I'm sorry, but I—"

"If you're worried about your fugitive friend, I have no interest in sending her back to Yerin." The Resero woman sighed through the transcom. *"I can even mark every security video with her in it as classified if that makes you feel better."*

Bribery, Grandmother's voice whispered, but Zahira felt her resolve stagger. What did the woman want that was worth all she was offering? The fellowship for Jo, covering up evidence of Zahira's presence...

Jo grabbed the edge of the countertop and leaned back. "Is the lab data really that important?"

"It's important enough that I agreed to work with the D.I.C." The Resero woman paused to let it sink in. *"I think you know how my uncle and I feel about them."*

Zahira glanced at the cryptoscope's control tower. Barely over half complete. It seemed likely Jo would give in before it finished running.

"What about the Boliska?" Nik cut in, his voice sounding as skeptical as Zahira felt. "If you've joined forces with the D.I.C., you should have their interrogations to work from."

"Boliska? Interrogations?" Her confusion sounded sincere. *"I don't know who you ran into, but when the D.I.C. got there, there was no one."*

No one? Nik hit the mute button, and they all turned to Pekke, who furiously texted on his trancom. A brief pause and his face fell. "She's telling the truth."

No. Zahira clenched her fist hard enough for her nails to dig into her palms. That couldn't be. Surely, the ceratopsid would have plowed through and destroyed the sliding room. If they'd gotten away... If the D.I.C. had no way of tracking them...

"It's up to you," Jo said firmly. Though she still gripped the edge of the countertop, her eyes focused on Zahira. "I'm not putting you at risk without your permission."

A million thoughts raced through her head. Grandmother's murderers sliding free. Every lecture she'd been given about prioritizing safety over revenge. The hatari who were presumably still in the Boliska's hands... "I need some time to think about it." She felt herself nodding, though, and the words *'Yes, certainly'* hovered on the tip of her tongue.

Jo nodded back and unmuted her phone. "We'll see if there's any more data from the lab we can pass on. Descriptions of the Boliska, at the very least."

"Any help would be wonderful. I'll be in touch about the fellowship."

The Resero woman ended the call, leaving the whoosh of the cryptoscope's arms as the only sound. Nik and Pekke occasionally glanced to Zahira, but neither of them said anything. What could they say? Sorry the trip to the lab was an utter failure and the bad guys got away? Empty promises that the D.I.C. could catch them without the scanner data? She felt more lost than when the hatari scan had started. At least then she had some idea of a plan of action, even if it was just letting the results guide her next move. She watched the arms spin down, with one irrational part of her still hoping it held the answer.

A hologram flashed into existence above the arms, portraying a familiar array of planets. Tiny green dots speckled Yerin and a few more hid among the outer planets, but there, right in the center of the map, burned a cluster tight enough and bright enough to shine like a miniature star. And it lay right in the center of Jo's golden cloud.

CHAPTER TWENTY-EIGHT

— • —

NIK

P ekke's eyes found him as soon as the cryptoscope's arms settled to the ground. The physicist had said Jo wouldn't be able to let go of her invention. That she wouldn't be able to say no to requests for help. The glowing spots of the scan results were all the test he needed. What she did now would either prove Pekke wrong or lead her straight into danger.

She should have been focused on the fellowship. It was all they'd ever talked about wanting: an actual lab and research grants. No more freelance repair work to afford secondhand parts. If Nik managed to sell a few papers analyzing the nguvu cloud, he could join her. It'd be just the two of them—plus the numbers, of course, and the occasional 'research' trip that doubled as a vacation. But somehow all this talk of conspiracies and potential disasters had shoved that aside. Had convinced his friend she needed to save the world.

His heart pulsed an irregular rhythm in his chest. He had hoped he'd have more time to talk her back down to earth, but Jo had already squeezed past Zahira to the console tower. Her fingers stuttered across the keyboard, their quick typing punctuated by the mashing of the backspace key. She had to have noticed what he and Pekke had—that the hatari cluster appeared to line up with the accumulating nguvu. A few bated moments and the golden cloud blinked into existence, confirming their suspicions and Nik's fears.

"Wish I could say I'm surprised." Pekke took a deep breath and slid his hands into his pockets. "At least I'll be able to tell Zave I told him so."

"But how?" Jo's voice was barely over a whisper. If she'd considered taking the fellowship, the thought was now leagues from her mind.

"I suspect the Boliska started collecting nguvu to breed their expensive little pets." Pekke cleared the distance between the counter and the projection in two strides. "This natural swirl around Yerin is the only reason the planet has viable eggs. Without their own supply, the smugglers had a problem. Yes, they could bribe some officials to look the other way, but they were still limited to a few hatchlings here and there. If too many disappeared, someone would notice."

"But with how volatile nguvu can get, a breeding program hardly seems worth the risk." Nik tried to meet Jo's eyes. He had to bring her back to reality. What were the two of them supposed to do against a smuggling ring?

Pekke smirked. "Yerin charges ten thousand monettes just to look at one. How much do you think the black market would pay for a partial hide? A fully-mounted hunting trophy? Better yet, a living, breathing spinosaur? Collectors were probably snapping up as much as the smugglers could supply and clamoring for more."

Zahira gave a worried glance at the glowing green cluster at the center of the clouds. "So the hatari..."

Pekke nodded. "Not sure how well it works, but I can see them wondering what would happen if they had a hatari or two curled up with some eggs. It might not be very efficient, and possibly dangerous if they need the hatari conscious, but how else are they going to provide nguvu off-world?"

Jo's eyes jumped past Nik to the projection. "Unless they found a device that could store it."

"Bingo." Pekke lifted a finger to stroke his chin like a smug detective in a hologram novel. "I'd bet my best lab that they have the Resero project."

And Nik would bet his left arm that their base would be a thousand times more secure than the moon lab they'd barely escaped from. He couldn't let the others talk Jo into raiding it. He put the kettle on, hoping tea might calm Jo even if the action of making it failed to calm him. "Smugglers, nguvu clusters, and government bribes? Sure sounds like a job for the D.I.C." He tried to meet Jo's eyes again, but she looked away.

Pekke helped himself to a clean mug. "That would indeed be the safe plan. I'm not a fan of the Department myself, but it could be called for here."

The situation certainly didn't call for people whose prior biggest adventure involved touring a hovercraft factory. Before Nik could push his point home, Zahira stepped forward to put herself between Pekke and the glowing green dots. "And what about the hatari? We don't know that these are all captives. As far as we know, the cluster is just as likely to be a peaceful commune as the Boliska base."

"Is it though?" Pekke motioned over her shoulder. "I can see the individual dots being escapees, but the cluster? No fuzzy green lines leading on or off. Not even little trails suggesting movement around on the planet. That's a little suspicious, don't you think? And even if wasn't, their overlap with the nguvu cloud can't be a coincidence."

He offered her a mug, but she pushed it away. "They could be protecting themselves."

"By gathering enough nguvu to short circuit a city?"

"Would you blame them?" Jo looked up from the console to meet Pekke's eyes. "They've been persecuted, denied basic human rights, and possibly enslaved. You've seen how the Boliska have no issues kidnapping and killing to get what they want."

Pekke's voice went sharp and low. "I've seen more than you could ever know." He met Jo's defiant glare until she looked away. "My point isn't whether the hatari would be justified in using a nguvu net for defense, but whether it makes any sense. And it doesn't."

Nik saw his chance to further weaken Jo's resistance. "If Zahari's right and we do nothing, the hatari can keep going about their daily lives in peace. All well and good. But what if she's wrong? What if we don't tell the D.I.C. what we know and the Boliska keep growing their battery of captives?"

He strolled over to put his hand under the hovering image of Yerin.

"Hundreds of potential victims. And as bright as the planet is with nguvu, it's nothing compared to the cloud growing around that cluster. We already have systems failing randomly thanks to the buildup. Imagine if they had a dozen more hatari? Hell, even one or two might be enough to nudge these few pockets into striking a planet."

Pekke sipped his tea and nodded in agreement. "We've been extremely lucky so far—only a few burns and broken limbs from over three dozen strikes—but one unfortunate hit could be fatal."

In spite of all the reasoning, Jo's hands and jaw remained clenched, mirroring Zahira's posture. Nik would have to convince the hatari if he wanted to convince her. He'd prefer half an hour to work up a slideshow and supporting note cards, but it looked like he'd have to wing it. "I'm not saying we have to give the D.I.C. all of this data," he said, taking a step back from the projection. "Or any of it, really. We simply give them the location of the cluster and say there might be hostages involved. Or that the Boliska are trafficking people for lab experiments. That way, they know to treat the captive hatari as trauma victims." He noticed Zahira's shoulders loosening and passed her a mug of tea. "And you and Pekke can start the process for getting rights for hatari from the Council. We don't reveal the locations of anyone else. Whether they want to come forward to testify is up to them."

Zahira seemed to accept this argument, but her hand lingered on one of the cryptoscope's arms. "How can we be sure no one else will come after them? That the hatari who don't want to be found won't be?"

"We could certainly delete the data, if that's what you want. And I think all of this has shown the cryptoscope shouldn't be taken to market." He sent a sharp look to Jo. It pained him to suggest taking her project, her baby, away from her, but better that than seeing her constantly torn on whether to use it and never moving on to something new. "Once it's out of the picture, conceivably, no one would be able to track hatari any better than the Boliska already does."

Zahira nodded, but now it was Jo's turn to hesitate. She didn't speak, but Nik could tell from the long, sad look she gave the cryptoscope—the project she'd spent the better part of three years on. The prototype Pekke said would drag her into trouble.

"We wouldn't have to scrap it, Jo. Just... store it long term. Maybe Pekke could keep it in one of his safe houses in case we need it down the line?" He shot the physicist a look that he immediately picked up on.

"I'd be more than happy to oblige." Pekke gave a small bow of his head. "And we could write up a contract giving you access should you ever change your mind."

Jo's eyes darted around the room, meeting Nik's briefly with a pained look that sent a chill down to his stomach. He swallowed. He hated seeing her so downtrodden. So resigned. He'd need to get her brainstorming ideas for her fellowship to distract her.

"I guess that's settled, then." Pekke clapped his hands together and gave them a quick rub back and forth. "We get the coordinates to the D.I.C.—I suggest via my friend Zave, as we haven't verified the caller was indeed Miss Resero—and then we start the process to get hatari officially recognized. In a few days' time, if it all works out, we should see the nguvu clouds fading and all the captives free."

Nik nodded and gave Jo a reassuring smile. She gave a half smile back, but it did nothing to quash the feeling he'd done something horribly wrong.

Chapter Twenty-Nine

Pravi

Barely an hour after her call with Jo, Pravi had a message from Munus saying the inventor sent coordinates through another consultant. Though she found the quick response reassuring, it hadn't come directly. Jo didn't trust her enough—yet. Still, even if Jo had sent the coordinates directly, what could Pravi do with them? Wish herself there?

At first, Munus' lack of follow-up sent worries scurrying through her mind. Would he cut her off now that he had what he wanted? Had she traded her chance at the prototype for the Department's empty words? A message early the next morning doused her fears. "Be ready for strike briefing in an hour." The words glowed on her transcom screen like a promise.

But what ever should she wear? This would be her first strike mission as a legitimate D.I.C. consultant, and Pravi spent a good ten minutes staring at her ready room. Her Z73 plasma rifle had been her go-to accessory, but it had more of a vigilante look to it, and even in its back holster, it stuck out a bit too far for the D.I.C.'s little sliding closet. Her mini pistol was serviceable, if a bit wimpy-looking compared to the Department's standard issue. She needed something not too flashy that still had a respectable heft to it. Her eyes fell on her uncle's 833 Magma. Dual-barrel, high capacity, and barely longer than her forearm. There was a good reason it had been his favorite. Highly reliable with a quick re-load, the dark-gray phosphate finish still shone from its last cleaning. She tossed the holster next to her body armor.

Was she being too presumptuous, bringing her own strike gear? Xander had always brought his own. He liked to say the Department's smelled too much like burnt tires. And besides, did her first impression with the strike team really matter? If she ended up having to smuggle out the prototype, it's not like she'd ever see the agents again. At least not when they were on the same side. She reached for a ready bag from the locker, its black fabric bulging with supplies to stick in her vest's various pockets. The armor she'd bought for Jo sat on the shelf above it, tags and packaging still on. *Always have a backup plan*, Xander used to say, *and a backup plan for your backup plan*. Maybe under the guise of the fellowship, she could give Jo some training. Clever as Munus might be, it wasn't the same as having a partner. She knew where he'd stand if it came down to her versus the D.I.C.

Her transcom glowed from the bench. A quick swipe showed more details on the meeting plans, sent from Munus' secretary. The gist was that Pravi would be part of a minor team launching from her patio. She drummed her fingers beside the screen. The location was undoubtedly convenient, but it meant she'd be running support rather than point. In addition, Munus would have a buffer between her and the D.I.C.'s master plan. He might even get the prototype off the base before her team got on.

Too late to worry about it now. She started changing into her gear, letting the ritual of buckles and zippers calm her nerves. Whatever happened on the base, she could roll with it. Flashlights, compression packs, emergency flares... Her pockets filled with the resources Xander had declared vital. Plus a few extra throwing knives and a pen-sized pistol.

Pravi was ready a full twenty minutes early. Lightweight body armor zipped down to her wrists and up to a mock turtleneck height around her neck. She spent five of her extra minutes reworking her hair into tight braids that would fit more snugly inside her helmet, should she need it. Which she doubted. Agents had already trickled into the staging area, dressed in navy jumpsuits that looked little better than scrubs and carrying cases of evidence bags and scanning equipment. Her gut had been right about being part of the cleanup crew. She gave the Magma one more check before tucking it back into its holster and picking up her helmet. As the tech crew was assigned an armed guard, she shouldn't be the only one with a weapon, but there was a good chance she'd be the most experienced should the need arise to use it.

Most experienced... The thought froze in her head like a buffering screen. Could she use this to her advantage? If Munus had assigned her crew to logging the evidence—making them responsible for securing the prototype—what would prevent her from absconding with it? In a standard strike team, she'd be guarded like a hawk. A dozen blasters pointed in her direction the second she gave so much as a hint she planned to take it. But in a lab crew? They tended to get right into work collecting evidence and leave the security to the token pair of armed members. Could this be Munus' way of doing her a favor? Or was this another test? She shook her head. No time to analyze now. Though the cameras still showed no sign of Munus, she set her house's alarm systems and headed for the patio.

At the end of the path, Agent Yuri let her by with a nod, his quick analysis of her armor seeming to end in approval. As for the equipment techs, they barely made eye contact as they scurried out of her way. Exactly the reaction she wanted. If she was lucky, they'd be too busy avoiding her to pay any attention to what she was doing. She counted nine equipment techs and two uniformed guards, their activity centered around the command tent. Evidence kits had been stacked on either side of the entry flaps and along the patio's edges. Dozens of black and orange bins, marked for various explosive and biological hazards. Half had small anti-radiation markings. Pravi ran a finger down the nearest stack. One of them was undoubtedly meant to hold the prototype.

"Consultant Resero, I presume?" A broad, gray-haired man strode forth from the tent with his hands clasped behind his back. He wore the dark green uniform of the Interplanetary Defense Force, with a few extra pins above his left chest pocket. No weapons or armor, suggesting he was there in a supervisory role. He seemed to notice Pravi's surprise. "Given the possibility for large, reptilian hostiles, Munus and I decided a joint maneuver would be best."

Calling in the army in case of dinosaurs. Pravi bet the soldiers were having a field day with their briefing. "Honor to serve with you, Colonel....?"

"Just Colonel is fine. Munus sends his regrets, but he had a more pressing matter to attend to." He nodded for his assistant to hand her a data pad. "Agent Jandra said you need to sign this before you leave."

A quick glance showed it was the same release of liability Pravi had tried to use to ditch her D.I.C. guard when Munus first showed up with his team. *'I hereby decree that I am leaving protective custody of my own volition...'* Now, the words felt more like a field trip waiver than a declaration of independence. She read through the page-length document carefully to confirm Jandra hadn't added anything malicious before signing her name.

"Perfect," the colonel declared when the data pad was back in his assistant's hands. "We have the comm system set up inside, if you'd follow me."

The command center had undergone a makeover in the hours since Pravi had last been inside. Jandra's desk was nowhere in sight, and rows of screens filled Pravi's corner. A paper- and tablet-filled folding table squatted in the center of the room, with a half dozen agents and a pair of military aides scurrying around its edges and back and forth to the corner's mounted screens.

The colonel waved aside a pair of techs and had them bring Pravi a modulator to add to her transcom. "Channel seventeen has the general mission chatter, and sixteen is for your team only. Let us know if you need any help securing the, ahem, asset. Twenty-nine is set as a private link between you and command."

Pravi nodded. So that was how Munus wanted to play it. The containers outside had made her suspicious, and this confirmed it. They expected her to turn over the prototype so her lawyer would have to cite Xander's will and sue for its return. The "right" way. The "legal" way. Because the department thought they had the sole right to decide what was and wasn't too dangerous for personal use. Never mind that all the appeals would take years to sort out, all while the prototype sat dusty in some warehouse, waiting for a corrupt agent to sell it on the black market. Well, two could play at that game. Why couldn't she cut out some of the middle steps and have the D.I.C. try to explain in court how Pravi could "steal" something she already owned?

Pravi shifted the helmet on her hip and followed the colonel to the command table, trying to keep her rebellious thoughts from making their way to her facial expressions. Neither the colonel nor the stout soldier he introduced as her team leader seemed to notice.

"Lieutenant Fivewire will take good care of you," the colonel was saying, his voice skimming over the obvious codename with ease. "He'll serve as your escort in and out, as well as cover the briefing. All systems go in eight minutes."

The colonel left and Fivewire handed her a tablet, a smaller one with a wrist mount and a screen twice the size of her palm. The screen showed a map with five buildings: one shed-like garage, three giant holding pens, and a sprawling one-story affair marked as 'Research Facility.' Fivewire laid out their plan, swiping between video feeds as he spoke. They'd arrive on the compound's northwest side after Strike Team Six cleared the area, then head for the Research facility. He walked her through the approach and which signals meant an area was safe to enter. Everything followed what her uncle had taught her.

But at the research building, their plans diverged. The D.I.C. liked to work methodically, checking rooms one by one in a standard search pattern, but from the window and roof layout, Pravi suspected the first half would be all incubation and nursery rooms. The back end was better set up for grounding and shielding, and where the greatest precautions were, the prototype was most likely to be. Let the D.I.C. waste their time classifying every microscope and holding cell. She was going after the real prize.

"Two minutes til go time," a tech called out. The chatter over the comms quieted, leaving space for a final check that all strike teams were in position. Fivewire escorted her to the sliding room door flaps—in front of a half dozen techs waiting in line—and gave the confirmation for their team.

"All teams standing by," a woman's voice reported over the comm. *"First wave go in twenty... nineteen... eighteen... "*

Pravi swiped through her wrist pad to follow along, finding over three dozen camera feeds. The first five looked to be from surveillance drones, hovering just outside of the base. Dark blue trees obscured most of the ground, but now and then one of them shook like they'd been hit with a gust of wind... or like something big had walked underneath them. Another dozen screens showed military teams crammed into sliding rooms, their weapons in ready position while the cameras panned back and forth down the line like the wearers were giving instructions. A few screens showed nothing but darkness, and others appeared to be hidden behind ghillie suits, with bits of leaf-like camouflage dotting the camera's edges. Pravi guessed their owners had infiltrated the perimeter, ready to pop up mobile sliding stations the second command sent the order.

"Three... Two... One... "

A mass of leaves on Pravi's screen popped up into a *cylindrical* frame, with thin wires along the top and fake branches sticking out along the edges. The first pair of soldiers arrived within seconds of the pieces clicking into place, and they barely had their feet out before the next pair appeared. Camera feed after camera feed showed teams creeping through underbrush and along tall metal fences.

Pravi's hand hovered over the Magma's holster. Her adrenaline had spiked during the countdown, and she fought the urge to charge into the sliding closet. On missions with her uncle, she never waited past the countdown. It'd be "Approach—Cover—Assess—Repeat." Or possibly "Shots fired—Target down—Secure all limbs with restraints." Every moment spent moving or analyzing. Every second required her mind and senses on alert.

Cracking branches and screams echoed in her headset, and she scrambled to find the camera feed matching the audio. *"Man down. Assistance needed in grid 7E."* Labored breathing and blaster shots filled the feed as she spotted the source. Streaks of light and dust obscured most of the view, but in the background she made out a half-open gate and a massive theropod trying to stagger back through as its teeth and shoulder dripped with blood.

The lab techs shifted uneasily as another request for assistance came across the comms, this time in 9G. The response was quick, but unhelpful. *"Strike Team Eight is engaging a gorgosaur. Unable to provide relief."*

"Sorry, S.T. Ten is locked down as well."

The coordinator called out orders to other teams, but it wouldn't be enough. Though open, the gate on the feed had been intact. Pravi could only assume the smugglers had released the reptiles on purpose, buying themselves time to set up defenses or plan their escape.

Across the command tent, the colonel watched the main screen with a worried frown. Dots of light showed the strike teams' positions within the compound. More than half of them blinked orange or red.

"Send me in," Fivewire said at the same time as Pravi. She looked at him with surprise. She wanted to get in before the prototype got carted out with the rest of the evidence, but what had him so antsy?

"Team Three, are you able to make it to Team Two for support?" the coordinator asked in their ears. A crackling line replied, *"Negative. Team Four's spinetail is blocking our path. Can we get some drone support?"*

"They need all the help they can get, sir," Fivewire insisted, stepping forward to get his commander's attention. He had his shoulder between the colonel and Pravi as if to signal that she wasn't important. "Sawhorse can bring Ms. Resero in once it's clear."

"Sawhorse doesn't have the clearance. You had your briefing."

So he was eager to get out of babysitting duty. As if she needed babysat. Pravi hooked her thumb on the end of her holster and straightened her back to look as imposing as possible. "Fivewire could bring me now."

"As much as I'd like to Ms. Resero—"

"If you've heard anything about my uncle, Colonel, you should know we Reseros can handle ourselves." She spread her hands as if to offer her gear as proof of her readiness. "Not to mention I already signed a waiver."

The comm line seemed to increase in volume. *"Colonel Brandon, could you send backup to 9F?"*

"I have a small team I can send through Circle Eight," the colonel agreed with a sigh. "Let S.T. Nine know they'll be coming from the north-west."

"Roger that. Lieutenant Swift, what's your team's ETA?"

The comm chatter continued as Fivewire ushered Pravi into the sliding closet before the colonel could change his mind. His movements were stiff, but if he bore any grudge, it didn't stop him from linking arms for the slide. "Three... Two..."

She barely had her helmet on before he said "One" and the world went black. Forty-seven long moments later, it flashed back in shades of cerulean and brown.

Fivewire released Pravi's arm and raised his blaster. A thin layer of camouflage gauze separated them from a dense forest of everblues and fern-like undergrowth. He checked his wrist to confirm their heading and motioned for Pravi to follow. She obliged. Every step behind him was a step closer to the research building. According to the map's grid, it was only three hundred meters from the corner of 9F.

"Drone support inbound to grid 7C," the comm hissed in her ear. Mere minutes later, distant sounds of heavy impacts and explosions shook the ground to the west. Fivewire and Pravi quickened their pace. Blasterfire filtered from trees to the south, and Fivewire adjusted course to meet it. The breeze carried a metallic scent.

A dozen meters in, the agent held up a hand for her to stop. "Raptor," he signaled. "In the bushes up ahead."

From what Pravi could see, the raptor crouched behind a fallen tree, slowly bleeding the strike team of ammo. Two, maybe two and a half meters tall. Nothing a strike team couldn't handle on its own.

"Team Nine?" Fivewire asked into his comm. They got a flurry of blasterfire in response.

"Half our team is down thanks to a stegasaurid," a woman's voice said in her ear. *"Could you get this asshole off our back so we can move the wounded?"*

Pravi launched into motion before Fivewire finished saying "Roger that." She had the advantage of angles, and the deep orange of the raptor stood stark against the blue of the trees. Two shots in quick succession, one burst of red at its neck and another on its back. Neither kill shots at this distance, but she had its attention.

The raptor hissed and charged, leaving the safety of the fallen tree. Team Nine tore apart the foliage as it ran, whole ferns turned to confetti, but it barely staggered. A miscalculation on Pravi's part. Long, angry teeth were on her before she could get another three shots off.

She rolled behind the nearest tree as claws tore at her armor. Jaws gnashed at branches she put between them. More shots, this time from Fivewire. Heavy ammo thumped wet and heavy into hide. Pravi scrambled to get out from underneath as it fell. Red against orange against blue. Branches snapped like bones beneath it, and she tried not to think about what would have happened if she'd moved slower.

"What the hell was that?" In his anger, Fivewire gave her only a cursory check for injuries. "Do you have some kind of death wish?"

Pravi pushed him aside, calming her racing heart with a quick reload of her blaster. "Let's just call it a calculated risk, shall we?" A split moment decision. If she had let Fivewire take charge, he'd be calling the shots from then on. But one reckless move on her part would put him on edge. Have him too concerned about what big moves she might make to pay attention to the small ones. "You're all clear, Team Nine," Pravi shouted into the brush.

Before Fivewire could argue that they should stay to help with the wounded, blasterfire crackled in the comm line. *"Strike Team Six could use some help on the compound's north side."*

"Lieutenant Fivewire and Consultant Resero on our way," Pravi responded. Too bad her helmet hid her grin.

Fivewire looked like he wanted to challenge it, but the dispatch coordinator was already taking Pravi's promise into account.

"We should report back," he whispered once they were a dozen meters away. "The colonel only gave us permission for one support mission."

"Call it in if you want to," Pravi countered as she slipped through a patch of waist-high brush. Flashes of light in the trees ahead suggested they were closing in on Team Six's location. "It's like you said, they need all the help they can get."

Fivewire gave only silence as a response. Now that he'd made it on site, he wouldn't want to be sent away any more than she did.

An impact hit a nearby tree and Pravi ducked to avoid the flying slivers. Her companion rolled for cover and raised his blaster.

"Team Six, is that you firing into grid 7D?" he asked in the strike team's channel.

"Yeah, sorry. Didn't realize you'd get here so fast. We've got four or five hostiles in the research building pinning us down, and we thought one of them was coming around to flank us."

"Nope, just us. We'll see if we can get them to ease up on you." To Pravi, he added, "Any chance you have eyes on that building?"

She wanted to answer, *'No, I'm not injured, thanks for asking,'* but held her tongue to stay professional. Instead, she moved a few fern leaves out of the way and checked the map to make sure she faced the right direction. "Negative. The trees are too dense."

"Okay, how about you stay here and I edge around the west side and assess the situation."

"Or... we could try a Hamlock maneuver."

He froze mid-step to the west. "How do you know about Hamlock maneuvers?"

"Maybe you'd know if you had actually read your briefing." Rather than rib him further, Pravi checked that her Magma was clear and ready for action. "I'm thinking you run point, using the equipment shed, trailer, and outhouse as cover."

The three locations arced around the research building's west side, with no more than five meters in between. Perfect for a two-person team to alternate between drawing the enemy out and taking shelter.

Fivewire nodded to the Magma. "How good are you with that thing when your target isn't a meter wide?"

"Better than you'd think."

"That leaves a pretty wide range between sniping the defense at a hundred meters and me bleeding to death on the gravel."

Pravi grinned. "Let's hope it's closer to the former."

"That's not very reassuring."

"It would be if you'd read the briefing."

A drumroll of blasterfire stole any chance for her companion to give a sassy retort. Once the 'pew' and ricochet noises stopped, Fivewire gave the signal to begin.

They started west first, keeping a good distance from the section of woods that had been riddled with crossfire. It didn't take long to see the first building. The ferns turned to gravel at the edge of the trees, leaving a clear view of a metal panel shed just big enough to hold three two-person ATVs. Far past it stood the south holding pen, or at least a building tall and sturdy enough to hold a small herd of sauropods. The research building lay long and low to the east, with small windows on its northern half. They had a clear view of the main entrance, the side opposite where Strike Team Six had been pinned down.

"Any sign of hostiles?" Fivewire asked.

"Negative." Pravi didn't see much sign of anything. With a surprise raid like this, she expected a few signs of chaos. Something like abandoned packs, ATVs left outside the shed, maybe even a burn or blood spot on the gravel. But other than the research building's entrance, the compound looked nearly pristine. "You ready?"

"Ready as I'll ever be." He gripped his blaster tight and took off toward the equipment shed.

Blaster fire rained down on the woods, mostly aimed at the strike team's location. Pravi marked the origination points with the barrel of her gun.

"I don't think they saw you," she whispered into the comm. "Looks like two at the front door and two at the windows."

Fivewire breathed heavy into his mic. *"Any at the side windows?"*

"Not that I saw."

Fivewire took off for the trailer, blaster shots peppering the gravel at his feet. Pravi marked the shooter and pulled the trigger before the blasts could get any closer. The side window shattered. "Guess there was someone there." She let off a few more shots at the other hostiles before creeping three meters to the side.

"Thanks for that." Fivewire's voice held no trace of gratitude. *"These side rooms seem empty, but I'm going to head back to you to be sure."* If there were hostiles in the other rooms, they'd expect Fivewire to head

for the outhouse next. And logic said hostiles crouched somewhere in the side rooms. With all the defenses they had, the smugglers wouldn't be stupid enough to leave a whole direction unattended.

Fivewire raced back, but the only weapons aimed at him came from the front entry. "You got the windows figured out, or do I need to run back?" he asked.

She merely shook her head. There had to some sort of defense on that side, didn't there? She pulled out her scope and checked the roofline. No signs of snipers or turrets, or really anything but a half-dozen satellite towers... She cursed under her breath. "They have their own sliding port."

"Sliding 'ports'," Fivewire corrected with a curse of his own. He gestured to the top of the holding shed. "The shady devils set up their own escape routes." That changed things a bit. Here she'd thought they had to worry about the smugglers disappearing into the mountains, but instead they were disappearing into Stringspace. Her only consolation was that transporting a wild animal would be significantly more time-consuming than simply setting a nav and sliding away.

"We've got them on the run," Team Six's leader announced over the comm. *"Ecks and Wai, cover me. Rafters and I are going in."*

Pravi moved to join them, but Fivewire motioned for her to stop. "Just let them clear it," he said. "We did enough to get the plan back on track."

"Did we, though?" She aimed the Magma at the ground to reload. "Are they really on the run, or were the defenders finally cleared to leave?"

"Leave?"

"Sliding port, remember?" She started through the ferns toward Team Six's location. The strike had been going on for what, twenty or thirty minutes? How many people could they evacuate in that time? How many tripwires could they set? She could only hope the prototype still remained.

"First three rooms are clear. Two hostiles seen running into the room at the end of the hall."

The area Pravi had guessed was the main research hub. "Consultant Resero entering zone 7D," she announced on the comm.

"Roger that," a man's voice answered. Hopefully, his acknowledgment meant she'd be safe from friendly fire. She left the safety of the woods at a half-run, half-crouch, with Fivewire following not far behind.

"I swear, if you get killed right now," he whispered, "the only flowers on your grave will be made of those briefing notes."

"I'll take that into consideration." Pravi waved to the agent on guard, who let them by with one look at Fivewire's uniform. She'd done too much to end up late now.

Inside, the hallway stood narrow enough she could have touched her elbows to either side without lifting them all the way. Beige walls and brown-tiled floor. Smoke drifted from a door halfway down and to the left. A wastebasket fire, from the smell of it. All ink and evidence docs.

"We've got wires." A soldier near the far end motioned for her teammate to stop. "I think these last three rooms are set to blow."

Good thing someone checked for it this time so they didn't have a repeat of the lab. Pravi crept closer, but all she could see was doors barely edged open.

Fivewire pushed past her, pulling tools and a canister from his vest pouches. "I'm on it. Let the Colonel know we're almost ready for Phase Four."

One of the soldiers nodded. Phase Four was presumably the lab tech wave, so she had maybe ten to fifteen minutes before this corridor was crawling with D.I.C. She slipped out her scanner.

"That's one done," Fivewire announced. "Lucky for me, they were in a rush when they installed them. These first two don't even have the sensitivity set yet. Only the last one should give us any trouble."

The scanner beeped, but Pravi froze, running his words back through her mind to make sure she heard them correctly. Had they planted at least two of the explosives that day? One she could understand. But multiple? Not when you had fifteen minutes to evacuate and destroy the evidence. You only did that when you knew you had time. She took a couple steps back and surveyed the hallway again. Gouges, running up and down the tile. Dings and dents in the doorways, suggesting equipment moved in a rush. She nudged open the nearest door to find the room empty. Only a small cabinet remained with some dust and a gum wrapper on the floor. The next three rooms were the same. They'd had warning. Maybe not much, definitely not the whole night, but at least as much as she'd had. She slammed her fist into the doorway and switched her comm to channel twenty-nine, the private link to command. "Code 63," she whispered. "Someone leaked the intel."

The line was silent for a moment. *"Are you sure?"*

"Positive. You can send over your crew, but there's a good chance the evidence is gone."

"And the asset?"

Pravi fingered the scanner. It showed traces of the prototype's signature coming from the end of the hall. "I haven't checked all the rooms yet, but the ones I've seen are empty."

"Keep us updated."

"Last one's all clear," Fivewire announced, waving a puff of vaporized gas out of his face. He slipped the canister back into his pocket. "Man, I love this stuff."

Pravi pushed past him as if to inspect his work. "We've got a leak," she whispered. "Keep this room clear until the techs get here."

"Roger that," he whispered back. "Does command know?"

She nodded, though she suspected he was already switching the channel on his comm to confirm.

The final room was massive, wide enough to swallow an average house. Thick wood studs ran from a bare concrete slab to the rafters, covered everywhere with a thick wire mesh instead of drywall. Industrial lights lit only the floor, but the shadows held traces of wires and sensors. She wouldn't be surprised if the whole back half of it could be used as a sliding port. Dust covered the floor in patches, with streaks from wheeled equipment and work boots. Most of the space had been emptied, minus a handful of storage lockers on the wall behind her and an abandoned cabinet to her left. The cabinet lay sideways on the ground as if the people moving it suddenly decided they didn't have enough time. If she and Fivewire hadn't stepped in, the whole room could have been clear.

"Anything yet?" Fivewire asked from the doorway.

"Not that I see." The scanner led to the abandoned cabinet, but she wasn't ready to give herself hope yet. She released a bit of her frustration by shooting the padlocks off the lockers. Inside the first were some tranquilizer darts and a couple rifles. Another held medical equipment like IV needles, protective equipment, and tubing. As for the third... Pravi's breath had never caught so hard. One of her uncle's storage cases, clearly marked with an X and an R right above the broken lock. Her fingers fumbled to find the wand-like prototype still inside, void of nguvu batteries, but fully intact.

"We're going to need some of those storage bins," she told Firewire in case he'd seen her reaction. "The type O59 and VL3 at least." Neither was what the prototype needed, but their hazard ratings were high enough to explain the way she'd frozen at the sight. She slipped the prototype up under her vest and moved on to the next locker. More bins and cases with broken locks in this one, suggesting they'd been stolen or confiscated. Passports... IDs... some stacks of cash. She'd leave them for the lab techs to log and classify.

A quick turn back to the fallen cabinet and her heart rate escalated. She couldn't be that lucky, could she? Everywhere else they'd failed. Securing the reptiles. Capturing the smugglers. Finding definitive evidence of who they were bribing and where... But one look at her scanner said the batteries were indeed inside.

"Munus says there's been another incident," the colonel reported in her ear. *"One your contact's model didn't predict."*

"Understood." She turned off her comm to mumble a few curses. If a mole at the D.I.C. had leaked the strike information, what else did they know? She had to warn Jo. "Hey Fivewire? I think we're going to need those Class 1060 cases."

"You found the asset?"

Pravi shook her head and pulled off her helmet. "There's traces of nguvu, though. I'll have to take off my comms so they won't get fried." She stripped off all her electronics, leaving only her personal transcom and scanner within reach. If she could pull this off, she'd use the scanner's secret nav device features for the first time. She searched through the cabinet quickly and methodically, setting aside every bin that didn't have the right shielding. Her fingers cupped a small metal box.

Fivewire said something, but it was gibberish without her translators. Pravi pointed to her ear without looking up. She had the batteries now. Their short-lived partnership was over.

He said something again, and she gestured to the bins around her while covertly installing the batteries with the other. She slipped her transcom back on her wrist and in her ear. "What's so urgent?" she asked.

"I think you need to stand back now." His voice was firm, but not unkind. "The colonel said to wait for the techs."

"Oh. Okay then." Pravi moved the cabinet door off her lap and stood back slowly. "Are they bringing the cases I asked for?"

He nodded, his eyes watching her suspiciously.

"Good. Good." Her eyes scanned the room, assessing her options. "You think we should check for sliding signatures? They probably used a waypoint, but it couldn't hurt, right?"

He shrugged.

"Worth a shot, I suppose." She retrieved her scanner slowly, keeping both hands in Fivewire's view the whole time. "My uncle and I got lucky with it once. Practically solved the whole case."

"Is that right?"

"Yep." She pulled out the scanner wand and started waving it back and forth over the floor. Her heart pounded, but it wasn't too hard to call up her nav app as she worked. The prototype buzzed against her stomach, signaling that it was ready.

Fivewire watched her uneasily, but his posture said his focus remained on guarding the door.

A few more swipes and she risked sliding her hand under her vest. The prototype's sensors felt warm against her fingers, and once she had them all lined up, sensation poured up her arm. Hundreds of tiny strings tingled at her senses. Fuzzy and cold. Sharp and smoky. She struggled to keep calm with the sudden rush of sensations. A fiery string burned into her mind, stronger than all the others. Suddenly, all her uncle's instructions on how to slide made sense.

"Hey Fivewire?"

"Yeah?"

"Tell Munus I'm sorry." She reached for the fiery string and pulled.

CHAPTER THIRTY

— • —

Jo

J o took a deep breath and pushed against one of the cryptoscope's limbs until the center joint hinged upward. If she planned to give up her invention, better to do it quick. Nik and Pekke wouldn't be back to help move it for hours, but she'd already locked half the arms into place. It was temporary, Pekke had assured her. She could get it back at any time. Still, the click of the locking pins sounded final.

Behind her, Zahira tapped her spoon on the side of her cereal bowl and watched as a clump of soggy mush slid off the surface. Twenty minutes ago, the grain meal had been warm and fragrant, but it seemed the hatari only had the stomach for stirring it. "Do you think the D.I.C. found them yet?"

"I guess they could have." Jo grabbed the next limb and readied its center joint. "Pekke seemed to think the Department would move fast. Possibly while we were sleeping."

It was crazy to think only half a day ago, they'd broken into the Boliska's lab, released a stampeding ceratopsid, and free-slid into a swamp. With all Jo's tools put away, the only real proof it happened was the muddy laundry piled in her bathtub and Zahira sitting groggy-eyed at the counter.

The hatari's spoon dropped into the bowl with a *plomp*. "Maybe we should check the news. That sort of thing would make the news, wouldn't it?"

"I suppose it could." Jo inserted the next locking pin and tapped her transcom screen. Nothing from Pekke yet. "I'm sure we'll know as soon as there's something to report."

"Or as soon as there's something to find." Zahira started swiping on her own screen, her breakfast forgotten. Her movements quickly grew frustrated. "Ulg, why is all the news about some sliding station on Donli?"

A sharp knock at the door froze both her and Jo in their places.

"Do you think it's Pekke?" Jo whispered.

Zahira threw her an irritated look. "How should I know? You didn't open it yet."

"Well, he didn't text first." She hated when people didn't text first. She considered checking her camera, but whoever it was knocked again, this time with more urgency. She wiped her hands on her coveralls and strode to the door, fully intending to open it only a smidge.

Pravi Resero shoved it wider. "Hey, sorry to barge in like this, but I was in the neighborhood and thought I'd say hi." A weird voice in Jo's translator added, *'Blink twice if you're in danger.'*

"Um, what?"

"Oh good, looks like I beat them here." Pravi pushed the rest of the way in and closed the door behind her. She wore some sort of combat pants and had a blaster pressed against her thigh. "I'm thinking we should start the fellowship early, if that's alright? Just throw a bag of necessities together, and we'll be on our way."

"A bag of... Early? What are you talking about?"

Pravi dropped a backpack to the floor and started rifling through it. Jo hadn't even noticed her bring it in because, well, her eyes had been fixed on the blaster. To her horror, Pravi set another, much larger blaster on the floor beside her, joined shortly by a dark-green military helmet. "Long story short, there's a mole in the D.I.C. They tipped off the target before we got there, and if they knew about the mission, there's a decent chance they know about you, too."

"Me?"

"Yeah. See, the D.I.C. keeps a log of who gives them what information. And you gave them the coordinates. So you think you can pack a bag up quick? I have a nice safe house wai—"

Zahira's chair scraped against the tile. "What do you mean, they tipped off the target?"

"I mean they knew we were coming before we got there. Booby traps set. Evidence removed." Pravi tossed a black band at Jo. "This nav is a burner. Leave your own behind, and turn off any device they could track. You have a security camera set up to watch the door, don't you?"

Jo nodded and swiped to the app on her transcom.

"But what about the hostages?" A buzz of energy sizzled around Zahira's words. "What about all those people held captive on the base?"

The zipper on Pravi's backpack froze halfway closed, and she looked up with a face as baffled as Jo felt. "No one told me anything about hostages. Other than a few guards, the base was deserted when I got there."

A string of Yerian expletives flooded Jo's translator, with side notes about dead cattle and the reproductive habits of sand moles. Normally, Jo loved the notes, but she was too busy stringing her own curses together to listen.

"We'll find them," she assured Zahira. "We'll just have to find them again." It wouldn't be that hard, would it? Unless the Boliska had miraculously developed better nguvu shielding during their flight, a cryptoscope scan should show exactly where they'd taken the hatari.

"I'd be more worried about myself if I were you," Pravi pulled on a padded vest and threw her backpack over her shoulder. "They've been pretty thorough about covering their tracks. I wouldn't be surprised if they were right behind me."

As if in answer, a fist pounded on the door, sending a rush of adrenaline up Jo's spine.

Pravi readied the larger blaster. "The camera feed," she hissed.

"Jo, Zahira, are you in there?" Pekke called through the door as his face popped up on her screen. "It's kind of urgent."

Oh, thank the strings. "Yes, yes. Just a moment."

She threw open the door, barely registering Pravi's move to hide behind it.

"Blessed stars." Pekke gave a heavy exhale as his eyes landed on her and Zahira. "I worried I wouldn't find you alive. I don't have much time to explain, but—"

"There's a mole in the department." Lines of nguvu swirled across Zahira's arms as she closed the door behind him. "I thought you said telling the D.I.C. was the right move?"

"I thought it was! How could I have known the Boliska had an inside man? I thought—Oh, nevermind what I thought. We need to go. Now. You can scold me all you want once we get to the safe house."

"And how safe is this safe house?" Pravi stepped out from behind the door, blaster in hand. "Seems to me anyone who knew about the location is a suspect."

"Are you implying that I'd leak it?" Pekke turned to face her, pausing only briefly when he spotted her weapon. He lifted his hands in a half-hearted surrender. "So nice to make your acquaintance, Ms. Resero. Do you always introduce yourself at blasterpoint?"

"I hardly have it aimed at you, now do I, Dr. Froum? Though I can't say you've given me a reason not to. Especially with that lovely little weapon in your pocket."

Jo's eyes followed Pravi's gesture. Sure enough, there was a small, barrel-sized lump at the untucked side of his shirt. She had a sudden feeling she should do something. They were supposed to be on the same side, weren't they? Not staring each other down while fully armed. There was no telling how much blaster fire would throw off the cryptoscope's calibration. And if they hit a trans-world sensor...

Zahira huffed and rolled her eyes. "If you two are going to shoot each other, could you at least wait until Jo and I are out of the room? We'll need someone alive to save the hatari."

"I'm fine with calling a truce if she is," Pekke said.

Pravi didn't holster her weapon, but her posture softened. "I suppose we can fight over where to run to once we're safely to a sliding station."

"A sliding station seems like an excellent idea." Pekke lowered his hands slowly and turned to face Jo. "Is the cryptoscope ready to go?"

"Almost. I have all but one of the arms locked in, and I still need to install the transport repeaters." Please let their truce hold until that was done.

Pekke nodded. "I'll get the arm locked in if you want to grab a bag of clothes." He turned to Zahira. "I trust your bag is already packed?"

"I, uh... No." She looked guiltily down the hall to where her backpack sat in a bucket waiting to be laundered. "We haven't gotten the swamp out of everything yet."

"You can borrow one of mine," Jo chimed in. She nudged Zahira toward the bedroom, hoping if they moved fast enough, Pekke and Pravi wouldn't get the chance to tick each other off and start blowing holes in her apartment. "I have some extra clothes, too, if you need them."

Once she reached her dresser, it became clear Jo didn't have a clue what she needed herself. Underwear? Socks? She passed her old backpack to Zahira and started shoving random bits of clothes into a large equipment bag. Would this be a camping trip-type situation? Did she need coats? Boots? Layers? What did you pack for going on the run?

Zahira grabbed her arm as she reached for a third set of coveralls. "We can buy anything we forget," she whispered. "I—well, Grandmother and I—we had enough saved for two. You don't want to be overloaded right now."

"Oh. Yeah." Jo mumbled. Of course Zahira would know how to handle the situation. She shoved the clothes down and forced the zipper closed.

Miraculously, her living room was still intact when they returned. Pekke's blaster had remained in his pocket, joined by an assortment of Jo's wrenches and tools. Next to him, the cryptoscope hovered on top of the lift, its base strapped on with a web of cables and bungee cords. As for Pravi, she still held her post at Jo's door, keeping half her attention on the physicist and the rest on the security camera.

"All set?" Pekke asked. He handed Jo a bulging equipment bag, packed with everything that hadn't fit in his pockets. "I put the transport repeaters on top. I'm thinking we should install them in the hovercraft rather than wait here to get cornered."

"Too late," Pravi cut in. "We have three goons inbound from the south entrance."

"What?" But Jo had just gotten—Someone had to have a plan, right? She looked to Pekke and Pravi, but they were looking at each other.

Pravi broke the silence first. "Back up to the hall and keep quiet. We might get lucky and they'll leave on their own."

Pekke nodded, and before either of them could protest, he ushered Jo and Zahira to the side. They held their breath as, for the third time that morning, someone rapped on Jo's door.

"Jo? Jo Incerti?" The Boliska's goons knocked again.

Pravi signaled that they were armed with two blasters a piece, and Jo quickly did the math. Three goons times two weapons—add in three more between Pekke and Pravi—that made nine deadly threats to her apartment and the cryptoscope. That left little chance either of them would survive.

Pekke motioned to the window. *Could we get out that way,* he mimed.

She shook her head. The patio wrapped around, so no risk of falling to their deaths, but the only window that could open wouldn't fit the cryptoscope.

Another rap at her door. "We know you're in there. We just have some follow-up questions about the information you gave the D.I.C."

Pekke mimed swinging a chair at the windows to make a big enough opening; but with how thick the glass was, Jo doubted a chair would do more than set off the glass breaker alarm. And even if they could break through, the patio had only one exit. Her eyes searched the room for another option. She needed the Boliska away from her apartment, and though breaking through the window would certainly do it, the Boliska would probably cut them off, anyway. Unless...

Unless the Boliska only thought they were escaping through the window?

There were other ways to set off the glass-breaker, ways that didn't involve swinging a heavy chair to mediocre results. She motioned to the others to hold their positions and headed for the far kitchen cabinet. The bottom shelf held a stack of hand-me-down plates, a worn medley of glass and ceramic that her aunt had given her. She never used them much—not with all the takeout Nik brought over—and anyway, this was an emergency, wasn't it? After a whispered apology to her aunt, she slammed the stack into the ground near the workbench, sending shards skidding across the tile. A siren rang out from the ceiling alarm and the Boliska goons hammered the door in reply.

"Quick, this way," she shouted. "Careful of the glass." She signaled for the others to remain in place as she shuffled through the shards toward the window. Several snapped under her feet.

The door shook again, this time followed by a single blaster shot. Jo shuddered. Hopefully, it'd take more than that to breach the steel frame. Another shake of the handle, then the slam of a shoulder, and silence.

"Well, that's one way to get rid of unwanted guests." Pravi powered off Jo's transcom and tossed it back to her. "They're heading for the main entrance. Better get moving before they discover our feint."

No one had to tell Zahira twice. She grabbed a kitchen knife on her way to the door.

"I'll take the cryptoscope," Pekke offered, moving to maneuver the lift. "I'm parked on level 17, so we can head for the elevator. Unless Ms. Resero's ride is closer?"

"It is, but it can't hold that thing." Pravi opened the door and motioned Pekke and the cryptoscope through with her blaster. "To the elevator we go."

Jo followed up at the rear, the shards stuck in her boots clicking against the tile with every step. If she forgot anything, or had left some tool vital to rescuing the hatari, it was too late now. She took one last glance inside before Pravi closed the door behind them.

"I'd move faster if I were you." The palm of the woman's hand shoved into Jo's back. "They'll be back through those doors in ten seconds max."

Up ahead, Pekke and Zahira had made it halfway down the hall, with the latter making a beeline to the call button. The elevator door opened before they reached it.

"Nik!" Zahira called, a mere second before Pravi yelled, "Duck!"

Jo's knee slammed into the carpet as something hot passed inches from her back. Blaster fire filled the hall, louder even than the siren.

"Jo!" Nik's voice called out from somewhere in front of her.

"I'm fine," she mumbled to the carpet. Her kneecap still tingled from the impact, but she waved him off. How could his timing be this bad? Yet another example of why people should text first.

A rough arm looped under her elbow. "Up we go." The lights flickered, and Pravi shot behind her as she helped Jo half-run, half-crawl the last few meters to the elevator. "Hopefully, your siren brings someone soon. Any idea of the local response times?"

"I... uh..." Shit. The last time she dropped a tin of screws, had she reset the override? She'd never had anything but false alarms. Lots of false alarms. "There's a chance it's not attached to the system."

"Are you kidding me?" Another shot whizzed past their heads, and Pravi returned fire.

Pekke pounded the elevator buttons as they crossed the threshold. "Come on. Come on. Another minute, and I'll have more holes than a Frinelli war costume."

The door seals clicked shut and Pravi collapsed against the wall. "Should have gotten the shirt with the wave pattern. It hides scorch marks better than the paisley." Her blaster released a thin trail of smoke from the barrel. "Though it also helps if you're firing back."

"I got a few shots off." Pekke poked at a frayed patch of fabric on his shoulder. A metal mesh shone through where the fabric had burned away, and he winced like a bruise had sprouted underneath. Was he wearing a blaster-proof shirt? Like the ones on the Norian shopping channel? "Glad to know these things aren't just for gullible tourists."

"I still prefer the military version." Pravi pulled the release on her blaster handle and popped a new cartridge in from her vest pocket. "Anyone else injured?"

Though her knee was bruised, Jo shook her head. It wasn't the same as getting shot.

"I'm fine, but Nik got his muffins mashed." Zahira made the kitchen knife dance between her fingers. "Some timing he had there. An extra few minutes either way, and he'd be a permanent resident of the hallway."

"You're hurt?" Though Jo scanned her friend for injuries, the only damage she spotted was a crunched takeout box in his hands. A sweet-smelling blue syrup leaked out the side.

Nik shrugged sheepishly. "Brivnian pastries. I was in the neighborhood when I heard about Donli, and I thought—"

"Donli?" But what did that have to do with bringing breakfast?

He cast his eyes to Pekke and Zahira. "I guess you haven't heard..."

"And here's our stop," Pekke announced as the door dinged. He pulled a small key fob out of his pocket. "I'm just a few spots west of the entrance, third row down. Blue quadfan. Can't miss it."

"But what about Donli?" Jo had a sinking feeling in her stomach—Nik wouldn't have brought her breakfast for no reason—but everyone rushed out before the elevator fully opened, guiding the lift and lengthening their strides. She swallowed her question and joined them.

Half the seventeenth floor served as the building's main parking garage, laid out in a grid of numbered spots. They dodged around hoverbikes and bi-fans as the space above remained eerily quiet. Seven meters of maneuvering space, and no hovercrafts there to maneuver. The bare, waffle-like ceiling did little to muffle the echo of their footsteps, which had grown louder than their half-dozen feet.

"We have hostiles incoming." Pravi turned and fired two shots at the stairway entrance. "Get to the hovercraft. I'll keep us covered."

"But how could they track us?" Pekke took a sharp left turn, barely keeping the lift stable as the cryptoscope tipped. He clicked his key fob and something beeped ahead of them.

"Maybe they have heat goggles. Or resonance scanners. Does it really matter?" Pravi ducked behind a rusty-red tri-fan and took a few more shots at their pursuit. "We'll lose them as soon as we get into traffic."

Pekke's horn beeped again, beckoning them closer. A deep blue ramp finished lowering to the ground as blasterfire rained on their feet. Pekke and the lift charged upward, followed closely by Zahira, Nik, and Jo.

"Seat belts, everyone." The physicist slipped into the driver's seat at the far end. Sensors and motors started whirling. "There should be a few hooks in the floor to help secure the cryptoscope."

While he got the fans ready for launch, Jo and Nik set to work. They had little space to maneuver—even locked into place, the crypto-scope's arms brushed the seats that lined the walls to either side. While Jo got the two hooks by the rear ramp, Zahira scrambled past her to the seat behind Pekke, latching the nearest lift strap before strapping herself in.

Nik got the final hook as blasterfire shook the hull.

"Hopefully that'll buff out." Pravi hopped onto the ramp and hit the button to shut it. She shot two more rounds before ducking the rest of the way inside. "Ready to launch when you are."

"Roger that."

Jo threw herself into a seat while Pekke pressed a few switches in the cockpit, pulling the craft upward as the ramp sealed into place. She sighed in relief. In the rearview camera, she spotted three burly men standing near their parking space, growing smaller as the hovercraft sped for the exit. One held a bleeding arm and another a transcom.

Pravi climbed nimbly over Nik and the cryptoscope to reach the co-pilot's seat. "We have company."

The hull shook as a small gray bi-fan flew into view in the rearview mirror. How the hell could the Boliska still be on their tail? The lab crew had been small, only four guards and their leader, yet somehow they now had a full team to come after her and the cryptoscope? She and Zahira exchanged glances. With the D.I.C. compromised, it'd be harder to get the hatari out than they'd thought. Not to mention the damage the unchecked nguvu cloud would cause.

The hovercraft shifted suddenly to the left and a flash of plasma shot in front of the windshield. "Hey, Jo?" Pekke's voice sounded as tense as a jammed up rotor. "If you could get the cryptoscope ready to slide, that'd be great."

"What? Now?"

"No, after they shoot us out of the sky."

Jo removed her safety restraint and crept along the floor. The ground rolled beneath her, whether from Pekke dodging unseen blaster shots or just zipping through traffic, she couldn't tell. She heard Pravi's seat belt unclasp as well, and the woman soon had her head and torso out the passenger window. Her larger blaster followed. This day couldn't be real, could it? Did they really expect Jo to install transport repeaters in the middle of a high-speed chase?

As she worked on screwing them in, the hovercraft tipped again, this time to the right, sending a bolt flying from her fingers. Thankfully, she found it within seconds, snagged on a curved metal track embedded in the rubbery floor. But something felt off about the track. It continued around the hovercraft, surrounding the cryptoscope in a two-meter-wide circle. She looked up. Dozens of cameras and sensors observed the room from recessed nooks and pockets. Strips of red lights ran down the walls where the ramp met the rows of seats. Her eyes went wide. "It's a built-in sliding station."

"Yep." Pekke checked his rear-view camera. The gray bi-fan hovered two cars behind them. "I meant it as a back-up plan, but I'm not sure we can shake them."

Who the hell prepares for that? Jo pulled her tool bag closer as the craft veered left, and she toppled, slamming her shoulder into one of the cryptoscope's arms. "Could you be careful up there?"

"Sorry, just trying to keep us alive."

"At least give me a warning..."

"Turning now."

Jo flattened against the rubber matting. The floor pitched right and her stomach rolled. "Thanks." She swallowed back hover-sickness and dug out a field modulator to program the repeaters.

"Hey, Nik?" Pekke called over his shoulder. "Check the hatch under your seat for the untraceable navigators. Should be a big, black bag, kinda tucked to the side..."

"Got 'em."

"Good. Pull up the main screen. Brace yourself, Jo."

The craft dipped downward, and a pile of parts spilled from her tool bag, rolling with the floor. Jo covered her face and head, but the rest pummeled her side and back.

Pekke glanced over his shoulder. "Something wrong?"

"Just a metal avalanche."

"Is the cryptoscope okay?"

"Yeah, my crushed ribs are doing fine. Thanks for asking." She stretched her arm back to the base, flinching at the jagged pain in her side. She slid her right knee forward, relaxing the bruised muscle.

"Turning."

The craft veered right and the tools slid left. Nik unfastened his restraint to help Jo collect them.

"Do you have those navigators ready?" Pekke called over his shoulder.

"Affirmative." Nik tossed the last wrench in the tool bag and strapped it in next to his seat.

"Set them to these coordinates: -18.1 Awt, 27.8 Vien." He checked his monitors for pursuit. "41.27 North and 96.027 West."

"Got it." Nik repeated the numbers back.

"Perfect. How about you, Jo? Almost ready?"

"Just need five more minutes."

"I can give you three."

Jo spun to her back, pulling out the modulator's probe.

"Short dip," Pekke called.

Luckily, her arms were too tangled with the machine to feel the shift. She poked at the newly-installed repeaters, setting them to recognize each other and her nav.

"Let me know when you're ready so I can run the pre-scan. The exit ahead looks as good as any." He turned and Jo recognized the bright billboards of the Mid-City Mall as they flew through the arch to the parking garage.

She pocketed the modulator and its probe. "Last one done."

"Perfect. Might want to get inside, Ms. Resero." Pekke hit the switches to land and unlatched his restraint. "We only have a short period where they lose visual. Everyone ready?"

Chaos filled the next sixty seconds, with Pekke jumping over his seat before the landing gear had even settled, Pravi chuffing her blaster inside her backpack, and Zahira fumbling to buckle on her nav. Nik freed Jo's equipment bags as the lights flickered. It was now or never. They linked arms and reached for the string, a bold buzz at the back of Jo's mind.

She gasped for breath as bright lights filled the surrounding room. Her first thoughts went to Nik and Zahira, then the cryptoscope. Everything appeared to have made it.

"This neutral enough for you?" Pekke untangled himself from the cryptoscope's arms and gestured to the wide space around them. Hundreds of active circles saturated the white tile floor while skylights filled the arched ceilings. "A nice public space to have an argument."

"Or I could just concede." Pravi wiggled out of her helmet and clipped it to her pack. "I suspect your safe house will do well enough."

She started for an exit circle and Pekke followed her. "Oh? And what happened to 'just how safe is this safe house'?"

"I left you a half dozen openings to incapacitate me and you took none of them." Pravi pulled out her transcom and swiped away a few notifications. "So either you're inept, or you're an ally. And seeing how you flew three blocks with only one fan fully functional, I doubt it's the former."

Jo's jaw dropped. "Flew... three blocks... on one fan?"

"It doesn't matter now." Pekke waved away her words to dial in their next destination. "The important thing is getting the cryptoscope up and running so we can check on the nguvu clouds."

"The nguvu clouds?" But she thought the hatari would be more important at the moment. Surely the Boliska wouldn't have be stupid enough to start the collection back up this soon after relocating.

Pekke pursed his lips. "We'll talk about it when we get to the safe house."

"Or we can talk about it now." Donli. Wasn't that the name both Zahira and Nik had mentioned? She restarted her transcom and entered it into the search.

"I really think you should wait," Nik whispered too late. Pictures of stretchers and ambulances filled her screen.

"Death Toll Reaches 50 after Field Fluctuation at Sliding Station." Her stomach sank with every detail on the news scroll. They'd tried to help things, to stop the incidents altogether, but they'd only made it worse.

CHAPTER THIRTY-ONE

— • —

ZAHIRA

It took Zahira a minute to realize why Jo had frozen. Her heart still raced from adrenaline and all she saw on the inventor's transcom screen was reports on the Donli sliding station, the same incident that had flooded the news pages that morning. Jo's screen played a particularly gruesome testimony, a shaking woman describing bodies merged with benches, tiles, each other... All thanks to a fluctuation in a navigation server's cooling field. In the background, white sheets covered the stretchers trickling out of the station. Only after a glance to Pekke and Pravi did her mind slow down enough to process the words. *Field fluctuation.* It'd been caused by the nguvu clouds.

"But shouldn't the collection be off?" she asked Pekke, keeping her voice to a whisper. She'd been too wrapped up in getting to safety to consider whether the D.I.C. raid had other side effects. "If the Boliska slid away with their equipment active..."

Pekke shook his head. "No one as careful as they've been would be that sloppy. My guess is they missed sealing up a container or two, or otherwise had enough of a residual field to pull two clusters together as they fled the D.I.C. We can't know for sure until we run a scan, though, and even that won't be definitive."

Zahira fingered her backpack strap. Of course the Boliska stranding themselves mid-slide would be too much to hope for. If her enemy had indeed made a successful escape, they'd only suffer a minor setback. But maybe that would be enough for now. Maybe having to regroup would throw the Boliska off-kilter long enough for Zahira to plan her next move. To make an offensive.

She plucked Jo's transcom from her hands, breaking the inventor's trance. "Let's save the wallowing for when the crypto-thingy is running, 'kay? Unless you want to read about an even worse disaster." Rather than wait for Jo to respond, she tucked the transcom in the inventor's pack and linked arms. They had to keep moving. Had to find the Boliska's weak spot as soon as possible and hit it with as much strength as they could muster.

As Pekke shared the coordinates to his safe house, Zahira gave Jo's hand a squeeze. "It's not your fault, you know. Even if we'd done nothing, a cluster would have hit a station eventually."

The inventor shrugged and fiddled with her nav device. Zahira guessed Jo would feel guilty no matter what she said, but it wasn't like the Boliska didn't have a body count before the clusters. Not with how Grandmother had talked about them. Not with how easily they resorted to kidnapping and blackmail.

Pekke sent the frequency through the chain of arms, a quiet, itchy one that smelled a bit like soap and stale bread. She grabbed it and amplified it, sharing it with Jo as the inventor had shared with her during their slide to the swamp. A bit of trust flowed there, too. Trust in Jo, and maybe a touch of hope that Pekke and Pravi's offers of alliance didn't hide too many secrets.

They arrived in a room three meter square, with barely enough room for them and the cryptoscope. A dim strip of lights lit one of the wood-paneled sides, and a small vent in the ceiling carried the scent of old socks. The only door was behind Pekke, and its metal frame had a complicated keypad for a lock. Somehow, she wasn't surprised his safe house would have an entrance like this. She and Grandmother had always laid low—small apartments with shared entrances and a myriad of window and fire escape exits. Never nice enough to tempt a thief, and certainly never secure enough to look like they had something to hide. But Pekke... She could only assume he'd learned his covert moves from holofilms. After scanning his retina and entering a six-digit code, he slid up a side panel instead of hitting the accept key. The door clinked open.

He eased it toward him with a tug of the keypad. "Careful, the knob releases knockout gas if you turn it."

Of course it would. Couldn't be too careful. She made certain to keep her distance as she edged around the cryptoscope to be the next out the door.

"Sorry about the dust." Pekke switched on a nearby table lamp and wiped its shade clean with his sleeve. "I haven't been here in a few months, and even then only to check if the plumbing had leaked."

The place didn't appear to have suffered from his neglect. Sure, the air was a little stale, and the couch and end table could do with a dusting, but the windows looked out to a sturdy fire escape and their latches appeared well-oiled. On the opposite side, a tiny kitchen stood with a full view of the living room and main door. The hallway adjacent stood clear of any furniture that could hinder escape.

Pekke put his hands in his pockets and rocked on his heels. "So, um, the bedrooms are down the hall. Only three, I'm afraid, as I wasn't expecting any additional visitors."

He gave a pointed look at Pravi, but she pretended not to notice as she inspected the same things Zahira had. Escape routes. Defensive positions. Possible points of attack. Jo and Nik followed up behind with the lift and cryptoscope rattling away. Whispers said the inventor was filling him in with details about the mole.

"There are two bathrooms," Pekke continued, "one in the hall with the bedrooms and one in the basement shooting range. I can show you how to access the stairs once you're settled."

A shooting range? Now that was a safe house quirk Zahira could appreciate. Maybe she'd be lucky and it'd have one of those secret arsenals, too, the kind with a whole assortment of weapons that slid out from a closet or bookcase. She scanned the rooms for hints of a weapons cache, only to find Pravi's eyes following her. The Resero woman was sizing her up just as much as she was sizing up the safe house, and Zahira knew she should do the same. How much could she trust someone who carried two blasters and didn't flinch at a firefight? Who landed clean shots on a bi-fan from over twenty meters, despite high speeds and unstable driving?

Jo might have been distracted with her cryptoscope, but Zahira had watched as Pravi took out not one but three of the Boliska's forward guns. If it weren't for her, they would have been road debris less than a kilometer from Jo's apartment.

Pravi peeked her head into the hallway and nodded to the far bedroom. "I'll take that one."

Zahira followed her gaze to find a room with a queen bed, a hefty dresser, and two windows leading to the fire escape. An excellent choice if Pravi thought the others might betray her. Or if she thought their goals might drift too far apart. The door opened inward and the dresser could serve as a barricade as she made her escape. Zahira might have chosen the same. She shouldn't have been so surprised that Pravi would stay. Sure, the woman had her own safe house, but so did Zahira. No doubt she'd also concluded that the benefits of being on site—like early access to new information and scans—outweighed the security of having her own space.

Zahira took little time selecting from the remaining bedrooms. The middle one had a larger bed, dresser, and window, but she didn't trust Pravi enough to have only a single wall between them. The third would serve her purposes just as well, if not better. It held a five-drawer bureau and an asymmetrical bunk bed, with a twin mattress on top and a full-sized one on bottom. Three windows wrapped the corner, and the bench below them held a collapsible escape ladder. Not as efficient as a fire escape, but that also meant no one could surprise her from outside. She went back to the living room to retrieve Jo's pack.

"You're bunking with me," she announced, keeping one eye on Pravi to see if the woman would protest. "I'll even let you pick which bunk."

"Uh, top?" the inventor answered through a row of screws held in her lips. She quickly finished whatever she'd been working on and slid out from under the cryptoscope. "I'd assumed one of us would take the couch? Or Nik and I could share the multi-bed room."

"I think this works better for privacy." Zahira put Jo's bag over her shoulder and cupped the strap with her thumb. The sleeping arrangement would work better for getting the inventor out safely, too. If they lost the cryptoscope in a raid, she could have Jo make a new one. Not to mention, Jo was Zahira's best chance at finding a way to hide from its scans. "Unless you'd rather not bunk with me?"

"Um, no, it's... it's fine. I hadn't expected it, that's all." She glanced briefly at her transcom, then reached for a spanner before putting it back and selecting another. "There's a lot about today that I wasn't expecting."

Like ending up in a safe house with two highly-skilled operatives they knew little about? Zahira glanced from Pravi to Pekke before tossing Jo's bag on the top bunk. Yeah, she hadn't expected that either.

Pekke's transcom buzzed from his pocket and he quickly pulled up a message screen. "Zave says they confirmed nguvu as the culprit on Donli. Though the readings were no higher than before, the strike hit one of the navigation computers."

Zahira crossed her arms. "So, what's the plan to stop them?" That's why they were here, right? Five near-strangers, thrown together by the Boliska and their nguvu collecting.

"Well." Pekke inhaled. "First, we need to update our map of the clusters. See if there are any more that are ready to collapse or collide. Then we work out a way to drain them. Once we've neutralized the imminent threat, we can move on to the next step."

"Which is rescuing the hatari, yeah?" She looked around the room, trying to meet the others' eyes, but Jo and Nik kept theirs on the tools. "We're not going to just let them rot in captivity while we go chasing energy clouds that might back up a post office or something."

"Donli Station was more than a backed up post office—" Jo started.

"Donli's also the exception." Zahira felt the nguvu rise in her chest and she fought to repress it. "How many strikes hit before now, with how many casualties? The hatari are in danger as we speak. Or have you forgotten they're the ones causing the clusters?"

Pekke put his transcom down and took a deep breath. "Zahira, I know this is important to you. The hatari are important to me, too. And we *will* rescue them. I promise you that. We just need to be sure we won't cause a domino chain of strikes when we do."

"So we just need to collect all that stray nguvu, right?" Zahira un-twisted one of her coils from her hair and set it on the counter with as much force as she dared. "Well, here you go. Size this up and put it at the center of the clusters."

"It's not that simple," Pekke said at the same time Pravi whispered, "Where in the strings did you get that?"

Before Zahira could even think of snapping the coil back up, Pravi had it in one hand and a wand-like device in the other. Wires and computer chips glowed orange under a clear, poly-alloy shell. The woman held it out to Zahira, her thumb tabbing on the bottom end of the wand. There, tucked underneath the first of the finger sensors, sat two coils identical to hers.

She stepped back, suddenly aware of the exits as well as the knife she'd smuggled from Jo's apartment. "We didn't steal them, if that's what you're wondering. I watched Grandmother spend years refining the design and the alloy and—"

"Dr. Evike Citanae. Lead Professor of Metallurgy at Jaana University." Pravi took a deep, unnerving look straight into Zahira's eyes. "Or at least she was, before she took a sudden retirement and disappeared from the scientific community a few decades ago."

"Twenty-three years ago, to be precise." Right after she realized her granddaughter was hatari. Zahira returned Pravi's stare. She hadn't heard Grandmother's real name in years, not since they'd stumbled across an old picture of hers in a library in Jaana. She'd always been Dahra or Inoa or Edetta, or some other alias Zahira would forget, which is why she'd stopped using them altogether.

Pravi set the coil back on the counter and tucked the wand under her jacket. "Xander gave her the credit in his notes. Said he'd never have gotten the wiring right without her, either."

"Good." Grandmother deserved for all her sacrifices to be recognized. Deserved so much more than Zahira could give her.

"So he did know her," Jo whispered. She'd watched the wand with intense interest. "I knew it couldn't have been a coincidence."

Pravi drummed her fingers on her holster. "There might be more in his notes that could help us. If only I had parted with the D.I.C. on better terms."

"The D.I.C. has your uncle's notes?" Pekke asked in surprise.

"The D.I.C. has my house and my house has the notes." Pravi's eyes turned back to Zahira's. "My house also has a nice arsenal for breaking out the hatari. Too bad I can't carry it all out on my own."

Zahira knew in an instant what Pravi was offering. Help retrieve the notes, and she could keep what she could carry. Pass whatever test the woman had planned, and she'd earn her help with the strike.

Pekke raised an eyebrow. "How dangerous is this retrieval?"

"Not too bad, presumably." Pravi didn't take her eyes off Zahira. "So long as the Boliska's mole hasn't helped their friends sneak past the D.I.C.'s defenses."

Given how quickly they'd reached Jo's apartment, Zahira knew better than to count on that. On the other hand, she didn't want to wait until the clusters cleared to plan an attack. "How do I know I can trust you?"

"Oh, you don't." Pravi pulled out her smaller blaster and checked the cartridges. "Do you know how to handle one of these?"

Zahira nodded. Though they'd never kept one in the apartment, Grandmother had taken her to the shooting range a few times.

"Good." Pravi put the weapon in her hands and started for the front door. "If you do end up needing it, try not to hit me."

"But I haven't agreed to come."

"Sure. That's why you're already three steps from the counter." Pravi grinned. "We'll be back in an hour, Dr. Froum. Jo has my number if you get the scan of the clusters before then."

Zahira wrapped her hand around the blaster's grip. Every memory of Grandmother told her to stay back. To stay safe. But Evike Citanae hadn't held back when her granddaughter needed her. Hadn't taken the safe route of waiting for someone else to fix things. She tucked the weapon in the side pocket of her backpack and joined Pravi for the slide.

Chapter Thirty-Two

— • —

Nik

Nik watched as Zahira closed the door to the sliding room behind her. A normally cautious person setting off with someone she'd just met? Yeah, that tracked with how things had been lately.

Jo went back to setting up the cryptoscope, and Nik leaned in toward Pekke. "So Jo said something about a mole in the D.I.C.?" Due to the shock of Donli, she hadn't been super clear on the details when he'd asked.

"Unfortunately, yes. Someone tipped off the Boliska before the raid started." Pekke nudged the coil Zahira had left on the counter. "Zave's contact said that based on the fading traces of people and equipment, they must've had at least an hour's warning."

So the people at Jo's apartment had indeed been Boliska. Good to know Jo hadn't found new enemies to run from. He slid his hands in his pockets. "So what's the plan, then? How long does Jo need to stay here?"

"I'd say until we take down the Boliska, at the very least. Past that..." Pekke shrugged. "She's welcome to stay as long as she wants."

But why would she want... Oh. He meant if Jo couldn't put down the mantel of hero. If the failed D.I.C. raid had convinced her not to leave the cryptoscope's fate in another's hands. What was it Pekke had said during their escape from the lab? *'Sometimes the quietest people are a mere opportunity away from becoming vigilantes.'*

Jo muttered something under her breath and pried at a stuck travel latch with a screwdriver. From the look on her face, she'd locked in on her task, unable to notice anything else. Not that she'd snagged her sleeve on one of the cryptoscope's joints, nor that she'd stepped in the pack of muffins at some point and had left a trail of blue all over the rug. Until she had the cryptoscope running, all that mattered was ensuring another Donli never happened. And after that... Nik's chest tightened. Knowing her, she wouldn't stop until she personally watched the hatari freed and the Boliska carted off to jail. Even if that meant more firefights and high-speed chases. Even if it meant never going home.

He turned back to Pekke and stuffed his hands in his pockets. "What would you do if you had the chance to do it over? If you could save your friend before she was framed?"

"Are you asking if I'd still try to talk her out of investigating the inconsistencies?" Pekke glanced at Jo and shook his head. "I don't think I could have, no matter what I tried. The only thing I'd do different is say 'yes' when she asked me to join her." He gave Nik an apologetic smile and cleared his throat. "The thing is, deep down, everyone wants to make a difference. We want the things we say and do to matter. It's just that when it comes to the hard things, the risky things, most people feel like they can't do anything. Like there has to be someone better suited to solve the problem. Once that illusion breaks, there's no going back."

Nik took a deep breath and nodded. The D.I.C. were supposed to be the experts. They were supposed to be the ones tracking down the Boliska's base and rescuing the hatari. But giving them the coordinates had only made things worse. "So what do I do now?"

Pekke leaned forward on the counter and nudged Zahira's coil toward Nik. "A good first step would be helping me turn this into some sort of nguvu grounding rod."

"No, I mean with," he tilted his head toward Jo.

"Ah. Well, I certainly wouldn't tell her she's making a mountain out of a musk wasp nest." Pekke gave a tight smile, wincing at the memory of having said just that. "But let's be honest here. Forget about Jo. Do you really think that you, Mr. Let's-Just-Hit-The-Boliska-With-The-Sphere-Case, can go back to normal now? After the lab, when you found Jo missing, your first thought was to ambush the people chasing us. Is that the thought of someone destined to grade papers and fact check others' research?"

Nik stared at the countertop. He'd wanted to go back to exactly that, hadn't he? So he could pretend none of this ever happened. That being chased by smuggled dinosaurs and Boliska agents and hostile hovercraft had been some hologame he'd spent too much time playing. Their old life had been safe. Predictable. He didn't want the world to need him. If he and Jo were the hatari's best hope... He shook his head. "My ambush plan was asinine. You said so yourself."

"Eh. You gotta start somewhere." Pekke pulled a slip of paper out of his shirt pocket and scrounged a pen from one of the kitchen drawers. "Do you think I was this awesome before my friend's misfortune? I could barely make eye contact with a D.I.C. agent, much less help her hide from one. No safe houses. No fake IDs. I certainly couldn't have handled a blaster, much less shot at someone. The only fighting experience I had was a few Rygalian martial arts classes when I was six." As he spoke, he started scribbling different hooked helix shapes and then crossing them out. From their shape, they looked to be designs for absorbing and grounding the nguvu clouds.

"Might be worth trying a lightning rod at the center," Nik said without thinking. "Then you could spiral a larger coil around it."

Pekke grinned. "See. You're not as bad at this as you think you are. Now we just need to rig up a prototype or two and pass them to Zave when the nguvu data is ready."

Nik leaned back from the counter. "Brainstorming isn't the same as flying a hovercraft on one rotor."

"Oh, isn't it? A bit of pattern recognition, a bit of spread out awareness. Noticing how the whole thing wants to shift and how a slight change can correct that. Past that, it's just practice. Lots of practice. Did I mention that there's a shooting range on the lower floor?"

Nik glanced at the helix sketches. This was much more complicated than Pekke made it out to be. Nik was a college professor, not a radiation mitigation specialist. His rough grounding rod sketch had as much chance of magically fixing the clusters as a few rounds in the shooting range had of making him an ace. But he supposed he had to start somewhere. He slid the pen and paper closer to himself. "Here, let me take some measurements and see what I can come up with."

Pekke grinned and turned to check on Jo, who had moved on to recalibrating the sensors. Nik watched her adjust the sensitivity with one wrench in her hand and another between her teeth. She did seem to want this, didn't she? She moved differently. More focused. Like lives depended on it. Nik guessed lives did depend on it. His mind drifted back to the helixes. They'd been a rough start—no sense of scale or placement or metallic makeup. The latter could be fixed by analyzing Zahira's coil, but they had no guarantee it'd work for higher nguvu levels; especially levels high enough to override sliding station safety measures.

Nik flipped the paper to the back to start two neat columns. One, a list of which measurements to take from Zahira's coil, and the other a list of benchmark tests they could complete before assembling a full-scale prototype. By the time he had the paper filled, Jo had the cryptoscope calibrated and ready to run.

Pekke looked them both over and rubbed his hands together. "Perfect. Who's down for lunch while we wait for the scan?"

Jo shrugged as she hit the start button, but her stomach growled. She must have been smelling the muffins the whole time she worked, and her body wouldn't let her ignore it anymore. "I guess I could eat something."

"I'm down, too," Nik said. He'd eaten before his run to the bakery, but that felt so long ago now. Back when he thought the only change he needed to adjust to was Jo taking the fellowship. Back when he'd thought a simple text to the D.I.C. could fix everything.

Pekke flipped out his transcom. "Preferences, then? Soup? Sandwiches? Those little grain rolls with the green wrapping?"

"I... don't know." Jo collapsed onto the couch. "Do you want to text Pravi and Zahira and see if they want anything?"

"I could... Though I imagine they have their hands full. What with the D.I.C. and all." Pekke tapped the screen with his finger. "Best to get a few extra items and not bother them."

"General groceries would be nice," Nik chimed in. "Given that we'll be staying a while."

Jo gave him a confused look, and he shrugged. She'd probably expected him to argue for leaving as soon as possible. He was a bit surprised himself, but it felt like the right thing to do. "It'll be easier to test the grounding rods from here," he offered.

"But what about your job?"

"I can get a sub for finals week, and grades are easy enough to do remotely." He could decide about next semester later. Once he had more time to plan. He hadn't realized it, but his subconscious was already working on other things to clear from his calendar. Blaster safety classes could replace his weekly laser tag meetup. Fitness classes could fit between an earlier waking time and a shorter brunch. Or he could see if Pekke had recommendations on that front. He didn't know how to drive a hovercraft, but he could learn that, too. Part of him still hoped this would be a one-off for Jo. A daring hatari rescue followed by a quiet retirement to her lab. But if it wasn't, if Pekke was right and this was just the start, he had to be ready for even more daring escapades. The world, and his friendship with Jo, might depend on it.

CHAPTER THIRTY-THREE

— • —

PRAVI

What equipment did one need to save the world? Pravi's mind raced as she and Zahira arrived in the ready room sliding closet. Weapons, of course. And body armor. She peeled her fingers from the transport wand, reluctant to part from the warm hum of the strings. No books could have prepared her for tasting the sharp tangerine of her home string. Or the way its insistant buzz smelled like an aquarium. For how much more vivid the world felt with it in the background. But she had work to do, and that meant waiting to enjoy her freedom until she'd rid Stringspace of the nguvu threat.

Pravi pushed open the door to her ready room and her hand went straight to the hook of empty duffel bags. Covert surveillance equipment was a must, and maybe a few field scanners and first aid kits. She scanned the shelves for more ideas of what to pack, only to find Zahira still standing in the doorway. "Feel free to grab a duffel," she said, pulling the hatari out of her reverie. Pravi remembered having the same feeling of awe the first time her uncle had let her in. Polished metal and military gear everywhere you looked. Rows of blasters and ammo laid out like a candy store for vigilantes. "The weapon cases are in the bottom drawer to your left."

Zahira grabbed a duffel and hurried to the nearest supply cabinet. Pravi watched as the hatari perused the labeled shelves and drawers. The Lufus 550 might be a good starter weapon for her. Or the Nexx 33. Though small in statue, the way she moved suggested she could handle something hefty. An A7-mini could make a good secondary.

Pravi pulled ammo for each and checked the security feed to see if anyone had noticed their arrival.

To her surprise, the command tent in the side yard appeared quiet. Eerily so, with how active it had been mere hours before. All that remained of the soldiers' presence were a few trampled leaves in the flower beds and impressions left by the stacks of evidence bins. The stark absence of their equipment sparked hope that the D.I.C. had given up entirely. But no such luck. Agent Yuri stood at his post on the side walkway, and the stakeout car still waited across the street. Neither of them appeared on high alert, but Pravi couldn't risk staying too long. She motioned for Zahira to pack the ammo and body armor as she slid in an earbud to check the audio feed in the stakeout car.

"... by the makers." Agent Clive's voice sounded brusk through the still-undiscovered bug she'd left in the driver's side door. *"This seat is so stiff today. I almost envy Regi and his pile of paperwork."*

Leather creaked as Agent Beni stretched in the passenger seat. *"Is it really the seat making you sore, or is it the lack of delivery trucks to obsess over?"*

Clive's answer was sharp in spite of the crackling from the receiver. *"I do not obsess over them."* More noise from his chair suggested Clive was either trying once again to get comfortable or he had turned his back to Beni. Whichever it was, neither his words nor actions signaled that they'd noticed Pravi and Zahira sliding in.

"What are those lighter-looking things?" Zahira asked.

Pravi looked over and noticed her companion had already packed a handful of tactical knives and a riot shield on top of the armor and ammo. She followed Zahira's gaze to a top shelf. "The flash detonators? They produce a directional burst of seven million lumens. Highly dangerous. They can burn your eyelids off if you're too close when they flash."

"Oh."

"I'd grab three." Pravi headed for the far wall to select her own equipment while Zahira packed the detonators in the corner of a weapon case. It was a pity she, Nik, and Jo were so inexperienced. Although proper protection could mitigate the risk of using something like the flash devices, some of the cooler tech required a skilled handler. Like the remote-piloted drone support. Or the laser cutters.

Oh, well. Pravi would have to deal with the team she had. And that meant hoping a few extra smoke and flash grenades would be enough to turn the tides. She started packing them into a duffel with her gas masks and tranquilizer darts when her transcom buzzed. Munus.

Did he know she was there? She signaled to Zahira that she was going to take his call. "If this goes wrong, there's a chance we'll need to make a quick exit."

Zahira nodded and packed faster.

"Miss Resero?" Munus' voice had a hint of disappointment when she answered. *"I suppose this means you left of your own volition."*

"Yes. I felt I needed to protect myself and my property from the D.I.C.'s mole." Finished with filling her first duffel, Pravi tucked all the straps and corners out of the way of the zipper. "And I must say I found your absence during the raid a little suspicious."

Munus responded with a moment of silence. *"Would you believe me if I said I was shot?"*

"During the raid?"

"About an hour before."

Pravi's hand paused on its way to a fresh weapons case. "Pics or it didn't happen."

To her surprise, her transcom buzzed with a text mere seconds later. A picture of Munus, laid up in a hospital bed, one shoulder bandaged and his arm in a sling. *"What else could have made me miss my favorite consultant's first raid?"* He had a smile to his voice, but when Pravi didn't bite, he cleared his throat. *"Long story short, I've been having suspicions that this might be related to an old case file. When I went to interview a witness, I ended up here."*

"Do you think it was related to the mole?"

"Could be, but I don't think so. The witness is the one who shot me."

Pravi started pulling down blasters and arranging them to fit as many as possible. "So did my uncle work on this mysterious case?"

Munus took a deep breath, as if buying himself time to weigh what information to give and what to hold back. *"To be honest, it was the Penderfyn case. I expect you've heard of it?"*

Pravi searched her memory, but couldn't figure out why she recognized the name. "I can't say that I have."

"Your uncle refused to consult on it. Said there was too much doubt about the evidence to help track the culprit."

As if that narrowed it down. Penderfyn... "The one where modeling explosions turned into illegal tests of their model?"

"That's the one. The suspect claimed she hadn't run the test and that her models were intended for risk evaluation only. Turns out she wasn't lying about being framed."

"And this applies to our case how?"

"One of the models involved concentrated nguvu."

Pravi slammed her weapon case shut. "A tenuous connection at best." And one that made Pravi question whether Munus only wanted to keep her on the line. Still, her security feed remained clear, and Zahira had almost finished packing their third bag.

"I thought that too," Munus said with a sigh, *"until that lab we visited turned out to be the same lab she'd worked in and the suspect's son was seen in the same security line as your informants."*

Yeah, that sounded like pretty compelling evidence. She'd have to ask Zahira if she or Jo had seen anything.

Munus continued. *"You know what sealed it for me, though? The company that owns the compound we raided is tied to the one that funded their research."*

Well, shit. That would seal it for Pravi, too. She threw her Z73 rifle over her shoulder. "So what does that mean? Why would they care about how it explodes?"

"I'll answer that with another question. Why would the smugglers need to produce a nguvu cloud bigger than the one hovering around Yerin?"

Before Pravi could answer, another voice spoke through her ear bud. Clive's. *"You've got to be kidding me. What packages could she need when she's not even home?"*

"I'm going to need you to get to the point." Pravi signaled to Zahira that it was time to wrap up. Something in her gut said they'd already stayed too long.

"I'm saying they aren't just collecting nguvu for the lizards."

"I don't know, Clive. Maybe she forgot to cancel her grocery order?" The sound of creaking seats accompanied Beni's voice.

"I've told you." Clive countered, *"I've told you. Groceries are a green truck on Saturdays."*

"It's not too late, you know." Munus' words overlapped with Clive's. *"Just file an injunction to keep us from taking the prototype and come back to work."*

"Oh, it's that simple, is it?" Pravi pulled up the security feed to find the 'delivery truck' did indeed look suspicious. It also had two bulky-looking mailmen instead of one.

"They didn't go to the back, Beni. If the package is big enough to need two people, wouldn't they keep it in the back?"

Pravi's throat tightened. "We need to leave. Now." She picked up two of their bags and shoved Zahira toward the sliding closet. "Head back the way we came. Same stops, just in reverse."

"You're not coming?" To her credit, Zahira's question didn't keep her from following directions. She pulled up her nav dial and took the bags from Pravi.

"We can't both fit with all this equipment, and I'm not wasting our trip." Pravi also wanted to know how these 'mailmen' knew she'd come home when the D.I.C. didn't.

Zahira opened her mouth to say something, but a security alarm signaled a breach attempt at the front door.

"Miss Resero? Are you still there? What's going on?"

"Not now, Munus." Pravi hit the release for the stun gas her uncle had installed at the front entrance, but nothing happened.

"Main entrance compromised," the security system announced.

A seatbelt clicked in her ear, and Clive insisted he was going in.

"Please tell me you didn't go home."

Pravi ignored Munus to process all the other signals coming in. Her front camera was dead, having cut out before it got a good view of the invaders' faces. A strong floor tremor said they'd made it inside. If they had decent scanners, it wouldn't take them long to realize which room had the most shielding.

As for Clive, the camera in the side yard showed him crouched next to an unconscious Yuri. Beni appeared to be coming up behind, weapon drawn and aimed at the front door.

"Damn it, Resero, we didn't find the mole yet." Though Munus had said he was in the hospital, he sounded ready to grab his blaster and head for her house. *"What were you thinking?"*

"I didn't realize that was any of your business." Pravi confirmed that Zahira was fading from the sliding room and assessed her options. With Beni and Clive coming in for support, she didn't have to run. There was still the chance of catching one of the invaders alive and using them to find the mole. On the other hand, was the mole really her problem? She and her team had already decided not to pass any new coordinates to the D.I.C.

The door to the ready room shook, and Munus was in her ear again. *"Was that blasterfire?"*

"No, I just decided to do some renovations, and the demo crew suggested dynamite." Pravi looked again to the sliding closet, but sprinted for the equipment shelves instead. She didn't give herself time to second guess as one hand closed around a pair of flash detonation devices and the other pulled on a face mask. "You know, I've always wanted a sunroom."

"Pravi..."

In one motion, she unlatched and opened the door, giving herself just enough space to aim flashes both up and down the hall. Even with her eyes closed behind her shield, her eyelids flashed bright red. Something clattered to the floor as she slammed the door back shut and latched it.

"I swear, if you get yourself killed..."

The sound of blasterfire cut him off and booted footsteps thundered in the hall. Pravi latched the door and took cover on the side wall.

"You're under arrest by my authority as a D.I.C. agent." The speaker panted heavily as he spoke, and the wall's insulation made it hard to determine who it was. Agent Beni?

Someone else knocked on the sliding room door. "Miss Resero? Is someone in there?" The deeper voice made it clear it was Clive.

"Affirmative." Pravi lowered her blaster, but didn't put the safety on. "You might want to check whether they had backup on the way."

"Will do," Beni said at the same time a woman's voice declared it, "Unnecessary."

Jandra?

The audible sneer of the words could only belong to her least favorite agent. "Miss Resero, seeing as the safety of your home is compromised, I'm going to need you to come with me to headquarters."

Pravi put the safety on her blaster and gathered up her bags. "I'd rather wait here, but thanks."

"I insist."

"Don't do it," Munus whispered. *"I can't contact the team. All the feeds are dead."*

Pravi considered flipping the safety back off, but took slow steps toward the sliding closet instead. "Nothing short of a full security escort is getting me out of here."

"I don't think you understand." Four shots echoed from the hall, followed by two heavy thuds. "You can either come with me, or you can take the fall for two dead agents."

Pravi froze. Two dead agents? Had she...? Were Beni and Clive...?

"I think we found your mole," she whispered to Munus as she took the last step into the closet. It all made sense now. Jandra's obsessive scan for weakness in her security net. The gap in the D.I.C. cameras... "I don't think I'll be able to come back to work after all."

"I'm giving you to the count of three."

"Don't worry, just get yourself safe." Something rustled on Munus' end. *"I've been recording the whole call. She can't pin anything on you. The second my team gets there, she'll be under arrest."*

And Pravi would be gone by then. She pulled up her navigation dial, but her hand paused over the numbers. "What if you didn't arrest her?"

"What?"

Something heavy slammed into the ready room door.

"What if we used her to feed false information to the smugglers? Tactics Manual Chapter 13." Another slam and Pravi locked in her destination. "At least give me an hour to pitch the idea to my team."

"Alright. An hour, but no more." Munus' voice faded as Pravi ended the call and grabbed a string. The door burst open, but she was already sliding away, a plan forming in her mind.

CHAPTER THIRTY-FOUR

—.—

Jo

"**N**o, absolutely not."

Something about Zahira's tone sent Jo's heart racing, and she looked up from her equipment bag. She'd been taking stock of her tools while waiting for the cryptoscope to run, but the conversation happening in the kitchen area appeared far more important than finding out what Pekke had and hadn't packed. She dumped the arrangement of spanners from her lap and took up a defensive position between the argument and the cryptoscope's spinning arms.

"I understand how you feel," Pravi said, "but we need to keep our options open."

Zahira leaned back, revealing tightly crossed arms and a slight buzz to her coils. She'd been on edge since they'd gotten back from the supply run. "Open? Weren't we being open when we sent the D.I.C. the coordinates in the first place? How do we know there isn't a second mole?"

Pravi gave an exasperated sigh. "That's my whole point. This is the best way to find out."

"By doing what?" Zahira asked. "Trusting them again? Letting them cause another Donli?"

Jo blinked. Pravi hadn't suggested giving the coordinates to the D.I.C. again, had she?

"Of course not." Pravi's voice came out sharp, even more so than Zahira's, and she took a deep breath to regroup. "Let me back up in case one of our translators missed something. We're not giving the D.I.C. information. We're just... pretending to. We come up with some story for Director Munus to tell his team, maybe give them a little 'proof', and then he uses that to see if the mole has any friends hiding in the organization."

"And what if there is another mole? Can't they just flip the trap back on us?"

"How?" Pravi crossed her arms to mirror Zahira. "All we're doing is giving Munus a story. He'd be the one setting up the trap and risking his team."

The idea made sense to Jo, but Zahira's posture didn't loosen. For her, this had to feel personal. "And after? Let's say this little trap goes as planned, and it looks like Jandra is the only mole. Is that really enough to trust the D.I.C. again?"

"I don't think that's what Miss Resero is suggesting." Pekke's voice came from the hall, and Jo turned to find he and Nik were standing near the secret passage to the basement. "We do need to be realistic, though. Working with the D.I.C. isn't any more dangerous than the five of us trying to take on dozens of Boliska alone."

Zahari scoffed. "More dangerous for whom? Us or the hatari?"

"Us and the hatari. And the world in general." Pravi gave a heavy sigh. "Or did you forget there's a giant field of radiation hanging around Stringspace?" As if on cue, the cryptoscope pinged to signal the projection was ready. Pravi swept her arm toward it without looking. "The most important thing, for everyone, is getting rid of these clouds as soon as possible."

"Agreed," Pekke said.

Nik nodded as well, surprising Jo with how decisive he looked. He couldn't possibly have gotten on board with the mission, could he? After all that time he'd spent trying to trying to talk her out of it? What exactly had he been doing in the basement with Pekke?

Zahira pursed her lips as if to argue, but the discussion had ended. Everyone had turned to take in the newest scan. Jo had the sudden urge to give the hatari's hand a squeeze and tell her everything would be okay. That they'd figure it out. But she didn't know if she could keep that promise.

"Looks like we were right." Pekke took up position on the side of the projection closest to Donli. "They must have passed through this cluster here, setting off the strike, and continued on in that direction."

Jo followed the path of his finger. The main cluster had dissipated since the strike, but a defined streak stood out on the edge. If she ran another scan for the hatari frequency, she'd likely find the Boliska had made a stop in that direction. There might even be a base along that trajectory.

"What about this wispy bit over here?" Pravi asked. She gestured to a similar patch of nguvu a few worlds away. "Is this another place that could strike?"

"I don't think so," Jo answered. The patch of gold was barely bigger than her fist, and there'd never been a strike from a cluster that small. "But maybe the Boliska passed through that area as well?"

Pekke shook his head. "Wrong trajectory. They'd have to have zigzagged to get the wisp in that direction."

"Not if they split up." Pravi knelt at the edge of her wisp and looked toward the location of the raided Boliska base as if to line them up. "It would be a smart move, strategically speaking. Split your group and split your risk of being followed or discovered. We'd have a hell of a time finding them all, if it weren't for the cryptoscope."

"But we do have the cryptoscope," Jo pointed out. "So all they'd be doing is splitting their defenses."

"Sure, but they don't know that." Pravi stood and started picking her way through the projection. "Why was that Boliska team sent to your apartment if not to figure out how you tracked them? And to keep you from doing it again? Ah, here's another one." She pointed out another streak of nguvu, once again lining it up with the raided Boliska base. "That makes at least three. Four, if that bit over there is another one." Her arms crossed as she faced Zahira. "You still think the five of us can handle this by ourselves?"

Zahira didn't respond, but the buzzing at her scalp grew louder.

Jo felt a wave of apprehension as she edged closer to the projection. "Would they split up the hatari, too?" she found herself saying. "Or is there a chance we could rescue them first and leave the other bases to the D.I.C.?" Rescuing the hatari remained the highest priority, didn't it? For both Zahira and the growing clouds.

Pravi stopped her search for anomalies to consider the idea. "I suppose it's possible they kept them together. What do we know about their collection device? Is it individual pods or do they have all their hostages tied in together?"

Pekke shrugged. "We've only come across the product, not the process. But there is one way to be certain." He nodded his head from Jo to the cryptoscope's tower. "How about we send this scan to Zave and start a new one?" This time, he seemed to imply, they'd use the frequency for hatari.

Jo looked to Zahira to confirm she was okay with it. And not just because the hatari could take out the cryptoscope with a single touch.

"That's naturally the next step, isn't it?" Zahira gave a tight-shouldered shrug. "Can't argue about whether to share the data with the D.I.C. if we don't have it."

"It's just collecting information—" Pekke started to say, but Zahira shrugged him off.

"By all means, run the scan." She turned away from the projection as if washing her hands of it. "Just don't expect me to agree on what to do after." She grabbed one of Pravi's equipment bags and headed for her bedroom while Jo and Pekke exchanged glances. They'd be in for trouble if they split their approach.

"I've got this," Pekke said, starting for the cryptoscope's tower, "if you want to... you know."

Take the harder task? What was Jo supposed to do to get everyone on the same page? It wasn't like there was some calibration table that she could set everyone to. She took a wistful look at her crystal probes, then followed Zahira to their room.

Sounds of zippers and latches came from the bottom bunk as she entered, and dark gray and green boxes filled the area around the bag.

"What do you think?" Zahira asked before Jo could say anything. She didn't look up as she set grenades and ammo in little lines by her pillow. "Should we give the D.I.C. another chance?"

Jo bit her lip as she grabbed her own bag off the top bunk. "Well, as Pravi said—"

Zahira thumped a blaster-proof vest down on the bed. "I don't care what Pravi said. I asked what you think."

"I am hesitant to trust them again. You know, after Donli..."

"I sense there's a 'but'?"

The heavy buzz from the coils gave Jo an uneasy feeling, but the hatari appeared to want honesty. She set her bag on the dresser and started to unzip it slowly. "But... I also think we can't afford to count them out. There's only the five of us, and it's not like the D.I.C. will sit idle if we don't tell them anything." She wouldn't have entrusted them with the first set of coordinates if they'd had a reputation for being inept.

Zahira sighed. "That's my fear as well. That they might find the Boliska bases without our help and mess up our plans."

Jo nodded. At least if they kept the lines of communication open, they could coordinate new raids.

"Looks like we don't have a choice, then." With the duffel bag empty, Zahira cast it as aside and turned to inspect her equipment. She seemed to do a series of calculations in her head. "As much as I hate to admit it, we'll have to try Pravi's plan."

"Maybe it won't be too bad?" Jo offered. She tried for a reassuring voice, but her worries seeped through. "If the D.I.C. clears out any moles, that's a good thing, right?"

Zahira shrugged. "It's not just the mole. There might be some broader politics involved."

"Politics?"

"Politics." Zahira pulled up her transcom and started flipping through her tabs. "You remember the blond woman at the lab? The one who seemed to be the leader?"

Jo nodded.

"I found her." At that moment Zahira stopped on a news video, one taken on Yerin. "I ran across this while waiting for Pravi. Seems like the Boliska wanted to preempt any action from the D.I.C. by saying the base they raided was owned by 'rogue agents' and that they're working to 'unravel the corruption.'"

"That's what we want, though, isn't it?"

"Yeah, except the woman who's making those promises is the one who killed Grandmother."

CHAPTER THIRTY-FIVE

— • —

ZAHIRA

"*A* *lthough we are confident that all the rogue elements have been identified, we will continue to cooperate with the D.I.C.*"
Zahira's fingers tightened on her transcom as the news conference played. Though she sat on the bed surrounded by an arsenal, it gave her little comfort. *'Dr. Ulsta Feikasan'* the caption read, its bold text naming Grandmother's killer. *'Boliska Chief of Internal Affairs.'*

Cameras flashed and journalists took notes, oblivious to the most important fact: the blond woman's presence turned the whole news conference into a farce. *"I believe that a thorough investigation,"* she was saying with all the confidence of a con artist, *"as well as our quick, decisive action to purge the culprits, are the first steps to restoring the public's trust."* Oh yes, because Yerin could totally trust the ringleader to purge her loyal followers and not whatever innocent bystanders the Boliska still had.

Jo looked like she was going to be sick and shifted uncomfortably beside Zahira. She had to be thinking the same thing Zahira had when she'd first discovered the video—that Dr. Feikasan must have thought she was untouchable.

"We need to tell Pekke," the inventor's voice held anger and urgency. "He already gave her description to Zave. We just need to give them the name."

Zahira shook her head. Getting revenge wouldn't be that easy. "She's head of Internal Affairs in a major government department. Not even the D.I.C. can mess with local officials without substantial proof." Anything less than indisputable evidence, and Feikasan could sidestep or call it into question. Or flip it back on them. Like how the D.I.C. mole had tried to set up Pravi as an agent killer.

"But we do have proof." Jo's hand tightened on the edge of the bed as she turned to meet Zahira's eyes. "The lab data. Those scans prove Feikasan was there."

She'd almost forgotten about that. How they'd had the scanners recording everything. A bubble of hope surged into Zahira's throat, but she pushed it down. "She still holds a government office. The D.I.C. would have to jump through bureaucratic hurdles..."

"Not if they don't know she's a government official." Jo's eyes went sharp, and she started sketching out a plan on the bed quilt, using Zahira's supplies as pawns. "We can make them come at it sideways. Pravi said we need data, didn't she? Something to bait the mole with? We could give them the lab scans without telling them about Feikasan—after filtering out your resonance, of course—and from what Pravi said about Munus, there's no way he won't look into it."

"And that will lead him to Feikasan."

Jo nodded. "He can use the lab data to start building a case. Feikasan's resonance doesn't give him a name or a face, or anything that might clue her in until it's too late to stop him."

And while he pursued Feikasan, they could rescue the hatari. "But what about Pravi and Pekke? What if they're not on board with this plan?"

Jo gave Zahira a confused look. The inventor hadn't considered that possibility.

"By hiding the truth about Feikasan, Pravi would weaken her relationship with Munus and Pekke risks his credibility with Zave," Zahira explained. And as much as she hated to admit it, they needed both if they wanted to wipe out the Boliska completely.

Jo's voice went quiet again. "They're not risking it if they don't know."

Now it was Zahira's turn to be confused. Was Jo really suggesting what Zahira thought she was? That the timid, honest inventor would lie for her? Would risk her fellowship with Pravi in order to help Zahira seek revenge?

A heavy knock disrupted her thoughts. "Sorry to interrupt," came Pravi's sharp, no-nonsense voice, "but I need to give Munus an answer."

Jo's eyes flicked to Zahira, and she cleared her throat. "We're both okay with the plan now. We might even have some data to use as bait."

"Is that so?" Pravi edged open the door and leaned against the jamb. "Would this data be the reason for your change of heart?"

The question was directed at Zahira, but Jo answered. "Not exactly. I... well, we... You see, we took these scans at the lab..."

"I asked her to hide them before." Zahira crossed her arms and returned Pravi's intense stare. Kudos to Jo for trying, but lying to the Resero woman was not a job for an amateur. "And if it weren't for the failed raid and Donli, we might still be hiding it."

"Because it proves you were there." Pravi's eyes drifted down Zahira and back up to her face. "Because you don't want anyone having a resonance pattern to track you with."

Zahira shrugged. "Would you want that if you were me?" She channeled her feelings of defiance into her face and posture. Anything less might not sell the lie. "But Jo says she can filter my pattern out before we pass it to the D.I.C."

Jo nodded eagerly. Hopefully Pravi would read it as a strong desire to create a consensus and not as impatience for the woman to agree. Pravi had to see that using the lab data made sense. The mole couldn't help but be tempted to intercept it, and anyone they contacted for help would fall right into the D.I.C.'s net.

After a few tense moments, she tilted her head in a sideways nod. "I suppose that works. But Munus is going to need a small sample ASAP."

"I'm on it." Jo hopped up from the bed and gave Zahira a small smile before scrambling to the living room for her scanner.

Zahira didn't budge. Pravi's agreement didn't mean she'd fully bought their story.

"Promise me the risk will be worth it," she said, trying to balance out Jo's eagerness with a show of hesitation. Like Zahira was mere words away from changing her mind. "Promise me we'll get those bastards."

Pravi pursed her lips and pushed off the doorjamb. "I can only promise that I'll do my damnedest." Other than a brief exchange of determined glances, those words seemed to be the end of it. The cryptoscope finished running shortly after, confirming that the hatari had indeed been taken together to a new base. Zahira and the others would infiltrate it themselves, leaving the other bases to the D.I.C.

Whatever suspicions Pravi had about Zahira's motives, they didn't stop her from sending Munus the lab sample the second Jo had it ready. She didn't even give the full data more than a cursory glance as the inventor worked to clear it of Zahira's resonance. And why would she? They already had a way to track the Boliska's bases, and they already knew where the hatari had been taken. Still, Zahira didn't let herself relax as she helped Pravi and Pekke evaluate the hatari's location. The cryptoscope had placed them only an octave away, in a three-building compound in a remote industrial town. Satellite imagery showed no activity, but the images were old and Pekke couldn't get new ones from the D.I.C. without alerting them. The only thing to do was to check it out themselves.

A restless night and a light breakfast later, they all sat in one of Pekke's hovercrafts, half a kilometer away from their target, watching Pravi's transcom screen.

"We have Agent Jandra in custody," Munus' voice said over the line. *"Proceed with phase two."*

The blank screen switched to dual D.I.C. feeds from a dozen worlds away. Both overlooked a busy plaza, one from a rooftop view and the other inside the café where the lab data exchange would take place. Pravi had timed their surveillance mission this way on purpose, so that Munus wouldn't suspect they were already making moves against the Boliska. While he and his team trapped the mole, she, Zahira, and the others would run a reconnaissance mission of their own.

"The drone is making its first pass," Pekke said over his shoulder. He sat hunched in the driver's seat, the surveillance footage playing on the center console. Like the others, he wore head-to-toe body armor. After the fight at Jo's apartment, no one wanted to take any risks.

Zahira crouched in the back seat, wedged between a weapon case and a riot shield. A bag of magnetic climbing gear sat behind her, brought in case they encountered barriers to the drone. So far, it hadn't proved necessary. She and the others huddled around the two small screens, with Pravi's transcom showing views of a bustling crowd and Pekke's console sporting frame after frame of broken, weed-speckled concrete.

"Asset moving in," came the voice of one of the D.I.C. agents as his camera panned to where the plaza met the street. Zahira's eyes landed on a brunette woman in a navy jumpsuit, weaving hesitantly through the throng. If she hadn't known better, and if the inventor hadn't been sitting just one meter away, Zahira would have sworn it was Jo.

Pravi held a finger to the unmute button. "Did Jandra contact anyone before you arrested her?" she asked Munus.

"Not that we know of, but we are searching her office for secret comms."

The second D.I.C. camera meandered in the direction opposite the fake asset, checking for ambushes and assassins.

"That looks a bit like a guardhouse, don't you think?" Pekke tapped the corner of the console screen, pulling everyone's attention away from Munus' team. A small field office came into view from the drone's feed, sided in vertical gray planks and no more than five meters long and four wide. As they watched, a man in a green vest came out to stretch.

"Seems plausible." Pravi craned her neck to squint at something in the background. "Can you switch to thermal imaging? That long, yellowy building to the west looks a bit like a dormitory, don't you think?"

Pekke flipped a switch and the colors in the drone feed switched to grays, reds, and oranges. Three bodies warmed the guardhouse, while the long, low building Pravi had asked about flowed with a half-dozen reclined forms. The third building, and the largest, showed no color except on the myriad of antennae on the top. The walls had to be shielded.

Pravi tapped them with her finger. "That'll be where they're keeping the hatari. We just need to determine how many are inside, and then we can make our plan."

Zahira nodded to herself. It all seemed so simple now. One well-planned raid and she could free the hatari. On the D.I.C. feed, Munus and his team were only a few steps from taking down Feikasan and the Boliska. Her goal of revenge was as close as the walls of the hovercraft.

Pekke's transcom buzzed in the front seat. "Oh, hey. Zave has some info on those people from the lab." He swiped up a few times and then held it over his shoulder. "This person look familiar?"

Zahira's stomach tightened as her eyes met a picture of Feikasan. The blond woman looked younger than she had in the news conference, but there was no mistaking that cocky smile.

"Looks like she was a xeno-anthropologist before joining the Boliska." Pekke continued scrolling, not noticing that Zahira's heart rate had doubled. "Dr. Ulsta Feikasan. This says she got kicked out of a lecture post at Hamlin University for having quote 'controversial opinions.'"

He pulled up a video as Zahira's mind went elsewhere. How much of the lab data had Munus analyzed? If Pekke or Zave sent him the news about Feikasan, would he be able to connect the two? Would he have enough evidence to sidestep the bureaucratic hoops, or would his investigation get shut down before it could start?

"Well, that's a hot take." Pekke's voice cut into her thoughts, pulling her back to the Feikasan video. From the way her students reacted, it seemed the blond woman had something controversial about what constitutes personhood. Something involving the words *they're just not like us'*.

Feikasan cut the students' protest off quickly. *"My old roommate used to think that way. That we should treat all humanoids with the same rules, no matter how strange their mutations or evolution."* Her voice dripped with condescension. *"Her name was Elli Masterly, though I don't expect any of you to recognize the name. After our undergrad, she spent her sabbatical on Loras 2, studying the Waxxuns. Have you heard of them?"*

The students shook their heads.

Feikasan grimaced. *"Nasty creatures. Covered in matted fur and a second set of nostrils. Their whole world is barely a century into the stone age. I told her not to go, but she insisted she'd find a rich culture. That she'd prove the Waxxun are a species worth protecting. And do you know what happened?"*

One student sighed sarcastically. *"She was disappointed?"*

"She was eaten."

Pekke sneered and closed out the video. "Generalizing hundreds of species over one instance of cannibalism. Makes sense why the Boliska hired her to help with the hatari. Must be easy to get someone to go along with kidnapping and false imprisonment if they believe the captives aren't really people."

Pravi gave a pursed lip nod as Munus' voice crackled back on the transcom. *"I have good news and bad news,"* the agent said, clearing his throat. *"The good news is that we caught two wannabe abductors and found Jandra's secret comm. The bad news is she made a call about an hour before we arrested her."*

"A call to who?" Pravi asked. "Have you tied it to the abductors?"

"It was a call to the Boliska office on Yerin. Specifically, to the Department of Internal Affairs."

Zahira gave a sigh of relief. That had to be enough for Munus to get a search warrant, if not to bring Feikasan in for questioning. Hopefully, she couldn't claim some kind of diplomatic immunity before he tied her to the lab.

"Does that mean she's getting arrested?" Jo asked, a little too loudly.

Pekke's eyes shot to her. "Is who getting arrested?"

"Dr. Feikasan."

"I'm sending a team to investigate, but it seems their department head already left for an early lunch."

Jo's face fell. "So she's not getting arrested."

Pravi slowly lowered her transcom and turned to face Jo and Zahira. "Is Dr. Feikasan the department head?" she asked, her voice tense enough to imply she wanted the answer to be no. "Is that psychopath the one who Jandra contacted?"

Although Zahira maintained a hint of defiance, Jo could merely nod.

"And I'm guessing her resonance was part of the lab data?" A string of cuss words poured into Zahira's translator as Pravi unclipped her blaster and checked the cartridge. "Looks like this mission is turning into a full-blown raid."

Pekke held out a hand to stop her. "Now hold on a minute. Sure, the woman's crazy, but do you really think she'd go nuclear?"

"Do you want to risk it?" Pravi answered at the same time Zahira asked, "What in the seven hells are you talking about?"

Pravi stuck an extra ammo clip in her vest. "The Boliska are pretty efficient at cleaning up their messes. Now that she's been discovered, which one do you think Feikasan will hit next?" She nodded toward the center console, toward the dark gray building that housed the hatari. The antennae had a quiet violet glow.

No. Zahira repeated the word a dozen times in her head. This wasn't how it was supposed to go. Feikasan was supposed to be captured, or at least on the run. She and the D.I.C. were supposed to be distracted while they rescued the hatari.

Pekke gave a heavy exhale and reached to check weapons of his own. "You heard the woman. We're going in now."

Chapter Thirty-Six

— · —

Nik

N ik held back as the others hurried to tighten gear and straps. There couldn't be this much call for alarm, could there? Mere moments ago, they had been cautiously surveying their target and waiting on news from Munus. Had so much changed in Pravi and Zahira's brief exchange to warrant casting aside their chance to strategize?

"Am I missing something?" he asked Pekke as the physicist reached past him for a shoulder strap of grenades. "What reason would Feikasan have for killing the hatari now? They're out of the D.I.C.'s reach."

Pekke took a sideways glance at Pravi before adding a resonance scanner to his bundle. "You're thinking about three steps behind. Right now, the department's case is tenuous at best. Sure, Feikasan was at the lab, and she was contacted by the mole, but there's no solid evidence that she actually did anything. Conspiracy to commit a crime is like a tenth the sentence of actually having done it. Excuse me."

The physicist slipped past Nik to open the hovercraft's rear doors. As the ramp lowered and the equipment stacks shifted, a case of his collapsing energy spheres tried to roll out, but he caught the strap with his foot. "Now, let's say the D.I.C. gets witnesses. Victims. Hatari who can say 'That's her. That's the woman who milked me for nguvu like a dairy goat.'" Pekke reached down for the sphere case and dumped it in Nik's hands. "If that happens, she's going from six or eight years total to fifteen to twenty per count."

Nik absentmindedly threw the case over his shoulder and took the next thing Pekke offered without looking. His reasoning still didn't make sense. Even with the D.I.C. on her tail, Feikasan had no reason to wipe out the hatari. "Isn't the sentence for murder even higher?"

Pravi came up behind him to answer in the physicist's place. "Three or four counts of human trafficking, and she's already at life. Pekke estimates at least a dozen hatari taken." She motioned for Pekke to pass her one of the gray boxes. "If she removes the evidence, she has hope for a plea deal. But who knows, maybe we'll be lucky and she went after some other evidence first. You want to leave the hatari's lives to chance?"

He shook his head. Of course not.

"I didn't think so. Now holster up your blaster, and let's get a move on."

She nodded to his arms as she said it, and Nik followed her gaze to find Pekke had deposited a NW 3-27 in his hands. The canister port was still warm from the practice round before they'd packed it.

Pekke passed him a pouch of ammo. "A bit more time at the range would have been nice, but eh. What can you do?"

Indeed, what could they do? This was what they'd been building to for weeks, wasn't it? Finding the nguvu clouds, meeting Zahira, realizing how everything connected to the Boliska... The lab. The D.I.C. mole. Donli. If they didn't do something now, the death toll would continue to rise.

"Tell me we at least have a plan." Nik attached his blaster as Pekke had shown him the afternoon before, with the cannisters clipped onto his vest for easy access. They felt familiar in his hands. Too familiar. Pekke had said he chose the model because it was similar in shape and weight to the gun Nik used for paint-balling, but nothing he'd used with his friends had the potential to be this lethal.

Pekke took a face shield from the shelf beside Pravi. "I suppose we're going with something basic? Set up a couple of positions, then try to take out the comm towers and antennas. Maybe drop a small EMP from one of the surveillance drones."

"Something more contained would be better." Pravi scavenged through the equipment they'd brought. "A single EMP would have to cover half the roof to hit all the antennas, and who knows what it'd hit inside. Wouldn't want to send the nguvu device into meltdown."

Zahira had been loading her vest pockets on the other side of the hovercraft, and Nik noticed her pale at the words.

"What about the acid grenades?" he offered, seeing the chance to do something useful. Something that didn't involve standing around and thinking about how crazy this was. He'd helped Pekke pack the extra grenades under the hovercraft seats and he hurried to pull them out. "If I'm running the numbers correctly, the drones can carry three or four of them. That should be enough for both comm towers on the big building, plus one for the guardhouse."

"And they're quiet enough for the people inside not to notice." Pravi drummed her fingers on the center of her vest. "I assume Jo can pilot the drone, yes?"

"Yes?" Jo looked up from adjusting her own armor. Spanners and probes stuck out of the pockets at odd angles, interspersed with a lockpick set and two bands of smoke grenades. Goggles and a face mask covered her face, while another set of goggles rested above the first. If anyone was ready to dive head-first into this, it was her. Nik needed to borrow some of that energy. "You need me to do what, now?"

"Pilot the drone once the offensive begins." Pravi took a deep breath and laid out the plan again slowly, giving Jo the chance for each step to sink in. The guard building would be the first target drenched with acid, followed by the big building's antennas on the side farthest from the dormitory. No matter what went on with everyone else—and there was a good chance the guards would notice the second their comms went down—she couldn't stop. Any delay in deploying the acid would allow the Boliska to call for backup.

Once Jo had been filled in, Pravi and Pekke continued to lay out materials and discuss strategy. They would be five people against at least nine. Maximizing the advantage of surprise was essential. But would it be enough? Nik tried not to think about it as he clipped the grenades onto the surveillance drone. He'd already made his decision, hadn't he? Rescue the hatari and keep Jo safe. Time spent second-guessing himself would be better spent keeping everyone alive.

He checked over the drone's deployment clips twice before turning his attention to his own gear. Pieces of Pekke's collapsing spheres went in the lower pockets, while first aid kits slid into place at his left shoulder and right thigh. Zahira and Jo had gone through Pravi's assortment of goodies and picked out a few flash detonators and tranquilizer darts, but Nik stuck to the basics. Things like smoke grenades and a short knife he could trust himself not to fumble with. Things he could use from habit when the chaos started. And there would be chaos. As everyone suited up and stored essentials away in holsters and vest pockets, Pravi laid out a plan focused on cover fire and explosions. The more ruckus and confusion for the Boliska, the easier it would be to pick them off.

For Nik, his station would be to the east of the compound, across from the guardhouse. He'd help Pekke defend the drone until Jo could deploy the acid. An old industrial park could serve as cover, and once the comm towers corroded into useless heaps, they'd set off a series of charges in the abandoned buildings around them, drawing the security guards into their range of fire. As for Zahira and Pravi, they'd approach from the south toward the dormitory-looking building, taking out anyone drawn into the compound's defense. From there, they'd meet up with the others to storm the main building.

Nik's gear weighed him down as he crept through an old factory and into position. They'd left the hovercraft behind in the back alley, holding whatever weapons and tools hadn't fit in their pockets. An old concrete bench with a planter provided scant cover. It would have been nice to have some kind of flowchart of priorities. What if someone suffered a blaster wound during the initial assault? Was Nik supposed to run to their aid or continue covering the drone? What if their location was compromised? Should he have worked out a set of hand signals with Pekke? He leaned his back against the cold concrete and checked his blaster and ammo for the tenth time. There were over 300 worlds in the explored area of Stringspace. Someone, somewhere, had to have written a guide on how to be a vigilante. And if Nik somehow made it out of this alive, he planned to find it.

"Launching now," Jo's voice whispered through the com. A light whirr rose from the industrial park, sending the drone and their assault plan into motion.

No turning back now. Nik peeked out from cover to make sure the path remained clear. Across a dozen feet of gravel, the flat-roofed guardhouse stood silent on a cinder block base. No sign of any Boliska. He eased the barrel of his blaster up to aim at the door while the drone's shadow passed overhead.

"What's that buzzing?" Pekke asked at the same time Nik heard it—a soft hum coming from the drone's blades. It hadn't done that before.

They exchanged glances and for a moment, Pekke looked like he might slip from his spot behind an old dumpster and tell Jo to bring the drone back in.

"The screen's a bit fuzzy," she said before either of them could do anything. *"I think the main building is emitting some kind of field that's messing with the feed. Maybe to counteract the nguvu?"*

"Or maybe it is the nguvu." Pekke sighed into the com and signaled for Nik to turn his attention back to the guardhouse.

And good thing he did, because at that moment, the door edged open.

"Hold for a moment," Pekke whispered. *"The drone is still three meters from the antenna."*

And if Nik shot now, the guard could send out an alarm.

The door crept open the length of a shoe. "Yeah, it's louder out here," came a man's voice. "Pass me one of the TKs so I can check it out."

"Just treat it like a paintball match." Out of the corner of his eye, Nik could see the physicist taking aim at the door. *"Don't overthink it."*

A loud creak and the guard stepped out, his eyes passing quickly over the industrial park where they hid. Nik held his breath, praying he wouldn't look too hard. A confused expression passed over the guard's face and his neck turned upward. His eyes landed on the drone.

Someone fired, the shot echoing loud even through Nik's hearing protection, and the butt of his blaster slammed into his shoulder. Had he...? He found his finger tight on the trigger as the guard fell, backward and mouth open, a light mist of red hovering where he'd been.

The drone hummed louder in the heavy moment of silence that followed, louder even than Nik's heartbeat—its payload a mere meter from its target.

Nik's chest tightened. It was going to be too late. Even if the drone could drop its payload now, the acid would take time to corrode the antenna enough to be unusable. He fired blindly at the guard house windows. They needed to distract the guards for a minute. One single minute so the plan wouldn't fail. Heat blasted past his face shield to ram into the wall behind him. He fumbled to switch out the cartridges. This was nothing like a paintball match.

CHAPTER THIRTY-SEVEN

—·—

PRAVI

P ravi cringed. At first, she'd hoped the loud bang had come from
a piece of industrial debris, knocked out of balance when she
and Zahira planted charges on their way to their position. But as they
approached the windows facing the Boliska's base, more blaster shots
echoed from the guardhouse, confirming her fears. Mere minutes had
passed since Jo had signaled the drone launch. Pravi had hoped they'd
have more time before the guards noticed. Time to get closer to the
dorm building's exits. Time for Munus to get a team together and join
them.

She adjusted her heat vision goggles and took aim at the nearest spot
of orange. From forty meters away, the lounging form seemed more
like a low flame than a person. A half-dozen off-duty Boliska stood
or crouched in the surrounding rooms, their attention drawn to the
sound of blaster fire. As soon as they headed for the doors, a second
wave of shooting would start. She glanced toward the roof of the main
building, its shielded form quiet and gray. That's where she suspected
the hatari were kept. It'd be a while before the drone could make it
that far, given that it survived the crossfire. *Please let it survive the
crossfire.* She hadn't told the others, but the second antenna wasn't for
communications. It was a sliding satellite. To her relief, its metal was
still a cold shade of lilac, as it had been the three times she'd checked
on her way here. She needed it to stay that way, at least until the D.I.C.
arrived. Or until they could clear out all the Boliska and breach the
main building themselves.

"Hold your fire until the targets are fully outside," Pravi signaled to Zahira. She thought of switching to the comm channel with Nik and Pekke, but the continued staccato of blaster fire told her everything she needed to know. Two minutes in, their plan had already gone to shit. "I'll cover the exit closest to the guardhouse if you take the opposite side."

"Roger that." Zahira settled her blaster into place one bay down, its nose steady on the windowsill. Shards of broken glass cracked under her feet. The woman hadn't said anything since their plans had changed. Not since her move to corner Feikasan had put the other hatari at risk.

A deep orange blob headed for Zahira's exit. "Target inbound," Pravi announced, lining up her scope with the opposite door. "Might be a second one headed your way as well."

The lone figure racing for Pravi's exit seemed to move both quick and sluggish, and she steadied her breathing to prepare. *Concentrate*, her uncle's voice whispered in her ear. *Don't fire until you can make the hit.* One boot touched the gravel, then another. The door itself still stood open and in her way. It took two breaths for the boots to inch out of cover. Her fingers tightened on the trigger. The trusty Z73 shot true, piercing the blob's shoulder. Its second shot took the figure's knee before it even hit the ground.

Zahira's blaster stayed silent, and Pravi followed her aim to the doorway. Three or four blobs appeared to be in some kind of scuffle within meters of the exit. Like sunlight on water, spare flashes of yellow and orange danced in and out of the fray. Limbs, punching and flailing. The tallest ray had his back to the door, pushing the others away. Keeping them from running. She signaled for Zahira to hold her fire, to wait for the mob to win. But it was a moment too late. An ochre body tumbled past the blob guarding the door and into the woman's crosshairs. The ensuing blaster shot shook both the gravel and the bodies still clustered inside.

So much for waiting for everyone to run away in panic. The remaining figures inside were no longer fighting, and two had moved further indoors, possibly looking for some sort of barricade. Pravi counted four remaining targets. Four Boliska who could pose a threat when they tried to breach the big building's door. To make matters worse, a flash of blue caught Pravi's eye. The sliding satellite was warming up, either for someone else's exit or Feikasan's arrival. They didn't have time for an extended shootout. She needed to smoke the Boliska out now. "Cover me."

Before Zahira could ask what for, Pravi detonated the charges they'd placed. The sound of explosions echoed from empty factories and warehouse walls, covering her leap over the windowsill and out onto the gravel. The hatari recovered quickly from her surprise, aiding Pravi's mad dash for the dorm with shots at the windows and siding. Large booms shook the buildings to either side, while cracking concrete sent clouds of dust and debris into the air.

Someone shot back at Zahira as she ran. Someone skilled, based on how easily they'd pinpointed Zahira's exact bay in spite of the billowing dust. Flashes of light came from the far window of the dorm building, making Pravi suspect it was the man who had blocked the exit. She ran low to avoid his notice, skidding to a halt at the building's opposite corner. As she caught her breath, another window broke to make way for a second blaster. They weren't going to make this easy for her, were they?

She turned to circle to the dorm's other side, only to come face to face with a fallen Boliska agent. Blood seeped from his shoulder and knee. He groaned, and she considered her risk of exposure. If only he'd had the sense enough to play dead. Instead, he looked her straight in the eye and called for help.

Pravi scrambled to pull a sodden rag from her vest pocket and launched herself forward. The shock of it cut off the Boliska's words, and his fingers clawed at her gloved hand and face mask as the chloroform set in.

"Hey!" someone shouted from behind her. "Let him go!"

A blaster bolt hit the gravel behind her as if to make their point, but Pravi kept the rag tight over the Boliska's mouth and nose. She rolled, moving to put her limp hostage between herself and the blaster. Something cracked inside her vest.

"I said let him go!"

The second shot hit a meter from her hostage's feet, revealing a shooter still inside the dorm building, peeking through the cracked door. Only a shaking arm and blaster showed in the narrow space. Not a guard. At least, not an experienced one. She pretended to raise her arms in surrender, but tossed a smoke grenade instead.

The shooter jerked back inside as Pravi scrambled to her feet. Smoke hissed into a growing fog, and she realized Zahira's position had grown quiet. The only blaster fire came from within the dorm building and back by the guardhouse.

Well, shit. Pravi ditched the Z73 for two blasters meant for closer quarters. She had no choice but to keep pushing forward. Hopefully, Feikasan wasn't already inside the bigger building destroying evidence—or killing witnesses. She backed away from where the shooter had been. Her heat goggles showed three forms standing at the front of the dorm building, with a fourth lying still on the floor. It seemed Zahira had at least taken that one out before she went quiet. Pravi scrambled around the back corner as one figure broke off and crept toward the door. She considered throwing another smoke grenade, but what she needed now wasn't more cover. She needed to chase the Boliska out of theirs.

Her vest held canisters of knockout gas ready for the task. Chances were the Boliska would run out before it kicked in, but that would still give her something to shoot at. She broke the nearest window with the butt of her blaster and tossed one in. A couple clanks and a hiss, and the Boliska heat patterns turned toward the sound. They sprinted for the door and the thinning cover of the smoke grenade.

It wouldn't help them, thanks to her thermal goggles. As the third stepped through the door, Pravi took aim at the first. One shot to the knee, then one to the shoulder. Her third shot hit the second figure's back, but a blast of heat sent her fourth shot into the gravel. Fire erupted in her arm, and her blaster tumbled to the ground. Wetness soaked her sleeve.

She pulled back around the corner as the Boliska's next shot whizzed past where she'd been standing. Her head reeled and she couldn't feel her fingers. Shit. She shot around the corner with her other hand before fumbling for a tourniquet. Searing pain and nausea told her it was bad. Much worse than any light grazing or stabbing she'd experienced before. Thick warmth soaked the side of her vest as she slid down to sit against the siding. She'd need another smoke grenade for cover, but her face mask made her feel like she was choking. Her left arm hung useless by her side, and tying it off with the tourniquet only intensified the throbbing.

A blaster bolt hit the gravel near her foot, and she pulled her knees in tighter. Her heart beat into her throat and her stomach reeled, threatening to decorate the inside of her mask. She sent a few warning shots around the corner at the Boliska agent. That would hopefully hold him off for a bit. Her head tipped back against the siding. Deep breaths now. Dizzying pain pulsed from her arm, and her hand laid limp in her lap. She forced herself to look.

There was a bloody hole where her elbow should be.

Bile rose in her throat. Half the joint had been blown clean away, leaving oozing muscles and white bone. Her head spun and her gut twisted, and she barely got her mask off before her stomach emptied itself onto the gravel.

Boots crunched behind her. She whipped the blaster around the corner, shooting wildly. The charged rounds ricocheted off the ground in a cascade of sparks. It was only two meters back from her position, but it was enough. The footsteps retreated down the side of the building, raining cover fire at the ground beside her. She responded with another shot and dropped the blaster in her lap. It squished against her dampened clothes. Her stomach threatened to loose itself again, but she needed something to use as a sling. Although not the best option, she did have more bandages. Dizziness overcame her as soon as she reached forward.

She slid her hand inside her vest instead, hoping to find comfort in the sliding wand her uncle had made her. If worse came to worst, she could use it to free slide and find a hospital. But to her horror, her fingers hit jagged metal instead. It must have snapped in the scuffle. She was going to die here, wasn't she? The thought seemed almost comforting, like a soft pillow that would carry the pain and nausea away. But thoughts of the hatari tickled at the back of her mind. Someone had to save them. Someone had to pick up the torch that Zahira had dropped. She forced herself to put her elbow in a sling.

Blaster shots from the remaining Boliska decimated the gravel and nearby siding. She tossed another smoke grenade, but it wouldn't do much. It wasn't like she was going anywhere. The mere thought of standing sent stomach acid up her throat. The smoke could conceal knockout gas, though. She reached for a canister, wincing as her limp arm dragged across her thigh and out of the way of the pouch. There were only two left. Two chances to take out the remaining Boliska.

She reached for her face mask as the footsteps inched back along the gravel. She barely had it on when a bright light flashed blindingly through the smoke, burning deep red through the thermal goggles. She couldn't see. Couldn't tell which way was the corner or from where the next blaster shots were fired.

When her vision returned, the only thing she saw was a pair of black boots. Small and sturdy, like Zahira's. She fainted into the hatari's arms.

CHAPTER THIRTY-EIGHT

— · —

Jo

Jo dispatched the first canister of acid as fast as she could, panning the camera to confirm it hit its target before sending the drone toward the next antenna. Outside, blaster shots peppered the concrete walls, threatening to put holes in Nik and Pekke as well. She itched to help them, to pull them out of danger, but she had her orders—Antennas first. And this next target was special. Two spikes of metal, one thicker while the other stood tall, both with cross pieces running through their center. Pravi hadn't mentioned it, but Jo knew what that silhouette meant. The bottom of it would curve like a satellite dish, and inside, its wires would run to an array of cameras and a sliding port.

She angled the drone to it, trying not to drop the controller when explosions shook the surrounding buildings. She might not shoot blasters like the others, but she could keep Feikasan from coming and killing the hatari. More explosions rattled the rafters, shaking the chains that hung from them. Pekke had said the space was an old hovercraft factory, judging from the wide remnants of an assembly line and the giant loading dock on the far side. But for all Jo cared, it could have been a pitch-black basement. She focused on the camera and the camera only—the sliding antenna waited a mere dozen meters away.

Dust billowed at the edge of her screen, kicked up by a gust of wind. Jo course-corrected to take the force of the breeze into account. As the drone kicked up speed, a flash of light zipped by on her left. Then another overhead. It took a moment to realize they weren't on the screen, but inside. The third blaster bolt grazed the controller before she could roll to the side. The charred plastic curled, but thankfully it didn't affect the function. She looked back to the wall, where concrete peeled from a web of rebar. Blaster fire lit up the area outside the hole. *"Someone brought out an automatic,"* Pekke yelled through the comms. *"The concrete might not survive it. Watch out for debris."*

Nik fired a round before replying, *"Will do!"*

Jo flinched as another blaster bolt rammed into the wall beside her. She tucked herself back behind the old assembly line and hunched down over the controller. The drone had been so close to the antenna, but her roll had sent it veering off sideways. The camera now showed a figure at the dorm building. Pravi, maybe? They threw a gas canister or grenade through a window. No time to worry about it. She hit the toggle to spin the camera around, only to find she'd over-corrected. Her camera now faced the back of the guardhouse, watching a wounded Boliska lean against the siding, a weapon tight to his chest. She wished for a moment that the drone had come armed with more than acid. And in that moment, he looked straight at her—straight into the drone's camera.

Shit. "I've been spotted," she shouted to Nik and Pekke, forgetting for a moment that they were already pinned down. "There's a Boliska on the guardhouse's northwest corner."

"Guess you're going to have to fly fast." Pekke's breathing was labored and the sound of exploding concrete hammered in the background. *"Best I can do is a couple shots when the automatic reloads."*

But the drone was already booking it toward the second antenna as fast as its little rotors could go without unseating the canisters. Pekke's distraction wouldn't keep the guard occupied long enough. She stared at the camera, wishing the view of the gravel and roof shingles could give her some solution. What would Pravi do? Well, she'd probably break out a window and snipe the guard before he could take out the drone. As if Jo could pull that off. She did have a blaster, though.

A bolt grazing the drone's rotor made up her mind. It was a crazy idea, but she took off toward the loading bay doors, thumb holding down the drone controls in regular zigzags. The guard waited somewhere ahead and to her left, past the blaster bolts whizzing into concrete walls and the sound of scattered rubble. The doors creaked open with a swift kick. She waited only a moment for Pekke's distraction, then sprinted to the next building as his counterfire became her cover.

She had to be insane. Shots zipped past her legs and feet as she barreled shoulder-first into the next building's door. Dust poured from the frame, threatening to smother her even as it offered her refuge. But she made it inside, and the drone had survived another shot from the guard at the corner. She scrambled to find the right window. Broken glass shook in a half-dozen frames, adding another layer of debris to what had once been a showroom floor. Judging from how far the guard had looked in the camera, she needed at least the third window down.

A stray blaster bolt hit the roof beside the drone. How many more meters was it to the antenna? Three? Four? She couldn't trust Pekke and Nik to keep the guard occupied the whole time. He had to suspect what she was doing. She leapt through piles of rotting leaves, stopping briefly to correct the drone's course. A few more steps and she had a view of the guardhouse. A view of the guard's shoulder. A view of the blaster he had trained on the drone.

She raised her own weapon with a shaky hand. The first shot hit the ground. The second sent chips of siding flying. But it was enough to get his attention. She ducked before a blaster bolt took out the window's remaining glass. Chunks of window sill battered her controls as the drone cleared the last meter. "Second canister away," she announced through her mic.

Nik and Pekke didn't respond. Instead, the blaster fire near them seemed to grow even more intense, sprinkling the ground with heavy chunks of their cover. As she turned the camera to confirm the acid's deployment, dust filled that part of the screen. Her ears rang, making it impossible to tell who was shooting what.

"You got him!" Pekke shouted into the comm after what felt like hours, but was probably mere minutes. *"Main gunman is down. I'm heading in."*

The blaster fire by Jo's head ended abruptly, focused instead on the bootsteps that pounded across the pavement. As Pekke ran, Nik rained coverfire in response. Where the moments of radio silence had felt like forever, the next few minutes flew by in a whirl of blaster volleys

and shouting through the comms. Next thing Jo knew, Pekke called for
her to 'get this blasted door open.' He'd cleared the way to the main
building? They were into the final phase already?

Jo dropped the acid cartridge on the final antenna and lifted her
head from cover. Two of the guardhouse walls were now bare of their
siding, with whole panels littering the ground in pulverized chunks.
She hurried out to meet Pekke with the lockpicks as Zahira reported
in on the comm.

"Dorm building is clear," she said, her voice heavy and fatigued.
"But Pravi took a beating." The hatari turned the corner of the main
building as Jo's footsteps slowed. A half-dead Pravi limped beside her.

Pekke cursed and raced to help. "How much of the blood is hers?"

"Most of it, I think." Zahira slouched as Pekke took over, her chest
heaving to catch her breath. "Careful with her arm. I gave her a bag of
plasma, but I think she needs a lot more than that."

Pravi mumbled. "A surgeon and a few painkillers would do the trick."
A surgeon and a two-week stay in an ICU maybe. Her cheeks lacked
color and dark liquid stained half her armor. Yet somehow, the woman
had enough energy to flail her non-slinged arm at the main building's
entrance. "Feikasan."

Jo's stomach sank. Had the horrible woman slid in before she could
take out the antennas?

"We'll handle it." Pekke's voice sounded confident as he motioned
for Jo to pass him the lockpicks. "But first, Jo's taking you to the
hospital."

"I am?" But of course she'd be the one to do it. Everyone else could
actually hit their targets. That's why she'd been assigned to the drone,
wasn't it? Although she wanted to protest, Pekke was already sliding
Pravi's good arm over her shoulder and shooing them away. She'd been
voted out of the final battle.

"Take it nice and slow 'til you get to the hovercraft," Pekke said,
pulling out the first of the crystal lockpicks. "And text me when you
get to the hospital."

Before she knew it, he and the others headed inside, blasters drawn.
The door clicked shut behind them.

Chapter Thirty-Nine

—.—

Zahira

*Z*ahira held her blaster like a safety blanket. It was one thing to be running from the Boliska, defending yourself while looking for an exit. It was another to step into their hive and take them head on. Even attempting to rescue Grandmother had been limited to a grab and run strategy. But there would be no grabbing and running with over a dozen hatari to save. Pravi's injuries had made those stakes crystal clear. Her initial charge toward the dorm building had been exhilarating. It was like something out of a holonovel, and the only things that kept Zahira from watching with mouth wide open had been the need to provide cover fire and the rain of concrete and blaster bolts that followed. Buildings exploded left and right while Pravi practically danced through the crossfire.

Minutes later, Zahira had found an opening and charged in as well, heading for the other side of the dorm. She'd stumbled slightly when she came across her first kill. A blaster bolt had pierced the man's chest, his face frozen in wide-eyed panic. He'd been nothing but a blur of heat when Zahira shot him. Boliska weren't supposed to look like real people, you know? Certainly not like a stranger in a vest lying dead on the street. They also weren't supposed to yelp in fear while your partner tossed a gas canister into their hideout, sending them scurrying into a death trap.

But whatever qualms Zahira had about killing them disappeared the second she'd found Pravi. Blood soaked the woman's clothes while red droplets formed a small pool on the gravel. Zahira's thermal goggles had shown a burnt-orange form sneaking up on them, ready to finish his kill. It took barely a thought to throw the flash detonator and riddle him with burn marks.

What came next would be forever burned into her mind. Pravi fainting into her arms, her elbow bleeding through the compress. The way the joint dipped inward instead of outward. The paleness of her skin. Almost gray, like Grandmother's had been. Zahira shook the memory away as chills ran down her spine. She whispered a prayer to never see the others like that. That any gods listening or even the strings themselves would keep the inventor whole as she ushered Pravi to safety.

Her second prayer was for the hatari. That as the door to the main building creaked open, they weren't already too late. But her first glimpse inside with Pekke and Nik didn't encourage her hopes. Debris littered the concrete floor, with the light from the door hitting cracked circuit boards and smashed computer screens. Broken glass and metal fragments crunched under their boots while the sounds of smashing equipment echoed from further inside. As her eyes adjusted, she spotted two figures in lab coats standing at the heart of the destruction, wielding sledgehammers.

Pekke fired a warning shot at their feet. "Hands up and drop the weapons."

The lab coat on the nearest Boliska seemed to swoosh as he turned toward them, and his sledgehammer thunked into the shattered husk of a monitor screen. As for the second figure, she raised her hands without letting go of her wooden handle.

Pekke fired again, this time grazing her boot. "I said drop it."

She complied, and the quick fall of the weapon scattered a pile of broken glass.

While Zahira kept her blaster trained on the left-hand figure, the physicist took aim at the one on the right. "Nik. The cuffs. Right hip pocket."

Nik edged over to pull out four zip ties without lowering his pistol. The lab assistants seemed to quiver as he moved. Not in fear, though, more like they weren't visually in focus. Like a mirage. Zahira squinted, and it took a moment to realize what was happening. *They were free-sliding.* Her and Nik's blaster bolts went whizzing past where they'd stood, leaving the energy blasts to crackle into the wall behind them. Strings of curses raced through Zahira's mind as Pekke rushed forward to scan the area. Even if he sent the readings straight to Zave, the techs would be long gone before the authorities could follow.

Zahira kicked at a broken keyboard. They couldn't be too late. The Boliska couldn't possibly have moved that many hatari in the time since their siege began. She scanned the room, taking in as many clues as possible. Vacant desks and bare cabinets lined the space near the entrance, with wires dangling from the former and empty boxes toppling from the latter. The floor between them held nothing but debris. The other side of the room, however, looked intact. She hadn't noticed when they first entered as her eyes hadn't yet adjusted, but ten meters away, little lights blinked from pod-like devices, all set in a circle around a giant, glowing column. As she watched, an amber bolt of lightning zipped from the column's base to its crown, disappearing into a tangled mess of cables and conduits. A thick blanket of black mesh separated her from both pods and column, closing them off like a cage. A giant, shielded cage. And it seemed to flicker with movement.

Zahira raised her blaster, ignoring Pekke's signal to hold back. Let him and Nik worry about whether any of the computer evidence had survived. The pods were people-sized. Hatari-sized. Had they... Could this be how the Boliska hooked them up to collect radiation? Was this column, this nguvu-colored hulk, the device Jo had been searching for? Coral lines rippled from the furthest pod, beckoning her forward. Curling, darting lines like the ones on her own skin. She crept toward them, noticing for a moment that the mesh gate had been left open. Could she dare hope that the lab techs hadn't determined the captive hatari to pose much risk? That they would have saved them to deal with after all the other evidence? The flashing status screens seemed to give a resounding "yes." Thin lines traced out heartbeats and brainwaves. Blood pressures and blood sugars. Line after line of data that Zahira understood to mean one thing: The hatari were still alive. They were safe. Pekke and Pravi had kept their promises, and Nik and Jo had helped achieved the impossible.

Sharp metal bit into her neck as someone pulled the blaster from her hand. "I'll be taking that," Feikasan's voice came sharp in her ear. "Tell your friends if they come closer, there'll be more than just computer debris to clean up off of the floor."

That's when Zahira finally noticed it. A dark, quiet sliding port tucked into the corner between the mesh and the exterior wall. Pravi had been right that the Boliska's head would come to tidy house. That Feikasan would be spooked by the lab data. All the work Jo had done with the antennas hadn't been enough to stop her. Or, at least, it hadn't been fast enough to stop her from coming. The port's lights were dead now and Feikasan's attack had come from the opposite direction.

"Zahira?" Pekke's voice called from back outside, near where he'd crouched to take the readings. "Did you find something?" He made it halfway to the gate before stopping dead in his tracks and signaling for Nik to do the same.

"This feels familiar, doesn't it?" Feikasan pressed the knife deeper, angled so that if Zahira tried the move she'd used in the lab, she'd slit her own throat. "You know the drill. Weapons. Drop them."

Pekke hesitated, but Nik lowered his slowly to the ground. He seemed to be searching the room for other options.

"I said lower it or she dies."

"Bold of you to assume I care." Pekke took a step forward and raised his weapon higher instead. A ploy? A move to call Feikasan's supposed bluff? She'd already killed an innocent grandmother, for strings' sake.

"Oh? You're claiming you don't care?" Pain dug into Zahira's neck, followed by warm droplets. "Not even a little?"

Pekke averted his eyes, but not his blaster. "I'm here for information. You give me that and you can keep her."

The blade pressed deeper, letting a thick trail of blood creep down her neck into her shirt.

Nik tried to force the physicist's weapon down. "Pekke, you're killing her!"

Pekke shook him off. "You think dropping my blaster will save her? What if it was Jo out there? It's been two years, Nik. I haven't heard hide nor hair of Sadie for two years."

Sadie? Suddenly it clicked. That woman who'd been framed. The one Pekke kept mentioning. Zahira cursed herself for a fool. Of course he wouldn't have done all this, risked all this, for some random stranger. His friend had been the whole reason he'd found out about the hatari, hadn't she? His reason for following the nguvu trail.

The pressure from Feikasan's knife relented. "What do you want then?"

"Tell me everything you know about Sadie Penderfyn and the explosion mapping project."

Zahira's captor scoffed. "The explosion mapping project? What, you think I'd be dumb enough to give a confession?"

"I couldn't care less how you're involved. Just tell me what you know." Pekke sighted-in his blaster. "Is Sadie alive? Where's Henri Anuul?"

"I wouldn't know about Penderfyn, but as for Dr. Anuul, well... Given as he was dumb enough to shoot a D.I.C. director, he's probably at the bottom of a lake somewhere."

"Tell me where Sadie is, then."

"I said I've never met her."

Pekke fired at her feet, causing the blade to twitch against Zahira's neck. "Never met her doesn't mean you don't know where she is."

"All I know is that her brat was at the lab." In her frustration, Feikasan's knife pressed deeper again, this time slicing a few fingertips below Zahira's ear. She shivered as wetness rolled toward her back. "He left when you did."

"Rafe? Rafe was at the lab?"

Rafe? Wait, the little brown-haired kid with the comic book obsession? All this because Zahira had forgotten to pass along his message? "He was at the swamp with Jo and—"

The blade cut her off. "He absconded with papers from Anuul's locker. I imagine he and his mom are still trying to prove her innocence." Feikasan sighed. "You want to put down the blaster now?"

"No." Pekke's voice sizzled with anger. "Not until I know where Sadie is."

"She said she doesn't know." Nik motioned for Pekke to calm down. "There's no need to escalate things."

The physicist gave him a look that was almost a snarl. "What do you care? Jo's safe, isn't she?"

"Yes, but Zahira's not." The moment he spoke, the moment where Pekke slightly lowered his blaster and Feikasan lowered her guard, Nik tossed something small, metal, and glowing. Zahira recognized it as one of Pekke's spheres at the same time her captor did. Had Nik assembled it while they were distracted? She had no time to question as Feikasan dragged Zahira into her dodge, dropping the knife to a less dangerous position. She moved from both instinct and practice, shoving the knife arm away as she ducked and rolled in the other direction. The sphere clattered to the floor in an array of sparks. As Zahira's hand reached her blaster, a siren blared from the mesh fence.

The gate swung shut before Nik and Pekke could reach it.

"I'd be careful with that if I were you." Feikasan motioned to Zahira's blaster, then stepped behind one of the pods. "There's a lot of sensitive equipment in here. You wouldn't want to cause collateral damage."

Zahira considered for a moment whether the blond woman would be bluffing, but the truth was the place had to be crawling with nguvu. If it blasted back into one of the pods... "It doesn't matter," she said, keeping her weapon raised. "The D.I.C. will swarm this building any minute. Hell, they could be out there already."

Something beeped from the back of the pod. "And I'll be gone when they get here." Feikasan smiled. Lights flashed from the other pods, blinking in unison. Resonance repeaters. Evidently, Nik and Pekke hadn't been the ones dragging the conversation on for time. The center column now stood silent, dark except for two tiny lights at its base.

Her heart skipped a beat. Feikasan had shut everything down for transport. "You're not seriously going to freeslide with all of this?"

"Freeslide? Oh, heaven's no." Feikasan had moved fully out of sight, sharp nails tapping away on a screen. "Where'd you get that idea? Because one of your friends took out the antenna?" When the nail tapping stopped, something above them started to grind, like a giant hatch opening in the roof. Another sliding antenna. "As if I wouldn't have a backup."

CHAPTER FORTY

— • —

PRAVI

Pravi and Jo had made it halfway to the hovercraft when the grinding started. The trek had been slow going, with Pravi hobbling along with two med shots' worth of energy and an extra wad of bandages tucked into her sling. She'd protested at first, of course—that her arm wasn't as bad as it looked. Or that Jo should leave her and go in with the others. The typical self-sacrificing heroics only achieved through a heavy dose of adrenaline and blood loss. But her fatigue and pallor won out in the end. Even with Jo's help, there was no denying the effort of every step, the way her feet dragged across the gravel as if it were an ankle-deep swamp. The guard house and fallen Boliska were mere blotches at the edge of her vision, tilting this way and that as the ringing in her ears begged her to give up and collapse. She assumed the grinding was just her body upping the ante.

Until Jo hesitated as if hearing it too. The inventor turned to check the door where Zahira and the others had disappeared, then turned to the sky. A D.I.C. helicopter? A drone? Pain and nausea kept Pravi from turning too, but Jo's face said it all. Something had gone terribly wrong. "You said that antennas take priority, yes?" Jo's voice held a hint of panic, and she shuffled Pravi toward the crumbling planter Nik had used as cover.

Antennas? Hadn't Jo dosed them all with acid? Before Pravi could break through her mental fog, Jo leaned her against the planter and turned her toward the sound. Two uneven prongs rose from the big building's roof. Her response came out like a groan, "Pulse grenade. Left hip pocket."

It wasn't an EMP, unfortunately, as the initial surveillance mission hadn't required one. But the power would be enough to prevent the Boliska's escape for a few minutes. At least until their system reset. She could only hope it provided enough delay for Zahira, Nik, and Pekke to get the situation under control. If only she weren't so injured. The best move would be taking out the antenna with other means once the pulse kicked in.

Jo dug the grenade out with as much speed and care as she could manage, which meant a short spasm of pain shot from Pravi's arm to the back of her neck. She clenched her teeth to suppress a yelp. "Flip the switch, then toss it as close as you can. Two second delay."

The inventor nodded and ran off, leaving Pravi to breathe through the discomfort. What she wouldn't give to have Munus and his team there. All that time she'd spent trying to get rid of them, and now that they were actually useful, they were nowhere in sight.

A loud thunk and a skittering turned the antenna's grinding to a creak. The inventor's aim had been a bit off, but it didn't matter. Grenade shrapnel rolled off the roof, and the antenna fell silent.

Jo raced back, heading for the hovercraft rather than stopping to pick up Pravi. "How much time do we have before the restart? Five minutes? Ten?"

"Five. Where are you going?" Whatever Jo replied was lost in the echoes of her footsteps, and Pravi found herself entirely unable to follow. Well, shit. Now she was really stuck, with no chance of making it the last twenty meters to safety, nor of turning back to help Zahira and the gang make the best of the delay. Her only company was the nauseating breeze and the two wavy blotches of Boliska.

Wait. Two wavy blotches? Hadn't there been three guards? Pravi could have sworn, foggy as she was, that there'd been someone lying at the corner of the guardhouse. But now, all that remained was a bloody patch of gravel. Before she could wiggle her transcom free to warn Jo, a blaster buzzed at her ear.

"Hands where I can see them." The missing Boliska's voice was loud and shaky, hinting at the worst trait a captor could have: Desperation. "Don't even think of yelling for your friend."

Pravi slid her hand away from her comm and lifted it slowly into the air. Hopefully it was clear why her other arm wasn't moving.

"Where's your transport? Is it a hovercraft or a portable sliding station? Is there a PIN?" The questions tumbled from his mouth fast enough to make Pravi's head spin. "Is there anyone guarding it?"

"I... I'm sorry." She played the injured and confused card, which wasn't too hard as she was maybe three minutes from the med shots wearing off. A weary sigh and an exhausted tilt of her head were not only called for, but also exactly what her body wanted her to do. "I don't understand... what you're asking."

"Transport. You know. Vroom vroom, slidey slidey."

Pravi hid her urge to laugh with a cough. "Transport? Like a bus?"

"A bus? You took a bus with all your blasters and grenades and everything?" The guard shook his head and waved the blaster at Pravi's face. "Tell me where your transport is."

"Yes, yes. Transports transport." He must have suspected they had backup inbound and wanted to get out quickly. Pravi gave an exaggerated yawn and waved her hand toward the other side of the guardhouse. "There-ish... Big green thing. With four of those... spinny things." She slowly closed her eyes as she spoke, leaving just a crack to watch the guard with.

He anxiously scanned the area, especially in the direction Jo had disappeared to. One hand, the one without the blaster, pressed against a bloody spot where his chest met his shoulder. She couldn't tell how bad the injury was with his hand there, but red tinged his fingers. More blood showed on his upper thigh.

"And you're sure it's unguarded?" He didn't wait for her to answer before creeping away, which was fine because Pravi didn't plan on saying anything. She continued to play unconscious, trying her best not to look like a threat. Hoping that he'd be gone before Jo got back.

Four steps away, he stopped and held perfectly still, as if listening for something. Had Jo made some noise? With all the ringing in her ears, Pravi would have been lucky to hear a freight train. She gave a heavy sigh and wiggled as if trying to get comfortable, stirring up the gravel. The guard's eyes turned to her sharply and his hand tightened on the blaster grip. Did he believe her ploy? That whatever noise he heard was only her? The way he raised his weapon suggested he had, but that he also wasn't leaving her alive to blow his cover. His hand was shaky, but his barrel lifted to point at her face.

A crunching of gravel and something launched itself from the abandoned factory. A blur of green coveralls and a vest swung wildly at the guard, knocking away his blaster with a heavy black bulk. He stumbled back. Jo swung again, missing his stomach with the sack of magnetic climbing gear.

Was this some fever dream? Had Pravi lost consciousness and started hallucinating that her potential protégé was already a resourceful fighter? No. Because now Jo was losing. The heavy bag had thrown her off-balance, and the guard had grabbed her by the arm, pulling her into a choke hold. "His shoulder! Hit his right shoulder with your own!"

The inventor obeyed, but the guard moved faster, dodging her thrust while weakening his hold.

"His knee! Kick right above his left knee!"

The guard dodged again, but Jo misheard the order and kicked right instead of left. A flub, but a lucky one. The guard lost both his footing and his grip on Jo while she stumbled away.

"Drop the bag. Do you have something lighter?" Pravi felt the med shots wearing off, but she struggled to stay in control. "Pepper spray? Maybe a knife?" She hesitated to mention Jo's blaster in case the guard lunged for it first. But Jo seemed to have thought of something already and struggled to get it out of her pocket.

The guard charged as Pravi shouted, "Dodge left," sending whatever it was shimmering to the ground.

Jo fell after it as strong hands gripped her ankle. She was already kicking before Pravi could give the order, making grazing attempts at the guard's face. His nails seemed to dig into her calf, but her hands closed on whatever she'd dropped. A tube of some sort.

"Hit his neck!" Pravi ordered.

The man flinched to guard the back of his neck, leaving the front of his chest open. Jo slipped something from the tube and slashed with all her might. A white light crackled and snapped, sending spasms through the guard's body. One of Pekke's energy spheres? Or just part of one? The guard seemed paralyzed as Jo fished out a set of cuffs.

Pravi leaned back against the planter. She'd done it. This meek inventor, this scrawny little lab rat, had overpowered someone. Had fought for her life and won. If Pravi wanted a partner to replace her uncle, Jo might just be it. Grinding echoed from the big building, pulling Pravi free from her latest rush of adrenaline. "The antenna!" she called. "Get the climbing gear."

Jo looked up with wide eyes and wiped dust from the corner of her mouth. To her credit, she only froze for a moment before she scurried for the bag. Pravi watched as she hurried for the building, pulling out the magnetic grips.

Even with success within their reach, the darkness closed in on Pravi, threatening to steal her consciousness. She barely noticed her transcom buzz against her thigh, signaling a message from Munus. Even if she could reach it, she was too dizzy to make out the words. But if she had seen it, she would have relaxed even more against the planter. It read: *"We're here."*

CHAPTER FORTY-ONE

—·—

ZAHIRA

"**W**hat. Did. You. Do?"

Feikasan brandished her knife for the third time since the grinding had stopped, and once again Zahira second-guessed her decision to hold her fire. But as had happened before, her foe hopped quickly back behind a pod to tap wildly at the screen, leaving Zahira with nothing to shoot at. It did leave her free to go back to what she'd been doing, which was taking out the resonance repeaters on the other pods. Frying the main node would have been faster, but Feikasan had given no clues to where she'd stashed it.

Zahira reached out to touch the next tiny, blinking device. It still wasn't clear what had frozen Feikasan's spare sliding antenna, but whatever it was had backed the woman into a corner—a corner that would result in a dangerous free slide if pushed too far. Like if Zahira tried to attack head-on.

She had to focus on undermining Feikasan's plan instead, while keeping her nguvu discharge to the faintest of sparks. Somewhere, far beyond the mesh, Nik and Pekke rustled through drawers and kicked through the broken debris. She could only assume they were looking for some way to help. The physicist's prior attempt to break in had resulted in a nasty shock and a clattering of lockpicks.

She closed her eyes and calmed her breathing. Taking out the repeater took all of her concentration, leaving no room for error. Too much of a jolt could transfer to the pod itself, and who knew what that would do to the life support systems. She had to pay close attention to every wisp of nguvu swirling around her. The energy hummed through her coils and even in the air between the pods. Every hair on her body was raised. Every swirl on her skin had her attention. Once she was certain she could control the flow, she let the tiniest trickle free and pulled her hand away. The repeater died with a quiet zap and a puff of burnt-plastic smell. Six down, nearly a dozen more to go.

"I said to stop that." Feikasan's voice shook with frustration and her fingers slammed against the data pad.

Zahira closed the distance to the next repeater. "And I said to go throw yourself off Devil's Dune, but somehow you're still here." Strings, she wanted to shoot the woman so bad. She let out another zap, saving another hatari from Feikasan's transport web. She moved on to the next, but one of the pods started to hiss behind her.

"If you fry another repeater, I swear I'll slit his throat."

Zahira turned to find Feikasan's pod had opened, revealing a dark-haired man in his forties. Something about the shape of his chin scruff looked familiar. He'd been on Pekke's list, hadn't he? Amber lines danced across his pale neck, shying away from the Boliska's blade. She reached out to the next repeater in defiance. "How is killing him any better for you than leaving him behind?"

"How is me doing either any of your business?" Feikasan traced her knife down the unconscious man's clavicle. "Do you think he would care about you, should the situation be reversed? That he'd risk life and limb to keep you from this fate?" She gave a derisive puff of air from her nose. "He couldn't even keep his wife safe, much less you. The fire she died in was one he started, and he injured dozens more before we finally tracked him down. How cruel to make him live with that. To spend every waking moment as his wife's murderer. So much better to be useful."

"Useful?" By helping hatch dinosaur eggs? How much more useful could he have been if he hadn't spent his whole life running? If he hadn't built up fear and nguvu to the point he no longer had control?

Feikasan sneered. "Useful. Doing something that will help people instead of hurt them. Once my buyer—" The grinding started back up before she could finish her sentence, and she grinned at the sound of it. Zahira could only guess the woman was planning to ditch her witnesses and make a profit in one fell swoop. "Well, I suppose my buyer is waiting. Pity you don't have the sense to climb into one of those pods and come along too." She turned back to the data pad, careful to keep her knife pressed to the man's throat. But in her hurry, she turned her back to Zahira, revealing a small, black remote in her pant pocket.

The main control node. Destroy that, and Feikasan couldn't take any of the pods or hatari with her, no matter the state of their repeaters. Zahira waited for the blond woman to get caught up in her typing, then launched herself forward. One hand she readied to bat the knife away, but the other headed straight for the control node.

Only the second hand succeeded. As her fingers wrapped around the node, Feikasan's blade swiped toward her face, grazing her cheek. Pain and warmth sprouted from the cut, but she rolled away before it traveled further. She started to fry the node, but Zahira had to duck under another slash, and Feikasan dodged the returning kick. The following blows were evenly matched, and Zahira traded a heel to her opponent's gut for a slice across the arm. Feikasan slashed where Zahira rolled, and Zahira punched where Feikasan stabbed.

Through it all, Zahira couldn't quite make it back to her feet. Cold concrete chilled through her clothes, and wires threatened to trip every attempt to stand. Even as she kicked away Feikasan's blade, the woman was on top of her, ready to press her arm against Zahira's throat.

"Any last words?" The woman taunted. "How does it feel, knowing the second you're unconscious, you'll be in one of those pods as well?"

Zahira opened her hand to reveal the melted control node. "I'm afraid I wouldn't make it very far."

"Why you—" A slam to the outside wall drowned out whatever curse words she had planned. Another slam followed, hitting higher and louder.

It was Zahira's turn to grin. "Sounds like it's too late for you to run."

As the outside wall shook, vibrating from whatever or whoever was moving up toward the roof, Zahira thrust against Feikasan with a sharp twist of her hips. They both rolled, stopping when they slammed into a pod, then rolling in the other direction as Feikasan held tight to either side of Zahira's vest. A sharp resonance barreled into her body, a string with a harsh odor and the taste of caffeine. The damn woman was trying to slide away and take Zahira with her.

Zahira fought back, not only pushing away the string, but shoving her current resonance back into Feikasan. So the Boliska head didn't want to meet her buyer empty handed? Zahira wouldn't let her meet them at all. The women struggled back and forth, shoving sharp resonance against smooth, and bland taste against caffeine. All the while, wires and concrete dug into their backs and hammering pounded into the roof.

The sharp resonance cut off suddenly, turning into a wisp in Feikasan's hand. "No!" The Boliska pushed away to escape, but Zahira held tight. She grasped the woman's shirt in one hand, close to her heart, and let go a wave of nguvu.

Whatever device Feikasan had to block nguvu in the lab proved no match for the energy pouring forth from Zahira. Her coils were full, and whatever more she needed, she pulled from the air. A tenth of it would have killed a normal person, but because of Feikasan's shielding, she merely thrashed in pain until Zahira let go.

Zahira wanted to kill her on the spot; to watch her writhe with nguvu and blaster holes. But whoever her buyer was, whoever waited for Feikasan at the end of that sharp, odorous string, posed a threat. And that threat meant she needed Feikasan alive. She cuffed her instead, imagining with each tightening of the zip ties she was strangling the woman's neck. Her only consolation was that the D.I.C. was more likely to listen if she wasn't standing over a dead body. Still, there was nothing stopping her from shooting the woman in the leg before department agents flooded into the room.

CHAPTER FORTY-TWO

— • —

Jo

J o collapsed onto the roof as D.I.C. agents poured from the surrounding buildings. A dozen bolts and a transversive flux belt lay scattered on her lap. She'd done it. The sliding antenna had been disabled and Feikasan was presumably stuck inside.

She spared a look to where she'd left Pravi. Had an agent stopped to check on her? The distance to the ground seemed so much greater now than it had going up, but Jo pushed back her fear until she spotted the woman's dark hair amid two med techs. A man in a navy jumpsuit watched over them, looking like some sort of captain or supervisor. While his face was stern, he didn't look overly concerned with Pravi's condition, which seemed to bode well.

The next thing to do was to climb back down. And not just because a D.I.C. agent pointed a blaster at Jo and ordered her to. The others were still inside, no doubt being harassed in a similar manner. Assuming that they'd survived. She tried not to think about it as she forced her feet and shaking hands back into the magnetic climbing gear. The clips were a bit unruly, and on the way up, they'd pounded something awful against the metal siding. But they'd gotten her up to the roof safely, and now they ferried her down into the waiting arms of a D.I.C. team. It took only a few minutes before her boots, as well as everything from her vest and pant pockets, made it to the ground.

"All clear here," the first agent said as he finished patting her down. He'd been calling out each item as he searched her, leaving no room for Jo to ask about her friends. "Might want the med team to have a look at her, though."

Did she really look that disheveled? Sure, she'd fought for her life, climbed a giant wall, and then dismantled a sliding antenna while it was charging up, but it's not like she'd been shot or anything. She started to protest, to ask if she could check on Nik and Zahira instead, but before she had the chance, the door burst open and a familiar voice called out.

"Has anyone seen Jo? Jo Incerti? She stands about up to here on me. Mousy brown hair. Loads of freckles?"

"Nik! I'm over here." She didn't see anyone with him, but her view was half-blocked by a med tech shining a light in her ears and nose. "Where's Zahira and Pekke?"

Instead of an answer, she got a look of relief. Nik pushed past the techs to pull her in close, then pushed her away for a moment to check for injuries, and finally hugged her again. "They're fine. We're fine. Everything's fine." He took a deep breath and squeezed her face into his shoulder.

He was alive. They were all alive. Jo hadn't realized how much she'd been holding back until globs of wet started trickling down the side of her nose. Oh, thank the strings.

"We did it, Jo. The hatari are all here and Feikasan's in custody." Nik pulled back, his voice holding a hint of concern. "How's Pravi? Did she make it to a hospital?"

As if Jo would have abandoned her for anything short of an emergency. "We didn't make it to the hovercraft, but she's with the med techs now. How'd things go inside?"

"Eh." He gave the med techs the side eye and wiped the side of his cheek. "It's a bit of a long story."

Once the techs finished scanning for broken bones and internal bruises, Nik shooed them away to explain what had happened. How Pekke had been willing to trade Zahira's life for information. How the boy at the swamp turned out to be related to everything. How Pekke's real motive all along had been finding his friend. The physicist himself walked in for the second half of the story, and by his silence, said he wouldn't deny any of it. Jo found she was already too full of emotion to blame him. She certainly wouldn't be trusting him again, though.

"I suppose you'll want the cryptoscope back," Pekke offered after Nik finished. When Jo nodded, he sighed and put his hands in his pockets. "Would you mind if I ran a couple scans first? Now that I know Rafe and Sadie were at the swamp, I might be able to find a sample."

Jo considered it for a moment as she leaned back against the siding. That was the sort of thing she'd made it for, wasn't it? To find missing people who might be in trouble? Although the past few days had shown her just how dangerous the cryptoscope could be in the wrong hands, it had saved countless lives, too. Things had looked bad after Donli, but they'd struck back. No more Boliska. No more nguvu collection. It'd take some time, but Pekke's friend Zave and his team could start dispersing the golden clouds in earnest. And the truth was, Pekke didn't even have to ask. It'd be easy for him to simply change the safe house entry code and use the cryptoscope as he wished. But he had asked. And besides, what good would it do to say no? They'd all made it out okay, hadn't they? And from the way Nik described it, Pekke being worked up about his missing friend had turned out to be the distraction they'd needed.

"I want my lawyer." The sharp voice came from the big building's door, followed by Feikasan cuffed and struggling against a pair of D.I.C. agents. Her right leg limped along, and her bandaged left dragged beside it. "She shot me. I was fully cuffed and sedated, and she shot me."

"I have no idea what she's talking about." Zahira's voice came from behind the door. She seemed to be holding it open for the agents. "I've only ever fired my blaster in self-defense. And I certainly wouldn't have shot an unarmed woman three times in the knee."

Feikasan practically spat in her direction. "Just you wait. She's a menace, I tell you. My lawyer will have a field day once he gets here. Excessive force. Unlawful arrest. False imprisonment—"

"Eighteen counts of human trafficking. Smuggling of Class C weaponry. Theft of government assets." The man who'd been watching over Pravi now strolled across the campus to join his agents. He had one hand in his pocket and the opposite arm in a sling. "Transport of non-native species without a permit. Intent to distribute said species.

Wanton destruction of private property. No, Miss Feikasan. I think the prosecutor will be the one having a field day." He motioned for the agents to take her away and turned his attention toward Zahira, Jo, and Nik. "Ms. Nacitè. Ms. Incerti. Mr. Placheny. It's good to put faces to the case files." He gave Pekke a nod as well. "Always a pleasure, Dr. Froum."

The physicist looked uncomfortable, but he returned the nod. "Director Munus."

Munus? Was he the regional director Pravi had been talking to?

The man rocked back on his heels. "You'll be happy to hear we've reopened the Penderfyn case, Dr. Froum. I trust you'll save both of us the trouble of filing yet another letter of appeal?"

"Appeal? You're going to clear Sadie's name?"

Munus shrugged, flinching when the movement tugged on his sling. "Let's just say new evidence has spurred a change of heart."

Nik cleared his throat. "And does that change of heart apply to us as well? Or will we be charged as vigilantes?" He'd said it fast, like he'd been waiting for an opening to ask, and now he looked braced for the worst. Thankfully, Munus shook his head with a small chuckle.

"How could a team of D.I.C. consultants be considered vigilantes? For all appearances, Miss Resero just followed orders, and the presence of hostages created probable cause. There will be debriefings, of course, and plenty of paperwork. But no. No charges." With that, he bid them farewell and started engaging the surrounding agents in conversation.

Jo looked incredulously at Nik and Zahira. Was that really it? All the rush, all the insanity of the past week, would turn into something as benign as paperwork? They'd spent the last three days tracking Boliska, trudging through a swamp, dodging a charging ceratopsid. She'd even run from a squad of assassins sent to her apartment, for string's sake. After all of that, was Jo supposed to go quietly back to inventing like none of this had ever happened?

As if reading her mind, Munus came back over and cleared his throat. "There, um, appears to be one more thing." He stared them each in the eye, holding it long to make Jo's skin crawl. "Did any of you come across two dozen barrels of nguvu?"

— · —

Afterward

If Pravi had to spend one more day in her hospital room, she would scream. It'd been five days since her surgery, and though she'd spent half that time groggy and disoriented, she was already sick of the stark white walls and the harsh smell of disinfectant. By all accounts, the elbow replacement had been a success, yet none of the nurses would even guess at when she'd be allowed to leave.

She leaned back and adjusted the strap of her sling. There was one good thing about the whole affair. She hadn't been forced to sit at the D.I.C. for hours, waiting in those godawful chairs while clerks pestered her with mountains of paperwork and asked her the same questions worded a hundred different ways. She'd had one single meeting with Munus, situated nicely between lunch and a painkiller-induced nap, plus two follow-up emails. Jo and the others hadn't been so lucky. The agents guarding her hospital room had said her colleagues were still in interviews when she got out of surgery, and that had taken six hours at least. Any more than that, the guards wouldn't say, no matter how much she badgered them. She was supposed to 'focus on getting well' and the agents 'couldn't comment on ongoing investigations'.

But she at least knew they were still alive.

She shuffled through her voluntary discharge papers, checking that every signature line and initial mark had been filled in. She'd met with a physical therapist. She'd been told what to watch out for regarding clots and infection. There wasn't a single reason for them to keep her there except for the question of how she'd get home. And the only person who would care about that was Munus.

Pravi's arm throbbed, the sutures tender even through the layers of bandages and pain medicine, and she set the papers down to wait for the nurse. She was getting out, with or without his permission. It'd be a whole lot easier if she still had her uncle's prototype. The last thing she remembered was shoving the transport wand's broken shaft up under her vest, but it hadn't shown up on any of the D.I.C. inventory lists. Even if they'd confiscated it, it should have been listed on one of the dozen forms she'd filled out, acknowledging which of her belongings had been taken into evidence. Even Munus claimed he didn't know where it had gone.

Someone knocked on the door, pulling her back to the present. It was a soft knock, much too timid to be a nurse or doctor. *Strings, don't let it be another flower delivery.* She'd woken up to a room full of the damn things, sent from mostly from Uncle Xander's old colleagues. The same colleagues who'd either contested his will or simply ignored her calls. Funny how things had changed now that Munus had promoted her to Senior Consultant.

"Come in," she called.

Blossoms peeked around the door, and Pravi prepared to send them away as she'd done with the others. But this bouquet was different. Not only were half the flowers crafted from scrap metal, but the vase carrier was none other than her protege.

"Jo?"

The inventor smiled sheepishly. "How's your arm doing? Director Munus said you might go home today?"

Well, he wasn't wrong. Pravi moved the discharge papers aside so Jo could set down the vase. "Tell me, what else did Munus say?"

"He, um. He said you might need a ride home." Jo messed with the flowers instead of making eye contact, and after a moment, one of the metal buds fell off. She fished out the stem and waved it over the nightstand.

Was the stem a scanner? What was she searching for, surveillance bugs? A blinking red light confirmed Pravi's suspicions, and Jo pulled a tiny metal capsule out of the drawer. She dropped it into the vase, where it gave a sharp snapping sound.

"He, uh, also said that the D.I.C. might pass on your case while he was on medical leave." She waved the scanning wand over Pravi's translator, but thankfully that was clean. "It's just his arm again, in case you're wondering. I guess he opened up the wound in his rush to get his team together."

In his rush to come to her rescue. He hadn't mentioned it during their interview, but she had noticed him holding his arm almost as tenderly as she held her own. "And did he say what he meant by 'pass on my case'?"

Jo shrugged and extracted another bug from the IV tower. "I guess a few of the agents still have questions about your uncle's prototype."

Which would mean they didn't have it. It would also explain the surveillance bugs. Pravi drummed her fingers on the nightstand. "Did you tell them anything? Give them a description or clues to what it runs on..." The inventor had been there when she'd shown the nguvu coils to Zahira. If she'd let that slip...

Another metal capsule snapped in the water. "Munus was the only one I talked to about it, and he seemed to know more than I did." He also knew enough to keep any documentation to the bare minimum needed for the case. Strings, it'd be easier if Pravi still had the damn thing. She could file for a disability permit or something, as she couldn't slide without it. The wand had to qualify as a transport aid at the very least. She held her questions until Jo finished her sweep of the room, but by then, the inventor was already rambling. Barrels of nguvu had gone missing, she whispered, and for now the D.I.C. wanted to keep it under wraps. Agents had grilled Jo and the others endlessly about it. Records confiscated from the Boliska base showed at least twenty-three unaccounted for, and Zahira had heard something about a buyer.

All thoughts of the transport wand disappeared as Pravi's mind went back to her transcom call with Munus. What was it he'd said? *Why would the smugglers produce a nguvu cloud bigger than the one hovering around Yerin?* If they'd only wanted it to hatch the giant lizards, they shouldn't have needed it to be that big.

Jo snapped the bloom back on the scanner and hid it in the vase with the other flowers. "So I'm assuming tracking down the barrels will be part of my fellowship? Munus said you applied to have me as a junior consultant."

Pravi nodded. She also had paperwork ready if Zahira and Nik wanted to join them as well. "I suppose this case is as good a start as any. If you're up for it?"

"I wouldn't be here if I wasn't." Although her voice was timid, Jo hefted both the vase and Pravi's duffel bag of clothes. "Zahira has a hovercar waiting outside and Munus sent me with your release papers."

Oh, thank the strings. Out in the hall, the agents standing guard weren't as happy about the release papers as Pravi was, but they seemed to pass muster. She and Jo made it to the exit with only a few suspicious looks and one agent's attempt to place a tracking device.

"Everything ready to go?" Zahira held open the door of the hover-craft as they arrived and helped Jo with the bag. "Nik said he had some final papers to grade and then he can meet us wherever."

Wherever indeed. It seemed even without her uncle's prototype, Pravi wouldn't be left stranded. She strapped herself into the passenger seat, trying her best not to grin like an idiot. "The research building on Rygal would be a good starting point. I imagine Jo's keen to check out her new lab space?"

The inventor flushed red against her freckles. "I won't hold you to it, now that I know why you offered. Saving the world is more than reward enough for me."

As if Pravi would go back on her word. "It's too late to back out now. The contract's already been typed up and sent to my lawyer. You're stuck with me at least until the fellowship's over."

"And that fellowship will be solving cases?" Zahira's eyes held their usual caution, but also a great deal of curiosity. "Like we did with the Boliska and their bases?"

Pravi nodded. "Exactly like the Boliska and their bases."

"I suppose you'll be needing this, then." Jo passed her a carefully wrapped bundle. "Munus snuck it into my belongings after the interrogations. He said he didn't want it falling into evidence."

Pravi's heart jumped, and she tore through the paper, ready for her hopes to be dashed. But inside she found not only the transport wand, but also fresh batteries and a newly mended shaft.

Jo flushed again. "Zahira had a few spare coils to replace the batteries, and the damage from the fight really wasn't as bad as it looked. Just a matter of taking the existing wire, adding in a bit of alloys, and..."

Pravi wrapped her fingers around the sensors as the inventor's words faded away. She had everything she wanted now. A team. A case. The chance to make it all work. The nearest strings tingled at her senses, ready to carry her and the others off on a new adventure. Smokey ones. Hazy ones. Ones that buzzed through her joints and smelled like kerosene. She had them all at the tips of fingers, and they tasted like endless possibilities.

Acknowledgments

There are so many people who helped make this book happen, and I would like to express my sincerest gratitude. Thank you to my husband first, of course. You say you don't "word good", but my best words wouldn't be possible without you. Thank you to my children, for your encouragement and for the rare times you let me write in peace. Thank you especially to Michael, for being my ~~guinea pig~~ I mean beta reader.

Thank you to my family and friends, for listening to me ramble about this book for years. Thank you especially to my mom and sisters for serving as beta readers on early drafts. I'm sorry I didn't figure out what I was doing sooner. Thank you to my writer friends on Discord. You also had to listen to me ramble, but without you, I'm not sure it would have ever turned into something coherent.

A special thank you to my critique partners, especially Michelle R. and Melisa H. An even specialer thank you to Melissa L, for being such a good sport that you read the darn thing twice. And lastly, I'd like to thank my editor, Bryan, for helping me polish my story into an actual book.

About the Author

Although she has a master's in architectural engineering, Candace Freilich much prefers building stories. Fictional worlds don't have to follow the normal laws of physics, and no one gets mad if you let a troll or a rancor into the basement. When she's not filling imaginary planets with dragons and interstellar wars, Candace enjoys sipping hot cocoa and pestering her children with mom jokes. Her other hobbies include singing off-key, taking her robovac on walks, and avoiding heights as if her life depends on it.

If you're interested in learning more or following her on your favorite social media platform, check out her linktree (linktr.ee/cfreili) or candacefreilich.com

Made in United States
Troutdale, OR
12/21/2023

16279303R00202